OF HOLLOWED STARS

FATE OF THE EMBERED
BOOK THREE

ROWYN ADELAIDE

Library of Congress Control Number: 2025918888

Cover Design: Rowyn Adelaide

Edited by: Katie Awdas, Spice Me Up Editing

Map Art: Melissa Nash

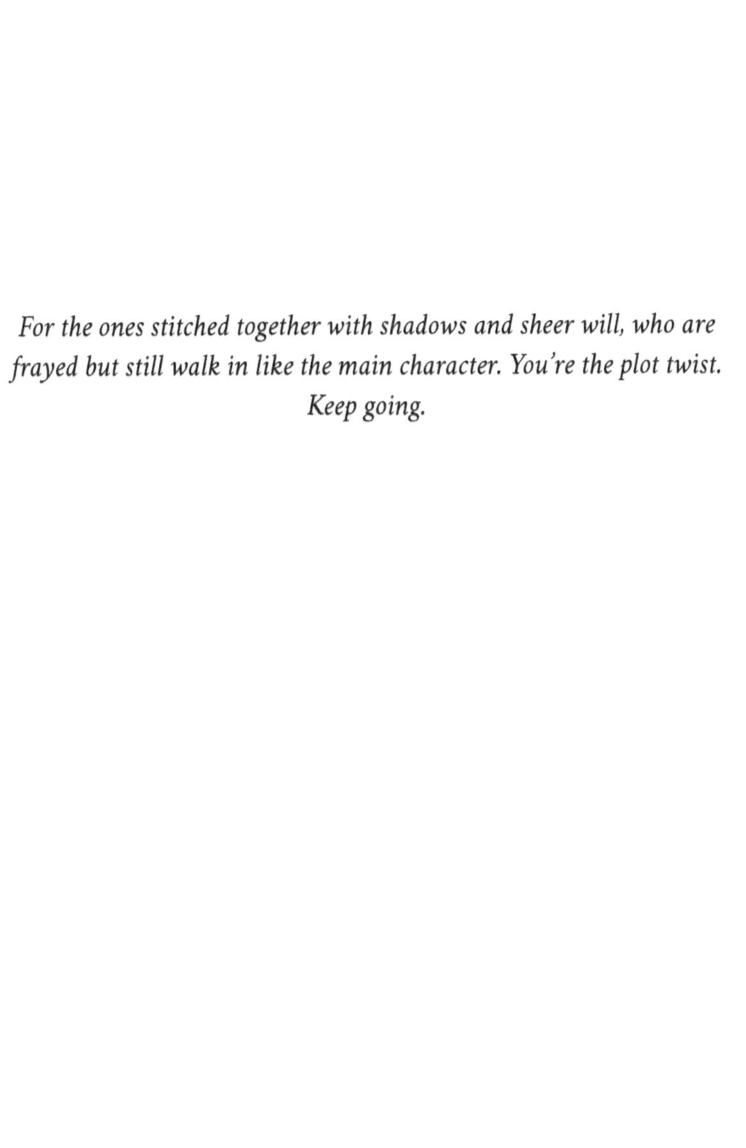

For the ones stitched together with shadows and sheer will, who are frayed but still walk in like the main character. You're the plot twist. Keep going.

There it shall linger,
    In the void where shadows creep.
    Beyond Nether,
    The nightmares decay sleep.

— ROWYN ADELAIDE

FATE OF THE EMBERED SERIES

Of Withering Dreams

Of Blooming Embers

Of Hollowed Stars

EXCLUSIVE UPDATES
FOR READERS

JOIN ROWYN'S AUTHOR NEWSLETTER

Be the first to learn about Rowyn Adelaide's new releases and receive exclusive content!

WWW.AUTHORROWYNADELAIDE.COM

PLAYLIST

Books are life. But so is music—at least to me! In no particular order, the following songs inspired me while I wrote this story. Below, come find me and my book playlists on Spotify!

- "Throne" - Saint Mesa
- "Take Me to Church (cover)" - MILCK
- "Catch These Fists" - Wet Leg
- "Black Sea" - Natasha Blume
- "Like a Dream" - Thomas LaRosa
- "Bittersweet Symphony" - The Verve
- "The Black Parade" - My Chemical Romance
- "Mr. Sandman (cover)" - SYML
- "Wicked Little Monster" - Veda
- "The Difference Between Medicine and Poison is in the Dose" - Circa Survive
- "Dream" - Roy Orbison
- "I Will Follow You into the Dark" - Death Cab for Cutie

- "Bringin' Home the Rain" - The Builders and the Butchers
- "Unraveling" - Muse
- "Bloom Baby Bloom" - Wolf Alice
- "Higher Love (cover)" - James Vincent McMorrow
- "The Summoning" - Sleep Token
- "Lose Control" - Teddy Swims
- "Out of the Shadows" - Ely Eira
- "Bury My Bones" - Amos the Transparent
- "Rise Up" - Andra Day
- "Through My Soul" - Enlly Blue
- "Blood In the Cut" - K.Flay
- "Your Rarest of Flowers" - Saint Avangeline
- "Sinners and Saints" - Andrea Wasse
- "The Wolf" - PHILDEL
- "Inside Out" - Eve 6
- "Bring Me to Life (cover)" - Brian H. Kim, Nxghtshade, and Satin Puppets
- "Eyes On Fire" - Blue Foundation

Of Hollowed Stars Spotify Playlist

AUTHOR'S NOTE

This is the third book in the *Fate of the Embered* series. Before diving into *Of Hollowed Stars,* you will want to read the series in order beginning with *Of Withering Dreams.* I am thrilled to finally get this story out into the world. I've always loved romance novels, especially ones with atmospheric world-building, magic, action, quests, and mystical beings. While some elements and names may be similar or very loosely related to Greek mythology, this is not a retelling or close representation of those tales or culture. This is a dark fantasy romance that was inspired by nature, magic systems, the world of dreams and imagination, Fates and Oneiroi (Dream Gods), mythology, etc.

At the back (*because spoilers*) of the book, there is a **glossary** and **pronunciation guide**. If you utilize the glossary and pronunciation guide, **PLEASE** be mindful that they are together and may contain **spoilers** if you look them up before reading.

Please enjoy the third installment of my dark romantasy series and keep an eye out for the rest. Read on for an important **content warning**.

CONTENT WARNING

Of Hollowed Stars is a dark fantasy romance (a.k.a. dark romantasy) with morally gray characters, explicit content, themes or hints of trauma and abuse, scenes with blood and gore, torture, violence, characters struggling with mental health and/or well-being, anxiety, grief, and other complex emotions. There are open-door sex scenes, talk of parental and loved ones' deaths, death, loss and grieving, cussing, characters with dark pasts and dark deeds, and supernatural elements.

Dark fantasy romance is a subgenre of fantasy romance that explores darker themes and worlds that may be considered disturbing, unsettling, traumatic, or frightening to some. However, it is not considered the same as dark romance, which often explores the darker side of love and relationships, power/control dynamics, fear, obsession, violence, abuse, etc.

I want to be clear that *Of Hollowed Stars* is NOT considered a dark romance.

I think the difference is important to note for those who enjoy dark romance specifically. I don't want to lead you astray if you were expecting certain tropes and themes that are often included in dark romances and the relationships therein.

Your mental well-being is important, so please review the trigger warnings before reading. If you are sensitive to scenes with the noted content, then this isn't the book for you. I want you to stay safe and to love what you read. If you decide to read this story, then buckle up and enjoy this enchantingly wild ride!

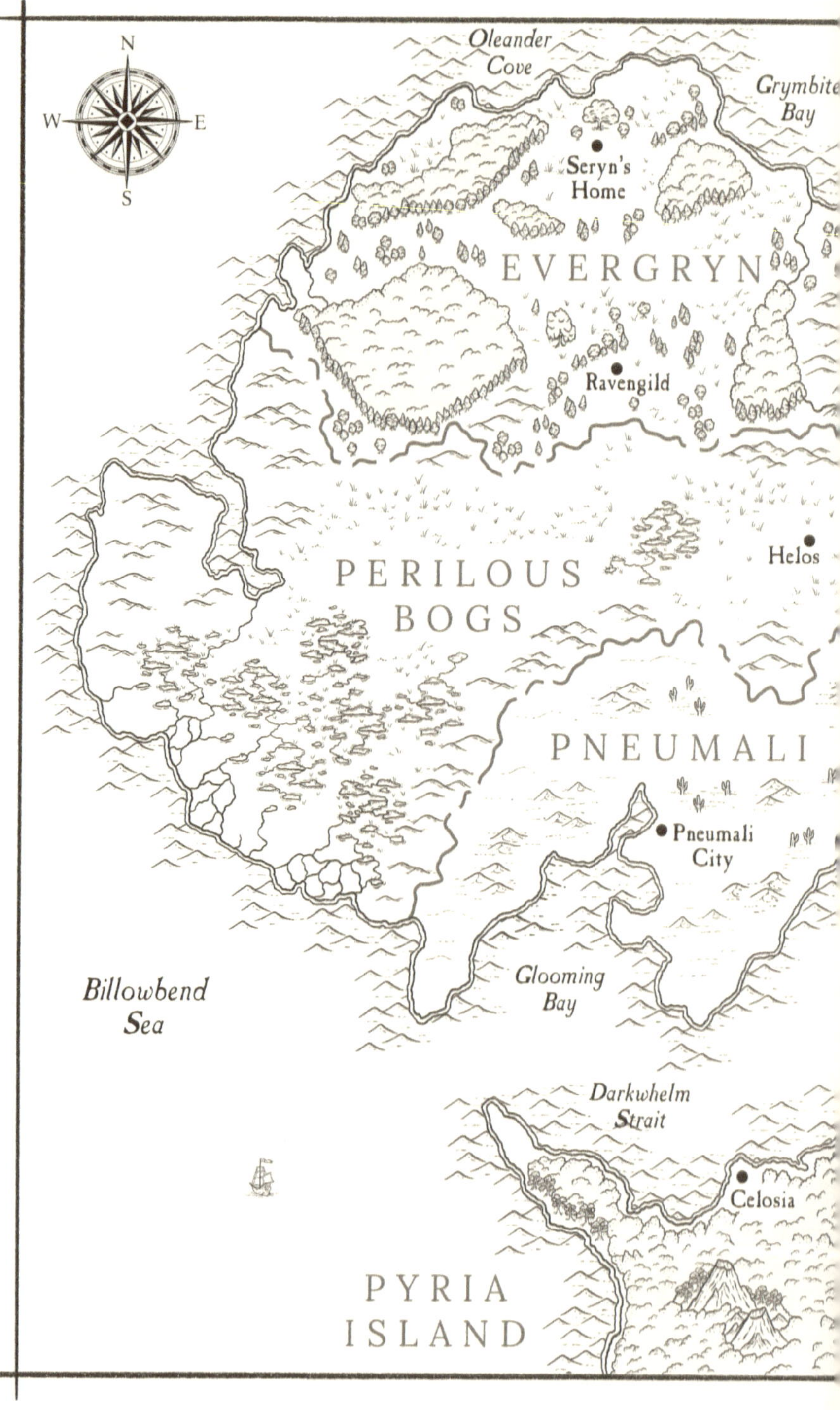

N
W E
S
Oleander Cove
Grymbite Bay
Seryn's Home
EVERGRYN
Ravengild
Helos
PERILOUS BOGS
PNEUMALI
Pneumali City
Billowbend Sea
Glooming Bay
Darkwhelm Strait
Celosia
PYRIA ISLAND

Ourea Peaks
Oneiroi Abyss
Lotus Loch
Inksalt Loch
Ceto
HAADRA
Aerides Loch
Gulf of Eidolon
MIDST FALL

PROLOGUE

MAYA AND MELINA ~ BACK THEN

The room was closing in on Maya Vawn. Or rather— *Nightshade*. A quiet snort slipped from her. In her twenty-eight turns of survival, she'd run from her lineage for so long that the feel of its tethers clung to her like chains, wrenching on her limbs.

She exhaled slowly, her heels pushing into the floor as she squared her stance. A flicker of memory stirred—Morpheus, slipping into her dreams like moonlight through fractured prisms.

It had been nearly a decade since her fated had first discovered the golden thread binding their souls, tracing it across the void of his prison. He had clutched it desperately, dragging himself through nightmare after nightmare to reach her.

He had been the one who spoke of the Fates' prophecies.

Who had urged her to escape.

To erase her name.

To become no one.

For her safety.

For the safety of her unborn children.

So, she had. With fear and regret fueling her, she had fled from the Perilous Bogs. Burrowed into the woodlands of Evergryn and buried her longing for home deep within her.

With every full moon, he had returned to her beneath the veil of sleep. And while he'd saved her—as nightmares bled in and dreams decayed across the realm—she had saved him, too. Held his sanity together. Kept his soul from shriveling into the darkness.

Their secret love had unfurled slowly, impossibly, in the shadows of the dreamscape, the *Somnis*. And three turns into their quiet, unseen devotion, they had made it real—consummated not in the waking world, but in that sacred place between souls and slumber.

Seryn was quite literally a dream come true.

Maya blinked hard, banishing the warmth of those memories as dread seeped into her bones.

In front of her, a feral grin dripped off Melina Harrow's incisors, her lips the color of fresh blood. The Elder relished this—the moment her prey realized they were cornered. Like a forest mouse scurrying between her talons, only to feel them close.

Maya's world narrowed to a single pinprick. Her fists clenched at her sides as she stood before Melina. She wouldn't be leaving this room a free woman, which she had known the moment she'd saved her daughter from Balor Drent earlier today.

Her time had come.

Melina watched the other female squirm, drinking in every flicker of resistance. Pets always thought they could flee. But their efforts were futile. No one escaped her—not when the game commenced.

She had learned to play hard. Long ago, she'd been caged,

helpless beneath the torment of Gryvak Leystaes' attention. Even now, the mere thought of her fated khorda infuriated her. But under that rage, a thin sheen of fear lingered, and it had nearly broken her.

Carved her into what she was now.

Now *she* was the one with the blade, and she would never let it go.

Maya swallowed down the bile rising in her throat, eyes flicking over the black silk and stone of the Elder's quarters.

She knew it was too late for her. Melina had seen her power; there would be no mercy.

But it was *never* too late for her children.

They were so young. Seryn only seven, and Letti just four turns old.

Her fingernails dug into her palms.

They would survive.

She would make sure of it, even if she had to claw her way back from the aether.

And Gideon. He'd do as she asked. He'd do his best. Watch over both his daughter and Seryn, despite knowing she wasn't his and unaware of who fathered her.

She cared for him deeply, but he knew her heart had already belonged to someone else. Nonetheless, he took her in when she'd been pregnant. Because he loved her and had from the moment he saw her in the Evergryn village.

Maya clenched her fists as if she could squeeze out the guilt seeping into her chest and then let her frantic thoughts shift.

She hoped the rune stone she'd embedded in Seryn's nape as an infant would hold. That her ember, if it ever awakened, would stay dormant. Regardless of whether either of her daughters were Druiks, Seryn was part Ancient, and her celestial gifts would have surfaced early on if not for her mother's precaution.

She would have been a target. Something for the Elders or the Ancients themselves to use. To play with as they saw fit.

"Sit," Melina cooed, her voice as silky as the settee she poked. The fabric threatened to split where the sharp tip of her nail dug in. Behind her, Balor licked his dry, cracked lips, already savoring Maya's pain.

"I'll stand," Maya replied coolly, lifting her chin. She wouldn't allow the Elder to break her. Just beneath her skin, her ember simmered, dark and twinkling like a star-strewn midnight sky.

Melina's head tilted, something between curiosity and trepidation flickering across her face.

"Ah, that's quite the backbone you have, Maya," she purred. "It's been a long while since I met someone with gifts like yours." Her gaze scraped over Maya's form. "I can almost taste it. Reminds me of *home*." She dragged her top teeth over her bottom lip. "Why don't you show me your bite?"

Maya's tense jaw twitched. Her energy pulsed, eager to oblige. But she stood her ground, urging her ember to hold steady.

Wait.

Endure.

Let her strike first.

Smoky tendrils crept around the Elder's silhouette, slithering toward Maya, testing, taunting, and prodding at her. Disgust churned in Maya's gut at the intrusion.

Melina's lips curled. "Come now. Do you need some encouragement?" She raised her hands. "We could bring your little ones in to play. Would you like that, pet?"

Fury ignited; Maya stepped forward.

Melina moved faster. With her palms thrust outward, shadows burst from her fingers and coiled around Maya's head in a billowing cloud.

With a garbled cry, Maya unleashed her gift. It flew outward, seizing the shadowy haze like fingers clutching a wrist, and ripped away the Elder's power.

Maya's ember was rare.

Born of something older.

Something *more*.

It could touch other auras as if they were solid.

Manipulate them.

Twist them.

Break them.

"Scion," Melina hissed, balking as her gaze snapped toward Balor.

The Akridai's power lashed out next, oiled and writhing.

Maya's ember swatted it aside as if it were a bothersome gnat.

The image of Seryn dangling above a raging river flashed behind Maya's eyes. Pure rage surged up her spine. She hurled Melina's aura back at her; the force slapped the Elder across her face, making her stumble and cough on her own creation.

Maya charged toward Balor. Her energy clamped onto the edges of his and twisted, winding it around his dough-like neck.

Tight.

Tighter.

His eyes bulged. His mouth bloomed a sickly shade of blue.

Maya narrowed her eyes. Loathing, grief, and fury all poured into her ember as it turned Balor's fluorescent tendrils against him, strangling him with the gift he used to hurt others.

But then—

CRACK.

A sharp blow collided with the back of Maya's skull. Searing pain sliced down her spine as she collapsed, her aura crumpling with her. Her grip on Balor's power faltered. She could have sworn she heard her lover's roar shatter through her mind.

Balor fell backward, gasping, dragging in broken, desperate inhalations. His fingers clawed at his throat, as if her hold still lingered there.

Maya lay still, her breath coming in shallow shudders.

Shadows crept in at the edges of her vision as she stared up at Melina, whose halo sputtered before sinking into her flesh. A metallic clatter rang across the floor as Melina dropped whatever weapon she had struck her with.

The Elder straddled Maya's waist, platinum strands falling around her face like polished guillotine blades.

"My, my," she murmured. "I didn't think we'd have quite so much fun, but you didn't disappoint." She sniffed delicately. "As much as I'd love to keep playing, I can't risk it. Not with you so clearly being my Scion."

A slow, languid sigh slipped from her lips. "And a deal with Phobetor tends to ruin the mood." She leaned in slightly. "It's a shame I can't send you to the aether … but a Scion's power is too tempting for him to resist, and he wants you imprisoned. No use to him if you're dead."

Blackness crowded the edges of Maya's vision.

Melina straightened with a shrug and flicked a hand at Balor. "Take her to the dungeon," she barked, smoothing her hands over her hair. "Prepare her for the Epiales Tombs. I'll be down shortly."

That name alone made Maya's faint pulse stumble. She remembered the lore of Epiales. The personification of nightmares. Phobetor's favored demon, long ago destroyed during the Nightbloom Sundering, had once been the Ancient's chosen companion. The shadow beast who suffocated dreamers with torment and madness. Perhaps the demon's spirit lingered still, because horror was already creeping along the edges of Maya's fading consciousness.

The Elder traced her forefinger down Maya's cheek, grinning at her. "Don't worry. I'll keep an eye on your girls for you."

Weakly, Maya lifted a trembling hand, but Melina smacked it aside before she leaned in once more. Her aura poured over Maya's face like liquid smog.

Yet, even with the threat of unconsciousness stealing away

reality, Maya's ember refused the Elder's invasion. Perhaps Morpheus was there after all, helping her gift deny access. Her eyelashes fluttered with effort.

With a frustrated growl, Melina bent to one side, and metal scraped across the stone before a cold, solid mass crashed against Maya's temple.

Then everything—light, sound, and any flicker of hope within Maya *Nightshade*—went utterly, violently dark.

1

DEMI-DAUGHTER

SERYN ~ NOWADAYS

The Dream Ancient had to be fucking with her.

"Da-daughter?" I stammered. The world tilted under my feet, and I locked my knees. My fingers flew up to skim Morpheus' warm hand as it cupped my cheek. A shimmer of recognition tingled under my skin.

My mind tore through everything that he'd said. Everything that had happened in the last days. The Nightbloom Sundering treaty that kept him and his brother Phobetor from crossing into each other's realms. His imprisonment.

Mama and Morpheus were fated.

Shallow breaths caught in my throat, my heart slamming hard into my ribs. This couldn't be happening. Not now. Not after Gavrel had sacrificed himself to the Void to protect me from Melina.

A broken sob tumbled over my bottom lip, and Morpheus' touch left me, his brows pulling together.

But there, the corners of his eyes and mouth were soft and curious.

Tender.

Kaden shifted closer to my side as Elders Strom and Guust stared wide-eyed at us. Everyone was still, a symphony of respirations dancing around us before dropping into the churning, metallic pool in the center of the pit.

A riot of emotions pummeled me. Smashed into my mind and bones like an explosion of rocks. As if I'd been the one trapped in amber all these turns until it shattered around me.

I'd lost Gavrel.

Devastation choked me.

I was Seryn *Nightshade*.

Anxiety sliced into my gut.

Yaya.

Fear.

Melina.

Rage.

The Withering.

Helplessness.

Father—no, *Gideon.*

Bitterness.

Images of all the times Gideon had scrutinized me as if I were a bug under his boot. His coldness. His disdain. His resentment. He'd never treated me with anything but callous obligation.

Because my mother had asked him to care for Letti and me, that final day in Surrelia, before she disappeared when I was seven.

"Take care of them," Mama pleaded.

Gideon lifted his chin, his expression softening as he met her gaze. "Of course, my love."

He'd *known* he wasn't my father but had raised me anyway. With a heavy dose of acrimony and reluctance.

I clutched the small bit of gratitude I felt for the man, letting it temper my disgust. But any lingering respect I had was dwindling by the second. He'd gotten Hestia culled and hadn't done a thing when the Akridais came for me.

I scanned Morpheus' countenance as his frosty eyes, so like mine, glinted with something close to affection. The strong, aquiline nose. The robust angles of his cheekbones and jaw.

A sculptor could have chiseled every bit of him; he looked like a marble statue brought to life, draped in gold. Perhaps he was after being trapped in stone for nearly a century.

No, he was real.

His words were real.

Beseeching.

I blinked several times, my knees threatening to give out.

The Ancient before me didn't blink.

It's true. Isn't it?

Morpheus was … he was my bloody father.

Damn me to the Murk.

"Holy fuckity fuck. You're a demi-Ancient?" Kaden squawked, his jaw halfway to the floor. "Please don't smite me, Ser. I know I can be a twat, but I've been your loyal idiot since we were two. Best friend privileges, yeah?"

A wry chuckle slipped from me, his joke breaking the spell I'd been under, tugging me out of the disbelief and confusion strangling me. The back of my hand lightly smacked Kaden's chest, and he smiled tenderly, wrapping his arm around my waist, supporting me.

Morpheus' eyebrows furrowed as he glanced at Kaden and then went slack as he looked back at me expectantly.

I bowed my head with a deep inhale and then stepped out of Kaden's hold. My fists clenched as I moved toward my … my father.

Before I could make contact, my attention snapped upward as the whir of the semi-translucent conveyor sounded from above. Inky energy writhed along its perimeter. Through the base, I glimpsed two blurry silhouettes.

Blue and yellow halos flared around Marah and Endurst. Morpheus' gilded aura rippled over him, and my nape thrummed in response.

As the disk descended, the glass cast a saffron tint over the flickering crimson above it.

"Wait," I ordered before anyone could deliver an embered attack. The familiar sound of friendly bickering floated down before its occupants were fully in view.

"The duuuuungeon," Breena sang as she wiggled her fingers and jumped, filling the space beside me. She slung her arm over my shoulders. "Betcha thought you could go on another dungeon adventure without me. Eh, Ryn? Fat fecking chance."

Kaden crossed his arms. "I think you missed out on a large part of the adventure."

"Not my fault the wyverns thought you couldn't make it without them. Besides, there's always another adventure." She winked at Morpheus, and his brows rose. "Who's this tasty morsel?"

Kaden coughed, and Marah's hands fluttered over her mouth.

"My Ancients, woman. Can't you see it's bloody Morpheus?" Rhaegar scolded, head shaking as he stepped off the platform and bowed low.

Morpheus lifted his hand, and Rhaegar rose, taking the spot behind Breena and ruffling her hair. She swatted at him before huffing and curtsying. "Well, hello there, oh, Ancient of Dreams. Did I hear right that ya knocked up Firefly's mom?"

"Bloody void," Kaden muttered.

Breena shrugged. "What? It's echoey down here. If he wanted it to be a secret, he should've whispered."

The corner of Morpheus' mouth quirked.

I glanced at Breena. "You heard right, but Gavrel—" I

stepped closer to the molten surface, and Rhaegar cursed under his breath, eyes narrowing in understanding. My breath hitched. "Is it … calmer?"

The substance's movements slowed, rippling like dark, metallic water in slow motion. All eyes were fixed on the opening.

"The full moon wanes. You need to go before it closes." Morpheus' gaze flicked between Breena and me, then landed on my hand.

He continued, voice low and urgent, "The ring … it's a conduit to the Oneiric realms, carving doorways through celestial borders. Mortals can only wield it under the full moon, when ember flows strongest. As my daughter, you might be able to portal outside lunation—or it could rip you apart."

Breena snorted and rolled her eyes. "Oh, is that all? Charming. I'm coming with you, Firefly."

There was no use in arguing with her. And no time, regardless.

Besides, I had no desire to discover firsthand whether my bloodline made me tear-resistant.

Morpheus leaned in, concern tightening his features. "Do *not* lose the ring. If you land in the Stygian Murk, you'll need it. That place was forged from raw, volatile aether with nothing to govern it. Like the tides, limbo expands and collapses with each lunation as it feeds on shifting ember currents. Without a celestial key like your ring, anything caught inside—Ancient or not—remains trapped until the next full moon."

I lifted my chin. "If they even survive that long."

Morpheus' shoulders relaxed, satisfied that I had understood.

Kaden pulled me into a tight hug, then Rhaegar followed, holding me at arm's length and squeezing my shoulders gently.

"Bring him home," Rhaegar instructed. "If anyone can, it's

you. We'll handle things here. Marek is determined to find Yaya."

A sad smile spread across my lips before I turned and then paused in front of Morpheus. He'd said he needed me to find my mother in the Void, which meant that's where he believed her to be. Hope glowed within me, casting light upon my resolve.

"I … I'll do my best to find Mama," I whispered roughly, remembering that my *father* also had a lot to lose if I didn't return.

Morpheus tucked a curl behind my ear, and I leaned into his warmth for a moment, realizing how starved I'd been all these turns for the nurturing touch of a parent.

He smiled, dropping his arm. "I've caught glimpses of you throughout the turns. In your dreams and Maya's. And I have no doubt you can do anything you set your mind to. Once you return from my brother's domain—and I know you will—we'll have time to learn one another. If that's what you wish."

I nodded and slowly stepped away from him, pressing my lips inward. I filled my lungs and grabbed Breena's hand.

She squeezed, grinning at me fiendishly. "Adventure time?"

My grip tightened on her fingers.

And then we jumped.

2

―――――

VENGEANCE

GAVREL

*M*y mouth dropped open, shock prickling along my skin.

The woman before me was surely an illusion, saying my name, interrupting my execution of Melina.

"How are you here, Gavrel?" She stepped closer, a look of concern sweeping over a face I hadn't seen in many turns.

Time seemed to have frozen, save for the floating specks of glowing cinders, the sporadic ebony flames that erupted from the dark terrain, and the frantic drumming against my neck.

This place was surely playing with my senses.

It *couldn't* be.

Close behind her, at least ten outcasts shuffled, their gaunt faces marked by a sickly pallor streaked with chalky black smudges, like they'd tumbled through piles of ash.

Most were human, but others ... I blinked.

Was that a bloody centaur? He was broad-shouldered, his tawny brown skin and hide slick with soot, and his pale, long

15

hair shining. One of his hooves clopped against the ground irritably as he leveled me with a flat, unimpressed stare.

Not an illusion, then.

The rest of the group's clothes were a mismatched mosaic of battered dark leathers that whispered tales of countless skirmishes and hard survival. I counted a dozen blades at minimum, each one carefully concealed, tucked in sheaths beneath frayed belts, strapped to worn boots, or nestled in vests cinched tight around ragtag forms.

Focusing on the woman once more, my shoulders tensed, and my fingers flexed against the hilt of my broadsword. "Maya? Is it truly you?"

"You have eyes, Comman—"

Without looking, I flung my arm down, the tip of my steel blade hovering precariously close to Melina's throat, effectively cutting off her words.

Maya's mouth twisted as she studied the Elder trapped below me before a slow smile crept over her face. "It's me, Gavrel. A mare wyrm wouldn't be as pleased to see the state *she's* in." With a wry chuckle, she jerked her chin toward Melina.

I shook my head, dislodging any further disbelief.

Seryn's mother looked unchanged, as if time itself had frozen, sparing her from its usual cruelty. Yet, survival had left its own mark. Dark shadows etched deep beneath her lash line, and her voice carried a rough, weathered edge.

She had always been beautiful, with fiery curls like Seryn's and eyes that missed nothing, sharp and clear. But the delicate planes of her cheekbones and jawline had hardened, forged into something almost blade-like, tempered against the blackened stones of this unforgiving realm.

It was her. I knew it in my marrow.

Bloody Ancients.

She reached for me as I sheathed my weapon, and I went to

her, our arms wrapping around one another. Maya leaned back, hazel eyes shining as she cupped my cheeks.

When I was young, she'd been a second mother to me as mine had been to Seryn.

My heartbeat stumbled at the thought of my khorda. What I wouldn't give for her to know her mother was alive.

For a moment, I closed my eyes, imagining that I could send the message along the cord binding our ribs, but I only sensed a faint twinge along the bony cage like the fading vibrations of a plucked fiddle string.

The image of Seryn screaming my name as I fell into the portal—as I left her—was burned into the back of my eyelids.

"Gavrel," Maya murmured, stepping away but resting one hand on my biceps. She nodded to someone in her crew, and he unclipped a set of thick manacles from his belt and moved toward Melina. "How did you come to be here? And what of my daughters?"

Her gaze was unwavering. Direct. Hopeful yet wary.

Before I could respond, ember burst from her, whipping around and behind me. I spun. Maya's glittering midnight ropes clamped around Melina's smoke-like energy.

"I wouldn't if I were you, *pet*," Maya warned, her power digging into Melina's as if it were a limb.

Melina bared her teeth, her aura writhing. "Do tell how you escaped the Epiales Tombs. I'm sure it's a tale for the ages," she taunted.

Maya didn't acknowledge the Elder. Instead, she simply nodded at a male and female as they emerged like shadows from the dim path behind the group.

My jaw nearly fell off its hinges, but I forced my mouth closed before I showed any sign of disrespect.

Vryka.

If I were right, these beings were the stuff of, well, nightmares. Creatures who haunted many mortals' slumbers. They had people looking over their shoulders in the night, fearing that their flesh and blood would be consumed before their screams could pierce the air.

The pair stationed themselves before the man holding the fetters. He didn't seem frightened.

Curiosity had my brows rising higher.

The sharp-eyed female, with cropped blonde hair catching the dim light, stood with a disinterested poise. Beside her loomed a stocky male, whose glower spoke of constant irritation.

Their eyes were black, liquid mirrors—depths into which one might fall and never return. A pair of soot-dark wings cascaded elegantly down each of their backs, ending in a talon that brushed against their calves. Veins of dusky sapphire traced intricate patterns across the wings' velvety leather, pulsing faintly.

Just a hint of white showed around Melina's irises.

She was nervous.

Excellent.

They moved closer to her, and a flash of cerulean-tipped black fire flared beside them, making the bluish gray of their skin appear lit from within for a moment, glinting over the brutal weapons secured to their bodies.

A lattice of leather straps crisscrossed the female's chest, leaving her wings unbound. The five-foot polearm rode at a slant along her spine, the slightly curved blade peeking past her shoulder, its haft locked into twin loops of iron-fitted leather. With one tug, the weapon would slide free. And she looked like she itched to free it.

The male's harness was nothing but blackened straps and iron clamps, built to bear the weight of the monstrous, spiked maul along his back. Its hammer-like head bristled with jagged studs.

"Go on, Therrok," Maya urged.

With crossed arms, the male hovered like a slab of stone over Elder Harrow. His dark eyes flicked between Maya, me, and the female at his boots, serving each of us with the same level of suspicion.

But finally, he grumbled and unlocked his arms, muscles thick and littered with scars, the ash settling deep into the old, cobalt-colored wounds, as if it *knew* he belonged to the ruin.

His scowl didn't waver. So much so that I wondered if it too was a permanent scar. His flaxen hair was shorn close at the sides, tight braids running along the crown and bundled at his nape.

The female vryka narrowed her eyes at him, and Therrok wrinkled his nose, snatching the cuffs from the other man, before bending over Melina and shackling her wrists. Rune etchings flared along the metal before disappearing. They were identical to the ember-blocking restraints in Morpheus' dungeon.

Melina pouted as her aura blinked out, and Maya allowed hers to evaporate.

"Clever, clever girl," Melina purred, jerking her wrists and making the metal chains clang.

"Shut your mouth, or I'll shut it for you," the short-haired blonde barked, grabbing the Elder's biceps and yanking her upright. Her wings rustled agitatedly with the movement.

A slow grin spread across Melina's lips, her lipstick smudged and fading. She leaned close. "Wouldn't that be fun?"

Clearly, she wasn't as wary as she had been moments ago. Or her mind was slipping further.

Without warning, the vryka's arm lashed out, her sharp black nails slicing the air before the back of her hand crashed against Melina's cheek.

I squared my feet and gripped my baldric.

A thin track of blood trickled from the corner of Melina's

mouth, mingling with the faded lipstick. She licked it slowly, silver eyes sparking. "Fun indeed."

The female's hand rose again.

"Enough, Thesa!" Maya snapped, her voice firm and commanding. Thesa froze mid-motion, jaw tight, tension coiling in her muscles before she dropped her arm, wrenched on Melina's chains, and marched off with her in the other direction. Therrok and the rest of her group followed.

My thumb rubbed the leather strap across my chest. "Quite the crew you have down here, Maya. How did it come about that you found me?"

She shrugged. "It's been a long while since I escaped Phobetor's nightmare prison, and I was fortunate to find the others during my time here." Her gaze lingered on her crew ahead. "Thesa was scouting, and she saw the portal spit you out. We hoped it might be another of Melina's prisoners escaping. It's rare, but ..." She shrugged, rubbing her lips together.

"Thesa and Therrok, are they siblings?"

She nodded. "They had childhoods I wouldn't wish on anyone, but at least they had one another."

Her eyes softened, likely thinking of her own daughters.

"I've only heard the myths of vrykas as a child. Are they ... Is there anything I should be careful of?" I asked, not wanting to offend.

Her head swayed from side to side. "No, they aren't like their kin. They left the capital—Nekrionn—long ago. Escaped the torment of their upbringing. But that's not my story to tell." Her eyes crinkled at the sides. "They won't drain you of your blood if that's your concern."

The thought *had* crossed my mind, but I'd take her word for it.

She went on, "I can't speak for the rest of the Void beings in this realm. I doubt I need to say 'watch yourself'"—she twirled her hand in the air—"*here.*"

I huffed a laugh and rolled one shoulder.

She swallowed. "This group. It might be worn at the edges, but we've been together a long while. Survived. Fought the nightmares clinging to our backs." She paused for a moment, gaze sweeping over the landscape. "Each of us, in our own way, was a prisoner. Of the Epiales Tombs. The Elders. Our circumstances. Death. But we found a way to fight back. Not to fade into the despair of this place. We found something to live for."

I followed her line of sight, trying to decipher what had kept her going. She'd been here for so long, I didn't think it possible. "And what did you find?"

Her eyes met mine, steady and unflinching. "Vengeance."

3

THE HESPIRA

GAVREL

e wound down gloomy switchbacks for the better part of an hour, descending from the plateau on which we'd started.

On a relatively flat terrace, I lingered for a moment and craned my neck to regard the escarpment we'd traversed. A flicker of opalescence dashed past my peripheral vision, but when I looked that way, only the bleak scenery met my gaze. My brow furrowed, shaking off the feeling that we were being followed.

This place was a dizzying maze of ledges, basins, and sheer cliffs, layered to confound and unsettle any unlucky soul forced to dwell in the nightmarescape.

I focused on sidestepping any sudden bursts of black fire and slick patches underfoot, having already learned my lesson; two clumsy steps had nearly sent me sprawling earlier.

The trick was to listen for the sputtering hiss of a blaze

igniting and to watch for the faint gleam along a stone's glassy fractures. Each was a warning of treacherous footing.

Maya and I spoke, but our words came in surges, truths spilling fitfully out between us like honey wine sloshing over the rims of overfilled goblets.

When it was my turn to listen, awe and pride swelled within me, warming me from the inside as gooseflesh prickled my skin in the chilled, stagnant air.

"Neoma is incredible," I said, avoiding a sharp boulder. "She's worked hard to bring the Korax together and turn it into something cohesive. I've no doubt that they will win the battles ahead."

A smile curved her lips. "She always had a way about her. People are drawn to her. They gather around her like ducklings. She never asked for it. It just … it just happens." Her voice hitched at the end.

A large shadow shifted behind us, and the centaur, Argedes, sidled next to Maya. He tossed his long, white hair behind his brawny shoulders, and his hearty chuckle ricocheted off the protruding rock formations. "Sounds familiar, eh?"

The corner of my mouth lifted. It hadn't taken long for the creature to warm to me. "Seems you have the same gift, Maya," I agreed.

She waved a hand as if batting away the notion, but Argedes was already sucking a breath in, burnished copper-hued eyes lighting up, readying himself for a performance.

"You should have seen us before she came along," he declared. "A lowly bunch of miscreants, hiding in any dark corner that offered scarce respite from the nightmares chasing us. Fighting off attacks and scavenging for scraps. Partaking in the most scandalous activities just to survive. Some more so than others." He winked at Therrok and threw his arms up dramatically, eliciting snickers from several of the others.

Therrok's eyes squinted as he looked at the centaur from the corners of his eyes, his wings twitching in annoyance.

Argedes ignored him, his hand sweeping toward Maya. "And then she fell from the sky, climbing out of the ruins, hair ablaze like wildfire, voice ringing across the abyss—"

"Get on with it," Thesa yelled from several paces ahead.

Argedes' long, pale tail flicked in the air. "And she spoke of prophecies, maintaining Kosmos' balance, and equality. Freedom."

A hush rippled down the line of misfits.

"She became our guiding star," he finished with a flourish. "Our evening star, *the Hespira*, if you will. At least that's the name people whisper when they talk of our exploits. The name seemed fitting for the stealthiest cadre of rebels who ever nipped at Phobetor's ankles."

Maya groaned under her breath. "Ancients help me. He exaggerates."

"He does not," Therrok muttered.

Argedes snapped his fingers. "See? The blood-drinker agrees."

The vryka's top lip curled back, exposing sharp incisors. The centaur guffawed.

Therrok shoved his shoulder against Argedes' flank. "Less theatrics. More walking."

Maya shook her head. "They do love a good prophecy."

"So, you're a believer?" I wasn't entirely confident in the Fates' predictions, but recent events were shifting what I thought I knew.

Her throat bobbed. "My mother taught me the scriptures as a young girl, and I passed on the knowledge to this group. Especially the Hollowed Stars prophecy. It's become a beacon of hope through the dark, a promise that Phobetor and the Elders' reign won't last forever. That balance will return. And so we fight, however we can."

We continued downward. The path narrowed between roughened cliffs and drop-offs that yawned deep into the abyss. When I grew quiet, Maya nudged my arm.

"Tell me more," she prompted.

So I did.

I told her everything. About the Korax and the attack on Helos. About the Elders and how dilapidated Midst Fall had become. Of Seryn breaking the amber boulder and of my plummet into the Nether Void.

I told her how Seryn's gift had awoken, of her daughter refusing to kneel before any Fate, and of her stubbornness and bravery.

Her steps slowed, awe sinking into her features.

We walked in silence for a few moments before our attention wandered to our left. A raging mass of red-orange water battered the jagged crags, the waves sliding off the obsidian stone so it gleamed as though coated with blackened blood.

"It looks like liquid fire, doesn't it? The Insomnis Sea is always a sight to behold," Maya mused.

A low rumble of agreement stirred in my chest as I scanned the horizon. Even in the ominous bowels of the Nether Void, the fabled sea was mesmerizing. You could lose yourself in its depths, whether in cerulean dream or persimmon nightmare.

Defiant, Phobetor's palace pierced the firmament in the distance, rising from its black-fire-opal islet. Unlike Morpheus' palace, no bridges led to its shining copper doors. Instead, a spine of dark stairs, from the entrance and to the sea, coiled around the base like a snake constricting its prey.

I narrowed my eyes. The sun, a black sphere rimmed in violet fire, crept toward the horizon, casting a silvery glow across the line where sky and ocean met. Light winked along the fortress' edges, making it come alive, shivering in anticipation.

We reached a lower gap and kept to the path skirting along a ragged cliff at our right, its looming face a constant companion. Overhead, a flock of massive, twisted birds cut across the dimming sky, their crooked wings stirring the cinders adrift in the air.

Trepidation skittered up my back, but I fought to keep from seeing an omen in the creatures as Maya's words echoed through me. I shifted my jaw, releasing the nerves settling in the hinges.

When Seryn was seven, Balor had dangled her over a cliff, the Surrelian River raging below. Maya had intervened, her power snapping out to catch her daughter and drive his ember back. It was sheer misfortune that Melina had witnessed the ordeal.

My lips pressed together at the thought of Balor until a sliver of satisfaction curled one corner. Seryn's blade had found his chest before I pulled Melina through the dungeon portal.

I glanced at Maya, her steps sure, focus unwavering.

No wonder her daughters were remarkable. The woman had survived the nightmare realm for over a decade.

On that fateful day during the Dormancy, she'd had a confrontation with Melina. And in the aftermath, she'd found herself imprisoned within the limbo tombs.

I frowned at the thought of the glass globes my brother had also been a victim of. "I can't imagine how horrible that was, Maya. Kaden won't talk about his time in them."

Her expression darkened. "I can still feel them sometimes. The nightmares. My worst fears. Living them over and over. It was so cold inside the orbs, but it also felt like my blood burned within me. And no matter how hard I fought to break free, the terror burrowed deeper into my bones. I saw my daughters— everyone I loved—dying in horrific ways. Every moment was pure horror slicing into my mind. I have no idea how long I was trapped."

I swallowed. "How did you escape?"

Her cheeks puffed with a long exhale. "Phantasos. One moment, I was inside the glass, the next, she was taking my hand, my prison shattering around us, and reapers screeching into the dark. She opened a portal and told me that the dawn didn't fear the night. That I had a part to play in what came next. That the balance had to be maintained. I didn't doubt her. Why would I?" Her hand swept across the air before her. "But then I was here. Nothing is ever simple with Ancients."

Bloody Ancients.

Despite Phantasos' help thus far, I wasn't sure the Ancient of Illusions could be trusted. Could *any* celestial being?

I swallowed, my throat dry and scratchy. Imagining Maya caught in an eternal loop of her daughters' deaths gutted me. "But you survived."

"So did you," she replied. "As will Seryn and Letti."

I released a slow breath, my thoughts shifting to my khorda.

Her face materialized in my mind.

Images of her channeling her power while she worked with the Augur.

The moment she shed her doubts and fully stepped into her gift.

When I took her against a tree, the night of the Moonbud Revelry, and felt her unravel in my arms.

The way she looked at me, as if she'd maim anyone who dared to wrong me.

Seryn softly humming whenever she tasted something she enjoyed.

"You love her," Maya stated as we trailed behind the others, and I squeezed my baldric tightly.

It wasn't a question.

I shut my eyes for a moment. If I didn't give the words shape, I could pretend they weren't true. Could endure the Void like Maya had done all these turns.

"I thought it would be Kaden," she added.

Irritation and grief crawled over my shoulders. My jaw ticked as missing my brother—my worry for him—curdled into something harsher. The thought of them *together* was a dull knife in my gut, the blade twisting.

She is mine.

"It was," I ground out.

I ran my tongue over my teeth, dropping my hands and flexing them.

Calm down. Fucking void.

A soft smile tipped up the corners of her mouth at my petulant tone. "You're her fated khorda, though."

With tension bunching my muscles, I regarded her fully, eyebrows lifting and the pang of my cursed rune burning behind my ribs.

Maya sighed. "I know what it is to be separated from your other half. And I hear it when you speak of her." She wrapped her arms around herself for a moment before letting them fall. "There's so much to tell. I … I've been away too long."

"She never gave up hope. That you were alive," I said, pressing the base of my thumb into my scar.

She crushed her eyes closed briefly before shaking her head as if dislodging something unpleasant. "I can't wait to hold my daughters in my arms again. Not a moment has passed that I haven't thought of Seryn and Letti. And Gideon—I'm grateful to him for watching over them."

Sourness lined my mouth, but I held in my words. Now wasn't the time to divulge what her husband had done to my mother. How abysmally he'd treated Seryn all these turns. Didn't protect her from the Akridais hunting her.

As if sensing my unease, Maya touched my wrist. "She isn't his, you know."

I flinched, steps faltering. "What are you saying?"

She continued forward, forcing me to follow. "He wasn't an easy man, but he was never cruel. He knew all along Seryn wasn't his, but married me anyway. I ran away from home long ago after I was gifted a warning … in my dreams."

My thoughts bumped into one another.

She looked up at the vermilion sky. "Morpheus is my khorda. That's who Seryn freed. I feel him. Here." She rubbed her palm over her heart, like I so often did. "Her *true* father." Her statements fell, crunching under my boots.

My heart knocked against my rib cage, jostling bits of memories and unanswered questions into place.

I cursed.

"Her ember. It … it all makes sense," I murmured.

"She's powerful, isn't she? I knew she would be. And what of Letti? Have they had a good life?"

"Mostly, yes. Gideon was always more caring toward Letti. And she's amazing, Maya. Bright and funny. Kind." I offered a smile, and her hazel irises looked almost gold. "Seryn—she's magnificent. Strong and clever. She's … everything."

Emotion choked me. The thought of never seeing the other half of my soul again—it was too much. Maya's eyes softened as her gaze swept over my face.

I pushed my shoulders back, swallowing hard when despair stuck in my throat.

4

MOURNING PASS

GAVREL

*A*s we neared the end of the towering wall, white dust speckled the cracked raven-colored path. The random sputter of dark flames lessened, and an inverted dusk settled over the sky in shades of hazy teal and clover.

Maya's crew paused, Thesa jerking Melina's chains so she, too, halted. She'd been unusually quiet on this journey, a gleam sparking in her silver eyes every so often.

Prickles rippled down my back.

"Don't say it," Thesa grumbled. She looked ahead irritably and then upward, almost longingly, following a steep byway haphazardly carved into the cliff face.

Maya shook her head. "You know well enough that the quickest route is through Mourning Pass. We need to make haste and hide *her*"—her chin jutted toward Melina—"before Phobetor finds us."

Thesa cursed but pressed forward regardless, flicking a displeased glance at the ascending trail one last time.

We rounded the corner, and a brittle crunch under my next step brought my focus to the jagged, ashen expanse before us. A field of splintered bones stretched across the terrain, jabbing and teetering on the edge of the cliff that loomed above the Insomnis Sea.

"Just ignore them," Maya directed, shoulders pushed back as she strode forward, disregarding the grinding beneath each step.

I followed her and the others, my boots crunching over bony fragments. "Ignore *them?*"

There was a shrill screech to my left. I whipped toward it, sword now in hand, and then spun to my right as another cry came.

There was no one there. The others didn't pay any mind to the rising cacophony of screams and pleas.

My eyes locked with the lifeless sockets of a partially crushed skull sitting atop a thick pile of femurs. Its jaw connected on one side as it flopped open precariously.

"Have mercy!" it shrieked, teeth clacking.

All right then.

These were the aforementioned *them.*

"Save me!" another skull cried as I sheathed my sword and caught up to the others.

"You pathetic fool. Shut up. They never help us," another responded.

They did not shut up.

I ground my molars together, pretending the sound clattering through my senses was my teeth and not the cracking of living skeletons under my feet.

The sobs and screams and insults followed us as we continued.

After what felt like an eternity, we reached the edge of a dark forest. Ghostly, barren trees with gnarled trunks and twisted branches scratched at their neighbors and the sky, as if desperate to tear free from the Nether Void.

A smattering of bone shards scattered across the obsidian gravel, crunching underfoot as we left the tormented wails of the Mourning Pass behind us.

"Welcome to the legendary Gloaming Weald," Maya murmured.

"The stuff of night terrors and neurosis," Thesa muttered, causing a few chuckles to ripple throughout the group.

"You might as well let me off my leash. You'll likely need the extra pair of hands." Melina wiggled her pointed nails in front of her.

Thesa tugged on the chain as she strode into the forest, making the Elder stumble. Something between a giggle and a snarl escaped Melina.

"Just focus on your path; don't let the shadows in the corners distract you. If you do, they'll take you, and you'll be lost to their deceptions," Maya warned.

"You'll be worse than dead, is what," Therrok added, his black eyes cold and assessing. "And you'll join your brethren in the Mourning Pass after the critters and trees pick your flesh from your bones."

My mouth pulled into a tight line as I braced myself and eyed the trees warily.

As we moved, an air of thick paranoia and dread crept among us. I kept my focus forward, willing myself to ignore whatever stalked at my periphery.

Again, variegated radiance glimmered beyond the trees, but I ignored it, unsure if it was the forest playing tricks on me.

Several rebels ahead, in front of Melina, a man's head whipped to the side. My chest tightened at the sound of his yelp. He threw his hands out as Maya and a few others called his name.

I made a move toward him, but Maya flung her arm against

my chest. "Don't!" she commanded. "Look forward. It's too late for him."

I stared straight ahead, ready to pounce, as something yanked his body to the side and into the shadows along our path.

As we passed where he'd been taken, there was nothing but a slinking darkness like suspended ink. So dark that it gobbled up the moon's eerie glow.

My eyelids crushed closed, and the hilt of my broadsword bit into my palm.

"Gaaaaaavrel," a rattling, throaty voice whispered in my ear. I lurched forward, eyes snapping open but fixing on Melina's platinum strands well ahead of me.

Ancients damn it, why couldn't the forest take her? It'd be doing me a favor.

We walked another dozen paces, and I concentrated on the scraping of gravel under my boots.

"Don't slow," Maya warned.

"Poor little Gavrel," the other voice whispered, this time from the opposite side. "Always following. Always failing."

I stiffened, eyes narrowing. No one else had reacted. They weren't hearing the creature.

Shut up.

Mist pressed closer, wrapping around my ankles.

"We're nearly there, Gavrel." Maya's voice seemed far away, as if I were underwater. Like I was soul-wandering, my astral body detached, floating with the suspended glowing ashes in the air.

"Let go," the voice crooned. "You can rest now. What do you have to lose? You've already lost everythiiiiing. You've lost herrrr."

An icy pressure gripped my ribs.

The pale trees faded away. Maya and the rest of the group evaporated like dark mist into the horizon.

No. Not her. I wouldn't—

I staggered, raising my sword. "Enough," I growled, swinging my arm, blade slicing through the shadows.

They recoiled with a reverberating hiss.

For a moment, I thought I'd won.

Then the sentient darkness surged back, and misty fingers coiled around my wrist, squeezing until numbness crept up my arm.

I tore at it with a snarl, muscles tensing as I ripped free and stumbled backward.

Pain exploded in my shoulder as something raked across it. I slashed high, then low. The dark billows danced around my blade giddily, toying with me like a cat with a dying mouse.

"Just lie down. You've fought enough."

No. No, I—

A fog seeped into the crevices of my mind. My limbs were numb. Sluggish. The tip of my sword clanged against the stones, and my knees buckled.

Get up! I bellowed deep within my soul. But my body wouldn't listen.

I shrank and shrank, my mind spiraling down a deep well.

"See how easy it is?" the darkness purred. "See how good it feels to stop fighting?"

Perhaps the shadows were right. What would it matter if I went into the abyss? Let it embrace me? What was the point of going on when I'd lost everything that mattered?

My home.

Kaden.

My purpose.

Seryn.

Nothing mattered except the blackness beyond.

I could simply walk into its embrace and be done with it all. Feel the pure relief it offered. Let it carry my burdens.

No! That isn't true, some distant part of me barked. *Seryn matters. My khorda …*

Clumsily, I wrenched my arm back, but the gloom cloaked me. Clung to me, inside and out.

Its fingers brushed against my flesh. My bones. The deepest parts of me.

I shuddered, and my sword slammed onto the ground.

The cold was so comforting.

The night so resplendent.

For a moment, I thought I heard the faint whisper of my name, but I ignored it, pressing my palm into the scar on my chest. There had once been something under there.

Haze crept into the edges of my mind. There *had* been something … something golden twined around my rib. Connecting my heart to something. Or *someone*? But I'd lost it, hadn't I? There was nothing but an empty hollow under my bones now.

"Come to meeee," the umbras beckoned.

My head turned. I was desperate to slip into the darkness.

Craved it.

Damp, inky fingers tenderly caressed the high angle of my cheek.

They were all I ever needed.

My eyelashes fluttered, and the shadows took my hand.

5

THE GLOAMING WEALD

SERYN

*E*very part of me felt like mush. A chilled breeze slithered over my skin, and the scent of burned iron filled my nostrils, thick and cloying. My eyelids fluttered, and the sky swam into view—a haze of cerise and peach mottled with flickering specks of darkness and the outline of the full moon.

But it wasn't the moon. *Was it?*

It was, but shadowy hues painted it. The stars were void-dark, the brighter ones ringed with sputtering purples. Perhaps the light bled inward, filling the astronomical bodies with their own ichor.

How long had we lain here, passed out? How much time had been wasted? Time I could've spent finding Gavrel. My mother.

With effort, I rubbed my eyes, thinking that my eyeballs must have bounced around my skull with my brain through the portal.

"Everything's arse over tits," Breena griped. I sat up, turning

36

toward her voice. She ran her fingers through her hair and tugged at the strands. "Are we inside out?"

To our right, a reddish sea thrashed, its splintering peaks capped in ebony. I rose, turning slowly, taking it all in.

The dark flames.

The heaving ocean.

On its fire opal islet, far in the distance, sat the transposed, yet somehow familiar, Gothic palace.

Yes, everything was off. Twisted. Backward.

But the realm spilled over the horizon in a way that felt like a memory.

A dream.

A *nightmare.*

This realm was eerily beautiful in a cruel way, like every gleaming edge would caress you, or cut you just for looking too long.

"Looks like we made it to the Nether Void." My tattered whisper flopped onto the soot-covered ground.

Breena groaned as she righted herself, brushing off her crimson leather breeches, eyes sweeping over the landscape. "Wish you were wrong, but I know you aren't."

A raspy, swishing sound hummed before a blue-tipped fire burst behind her, and she lurched forward with a squeal, grabbing my hand. "Let's move. No use waiting around, cooking our arses for the void beasties that come out at night."

We scurried ahead, dodging the rough pillars and jumping flames. Phobetor's palace loomed at our backs as we skirted the plateau's edge and followed a winding path downward. Below, a forest stretched—a sea of pallid branches scratching at the canopy like bony fingers.

The Gloaming Weald.

Magister Barden's teachings drifted back to me. This woodland was the largest of all the realms—even bigger than Evergryn—sprawling across half the darklands of the Nether Void's eastern coast. Its shadows teemed with as many beasts.

Every lesson had ended the same: Do not linger.

I swallowed and pushed my shoulders back. To our left, another cliff face rose, a jagged, black wall jutting from the trees. I closed my eyes, mapping the land as I remembered it.

The bends and boundaries unfolded in my mind: a vast plateau cleaved the forest across its middle, placing us on the path into its lower half. Far to the realm's southern reaches lay the capital. To the northwest, Phobetor's palace.

A flock of imposing birds flew overhead, their bones, limbs, and beaks ragged and protruding at odd angles.

Please don't be an omen.

I shivered in the silence. Even that felt sentient, as if the air were listening.

There were bound to be creatures hidden among the ghastly, twisted trees. But we'd clashed with monsters before; we'd endure whatever crept out of their lairs now.

We didn't have to wait long. An eerie hush crept behind us, skimming its fingers up my spine. Breena drew her blades and pushed her shoulders back as if she felt it, too.

Slowly, I turned my head, expecting to see creeping shadows or unusually gigantic creatures stalking us. I'd read about quite a few Void beasts or knew of the stories we were told as children.

I shuddered as nightmares danced through my mind and scanned our surroundings. "Do you hear that?"

"I don't hear anything," Breena muttered.

I glanced at her. "And that's the prob—"

Breena rammed her body into mine, cutting my sentence short and forcing me to lunge to my right.

"The trees! Run!" she ordered.

I picked myself off the ground in time to see a towering

trunk bending, branches clawing at the spot I'd been standing in.

"I've never read about the damned trees coming alive!" I yelled, running alongside my friend.

"Probably because the forest fecking clobbered 'em before they wrote anything!"

She had me there.

Roots tore through the soil like serpents, snapping rocks in half as they writhed to reach us.

Not every tree attacked us. But as we sprinted between the pallid trunks, some shuddered to life, their limbs whipping out to seize, smash, or pierce us.

A branch slammed down where Breena had been, splintering the black stone at its roots into a spray of shards. A stray bough grazed her right ankle. With a wince, she rolled, sprang to her feet, and kept running.

Another lashed at my ribs; I twisted aside, felt the wind whiz past, and nearly lost my footing on the slick ground.

We leaped over a tangle of roots as thick as our torsos. The earth trembled with every impact, branches cracking around us like falling axes.

Ahead, a wooden monolith groaned and bent low, blocking the path. Breena shouted, a sphere of sparking heat waves bursting from her palms and slicing through the bark.

I slid beneath the falling spray of splintered wood, the rough timber grazing my back, and pushed off the ground before the rest of the tree collapsed.

Another branch shot out and snagged my ankle. I pitched forward, teeth rattling, but Breena was there, her dagger flashing. She severed the grasping limb, yanked me up, and we staggered onward.

Every step was a gamble. One trunk leaned in to crush us; another split open with a shriek, jagged wood stabbing like a spear. The forest roared as if the trees shared a single, furious will.

My lungs burned, and my calves screamed. But none of that mattered. We would make it out of this. We *had* to.

Gavrel's face flickered across my mind. Not a memory, but a promise. I would not fail him.

Not again.

So, we ran.

We ducked and weaved, blades flashing when the branches came too close. The forest wasn't just alive—it was hunting us, and it would not stop until we broke.

But we wouldn't give it the satisfaction.

Shifting glimmers caught my attention. I blinked quickly, hoping it wasn't a trick.

There, up ahead, water was flowing.

Breena saw the river, too, and whooped, something between glee and a battle cry. She spun out of reach just as another tree swung an arm down.

The grin was almost immediately wiped from my face as a sharp tug pulled at my ribs and a scorching pain sliced over my neck.

Lurching forward, I stumbled out of reach of the attacking trees and fell to my knees at the bank of a narrow, fire-hued river.

Gavrel.

I wasn't sure how our bond worked exactly, especially with his implanted rune stone, but I knew something was wrong. My khorda was in trouble.

A ripple of desolation vibrated within me, mingling with jolts of energy down my vertebrae.

I clutched my chest, collapsing onto the dusty black pebbles. It was like something was trying to peel my astral form from my flesh.

My eyes clamped shut, and I knew Breena was beside me, screaming my name.

But all that mattered was my fated.

GAVREL!

His name tore through my mind. Or perhaps my throat. I wasn't sure. Shadows seeped along the backs of my eyelids.

No!

Fight!

In my mind, I imagined grabbing the golden thread that bound us and yanking on it with everything I had.

The bond shuddered—light against darkness, defiant and wild—and when I held my breath, the whole Nether Void seemed to breathe for me.

6

TYCHE MUST FAVOR YOU

GAVREL

*A*ll at once, something wrenched against my ribcage. So sharply it was as if invisible hooks latched beneath my sternum and yanked. My pulse slammed into the back of it, a violent, convulsive thud that tore through me like I'd been struck by lightning.

Every fiber in my body went rigid. Muscles locked so hard they were ready to tear from the bone. My spine arched against the cold earth, jaw clenching as a shockwave rippled down my limbs. My lungs seized, shuddered, and dragged in a trembling breath.

Then, with a sickening lurch, the golden thread pulled me back into myself, into flesh and sinew and the aching weight of my body as I collapsed against the earth with a gasp.

My vision flickered, swimming in and out of focus. I clung to the lingering tremors of our bond, letting it anchor me. My fingers curled reflexively, nails digging into the cold pebbles as sensation returned in stinging jolts.

The air reeked of sulfur. Shadows still loitered faintly in my periphery—ghosts that had ripped me apart and were irate at being denied the pieces of me they'd nearly claimed.

Fucking void.

Wide-eyed, Maya studied me, her hands squeezing my shoulders as I stood on shaky legs. "My Ancients. How did you come back?"

"I … Where am …"

Therrok clapped a beefy, blue-gray hand on my cheek in a way that reminded me of Rhaegar. If my friend had claws and wings. And a permanent frown. "They had you. Never saw anyone get loose, ya lucky bastard. Tyche must favor you. How ya feeling?"

"Like Kosmos reached inside me and released me from a swift death," I muttered.

The corner of his stern lips twitched, exposing an elongated incisor, like he expected the Ancient of Luck to appear and slap me for existing.

I blinked several times, clearing away the foggy tendrils still clinging to my senses. The lingering tug under my ribs vibrated, and I dug my knuckles into my scar.

A heady mix of terror and hope skittered up my spine.

Seryn.

Her name hit me harder than any blow ever had.

Maya's gaze softened as she released her grip, though she didn't step back. "You shouldn't be alive."

I huffed a humorless laugh. "That makes two of us."

She gave a slow shake of her head, scanning me, as if she might still find a hole where my soul should've been. "Phobetor's umbras don't make mistakes."

"Then he's losing his touch."

Therrok barked a short, gravelly laugh, the sound like a blade being sharpened against rock.

I rolled my shoulders, testing the weight of my body again. My skin prickled, gritty and itchy. But I was standing.

Breathing.

Whole.

Mostly.

7

OFFER US LUCK, OR I'LL
BITE YOUR NIPPLE OFF

SERYN

A rush of life-giving air filled my lungs. My body arched, every muscle shuddering, heels digging into the cold ground. Our khorda bond trembled, stretched taut, and then went blessedly slack.

I crumbled back to the earth, gulping down another breath. The taste was metallic, like a mouthful of coins. My throat burned with it, and my vision swam with fractured light.

"Ryn-Ryn!" Breena's voice cracked through the haze, sharp and furious.

I blinked at her scowling face hovering over mine, every line of her expression carved with worry she'd deny to her dying day. "If ya gi' me a scare like that a'gen, Ryn-Ryn, I'll kill ya."

Her accent alone almost made me laugh. *Almost.*

It always thickened when she was feeling big things.

Shakily, I sat up, ribs aching. She grabbed my arms, holding me steady. "Ancient's taint," she huffed. "You went limp like a corpse. I thought—"

I pressed my palm over her hand. "I know. Sorry."

Her nostrils flared. "Sorry? Bloody *sorry*?" She shook me off, muttering under her breath as she scrubbed a hand through her dark hair. "You're a fecking menace."

She was more rattled than I'd ever seen her. But when I reached for her again, she let me wrap my arms around her. She huffed into my messy curls and hugged me before helping me stand. She kept her grip on my waist as my legs wobbled.

"Our ... Gavrel was in some sort of trouble." The words shook something loose in me that I hadn't realized I'd been holding back. A sharp ache behind my sternum, an echo of his pain still lodged in my ribs.

Breena's thumb traced an idle circle against my waist. "By the looks of ya, I'd say he's all right now. Do you feel anything?" She tapped the spot above my heart.

I closed my eyes, searching inward, following the golden tether that had become my compass. It glimmered faintly and hummed against my bones. His presence was like a phantom at the other end of a long, unseen corridor. I could've sworn I smelled grymwood and leather—his scent.

I sighed. "Yes. He's alive."

She slipped her arm around my shoulders. "Brilliant. Let's find a place to get some shut-eye. Maybe not get eaten on the way."

That earned her a nervous laugh from me, and she grinned in return.

We stumbled along the riverbank, the current splashing orange-red and reflecting the inverted sky, the dark moon a splintered stain on its surface.

Mist curled over the water, thick and low. Each breath seemed weighted, like inhaling smog. My skin prickled. The trees beyond leaned, their pale limbs swaying without wind, as though they were watching us.

"Don't look at 'em too long," Breena muttered, glancing over her shoulder. "You'll start seeing faces."

"Comforting."

"Wasn't trying to be."

We walked for what felt like hours, but it hadn't been nearly that long. Time was sluggish and sharp all at once. My limbs grew heavier, and Breena limped slightly, favoring her left side, but she didn't complain. She never did. Maybe she would if she were dying.

"Tyche's tit," Breena groused. "I swear if that celestial wench doesn't give us a lick of luck soon, I'll bite her nipple off and feed it to the Nether fish."

I winced, snorting a half-laugh despite myself. "That's a very specific image."

"Motivation. Ancients like gratitude, right? Maybe they'll take fear instead."

"Or pity."

"I'd take that myself."

Nearby, something rustled, a slithering sound like vines dragging through damp leaves. Both of us froze. The sound came again, closer this time. My pulse stuttered.

"Don't," Breena whispered.

I had already drawn my dagger.

The movement came from the tree line—a squat shape, its outline shivering as if it were trying to decide what form to take. A cluster of glowing eyes blinked open across its surface, too many of them to count. Then, as suddenly as it had appeared, it receded, melting back into the dark.

We stood there, barely breathing.

"I really hate this place," Breena complained.

"Same."

We didn't speak again until we saw the hollow ahead. It was a shallow cave half-hidden by black reeds and dark, hanging vines.

I pointed. "Over there."

She squinted, mouth curling. "Maybe Tyche finally felt bad for us. I take it back!" she shouted her apology to the sky.

"She heard you threaten her nipple, most likely."

"Effective, though, wasn't it?"

Our laughter echoed strangely, swallowed too fast by the small, damp cave. Beads of glowing fungi lined the walls, casting a ghostly light. A few jagged stones jutted up from the ground, slick with some oily residue that smelled like rotting fruit.

I scanned the shadows with narrowed eyes, senses straining. The hum of mine and Gavrel's connection flickered again, brushing static along my veins. For an instant, warmth filled my chest, and I felt his breath against my ear, the weight of his hand against the place between my breasts.

Stay alive.

I gasped, but the warmth faded, leaving only my pounding heart.

Breena's eyebrow cocked. "You okay?"

"Just … felt something."

"Don't go swooning again. I can only haul ya so far before I leave ya for the trees."

I gave a weak laugh. "Understood."

We collapsed near the back wall, our arms propped beneath our heads. The cave's glow painted my friend in a pale blue radiance, sharpening her cheekbones and softening the rest.

"Sleep," she ordered. "Before something decides we're tasty."

I tried. Ancients, I tried. But my thoughts were a storm cloud. Every time my eyes drifted closed, the void pressed closer, whispering half-formed dreams of drowning in black water.

Somewhere in the darkness, a droplet fell. The sound rippled through the cave.

Plink.

Plink.

Plink.

I focused on the metronomic rhythm.

And I listened to my heartbeat and its echo. Gavrel's pulse synced with mine for three beats. The warmth of his hand ghosted over my shoulder.

Tears stung my eyes. I turned my head toward Breena. She was already snoring, with one dagger clutched loosely against her chest. I smiled.

The air grew thick, shadows blanketed us, and my eyelids grew heavy.

Before sleep took me, I whispered a prayer—not to Tyche, but to whoever still listened in this Ancient-forsaken place. "Keep him safe."

The shadows deepened, and my pulse steadied. For the first time since we'd fallen through the portal, I let myself drift into the fragile quiet between dreams.

And somewhere, far beyond the dark, my heart beat in time with his.

8

NETHERSHADE

GAVREL

"*M*aya, I … I felt our—" Scorching pain sliced through every nerve. I doubled over, bracing myself against the tops of my thighs. *Bloody void. This fucking rune needs to go.* "She's … I think Seryn's *here*."

Maya frowned, worry creasing her brow. But she didn't ask what was ailing me. Likely, the thought of her daughter being in this place held her attention.

"Lil' Nightshade came for a visit, then. The pieces falling into place, eh?" Therrok said blandly.

Maya glared at him, but he looked unbothered as he shrugged and squeezed her shoulder.

Maya closed her eyes for a moment, breathing in and out steadily. "Secure the Elder. Then you and Thesa scout for my daughter where we found him." She nudged her chin toward me.

"I'm coming, too," I said, moving toward the vryka.

The faintest sound of something between approval and annoyance fled him before he stepped back through some sort of illusion, ignoring me. The shimmery haze of its veil slipped over his bulk and sealed immediately behind him.

I scrubbed my hand down my face, my stubble rough against my skin. I was tired of this place. Its tricks and shadows.

"Maya. I need to find her."

"And we will," she replied, putting a hand on my shoulder. "Therrok and Thesa are my best, and you won't get far in the condition you're in."

I shook my head.

Her words were quiet, but firm. "Enough, Gavrel." Her hand dropped. "I've survived this realm for far too long. She's my *daughter*. Trust what I say. We *will* find her. But first, you need to rest. You're no good to anyone if you're dead on your feet."

I clamped my lips together, trying to do as she said. Fighting every urge within me that wanted to run into the gloom to find what was mine.

Fuck.

I hoped our bond was wrong. That Seryn hadn't found her way here. That she hadn't been stubborn and followed me into this nightmare realm.

But I *knew* she had.

Of course, the bloody woman had.

Fingers flexing and chin dipping, I studied the image before us of a dense thicket, nearly six feet tall with twisted roots and leaves as dark as midnight itself. Glossy berries hung like polished black pearls, clustered among delicate, semi-translucent black flowers—ghostly bells ringing a silent death toll. Neon-purple veins trailed over each fragile petal.

They were the most breathtaking flowers I'd ever seen.

Leaning closer, I watched as the blossoms trembled, and a prismatic iridescence shimmered and pulsed through the glowing veins, as if the bell-shaped flowers breathed in color itself.

Sucked in *life* itself.

Its aura reminded me of Seryn's.

"Nethershade." Maya touched the back of my arm and guided me through the embered illusion. The threshold shivered as we crossed it, a cool breeze sweeping over me like a sudden intake of breath.

"We bartered for the enchantment turns ago. It keeps wanderers far from our den. No one in their right mind would dare touch the nightshade down here. It's far more poisonous than the mortal realm's version. Excruciating pain. Vivid hallucinations. By the end, the poisoned beg for the aether to take them."

The corner of her mouth lifted. "Wouldn't recommend."

We stood outside a carved cave entrance, the veil already back in place behind us.

"Sounds fitting."

She raised a delicately arched eyebrow.

I sighed as the last of the void umbra's grip faded from me. "Nightshade protecting a Nightshade."

"Always."

Her words called Seryn to my mind again. I braced my mouth against a wry smile, and warmth spread over my chest.

A soft laugh spilled from her as she gave my wrist a gentle pat before slipping into the darkness like she belonged there.

And I was certain she did.

THE HESPIRA'S den was carved deep into the earth and stone. Maya guided us through winding tunnels; their gloom lit by countless smoldering motes suspended overhead. They flickered, forever on the verge of igniting, gathered from the cinders that drifted endlessly throughout the realm.

"I was lucky to find these caves long ago. Trying to survive in the forest or elsewhere in the Void is nearly impossible on your own," Maya explained, leading us into an enormous cavern with haphazardly strewn, mismatched pillows and low-top tables.

At least fifty of her crew milled about. Both whispers and lively debates filled the space. A fire burned in the center, warming the room and casting the shadows further into the corners. Passages were scattered along the walls, darkness obscuring them.

Maya waved her hand in a wide arc. "This is our main chamber." Various sets of eyes glanced our way before focusing on what they were doing, suspicion clogging the air. "Melina has been secured in one of the prison chambers. She'll be lucky if there isn't a threat to her life. She doesn't have any supporters among us."

"I should think not."

Maya's eyebrows lifted. "Not everyone here was her victim."

"But if they're part of your movement, they're against Phobetor ... and, in turn, the current Elders."

"You always picked up the nuances, Gavrel. Saw everything. Even when no one thought you were looking." Maya patted me on the shoulder and gave me a soft smile. "Hestia would be proud."

I gripped my baldric and coughed awkwardly.

"This way," she said, taking mercy on me. Maya moved forward, acknowledging those she passed with warm words. Everyone was drawn to her. Respected her. I wondered what she'd been through.

The corners of my mouth quirked. Like her mother. And her daughter. The Nightshade women were not to be trifled with.

We veered down various passageways, and I let my thoughts

drift. Let everything that happened in the last days settle within me. Reliving each second like grains of sand slipping through my fingers.

And every moment led to one thing.

One person.

Seryn.

I needed to find her. Needed her with me like my next heartbeat.

In agreement, the organ within my chest flipped.

If anything happened to her. I would fucking destroy this realm until all that was left was *me*—a single, brutal nightmare terrorizing anyone or anything that got in my way.

Maya paused at the entrance of another passage, curiosity and knowing sweeping over her features. "You can take the chamber at the end of this tunnel."

I thanked her, turning into the opening. My steps hesitated when she added, "Get some rest. We'll find her."

"There's no other choice," I agreed.

"You know … with Morpheus freed, so is dreaming. Thank you."

"For what? Seryn is the one who freed him."

"And you watched over her all these turns. Gave her the space to find herself. Loved her. For that, I'll always be grateful."

Words eluded me, and my neck warmed. I dipped my chin and rubbed my lips together.

Maya grinned and looked at the ceiling before tapping the wall. Her mouth opened as if she had more to say, but instead she turned and went back the way we'd arrived.

Without thinking, I shuffled to the pile of pillows and blankets in the corner, weariness pulling at my bones as I set aside my broadsword and sank onto the makeshift bed.

Memories had often been something I feared or regretted. Yet, as reveries of my khorda toppled through my mind like a shower of beautiful paintings from Surrelia, I held tight, relieved and grateful to have them.

My last thought before I fell headfirst into a dream was …

Stay alive.

9

IN OUR DREAMS

SERYN

The tunnel was carved out of the most luminescent moonstone I'd ever seen, so dazzling that even Morpheus' palace paled in comparison.

My fingertips grazed the walls, chasing the ripples of citrus-hued flashes that shimmered and vanished as I moved. Golden motes hung in the air, catching the wall's shifting gleam and scattering ethereal patterns across the passage.

What is this place?

A glimmer of light shivered along the wall, as if it were alive, beckoning me forward. My linen kirtle scratched against my skin; I didn't recall changing into it.

But memory unraveled in dreams. And I ... I was certain I was *dreaming*. It made sense that they'd returned now that my father was free. Did I recognize this as one because his blood ran through me?

Everything I'd been through in recent days tumbled through

my mind. What I wouldn't give for a carefree day … *or even just a warm bath.*

The thought barely formed before the air thickened. The moonstone's inner fire illuminated; lemon, mandarin, and chartreuse twisting until time itself seemed to bend. My senses slipped through my grasp like water between my fingers.

I blinked, and the tunnel dissolved.

In its place, an otherworldly pool stretched before me, its surface liquid gold beneath a veil of vapor. Tiny gilt sparkles danced in the mist. Moonstone stalactites dripped from the cavern's ceiling like melting stars, their fractured rainbows reflecting across the water.

My feet were bare now. The pool's edge warmed my soles, guiding me forward. I descended the first three steps into the spring, the warm water lapping at my knees. I inhaled deeply, steam filling my lungs. Somehow, I now wore a silken chemise, and my fingers curled into the golden fabric at my hips.

Gavrel's voice flitted through my mind. How my name spilled off his lips when something I said amused him. The moments he called me Asteria when his emotions were high.

I *would* find him.

It wasn't a choice. It was a fact. Something I would do or die trying.

Because he was my forever, even if that meant haunting the nightmare realm in search of him for the rest of eternity.

Closing my eyes, I skimmed my palms along my sides, across my belly. Tingles followed in their wake, but in my mind, they weren't my own hands—they were Gavrel's, strong and reverent —cupping my breasts, unyielding, claiming the desire that ached within me.

A solid warmth pressed against my back. Long, thick fingers closed around my waist.

My eyes flew open.

"No need to stop on my account, Asteria." Gavrel's voice

rasped low, roughened with want and something laced in remorse. His exhale grazed my cheek; his body anchored mine.

My heart somersaulted. Relief and lust tangled together. "Gavrel," I whispered, leaning against his chest. "You … you're here."

"I am. I'll always find you. Even in our dreams."

I choked on my next words. "You left me."

Slowly, his hands moved over my stomach, folding me into him. He kissed my temple, breathing me in as if I were his only source of air.

"It was the only way. She wouldn't have stopped. Forgive me."

I ran my thumb over the top of his hand.

He nuzzled my curls. "I … I thought I'd lost you." The words shuddered from him.

Steam cloaked us; the pool glittered against our legs.

"Never." I turned in his arms, his thumbs pressed into the slope above my backside, his fingers splayed across the round cheeks. I cupped his jaw, his stubble scraping against my skin. "You'll never lose me. I am yours. And you are mine. Until Khaos takes us all."

His emerald gaze traveled over me—my loose strands, the curve of my mouth, the fluttering pulse in my neck, and the necklace hanging between my breasts.

The tip of his tongue wet his bottom lip before he dragged his teeth over it. A shiver raced along my spine.

My hands slid down his neck, over broad shoulders, digging into the dark tunic stretched across his chest.

He descended another step, forcing me deeper; the water licked our waists and soaked the fabric clinging to our skin.

His right hand curved around my nape, his left squeezing my hip as he leaned close. "That's where you're wrong, Little Star."

His whisper brushed against my lips. Goosebumps raced over my flesh.

"Not even Khaos can take you from me. Because you're *mine*," he growled.

His lips crashed into mine, stealing my next breath. His tongue pushed into my mouth, tangling with my own as we devoured one another. Our kiss was rough and desperate and wild.

This was real. This *had* to be real.

I never wanted this dream to end; waking was an impossible, horrid thing.

I buried my fingers in his hair, pulling him closer still. His hands were all over me, squeezing, kneading.

Claiming me.

Heat pooled in my core, around me, through me as molten gold splashed around us. Steam caressed our heated flesh.

His grip tightened before his mouth pulled away. He nibbled and licked his way down my throat. My head fell back, the ends of my curls dipping into the water, and he bit the side of my neck. I whimpered, and his tongue ran over the sting, tasting me.

His hardness pushed against my stomach. I clawed at his tunic, tearing it off him. He yanked his soaked breeches down, cursing under his breath as the clingy fabric resisted him, then shoved them away and let them sink into the depths.

Gilded droplets trickled down his tanned muscles, slipping along the chiseled lines. I traced the rivulets down to the V that disappeared into the water, my teeth sinking into my bottom lip.

A low rumble reverberated in his chest, and he ran his thumb over my rune talisman. "You look like you came from this golden pool. A dream. A siren I can't resist."

"Then don't."

All at once, he dropped my necklace and tore the front of my chemise, and I gasped. The fabric fluttered away and sank as if it did indeed come from the liquid depths. He grabbed my bottom, and I jumped, wrapping my legs around his waist. His cock bobbed against me.

Hurriedly, he carried us to a flat moonstone boulder jutting out from the pool's edge. Spongy, lavender moss tufts scattered over the surface.

Our mouths met and retreated, tongues clashing, teeth nipping.

I *needed* him. Wanted him to ruin me before this dream ended.

He lifted me out of the water, placing me on the edge of the rock, legs hanging open on either side of his hips. Roughly, he gripped the tops of my thighs, pushing them wider and eyeing my slick center.

"Fuck, Seryn. You're so fucking beautiful."

I shuddered, leaning back on my elbows, the flora soft against my skin. He wet his lips, leaning down and blowing warm breath over my clit.

My head dropped back. His left hand trailed up my hip, my ribs. Until he found my breast and palmed it, his thumb and forefinger pinching my aching nipple.

Pleasure rocketed through my sex, and as a moan spilled from me, his mouth covered the throbbing bundle at my apex and sucked.

My chest pitched upward, but his palm splayed across my sternum, pushing me down before returning to my breast, toying with it as his tongue swirled around my clit.

"Gavrel," I groaned, tugging his hair. Anchoring myself in this steam-drenched moment.

"So delicious, and all for me. Only for me." His words vibrated against me as his right hand slid between my legs.

"Only for you," I agreed.

He rewarded me by slipping two fingers inside my wet heat while his lips and tongue worked my needy bud. Tingles pooled at the base of my spine, electric sparks shooting through my core.

It was too much.

I loved him too much.

Wanted him.

Needed him.

His mouth left me, and he nipped my inner thigh as his fingers pumped into me, his thumb flicking my clit.

I reared up again, and he let me, eyes boring into mine as my face twisted into a silent scream, air trapped in my lungs.

He leaned into me, sucking my other nipple into his hot mouth, left hand claiming my waist.

My hands flew to his shoulders as his right hand worked me, my need coating his fingers and my sex.

"Gav, I … I …"

"Let go, my star," he demanded, voice rough.

My desire condensed, everything in me stilling, my pulse, my breath. And with one final, firm brush of his thumb against my clit, I came undone. I screamed his name, and it echoed through the cave like a prayer.

"Fucking void. Come all over me, Asteria."

I convulsed, my center clenching in spasms, my fingernails digging into his biceps. Primal awe swept over his features as he watched me.

I was made of the glittering gold whirling in the heated mist.

And I was still ravenous.

I ran my hands over his chest. "I need you."

His damp lips parted, chest heaving. We were too far gone, and he was too tightly wound to be gentle.

Our time was too short.

We both knew we could wake at any moment. Such was the nature of dreams.

Without hesitation, he pulled his fingers from me, my core grasping at the loss as he gripped my waist and yanked me into the water. He kissed me hard once and then flipped me around, pushing between my shoulder blades until my cheek pressed into the warm stone and pillowy moss.

His palm glided down my spine before he grabbed my hips and tugged them up, positioning himself between my thighs.

"Hold on to something," he rasped. But his demand barely had time to land before he slammed himself to the hilt, driving a ragged moan from me.

My fingers scrambled to find purchase in the moss as my chest jerked forward, breasts bouncing as he pumped into my wet core.

Liquid gold splashed riotously around us as we moved, his front slapping into my bottom with each thrust, fingers digging into my hips.

From this angle, I felt every delicious inch of his erection. It was deeper, thicker. He reached one hand around and rubbed my clit as he moved within me. My nipples glided back and forth against the polished moonstone, and the hot spring water splattered relentlessly over my thighs and back.

Something coiled within my core as I felt the slick slide of his cock.

In and out.

My breasts were heavy; each brush of moss against them had my eyes rolling back.

His fingers swirled and tapped my sensitive bud.

"You. Are. Everything." Each thrust punctuated his words.

The sound of our slapping skin and splashing water sent jolts of lust prickling over my spine. My mind spun, vision blurring in a dizzying array of prismatic colors and shapes. Crackling ember flared around me, and his tattoo burst into life, our combined radiance lighting up the whole cavern like a supernova.

My center convulsed, and tingles shot down my spine.

He slammed into me over and over, groaning my name.

"Come undone. I want to feel you come apart."

And I did. I arched my back, rising as my core quaked. The orgasm scorched through me, and I flung my arms around his neck so I wouldn't sink into the water.

His cock jerked, swelling and throbbing before he spent himself inside me, groaning. His fingers jerked clumsily over my clit.

Tensing with aftershocks, he gathered me close before his muscles loosened and his head dropped to the side of my neck.

He kissed below my ear. "We'll find one another, Asteria. Stay alive until then."

I could feel my dream slipping from me. So could he. His embrace tightened.

"To the Nether Void and beyond," I breathed, my face turning to his.

"To the Nether Void and beyond," he echoed before placing a gentle kiss on my waiting lips.

My eyes fluttered closed, and we let ourselves drift into that unknowable elsewhere we so often promised one another.

10

MORMO

GAVREL

*S*omething was stinging my nose. Repeatedly. I swatted at the nuisance, figuring that would do the trick.

I was wrong.

"Bloody void," I grumbled, not wanting to leave the dream we'd shared. I'd had her in my arms. I could still feel her. Taste her.

Fuck.

I adjusted the hardness within my breeches, yearning for my khorda's touch once more.

I had to get to her.

She was here.

And alive.

For now.

And if she wasn't alive when I found her, I'd—

A sharp pain bit into the pad of my thumb. Whatever had been poking me chirped agitatedly. A flurry of splintered rainbows zoomed past my face.

"Ow!" I leaped to my feet, shaking out my bitten thumb.

All at once, a pixie appeared in front of me and stabbed the tip of my nose with one finger. "What the—How are you here, little one?"

It came out more of a scolding than I intended, and the tiny beast propped its hands on its hips, four lucent wings beating at the air furiously.

My eyebrows rose, remembering the flickers of light I'd seen on the journey here. "You … you've been following me, yes? You're quite a long way from home."

It squeaked, copper eyes flashing, its seafoam-green cheeks turning jade before it tugged on a strand of my hair.

"All right!" I groused, recognizing that it wanted me to follow. I strapped my sword to my back and rushed after the pixie. It was the leader from the Reverie Weald who had helped me find the portal home all these turns.

The beastie who seemed to have a soft spot for Seryn.

It shouldn't be here. Without its clan, it would be especially vulnerable in the Void.

But it must have stowed away. Tracked me here.

Or did it follow Seryn?

Was she close?

Was the pixie leading me to her?

I pushed myself faster through the twisting passageways, doggedly chasing the iridescent tail of the pixie's chaotic aura.

It stopped abruptly, and I almost slammed into the beastie before it flew upward, jabbing a finger at the empty cell. The barred door swung open, and familiar manacles lay discarded next to an unconscious young man on the floor.

He was breathing, his pulse steady when I checked it. But there was no time to waste. He would be fine until he woke.

"Melina," I spat her name like a curse before crashing through the tunnels, the pixie keeping pace.

We shot from the cave, my chest heaving.

The creature darted above the trees and disappeared. I ran in the same direction, clearing the nethershade illusion, not caring that night had fully taken root.

Melina would pray that a Void beast found her first.

She was to blame.

For *everything*.

Her deal with Phobetor cursed Midst Fall.

Destroyed countless lives.

Ripped apart families.

Why? So that she could live forever with immense power? So that she could control and torture others at her pleasure?

Bile rose in my throat. The burning sensation matched the ire and disgust I held within.

The Void umbras were nowhere to be found. I took in a long pull of air. The forest was quite tranquil when nothing was trying to steal your soul or eat you. I scanned the lattice of chalky branches.

Where was the pixie?

A flash of prismatic light zoomed past my cheek, and I paused, frowning.

"Get on with it, little one," I demanded.

It landed on my shoulder, tiny claws digging into the leather strap and then pointing ahead.

"Melina?"

With wispy white hair fluttering, it bobbed its head excitedly.

"Well done." It preened as I strode ahead, leaping off my shoulder and guiding me toward Elder Harrow's hiding place.

It wasn't long before we found her. She didn't even try to flee when she spotted me.

I cornered her between a tight cluster of pale trees.

"Couldn't stay away, Gavie?" she tittered, running her fingers up my biceps.

I gritted my teeth and pushed her away. With my sword in

hand, I grabbed her wrist. If she were in my grasp, she wouldn't have enough time to conjure her aura and attack without me knowing.

"Let's go," I barked, heading in the direction I'd come.

"Always in a rush, Commander. You used to take your time." She cupped my arm with her other hand.

Disgust lined my tongue, and I shrugged her off, my grip tightening around her wrist. I wanted to snap the bone, but thought better of it. Didn't need to give her an excuse to slow us down.

She did anyway, dragging her feet as we moved. Shadows moved at the corners of my eyes, and I pulled her behind me hastily, ignoring her rambling.

More movement. Fucking void. Were the void umbras back?

The crack of fallen twigs snapped nearby, and I spun, sword raised.

Melina yanked on my arm, pulling me off balance. A bulbous club whooshed past my ear. I twisted, steel flashing as I stabbed toward our attacker.

The strike clanged against an armored belly, reverberating up my arm until my teeth rattled.

"That's just mean," the creature grumbled, scratching his bulbous gut, his skin the color of gray-green mucksap. With a disgruntled snort, he swung again, the bludgeon swishing through the air.

Melina and I dove aside as it slammed into the pebbles, a spray of soot puffing around us. The ogre hacked, tongue lolling, wisps of pale hair fluttering along his ears.

"Enough, troll," rasped a voice from the shadows, scraping down my spine.

The darkness thickened, and she stepped forward.

The ogre's ears twitched. He scowled, slumping a little. "*Ogre*," he muttered like a sulking child. "You're no fun, Mormo."

Mormo.

The name pounded in my head. The bogey whispered in children's bedtime tales. Child-eater. Marrow-drinker. And here she was. Standing before me.

Fuck.

The sight of her induced a creeping sense of unease.

Two bent horns jutted from an exposed, ash-pale skull. Her skeletal face was sharp planes and hollows, nose flattened, and mouth pulled too wide, nearly to her cheekbones. Her pointed ears twitched. Despite the dark that filled her empty eye sockets, I sensed her stare as it raked down my body.

Her flesh stretched taut over every sinew, elongated muscle, and corded tendon. Bronze fissures glowed faintly like molten veins along her skin. Plates of the same metal fused into her shoulders, chest, and joints.

No need for armor when it's literally grafted to her, I noted to myself. My Order training filed the details away on instinct, fingers flexing around my hilt. I tried to measure her weaknesses, but there were none. She was built to brutalize.

Seven feet tall, her legs moved with a predator's grace. A tattered, dark strip of cloth hung from her waist like a funeral shroud, and her talons clicked against one another when she tensed her fingers around her scythe.

The ogre huffed. "But Master said alive or dead …"

"Preferably alive," Mormo hissed. "What good are they dead, you brainless lump?"

He grunted, shackling Melina in embered cuffs with a lazy swat of his meaty hand. Mumbling, he dragged her struggling form and his club behind him.

I lifted my chin. "I'm certain we aren't who you're looking for."

"On the contrary—"

I swallowed hard, shoving back and rolling out of her reach before she could finish. I leaped to my feet and swung my blade.

Sparks flew as metal met metal when she blocked it with her elbow. I kicked toward her knee, and she hissed, sidestepping. I slashed across her upper arm, and black bloomed along the bronze cracks.

Mormo clawed at me. Pain ripped across my palm from her counterstrike, but I slammed my shoulder into her side, forcing her to retreat a step. She growled, a wet, gurgling sound, before swiping her talons at me. I stumbled backward, catching myself against a tree; my blood smeared across the trunk.

Before I could strike again, the sweep of her curved blade cut the air and pressed against my nape, slightly nipping my flesh. Shadows coiled around her head like writhing hair, spilling from where her eyes should have been.

My pulse hammered. Even with a blade in my hand, my instincts knew the truth. Against her, instinct wasn't enough.

Leaning down, her lips peeled back almost to her ears, exposing rows of sharp teeth. Empty eye sockets locked on me. "On the contrary," she repeated, "You're *exactly* who we're looking for."

11

IT'S BETTER TO LOOK DEATH IN THE EYES

SERYN

"*P*leasant dreams, Ryn-Ryn?" Breena wiggled her shoulders, a saucy smile on her face.

Heat scurried up my chest as we made our way out of the cave and navigated along the river. The sky was a peachy shade with wisps of brownish-blue clouds.

Even in the day, this place cast a nagging sense of unease. A sensation of being inside out. Off balance.

I kicked a cloud of dusty pebbles, and they flew into the orange water with a splatter. "Did you dream?"

Breena spun, walking backward as she spoke. "I did! Nice little outing with my gran. Thanks to Daddy Morpheus, eh?"

Offering her a small smile, I shrugged.

"Every living thing probably dreamed last night. No doubt Uncle Phobe knows his brother broke out of his rock."

I still couldn't fathom my father being the Ancient of Dreams. So much made sense now. It was like a shadowed veil had been lifted; strips torn away bit by bit these past months.

My ember. My parents. My heritage.

Head dipping, I took a shaky breath. "I'm a bleeding demi-Ancient, Bree."

She walked in front of me, pausing abruptly, forcing me to stop. Gently, she nudged my chin up with the side of her curled pointer finger. "You are. And you're still *you*. Just might make others piss themselves in your presence. Let's start with Marek."

I chuckled. "Something tells me he won't be fazed."

"Maybe he'll be *fazed* when I finally stab him in his mireberries," she muttered as we continued.

I snorted, whacking her on the arm.

"I'm not entirely sure you'll stab his mireberries, Bree. Don't you love mireberries?"

"I will stab you," she muttered.

"You would never."

She bumped my shoulder with hers. "You have me there, but not about stabbing your cousin."

I chuffed.

We roamed in companionable silence, my thoughts drifting to Gavrel again.

Eyes softening, Breena glanced at me. "I'm sure he's safe now. Eh?"

I nodded.

And he had to stay safe until we found one another.

I sighed. Was I that transparent? My shoulders slumped. Yes, I probably was. Or maybe Breena knew me that well. I was fortunate to have her.

"But are *you*?" The crooning voice came from behind us. Breena and I spun around, blades half-raised. Though we froze as soon as we saw her. "Safe, that is?"

The female's golden-brown skin glimmered, rivulets of persimmon-hued water slipping over her torso. She was waist-deep in the river, sharp black nails trailing languidly through the current.

An intricate lattice of golden chains draped over her shoulders and chest, crisscrossing her biceps and barely concealing her breasts. Long, emerald waves spilled over her shoulders, gleaming wet in the dimming light.

My mouth worked before my mind caught up. "Are you … all right?" The words stumbled out, my tongue clumsy.

Breena's grip tightened, her voice low and clipped. "Who the feck are you?"

The stranger's eyes were gilded jewels, the pupils vertical slits of jet. She studied us patiently, body swaying.

When Breena and I took a step forward, so did she. The way her body moved was graceful, nearly imperceptible.

"You seem lost." The tails of her S's lingered in the air. "Let me help you. Pretty little things like you shouldn't be wandering so deep into the Gloaming … not when so many would be tempted to keep you."

Her words tugged at me. Both mine and Breena's wrists slackened, daggers drooping as if our arms no longer obeyed. Every tilt of her head, each silken syllable, pulled me closer. I dared not look away.

Through the haze, my energy thrummed restlessly underneath my scar. If only it would let me be.

She blinked, and a semi-translucent, ocher film shuttered vertically over each of her eyes. Air caught in my throat. The female smiled, close-lipped, achingly inviting.

We both stood at the river's edge now.

Then, all at once, the creature rose fully out of the water, and the illusion shattered. Her lower half unfurled in massive coils, a serpent's body gleaming with every verdant shade as she glided toward us.

If this was who I suspected … fleeing would make things worse.

My iridescence fractured around me, body bracing against the oncoming strike. "Don't run," I barked.

"Wasn't planning on it," Breena shot back. "Echidna loves the chase. So, feck if we'll give it to 'er."

Breena agreed it was Echidna, then. The mother of many fabled Void monsters.

Breena's halo erupted, and she hurled an orb of power at the beast.

Hissing, the creature twisted to the side, slithering onto the embankment. Her tail whipped out, sweeping our legs out from under us.

Breena toppled onto her backside with an angry snarl. I staggered but stayed upright—until her length snapped back, wrapping around me from thighs to chest within a couple of wheezing breaths.

I gasped, driving my obsidian blade into Echidna's scales, but it only angered her, her coils crushing tighter and tighter.

My lungs constricted, and I couldn't pull in enough air. Couldn't concentrate on calling upon my gift. Didn't know if my demise was rattling down my khorda bond.

Breena lunged forward, and Echidna's hand lashed out, catching my friend in the chest with a sickening *thunk*. She flew back, her body crumpling like a doll on the ground, daggers skittering over the stone.

Grinning, the beast's needle-like teeth were on full display as she rose. She lifted me high off the ground with her tail, bringing me closer to her gaping mouth.

Bloody fucking void.

I crushed my eyes closed.

I'm sorry, Gavrel.

"It's better to look death in the eyes," a rumbling male voice called.

My eyes snapped open, body stilling in mid-air. Echidna hissed, looking over my head. Air whooshed, and my braid whipped sideways.

"Or the teeth," another voice, feminine and acerbic, added.

Metal flashed in my periphery. The serpent monster shrieked, her grip slackening. Near my elbow, her flesh and scales split vertically in a slurping tear. "Leave me to my meal, you blood vermin!"

Another glint of silver. Echidna hissed again, her tail uncoiling. She lunged into the river, blood trailing behind her. My body was weightless for a moment, and I braced for a painful landing, but jerked as someone caught me by the vest and lowered me to the ground.

Breena moaned, pushing upright. "You know I love an adventure, but this is getting ridiculous." She snatched up her daggers and sheathed them, then raked a hand through her messy hair. "And who the feck are you two?"

Leathery wings folded behind them; weapons gripped tight, their blue-gray faces set in matching grim lines.

The male eyed me, one eyebrow raised. "Little Nightshade?"

The female's lips puckered. "Look at her. Who else could it be?"

Breena stepped closer to me as if ready to stab first and ask questions never. The female drove her polearm into the earth next to her boots, lip curling to reveal an elongated incisor.

"Vryka?" I breathed. Immortal void creatures who sustained themselves on blood and flesh. Legends said they moved faster than the eye could track, and they had the strength to crush bones.

I should have been afraid, but they had saved us. And perhaps I'd met too many living nightmares to be shocked any longer.

The male's nostrils flared, bulky shoulders rolling, neck cracking to the side.

"My name is Thesa," the female replied, slinging her weapon across her back. Her wings flicked once before settling. She tipped her chin toward her companion. "My brother, Therrok. We were sent to collect you."

They turned, heading back the way we had come.

"By who? And where are we going?" I demanded, following the pair.

"In the right direction," Therrok growled.

"Why don't you just fly us there?" Breena shot back.

"You have legs," he answered flatly.

Breena smirked.

I touched Thesa's shoulder. Her eyes narrowed, and I pulled my hand back. "Who sent you?"

"Your mother," she said matter-of-factly.

My next breath whooshed out, heart hammering.

"Your commander is with her," she added, marching on.

Breena laughed, tossing her gaze skyward. "Tyche, you sweet, beautiful wench."

"How fast can we get there?" I pressed.

"As fast as your meager mortal legs will carry you," Therrok declared.

12

THE MONSTER THE NETHER VOID FEARS

e followed the vrykas through twisting paths and rising slopes, winding up the plateau trail that split the forest down the middle.

"I've had enough of the Mourning Pass for one day," Thesa muttered as she eyed the cliff's steep drop to our left.

Screams and insults hurtled up the side, and I glanced over, grimacing when I noticed the field of living bones. I shuddered, grateful that we'd skipped that area.

As we moved, my nerves prickled with every sound, and Breena's chatter filled the silence. I didn't know whether she was trying to annoy our two guides or to keep me from sinking into the panic churning in my belly.

She bumped my shoulder. "Vryka, huh? Love that for us."

Thesa's wings twitched.

I tucked some curls behind one ear. "You said *my mother* sent you? That you're part of a group called the Hespira?"

Therrok nodded, heels digging into each step. "Your mother

leads us. And does a right good job of it. Brought unexpected allies together. Taught us to hope again."

"She taught us to remember we were more than prisoners," Thesa murmured.

Her words were so quiet, I wasn't sure if I'd heard them correctly.

Breena arched a brow, but then glanced at me. "Seems like rebel leading runs in Nightshade blood, Firefly. I'm impressed."

A soft ache spread through me, and I flexed my hands at my sides.

My mother was here. Breathing the same air as me. Fighting the same fight. Or so I gathered from the sparse replies the pair had offered.

"You all right?" Breena whispered.

I wasn't sure.

I was barely holding myself together.

"I just … I've waited so long for this." My words quivered as we reached the bottom, the dark forest fanning outward before us.

Therrok stopped abruptly, the handle of his spiked maul thumping between his wings. "As has she."

He pointed toward a massive flower thicket. The dark, translucent flowers were mesmerizing, their veins illuminated in pulsing rainbows. "Less fussing, more moving, lass."

"Isn't that nethershade?" I squeaked, recalling my studies about the deadly Void flower. I slapped Breena's hand as she reached for one of the berries.

She laughed, shaking out her arm. "I knew that. Just seeing if you'd stop me from certain death."

A wry chuckle lodged in my throat.

Thesa ran her tongue over her front teeth and stomped ahead, vanishing into a rippling veil, the image of the deadly foliage dancing over it. Therrok nodded toward where his sister had disappeared, his expression more than disgruntled.

I breathed in, and Breena weaved her fingers with mine. My exhale caught as we moved through the nethershade illusion, the secret cave entrance shimmering into view.

And the world narrowed to the shape of her silhouette. Auburn curls dancing over her shoulders. So like mine. The glowing cinder light dancing over her hazel eyes. So like Letti's.

My throat closed.

A hallucination—that had to be what this was. After all these turns, scouring every shadow, imagining her rising from the unknown, there she was.

"Mama." The rasping word drifted from me like a wish finally answered.

She ran, her arms closing around me, and our bodies sagged, relieved sighs mingling. When I pulled back, her hands framed my face, and her thumb brushed away a stray tear from my cheek.

"Little Star," she whispered, her lash line wet as her eyes roamed over my face. Her smile wobbled. "Look at you. Ancients, how I've missed you."

"I knew you were alive." My voice broke, and I took a shaky breath.

Mama pressed her lips together, hugging me again. For a moment, I let myself sink into her embrace—the impossible weight of finding her, the miracle of holding her.

Breena sniffled loudly and waved when my mother glanced to our side. "Breena Cadell. Best friend extraordinaire."

Mama smiled, and a watery laugh spilled from me. She hugged me tightly once more. "There's so much I need to tell you. So much time has passed."

"We'll have time."

"I hope so," she murmured, releasing me. Her expression shifted. The joy morphed into something urgent. "We found him, too, you know. Gavrel. He's here."

My heart stumbled at the possibility of getting to hold him again.

"Where is he?"

Her brow creased in thought. "I'll take you to him. He should've woken by now."

Suddenly, a young man burst outside, breathless. "They're—they're missing. I'm sorry." He rubbed his forehead. "She tricked me into removing her manacles, then did something to me. When I woke ..."

Mama's back stiffened; her voice clipped as she snapped orders. Therrok and Thesa took to the sky, while the young man sprinted to gather reinforcements and search the surrounding area.

"Melina's abilities are already waning." Mama ran her fingers over the top of her head. "That boy's brain would've been mush otherwise."

"Or she didn't want to waste the time needed to escape," Breena added with a shrug.

My jaw tightened, thumb rubbing the pommel of my dagger.

A breeze brushed my face; prismatic light twirled around my head before hovering in front of me.

"What are you doing here?" I asked, eyebrows lifting at the familiar pixie. It wagged a tiny finger at me, squeaking in rapid bursts.

"It wants us to follow," I called back, already chasing after the tiny pipsqueak. "Wait up, Pip!"

The beastie skidded in mid-air, wings buzzing, and shot me a grin so wide it showed every razor-sharp tooth. Clearly, it liked the nickname.

My mother and Breena hurried after me. Every rustle set my nerves on edge. Therrok had warned us that void umbras prowled the northern sector of the Gloaming Weald, but we'd been lucky with their absence so far.

Not much later, Pip spun in frantic circles, its glow flickering as it darted over a small clearing littered with snapped branches, churned gravel, and soot.

My attention shot to a tree ahead. A bloody handprint was smeared over its ashen bark.

The pixie hovered near it, wings beating frantically. Then, with a sharp chirp, it clutched its throat and went limp in an exaggerated faint. It cracked one eye open to check that I was still watching. Satisfied, it snapped upright again with a shudder.

"Gavrel," I whispered, pressing my palm to the mark.

Breena's hand squeezed my shoulder, and Mama stepped closer with a frown.

Therrok and Thesa landed behind us, their wings folding. Therrok stepped forward, eyes scanning the blood stain as he licked residual crimson from a fang. "We dealt with one of Phobetor's scouts."

"They've taken your commander and Elder Harrow to his palace," Thesa added. "This is their doing."

My vision tunneled.

Every muscle in my body tensed, fingers curling into fists.

If harm befell my fated, I would tear this place apart with my teeth and bare hands. Down to its bones.

I would become the monster the Nether Void feared.

13

BANESTONE

SERYN

"**G**ood riddance to bad rubbish," Breena blurted.

We were back in the Hespira's den, huddled in a meeting space. Marked-up maps on dingy parchment were strewn across the walls and a wide, flat boulder in the center.

The pixie rested safely in a chiseled hollow in the far wall. Its wings quivered as it snored delicately.

"Ascension is needed to maintain the balance," I mumbled, the words spilling out in a daze. I barely registered saying them aloud.

The Ancient of Nightmares had Gavrel. Plans whirled through my mind.

We'd all escape this nightmare.

We had to.

I unclenched my fists.

Breena rolled her eyes, pushing her hair aside and revealing her raven feather tattoo behind her ear. Letting me know, she *obviously* knew Ascension was Ancients-damned needed as a *fecking* Korax rebel.

Or, at least, that's what I assumed she was saying.

I stuck my tongue out at her, and she laughed. "A girl can dream. You know how much I love shoving pointy things into people who deserve it. And that twatsicle deserves it."

Thesa and Therrok glanced at one another, some sort of silent, sibling communication passing between them despite their unamused expressions.

The corners of Mama's mouth twitched. "Now that the Elders can no longer siphon from Morpheus, their stolen turns are catching up with them, especially outside of Midst Fall. Their ember will dwindle faster in the Oneiric realms, too." Her forehead scrunched.

Even though I hadn't seen it for many turns, I knew that line between her delicate eyebrows meant she was worried. She tapped her mouth with her fingertips. "And, yes, we need Ascension to occur, but it requires both the Elders' and the Scions' cooperation."

"Even if we can steal Melina back, she won't ascend willing-ly," I noted.

"No, she won't," Mama agreed. She cupped her cheek before her eyes brightened, and she snapped her fingers. "The amulet."

The Grim Twins—as I'd dubbed Thesa and Therrok—paused abruptly.

"No one's seen it in decades," Thesa grumbled.

Therrok itched a spot between the braids at his crown. "Not entirely accurate, Thes."

I was certain he was the only one who could get away with calling her anything but her full name.

His sister's eyes narrowed.

He shrugged. "I don't tell ya *all* the things."

She scowled in response. His mouth pinched as he looked at my mother, interest flickering in her gaze.

"Gryvak still has it?" she asked.

He shrugged. "Yeah. No one's stupid enough to steal it from Leystaes." Breena and my eyes darted between Mama, Therrok, and the rest of the Hespira crew gathered around us.

"Steal what? And who the void named their spawn Gravy Stacy?" Breena chuffed.

Thesa crossed her arms, still scowling at her brother. "Gryvack Lay-stace," she ground out as if she were teaching an unruly child how to pronounce the name. "The head of the Scourge."

Breena ignored her and rubbed her palms together. "So Gravy Stacy's gang has some pendant that will what? Solve our Melina problem?" She wiggled her eyebrows at me. "Adventure time?"

I smirked, shaking my head. Mama leaned into me and whispered, "I quite like her."

I smiled. "I do, too."

Straightening, my mother tucked her hair behind her ears, a flame-colored curl popped back out defiantly.

How I'd missed her.

I fiddled with the end of my braid.

"You've got moxie, Breena." My friend beamed at Mama in response. "But Gryvak isn't one to underestimate. He's in the business of smuggling. Trafficking. Relics, creatures, astrals— you name it. And he's brutal. Just ask Melina."

Breena rubbed her lips together, sealing in her usual quips. Apparently, my mother was the only one Breena would keep quiet for.

"What do you mean?" I asked. "Is Gryvak … Is he Melina's fated?"

Mama's mouth twisted into a frown, and she nodded.

I folded my arms against the pinch of sympathy for the Elder. Even though I understood how suffering could transform a person, I couldn't overlook all the atrocities Melina had committed in the past hundred turns. All the damage she had inflicted upon countless others.

Breena bumped her shoulder against mine. "She likely didn't deserve what he did to her then, but she does now. Let's not bloody forget that," she said, as if reading my thoughts.

"Can we get back to the Shadowvault Amulet?" Thesa groused.

Irritably, Therrok scraped one meaty palm over the rough stubble marring his thick jaw.

"Deep breaths, Rocky." Breena patted his massive shoulder, and it tensed.

Thesa took a step toward us, and I offered the female a placating smile, giving Breena a pointed look.

Her touch dropped from Therrok as she showed her palms to his sister. "New here, yeah? We don't know about your pretty baubles, eh?"

Therrok rolled his eyes. His voice sounded like bone shards crunching. "The amulet is legendary. Phobetor himself created it—a gift for Morpheus' wife before he offed her. But the lass wouldn't leave the Ancient of Dreams."

"If he couldn't have her, no one could," Thesa muttered so quietly I wasn't sure I'd heard her correctly.

"Didn't think the Ancient of Nightmares could love," I mused.

Mama sighed, her eyes wandering over the glossy cavern wall, jagged fractures glinting in the candlelight. "It wasn't love. It was envy and desire. The desire to hurt his brother—lash out —in any way he could."

Loathing radiated from her, but underneath … underneath, longing simmered. Her need to finally—*finally*—join her fated must have tormented her all these turns. I leaned against her, and she brought her focus back to me, offering me a sad smile.

If Phobetor knew Mama was Morpheus' khorda …

If he knew *I* was his niece …

Stop.

I wouldn't let fear ensnare me.

We'd do what we needed to regardless.

Therrok coughed, his boots creaking as he shifted uncomfortably. "The amulet … it's made of banestone."

Eyebrows rose around me. Others shook their heads. Breena put her hands on her hips, impatient.

He continued, "No one other than a descendant of Nyx can forge or wield the stone. Few have tried. All have been driven mad. The moment it turns from obsidian to amber, Nyxvein bumping around inside … there goes your mind. That mist feeds off your essence. Your greatest fears. It's what fuels the Nether Void." He stomped one heel into the obsidian—correction: *banestone*—beneath our soles.

"It's what the Dormancy pods are made of," Mama added. "The stone is harmless when dormant, like the pods. But there are active pockets of it, the closer you get to the capital. Stay as far away from them as you can."

"The Cradle of Nyx," Thesa mumbled, voice terse.

I recalled my lessons long ago, remembered being fascinated by the Nether Void's creation story. Magister Barden had described the event and Nekrionn in such vivid detail that day.

The Magister pulled out a hand-drawn map, pointing enthusiastically.

Kaden yawned, his chin propped on his knuckles. I rolled my eyes and shoved one of his elbows so his head bobbed. Magister Barden squinted at him, his finger stilling on the diagram.

"Apologies, Magister Barden," Kaden grumbled and then lightly kicked my ankle under the table.

I covered my mouth to hold in a combination of a yelp and a giggle.

The Magister tilted his head from side to side and continued our lesson. "The Cradle of Nyx is where the Primeval of Night landed after Khaos birthed her. Nyx fell through the aether until the dark took her. Nekrionn, the capital, formed around the impact, and it's where the Nether Void began. Every nightmare creature crawled out of that wound—"

"Nyxvein runs through it." Mama's voice brought me back to the present. "Feeds the land, feeds the beasts. It's their lifeblood."

"And where they watch others lose their blinkin' minds for sport," Therrok added.

Thesa crossed her arms, the top joint of one wing lifting. "That's the best-case scenario."

Nyxvein.

The word prickled under my skin. I rubbed at my arms, but the memory clung to me.

Inky mist sinking into my soul.

Filling me.

The thought of another Dormancy pod, of that darkness seeping inside once more, made bile burn the back of my throat. Then it struck me: this was my legacy. I could never scrub it out.

My fingers went cold, and I drew in a shaky breath. There was quite literally night in my veins. Nyx's veins. My *grandmother.*

And Hemeros, the Primeval of Day, was my grandfather. His light had once tangled with her dark when night and day brushed past one another. In that twilit moment, and with careless abandon, they'd conceived the Oneiroi.

Breena threw her hands up, breaking my musings. "You want us to find this ... this soul-sucking nightmare necklace? And what? Go bloody senile?"

Mama gently wrapped her fingers around mine. Surely, she could feel my pulse throbbing.

Therrok huffed. "No."

Breena smirked.

His chin jutted toward me. "That one has to."

Breena's wide mouth pulled into a frown.

My mother brushed her other hand over Breena's shoulder. And in a rare moment of softness, Breena relaxed into her touch, her features going lax.

Mama looked at me, her hand squeezing mine. "It has to be you, my love. As a demi-Ancient and direct descendant of Nyx, you're the only one who can wield it and trap Melina's ember within."

14

COME ON, BEASTIE

SERYN

A few days had passed since we had discovered my mother, riddled with moments of tender reminiscing, getting to know those in her cadre, and planning our journey to the capital.

All morning, we'd wound our way through the haunted forest, across the jagged lands where dark flames licked the stone, until we stood at the brink of yet another steep mesa. Belly fluttering, I peeked over the edge. Its side fractured into a winding descent that we'd be able to traverse with careful footing.

I scanned the expanse of jutting spires and barricades stretching outward. A thick stain of inky mist slithered over the intricate maze and seeped over the strategically placed walls that swerved and angled before us in a dizzying display.

Far ahead, the faint outline of Nekrionn's dark cityscape taunted us, like it knew we'd never reach its blackened border.

"It's a fecking labyrinth all right," Breena blurted, drawing her curved dagger.

I sucked in a breath, slowly unsheathing my own weapon. Its power vibrated against my palm, the iridescent mist languidly swirling within its faceted pommel.

"Stay close," I murmured, stepping forward with Breena on my heels and Therrok on my left.

"If she were any closer, she'd be a tattoo on your ass cheek," Thesa muttered.

Breena wiggled her eyebrows at her. Thesa's eyes narrowed further, which I would have thought impossible. A low, grating noise rumbled in Therrok's throat.

My mother had stayed behind with the rest of the Hespira. She had responsibilities beyond watching over me, and I told her so. She had only squeezed my shoulder, brushed my hair back from my face, and then ordered the Flints to tag along in her stead.

A smile tugged at the corner of my lips. Mama had changed, but not entirely. Maya Nightshade had always been an unshakable force, like Yaya. When I'd told her about her mother's capture, she had lifted her chin, certain that the eldest Nightshade would endure. Certain that she would be rescued.

And I'd make sure of it. Or perhaps, Marek had already found a way to get to her. Ancients, I hoped so.

The moments I'd spent with my mother over the past days weren't enough, but it was a start. Our stories had spilled out in the hours we shared. Stolen lifetimes condensed into unsatisfying abridgments. Whole chapters torn down to fragments, entire pages stripped to paragraphs, to fill one another in as best we could with the time we'd been given.

I sighed, focusing as we made our way down the slick incline, avoiding the dark bursts of cerulean-tipped flames and shifting piles of glassy gravel.

"So you're sayin' that if ya want in or out of that steaming pile of a city, you have to get through *that*? Every damned time?" Breena groused.

Therrok shrugged.

"And what creepy crawlies await us?" she asked.

I gawked at the entrance, its crudely carved edges like the yawning maw of a beast ready to swallow us whole.

"All sorts." He grinned, jutting a finger out one at a time as he listed the terrors lurking within the maze. "Ya know, stuff you were told about as a child."

"The Minotaur," Thesa added. The corner of her mouth curled.

I choked on my next inhale. "Excuse me, but did you say a bloody minotaur?"

"*The* Minotaur. There's only the one," she replied in a haughty tone.

"How has anyone survived the labyrinth with the Minotaur guarding it? Seems unlikely. Did you have any ambrosia smuggled in? Are you feeling right in the head?" Breena chided, poking her temple.

Thesa's knuckles turned pale blue as she squeezed her glaive. With a huff, her powerful wings flared out, and she soared high above us. "I'll see you on the other side, *humans*." She flew over the wall with a smirk.

"We're Druiks—she's a bloody demi-Ancient!" she shouted after the vryka. I frowned at her. She shrugged. "Damn imp."

Breena's mouth twisted into a scowl as she glared at Therrok. "You joining your sister?"

"Nah. It's been a time since I had some fun in the Minotaur's lair." His wide chin jutted forward, mischievousness rippling over his black gaze.

We moved through the doorway, and dread nestled under my skin. Or was it the hazy air itself?

I swatted some curling strands from my face, a breath

whooshing past my lips as I followed Breena to the left, away from the shifting shadows.

My palm brushed against the whittled rock wall, its chill sinking into my flesh as we twisted through lane after lane. Gummy vines, the color of pale, mauve-tinged bruises, coiled over the tops of the barriers like congealed flesh clinging to bone.

We didn't speak. Only listened—for the scrape of pursuit, for the hiss of beasts—but were met with the muffled whirr of an uneasy silence and the shuffle of our own feet, weapons, and clothing.

As we drifted into the heart of the maze, my pulse throbbed, too loud in the stillness. My ember vibrated against my nape.

It was too quiet.

Too easy.

Breena paused, her head tilting to one side as she turned. Her eyes narrowed. "Hear that?"

I did.

A discordant scraping noise emerged from behind me. I spun around, dagger ready.

Therrok's wings shivered, wide nostrils flaring before he glanced at the dusky path we'd left behind us.

All at once, a rush of dark, acrid vapor raced toward us, whipping my braid backward. The grinding roared nearer, shadows chasing us as the walls imploded, collapsing inward in a relentless sequence, as though the labyrinth were closing its jaws, ready to devour us.

"Move!" Therrok bellowed.

He didn't have to tell us twice. We burst ahead in the other direction, the grinding of rock chasing us.

I dashed beside Breena, our arms pumping as we rounded another corner. Her brunette strands whipped in a halo around her as she glanced back.

One moment, my friend was beside me, and the next, her

body flung forward, dagger flying out of her grip and clanging against the banestone.

I skidded to a halt, a glimpse of a familiar figure emerging from the darkness ahead, panic stealing my next breath. The pack of mare wyrms may have worn the faces of my mother, Hestia, Gavrel, and Letti, but they were soulless, insipid replicas.

"Fecking void!" Breena screamed, nails clawing at the earth.

I whirled in time to see Therrok rounding the corner, along with a wave of metallic-orange insects scurrying over the walls as they closed in.

Bloody tomb beetles.

I'd read about these little monsters. They didn't just bite. They burrowed and scorched their way through you, or whatever they nested in.

Therrok vaulted over our heads, leathery wings flaring as his spiked hammer swung down. The sickening, squishy thud that followed told me he'd hit his mark.

My dagger clattered to the ground as I lunged for Breena, her lower half already submerged in the soot-like sand. *Quick muck.* The surface quivered and collapsed around her, clutching greedily at her form.

My hands locked onto her forearms, heels digging into the ground while I yanked. She slid upward an inch, but no more than that. The rumble of the closing walls thundered toward us, shadows pooling at the edge of the bend.

"Kick your legs, Bree!" I shouted.

"Pull harder. I don't need my fecking arms!" she snapped back.

Terror jolted through every joint as my boots slipped. Slimy yet gritty tendrils coiled around her thighs, dragging her down. For the first time, horror swept across her usually unshakable visage.

Sweat burned my eyes, and my teeth sank into my bottom lip. Frantically, I scrabbled at the nearest vine, pale and clammy beneath my grip, anchoring myself. Breena's fingers clamped around my wrist, and I hauled with every shred of strength I had as the walls slammed shut behind her.

With muscles burning, on the verge of snapping, we both roared—auras flaring wildly in a fit of fear and fury.

At last, Breena tore free of the quick muck. We toppled backward, grabbing our fallen blades, stumbling to our feet, and surging ahead. Her aura burst around her, and she tossed a wave of scarlet heat behind us. A racket of clicks and screeches sounded, metallic shells shriveling in her wave of energy.

Therrok wrenched his weapon out of the flaccid belly of a mare wyrm. The beast collapsed with a wet screech, its guts sluicing across the path to join its fallen brethren.

"This way!" he hollered, already rounding another corner.

We raced after him, soles slick with gore, forcing ourselves not to think about how easily our bodies could be crushed any second. Ground to a pulp by the collapsing passage at our heels.

A shaky exhalation escaped my lungs as the rumble behind us dissolved into a billowing puff of dark mist, the corridor trembling but no longer closing in.

"Are you all ri—"

The words died in my throat. With my ember still vibrating around me, I caught sight of another swarm of beetles skittering over every surface, their flame-like auras crackling like sparks across flint.

"Don't let 'em stick to ya!" Therrok barked, his weapon smashing through the horde, crunching the palm-sized carapaces under our boots as we ran.

I yelped, swatting frantically as the insects scurried up my ankles, their hooked legs trying to needle through my leathers. Heat seared wherever they touched, as if their bellies were full of fire.

"Bloody void!" I hollered as razor-sharp pincers bit into the side of my thumb. I jerked my hand, and the fiery creature shot sideways, slamming against the banestone with a splat.

"Always with the fecking insects," Breena groused, skewering one mid-air as it leaped for her shoulder. The memory of the chasm spiders crawled unbidden through my mind, and I blinked hard to banish it while I tore a bug off her back. My stomach lurched, but I gritted my teeth and hacked through the swarm.

We battled free of the throng, leaving their shattered carcasses in our wake. Behind us, Breena lobbed an embered orb into the stragglers; the path blazed, tinged in cherry hues, and a chorus of clicks shrilled as the beetles blistered and popped in the heat.

We bolted down another path and skidded to a halt before a wall smothered in thorny red vines. The tendrils writhed, their barbs dripping with sap that sizzled as it plopped to the ground. The twisting ropes lashed out like greedy fingers, desperate to latch onto our flesh. Hastily, I jumped back, my blade slicing through a vine as it whipped toward my neck.

I spun around just as Therrok and Breena's silhouettes dissolved into a billow of inky fog. I called their names, but the silence swallowed my words.

Squinting, my gaze swept over the direction they had disappeared, anxiety tumbling through my belly as a wall of stone shot up from the ground, blocking me from following their route.

I clenched my jaw, forcing down the spike of panic as I studied the paths available to me now.

Slowly, I stepped forward, one foot in front of the other, navigating my way through the swirling darkness.

My gift thrummed around me, my star-shaped scar humming with tension. Goosebumps rippled over my arms, and my heart beat thrashed against my ribs. I'd had just about enough of this bloody labyrinth.

Coaxing my shimmering halo to sink within me, I drew a slow breath to the count of four, held it, and nearly choked when a grinding rasp scraped through the haze ahead. Hesitantly, I leaned forward, exhaling inaudibly, refusing to move until I knew what waited in the mist.

Come on, beastie. Let's get this over with.

15

TRY NOT TO DIE AGAIN, WOULD YOU?

SERYN

*A*s if answering my unspoken demand, a thundering growl tumbled toward me.

Fucking void.

There was nowhere to run, and frankly, any attempt to retrace my path would only draw more attention. I pressed my body against the wall, hoping to minimize the chances of a head-on attack.

A pair of crimson eyes materialized, suspended at least eight feet above the ground as the creature scanned the thinning haze with predatory focus.

Darkness eddied around the brute's hulking frame, floating cinder drifting in and out of its wide, bullish snout. Two gnarled horns crowned its head, scalping the shadows into ebony ribbons.

I gulped, fist squeezing tighter around my dagger. The silver hilt pressed into my bitten thumb, and a sharp sting shot through my hand as the skin split. I winced, blood beading

96

along the wound before melting into the cool metal. The faceted pommel flickered with molten iridescence, and every muscle pulled taut as fractured light danced across the swirling mist.

Air and iron zipped past my nose as the Minotaur swung its colossal double-headed axe, slicing downward through the chilled, twirling cloud my exhalation had formed. The weapon slammed into the stone, and cracks splintered from the impact.

Then, as if escaping, the fog crept away entirely. I grimaced as the beast's glowing gaze locked on mine. Its bulbous nostrils flared, and a guttural grunt reverberated through its chest as it jerked on the axe, dark cloven hooves bracing against the ground.

Corded ropes of muscle bunched and strained across its gray, human-like torso with each wrench.

Before it could free its blade, I dove to the side, landing in a clumsy crouch. The axe snapped loose, and the Minotaur swung its trunk-like arm, clearly aiming to send me to the aether.

I rolled as the beast stepped forward and sprang to my feet, slicing laterally across its thigh with my dagger. It roared, eyes blazing, as I sprinted past, boots hammering against the earth.

Behind me, the predator's axe whistled through the air, each swing matched by the thunder of its hooves and the frantic pounding of my heart. This couldn't be how I died. I wouldn't let it.

My family.

My friends.

Midst Fall.

Gavrel.

They *needed* me.

I tore through passage after passage, the Minotaur relentlessly stalking me through its lair. Far ahead loomed a thick pack of fleshy mauve vines. My tourmaline ring tingled around my forefinger, as if it already knew what I meant to do. I'd avoided using it in this cursed maze—couldn't risk reappearing in yet another trap.

But I was out of options.

After sheathing my blade, I sucked in a ragged breath and forced my legs to keep pumping. The beast's roar spilled over my shoulders. My thumb scraped over the ring, and I splintered into a sphere of fractured light, hurtling forward, ripping through space and time. My desperate cry broke free just as I reformed before the wall, fingers stretching.

The vines caught me as my body slammed into the rock, knocking the air from my lungs. Frantically, I clawed upward, boots scrambling against the knotted lattice, dragging myself over the uneven crest.

The air itself contracted, squeezing in from all sides as my vision tunneled, then snapped back into focus. Thunder rumbled through my ears, and I shook my head to quiet it. No—not in my head. The Insomnis Sea churned far below, its reddish-orange waves shattering and spitting in blackened sprays.

Chest heaving, I clung to the vines, digging my boots deeper into the tangle. The monster roared and slammed into the barrier, metal clanging against rock.

My palms burned, grip faltering. Pebbles and grit rained down, stinging my face. I pressed flat against the wall as it quaked, each tremor rattling up my spine.

I froze, muscles locking and shallow breaths fluttering in my chest. The Minotaur was going to break through. The sea would claim me. And with it, everyone I'd failed to protect.

I crushed my eyes closed.

Gavrel.

His face seared behind my eyes, every line etched in perfect detail. I pressed my cheek to the clammy vines, imagining my thumb tracing the furrow between his brows.

The tremors of cracking stone faded, distant and unreal.

Then my heart lurched. The thread between us yanked taut. My khorda was pulling—demanding my attention, commanding me to move. I gasped, jolted to life, sinew and bone warming, snapping into action.

I jerked my dagger free, hacking through a thick vine and holding tight just as the wall exploded into black shards. Nyxvein poured out in a writhing cloud, like ink swirling in water.

Instinct took over; I swung to the side of the opening, my fingers clutching a jutting cobble, pressing against the cliff face to anchor myself.

The billow flitted away, and the Minotaur's mammoth body filled the space, horns stabbing the open air. Its glowing eyes searched for its prey.

Searched for *me*.

Its axe carved a wide arc, the sharp edge snipping the end of a fluttering, wayward curl. The auburn strands floated into the chasm below, and a chill seeped over my vertebrae.

No.

Breathe.

You can do this.

My ember agreed and flared around me in a brilliant burst of radiance as I pushed my legs against the rock, running to the side just like I had during the Winnowing Trials.

The beast's hungry gaze fixed on me as I darted across the crag, like the deadly swing of a clock's pendulum.

Everything else—the wind nipping at my flesh, the vine slipping from my grip, the screaming sea—vanished. Left was only my will to survive and the urgent need to act. Seconds slowed, and my heart calmed. My gift condensed, branch patterns flickering down my wrists, flesh peppered with goosebumps.

The Minotaur's axe smashed into the wall above my head, severing the plant in two. Before the weightlessness of falling could claim me, I dove, hurling my dagger and a sparking orb of power with precision.

All at once, I latched onto the edge of the opening, grimacing as my knees crashed into the rock. After a brief scramble, I jammed the toe of my boot into a divot in the cliff face and braced myself.

The dagger buried itself in the Minotaur's eyeball with a sickening *thunk* while my ember slammed into the crook of its hock, forcing the joint to buckle.

The creature roared, its weapon spinning out of its grip and plummeting into the thrashing waves below.

Hastily, the Minotaur wrenched my dagger from its face, letting the blade fall to the stone. Bellowing and clutching its ruined eye, it stumbled, teetered, and then pitched over the precipice.

Its wail reverberated through the labyrinth and down into the abyss until the ocean swallowed it whole.

"Look at the fire tits on you, Firefly!" Breena skidded to a halt in front of me, a grin splitting her bloodied, grit-stained face.

Behind her, Therrok nodded at me, his frown slightly less frown-like than usual.

"Little help?" I huffed, hauling my body upward.

She bent down, grasping my wrists, but before she could drag me up, something grabbed the back of my waistband and hoisted me onto the ledge.

Breena and I toppled into a pile, shooting matching glares at Thesa as her wings settled gracefully behind her.

"Were you watching the whole bleeding time?" I snapped.

Her wings ruffled, and she sniffed, black eyes boring into mine. Her clipped tone followed her as she stepped over us and toward her brother a few strides away. "Try not to die again, would you?"

"I swear to the Ancients, I'm gonna chop her wings off," Breena hissed.

A tired chuckle rumbled in my throat as I rubbed my shoulder, kneading the soreness within while we caught up to the Grim Twins.

Thesa's body stiffened, but she ignored Breena otherwise.

"No, ya won't. You'll be friends before long," Therrok grumbled.

"How *dare* you?" Breena scoffed, eyes wide.

Therrok stretched his thick neck from side to side, wings lifting as he turned his head slightly. "Keep up. It won't take long for the Minotaur to regenerate." His eyes lingered on me just long enough to assess, then the corner of his lips twitched—a ghost of a smile that exposed one elongated incisor—before settling into his usual displeasure.

Recognition. Approval. Gone in an instant.

"Enough fun for one day, eh?" he snorted.

"Quite," I muttered, taking in the capital as we exited the labyrinth. I stood tall, drawing in a breath that tasted of smoke and iron.

Before us, a massive, tarnished bridge spanned a furious river. Beyond it sprawled Nekrionn, a nightmarish metropolis turned inside out; a dark mirror of Aion. Twisted banestone towers jutted at impossible angles, their spires tipped with verdigris-stained copper that caught the dim light in sickly glints.

A dark fog clung to every surface, and black-fire-opal paths coiled between the buildings, beckoning us forward.

My gift thrummed restlessly against my nape.

"Think you meant: 'for the *first part* of the day,'" Thesa groused, responding to her brother's earlier comment about enough fun.

"Fecking *quite*," Breena sniggered.

16

NEKRIONN AND THE SCOURGE

SERYN

The city was ominously alive. Hungry. It skittered over me like a spider in the dark, brushing against my skin. Every shadow seemed to twitch with its presence, every darkened alley a place it might have slipped through.

It left me with that uneasy feeling when the mind is caught between nightmare and anxious waking, unsure whether the sensation was real or imagined. Knowing only that if it had been real, the arachnid had moved too fast to catch—vanished into the night, leaving only the prickling memory of its touch.

"So, how do we get an introduction to Gravy Stacy?" Breena interrupted my wandering thoughts, and I chuffed a laugh.

Therrok narrowed his eyes, stomping ahead without a response.

Breena winked at me as we followed, Thesa trailing behind us.

We wound through the streets, haze caressing our cheeks. A

constant chill clung to my exposed skin, seeping under my leathers.

Breena and I turned in slow circles as we walked, our necks craning to take in the jagged, leaning structures. Fleshy mauve vines drooped between the towers, snaking through haphazardly carved windows. Every so often, I glimpsed pairs of eyes from those panes, following our progress.

Here and there, black and cerulean flames hovered around the vines like leaves, casting a dim, flickering light along the streets.

"Don't stare. Don't draw attention to yourself," Thesa bit out.

Breena rolled her eyes and slipped past to catch up to Therrok. I slowed, walking beside the female vryka. "You all right? My mother mentioned you grew up in the city."

"Yes."

"Do you mean … you're all right? Or that you grew up here?"

"Yes."

I pressed my tongue into the inside of my cheek and rubbed the back of my neck. "That must have been … interesting. Challenging."

Her nostrils flared, a faint shimmer of sapphire reflecting in her blackened eyes from the floating flames above.

"Do you have any remaining family here?"

She paused before the square stretching ahead of us and drew her glaive, the weapon's end clinking against the black opal ground. Its pointed blade stabbed at the air. "Therrok is my family." She jutted her narrow chin forward, and with a sigh, I followed her line of sight.

The piazza was a living, chaotic organism. Astrals and beings of every shape and size darted between stalls of strange, otherworldly wares. Whispers and shouts and snarls weaved together between the fog and commotion.

Therrok and Breena pushed through the crowds, heading toward a colossal archway at the other end. Thesa stomped ahead, and I trailed in her wake, careful not to make eye contact with anyone.

Several paces away, Therrok stopped to speak with a short, younger man. They exchanged hushed words, the man's eyes shifting restlessly around them. Therrok thumped a beefy hand on the man's shoulder before marching ahead again.

Someone bumped into my shoulder, a jeer brushing past my ear. "Watch yourself, *morsel.*"

My hand shot to my sheathed blade as I spun toward the source. A male vryka leaned close, sniffing me, crimson seeping over his ebony gaze. His bottom lip dropped, revealing glistening fangs.

He leaned in, and my blade snapped up, the point pricking the underside of his tapered jawline. Numerous salt-and-pepper braids hung around his gaunt cheeks.

"Watch *yourself,*" I snarled. "Unless you'd like a new hole in your head."

"I like my meals ... feisty," he purred.

"Enough. This one is off limits, Evyg," Thesa snapped, poking his shoulder with the blunt end of her polearm.

His attention flicked to her, one blue-gray nostril lifting, a pair of leathery wings twitching. "Welcome home, Thesa. Take better care of your toys. Or at least don't bring them into the Scourge's den." His eyes dragged down my body. Prickles scuttled over my back at the intrusion. "Unless you're offering her as a gift."

I bared my teeth.

He smirked.

Thesa slammed her pole into the ground at a slant, the blade whipping in front of my face, cutting the space between him and us. He ran a fang over his bottom lip, shrugged, and stalked off, his plaits snapping behind him.

Thesa strode away. "Keep close."

I hurried to match her pace. "I can handle myself."

"All right," she said, the tips of her wings relaxing, just a fraction. Coming from her, I took it as high praise.

"All right," I echoed as we reached the arch, an unspoken agreement settling between us.

Therrok and Breena waited at the top of a vast, semicircular stairwell that sloped down into a dark mist. A crowd pressed past us, surging closer, eager for a glimpse of whatever lurked below.

Breena clucked her tongue. "So, let me guess. We're heading down there. That where Gravy is?"

Therrok nodded, his usual irritation at the nickname vanishing. He was probably more concerned about our mission. Or being home. Likely both.

Descending, the vapor thinned as we neared a curved rim. My eyes widened at the scene before us, a throbbing sensation plucking at my pulse points the closer we got. Like invisible threads were drawing me toward the heart of the mammoth, black pit that lay below.

Therrok's gaze tracked the stairway as it stretched wider at the base, wrapping around the entire arena's rim. "The Cradle of Nyx."

Across the pit, a throne sat on a raised dais, etched copper gleaming between patches of green patina. In it lounged a tall, lean man, his athletic frame at ease as though he owned every eye cast upon him, pale gray robes draping over him.

His chin-length, mud-colored hair was swept behind his ears, a copper circlet perched atop his head. A chain of hammered metal coins draped around his neck, clinking melodiously when he shifted.

His aura was neatly tucked away, his expression carved in boredom. The rumor, Mama said, was that his powers hailed from Evergryn. But instead of healing, his ember could tear the body apart. My eyes narrowed as I studied him, disgust creeping into my assessment.

At first glance, his face was instantly forgettable; a man you'd pass in the street and never notice again. But his eyes told another story. They slowly scanned the stadium, dissecting each soul they lingered on, picking them apart, weighing their weaknesses, and measuring how best to use them.

My shoulders stiffened; every bit of me yearned to launch my dagger into his heart. But something told me it wouldn't reach its mark.

I fought the urge, unsettled by the unsolicited violence he sparked in me. "How do we get to him?"

"We don't. His gang—the Scourge—has this place locked down. You'd be dead before you took three steps toward Gryvak," Therrok said flatly.

"Then why the feck are we here?" Breena groused.

"Because I have a contact. She's meeting me here and will get us an introduction."

With a huff, Breena planted a hand on her hip. "Thought this would be more"—she dragged her thumbnail across her throat—"entertaining."

Thesa closed her eyes for a moment before stationing herself against the waist-high wall circling the basin.

Nearly half an hour passed before the leader of the Scourge rose. He clasped his hands behind his back and surveyed the crowd intently. A hush fell over the arena.

"Where's your contact, Ther?" Thesa hissed.

His brow furrowed. "She should've been here already."

My heart flipped. We *needed* to meet with Gryvak. Needed the amulet. There was no backup plan because there was no other option.

"Who would like to challenge the Cradle?" Gryvak's silky voice spilled through the space. Everyone stilled, excitement and fear thick in the air.

He stepped to the platform's edge, a false smile unnaturally curving his lips. It didn't fool anyone. Malice radiated from him. "Does no one want a favor from the Scourge? Your deepest wish granted?"

"This guy is definitely dipping into the ambrosia," Breena mumbled from the side of her mouth.

"What is with the constant talk of ambrosia?" Therrok rasped, biceps bunching as he crossed his arms.

"You should know," she shot back.

A wheezy huff rattled from his chest. "You make no sense."

She shrugged. "Sounds like you've dipped, too."

He grumbled unintelligibly under his breath, his wings ruffling agitatedly behind him.

Leystaes lifted his rounded chin, thin fingers smoothing back his already slick hair. "Come now. Let's not disappoint. Or shall I pick a volunteer?" A collective intake of breath rippled through the crowd.

"We need another way. Your contact is delaying us too much," Thesa said, already striding along the brim.

Breena grinned, rushing after her, practically bouncing on her toes.

Heads turned. Whispers spread.

"Thesa," Therrok growled. But his sister and Breena kept going, drawing more attention.

My scar throbbed, breaths quickening. If they didn't stop, they would surely be detained. Or worse—*volunteered.*

I darted after the pair, Therrok on my heels.

Movement dashed in my peripheral, figures closing in.

Gryvak's goons.

"We need to leave," Therrok snarled.

"We've got his attention, yeah?" Breena smirked.

And we did.

Leystaes' gaze pinned us, head tilted in what closely resembled mild interest. Then he raised one hand, crooking a finger. "The one in red will do."

Ice flooded my veins.

Breena.

Images slammed into me. Her body broken, eyes gone dull.

She wasn't supposed to be here. None of this was supposed to happen.

And it was *my* fault.

Everyone I loved paid the price.

Two beastlike creatures in pale robes grabbed Breena's biceps. "Get yer hands off me before I cut 'em off!" she snapped, thrashing against their hold.

No. Not her.

Me.

Before anyone could stop me, I vaulted over the rim. My stomach lurched as the sloping wall yawned below, ready to swallow me whole.

Breena screamed my name as a vapor-like mist swept over the top of the pit. Therrok and Thesa lunged for me, but they were too late. Their hands slammed against the barrier.

As I tumbled into the abyss, the banestone scraped against me greedily, its celestial energy needling at my skin, clawing at my essence.

Through jolts of pain and flashes of stone, I glimpsed Gryvak above. A small smile sliced his bland face. "Excellent. It appears we have a volunteer."

He settled in his throne, flicking his hand toward my friends as if they no longer mattered.

I was the entertainment.

The sacrifice.

Good.

At last, I reached the bottom, landing in a graceless heap. Ache pulsed through every limb. My eyelashes fluttered, fighting against the darkness crowding the edges of my vision.

"Let the games begin!" Gryvak drawled, each syllable a lance pinning me to the pit floor.

The crowd's roar echoed down the tunnel of darkness my consciousness had surrendered to.

17

THE CRADLE OF NYX

SERYN

*L*iquid iron slipped past my teeth and trickled into the back of my throat. My eyes snapped open, sight clearing as I propped myself up on trembling elbows. Pain flared in my ribs and singed along every joint. Wincing, I coughed and spat blood onto the glossy stone. When I touched my bottom lip, my fingertips came away slick with crimson.

My thighs shook as I forced myself to stand. A zap of energy met my thumb when I swiped it over my tourmaline ring. I straightened the necklace Gavrel had given me, sighing when it rested between my breasts.

Just breathe.

What horrors awaited me? Monsters? Feral animals? Other citizens?

I'd prefer beasts.

Desperation in mortals was something to fear; it sculpted humanity into wickedness. Ancients knew, someone with nothing to lose was dangerous, but someone with hope was even more so.

That's what Gryvak was selling in this endless nightmare realm: something to dream about. But the price was your soul.

The stone floor quivered under my boots, and I crouched low, keeping my balance. In the center of the pit, the ground pulsed with an eerie glow, trails of amber threading under the surface like exposed arteries.

The heart of this realm beat chillingly slow, as if it knew there was no need to rush. It would claim whatever it wanted in its own time.

My grandmother Nyx, the Primeval of Night, had fallen here. Reverence and dread tangled within me. I knelt on one knee and let my fingers touch the cool rock.

The veins of amber crept outward, crawling up the walls until molten gold covered the rim. Then the glow sank, pooling back toward the center, leaving the glassy channels behind.

Slowly rising, I held my breath in the utter silence.

Through the channels and then up the walls, Nyxvein slithered. Black, inky swirls spilled over the brim in a wave of creeping darkness.

I backed away from the walls, nowhere to go but inward.

I knew what came next.

Just like the Dormancy pods.

Do as we were taught.

The chilled, sticky tendrils found my boots first, and I crushed my eyes closed.

Just breathe. Let it envelop your body.

Its dewy fingers slipped beneath my leathers. My fists clenched.

Don't fight it.

Nyxvein crawled up my chin, prodded at the seam of my lips, and slithered into my nose.

Let it soak into your mind.

Breathe.

One. Two. Three—

Fuck that.

Something snapped within me. I wasn't a terrified little girl anymore. My eyes flew open, aura igniting.

The mist recoiled briefly, but then surged back harder, pouring into the hollows of my mind until darkness swallowed sight and sound. I was being torn apart from the inside. My body arched as my fingers dug into the sides of my skull.

I was the darkness.

And I screamed. And screamed.

Memories—laden in shame, fear, and guilt—washed over me in an avalanche. The Nyxvein burrowed its talons into tender places and unearthed all of my insecurities.

My knees gave out, and my aura disintegrated.

Defeat tasted bitter.

This is how I die.

In my grandmother's cradle.

I am nothing. This was all for nothing.

"True."

The familiar voice cut through my despair. A figure stepped out from the shadows, draped in a tattered, white dress, auburn curls snapping like a living thing. Her cheeks were sunken; her skin the color of ash.

I scrambled backward, heels scraping.

This couldn't be real.

She wasn't real.

The female smiled with my mouth. "*I* am real. And *you* are nothing."

The muscle in my chest pounded against my ribs while I pushed myself up on shaky limbs. Her words needled into the deepest corners of my being, unearthing the voices I'd buried. Thought I'd overcome.

I pulled my weapon free from its sheath. Nyxvein coiled

around her fist, condensing into a hazy replica of my dagger, its edges shifting like smoke.

Her thumb caressed the pommel. "It's no use. There's nowhere to run."

She was right … because how could I run from *myself?*

For she was some twisted manifestation of me. But her gaze was more feral. Unhinged. She looked like the version of myself I'd imagine if my freshly deceased corpse clawed its way out of the dirt and broke free of death's grasp.

Her eyes—mirrors of my own—sparked like cerulean flames reflected in banestone. They tracked me for signs of attack, just as mine did when sparring. I raised one eyebrow, clenching my teeth. She grinned, her pallid skin stretching unnaturally around gaunt features.

And then we both lunged.

The crack of our obsidian blades rent the air. The faint roar of the crowd's cheers broke through the veil above as we both spun away from one another, my plait whipping my cheek.

I slashed down diagonally as I faced her, and she feinted the other way, ducking and thrusting at my middle. Turning, I slammed my fist into her wrist and knocked her off course. My shoulder hit her flank, causing her to stumble briefly, but she steadied herself, boots scraping against the ground.

Her rhythm matched mine, as if she knew each move I'd make. Where my body ached the most. Where I'd attack next.

"Give up," she hissed. "You already have." Her dagger jabbed toward me, and I dodged to the side, the blade nicking along a rib. "You should've died in the Winnowing Trials."

Bile and insecurity burned my throat.

My blade whistling through the air, I swiped my weapon sideways, but a rope of Nyxvein wrapped around her waist, pulling her back in time.

Our breathing was in sync, chests heaving as we stared at one another.

"You're not worthy of your friends. Your sister. Mother. Gavrel. You'd be better off dead. Might as well save them the trouble before you get them all killed." Yellowing iridescence crackled around her like her aura had aged in the sun. It didn't glow as vibrantly as mine. "Or your ember sucks them dry."

Logically, I knew her words were false. But the fear that lingered in the deepest recesses of my mind flared, pushing my shoulders forward.

Maybe they would be safer without me.

Images slashed through my mind: Kaden, deathly pale; Letti, left alone; Mama's abilities exposed; Breena's ashen face.

She sprang forward, the edge of her blade skimming past my temple as I flailed to the side just in time. My arm whipped up, smashing into hers as she swung her weapon sideways, throwing her off balance.

The Nyxvein wobbled and tugged her back once more.

Her raspy cackle split the air. "He'll die because of you. They all will. You're a disgusting failure."

Another image raced through my thoughts. Gavrel's neck craned back, bones cracking at unnatural angles. Suffering. So much suffering because of me.

A sob caught in my throat, and I blinked, hand shaking as I held it in front of me. I breathed in, replacing the vileness coating my brain.

Breathed out.

A wisp of air brushed against me, and I imagined my fated holding me, whispering words of encouragement into my ear.

You are enough.

I straightened, mouth twisting into a stubborn slash. "Enough."

She laughed again, the sound like a cracked wind chime. "You'll never be enough."

She attacked, energy snapping around her.

I am you, and you are me! I screamed in my head. I wasn't sure if I was addressing my ember or the vicious clone before me.

Both.

In an instant, my opalescence zipped over me, branch patterns blazing on my forearms as an embered orb tore from my palms. Hers met it, and for a breath we suspended a massive orbiting star between us along a crackling string of fractured light.

My power pushed against hers. Pressure built in my spine, ringing clanged in my ears, and sweat dripped down my temple.

Her feet left the banestone, Nyxvein ropes lifting her. Fear fed her. For that's what fueled nightmares. Believing you were alone. Worthless. Broken.

But I wasn't any of those things. I loved and was loved. My life was messy and imperfect. But it was beautiful, and it was *mine*.

A raw, animalistic sound ripped from me, my gift surging forward, pushing against my double's. Her energy shuddered when mine overpowered it. Devoured it.

"You are nothing!" she howled, but the words were brittle.

She couldn't feed on my fears any longer. The darkness would not write my story. My broken pieces laid the foundation of who I was. And something new and fierce was built upon it. Something inexcusably resilient.

She fell to her knees, her form fading.

"I am enough!" I screamed, and with one final tug, I ripped her energy away completely, unraveling her as if she were made of thousands of dark cobwebs. Her body arched, arms flung wide before exploding into a twirling billow of Nyxvein.

All of the consumed power churned within me, and I dropped to my knees, bending over. With my next breath, my ember detonated—a bloom of light that tore through the misty barrier above like a supernova.

Silence slammed into me. Then the crowd burst into a thunderous applause.

Gryvak raised his hands, but it took a few moments for the crowd to settle. He didn't look pleased. "We have a victor. Bring her to me." He nodded at the sizable vryka by his side.

The male descended. *Evyg.* The male who had bumped into me earlier.

I tried to get to my feet and ready my dagger, but exhaustion weighed on my bones.

"Now, now," he chided. "As much as I'd love to see what you could do with that tiny blade, we don't have the time. He doesn't like to be kept waiting."

Before I could spit out any words, he scooped me up, wings beating against the air.

The world tipped, and I had no fight left to struggle.

He set me down in front of Gryvak, who looked at me like I was the soot beneath his boots. "Quite the show, pet," he sneered.

The way he said *pet* reminded me of Melina. Swallowing the bile rising, I stood, brushing off my pants.

I couldn't imagine the things he'd done to her and countless others. But sympathy had no place here.

"My prize." I met his steely gaze. "The Shadowvault Amulet."

His laugh was brittle. "How auspicious you are."

My voice rose so that most of the crowd could hear it, my words echoing across the expanse. "Does the victor not get their wish granted?"

The citizens cheered, the sound bubbling over.

Gryvak's features fell, and his gray eyes darkened. The corner of my lips curled. His twitched. I had a feeling that, if we were alone, I'd already be bleeding. But we weren't, and he was a man who needed control.

The corner of his eyes crinkled. "Of course, but the amulet is a rare prize indeed. I keep it close, but it requires something *more*—equally valuable—in exchange for me parting with it."

My eyes narrowed. "Which would be?"

With a victorious look, he snapped his fingers, and a female brought forth a small rose gold box. She placed it in my hand. I ran my finger over the etching of a droplet with the moon phases circling it before clicking it open.

Black satin cradled the teardrop-shaped banestone, smooth and dark as night. A pair of rose gold threads crisscrossed at the top and then wrapped down either side, not touching the stone. The crystal was suspended between the metal; an ebony tear trapped for eternity.

"I hear that my fated is in the Nether Void. I want her brought to me before the next Dormancy."

One of my eyebrows lifted at his statement. It would be fitting justice for Melina … to have to return to the male who made her. The one she murdered. I wasn't sure I'd be able to deliver, but I needed the amulet and would be far from this realm if we succeeded regardless.

"Deal."

He stared at me for a moment, his eyes too intense, trying to pick me apart, before nodding to the necklace.

A fleeting look of interest flickered over Gryvak's face when I fastened the necklace around my nape. The stone heated and vibrated against my sternum. He was likely calculating how he could use me. How he could keep me.

He knew I was unique.

But I realized it as well.

I was *more.*

Not only because of my ember, but because I was a *survivor*.

If he or any other monster came for me, I wouldn't be caged so easily.

I would keep fighting until every last nightmare was nothing but a bad dream that faded with the sunrise.

18

WIELD ME

SERYN

By the dinner hour, we'd made it back to the Hespira's den. While we shared a meal in the main cavern, firelight and embered cinder flickered around us, making the shadows dance jovially.

Breena and I sat on either side of my mother, cross-legged atop pillows. Hearty guffaws and chatter ricocheted off the walls, and a sweet buoyancy filled me, lifting my spirits as I studied the mortals and creatures in communion around me.

I swirled the navy spirits in my tarnished copper cup—noir-shade, as Mama had called it—its viscous liquid clinging to the sides. I took a sip. Tart dryness coated my tongue before warmth slid down my throat. Plates of unknown game and vegetables in rich, dark hues splayed across the flat boulder we sat around.

For being trapped in the Nether Void, this band of rene-gades, mismatched like the pillows we sat upon, were a lively bunch. Something about being condemned to a living nightmare for the rest of your days had a way of binding beings together like nothing else. As Rhaegar liked to say: the more we struggled, the more resilient we became.

Most inhabitants here were creatures native to this cursed realm or astrals summoned into it, their eternal torment the price of mortal sins.

Yet, many of the Hespira were collateral damage in the Elders' endless games, stolen from Surrelia, the Epiales Tombs, or Midst Fall. Some had earned Phobetor's ire through imagined offenses. Others had simply intrigued him.

My gaze drifted to Thesa and Therrok, perched on a long, curved boulder next to a blue-haired siren and Argedes, the hulking centaur. All of them were caught in a lively argument. Pip sat on Thesa's shoulder, and the vryka handed it a morsel of meat that the pixie gobbled up greedily. The corners of my eyes crinkled at the sight.

Not everyone who had been born here—or who once deserved to stay—was a monster. Some clawed their way toward atonement, reaching for the aether. Trying to be better. To *do* better.

Therrok drank from his cup, crimson staining his upper lip before he licked it clean. Gulping, I was reminded once more that the Grim Twins sustained themselves on blood. But my mother had been right—they weren't like their kin. I frowned, thinking of Evyg, hoping I wouldn't cross paths with that particular vryka again.

Argedes clunked one hoof against the ground to emphasize whatever point he was making, his muscular, human arms flying into the air in exasperation. Galeyn, the siren, smiled at his outburst and leaned back with crossed arms. Thesa's wings ruffled behind her agitatedly.

"They're likely arguing over who could take down Phobetor's guards fastest in a raid." Mama shook her head, lips curling in amusement.

"I'd put my coin on the siren," Breena muttered. "One croon and you're mucksap in their palm."

I chuckled. "Ah, you speak from experience then, Bree?"

"Maybe," she grumbled.

"Mucksap," Mama murmured. "How I miss it."

Breena chuffed a laugh. "Said no one ever."

With a wistful look in her eyes, Mama sighed, leaning back. "I miss home. The Bogs, I mean."

My heart pinched. I missed it, too. But also … "What of Evergryn?"

A soft smile tipped her lips. "Evergryn holds a piece of my soul as well. It sheltered us, gifted us a happy life despite everything. I have room for both in my heart."

I swiped my fingers through my curls, holding back the trembling avalanche of emotions threatening to spill free.

Things would never be the same.

Not Evergryn. The Bogs.

Everyone I knew and had yet to meet.

Me.

We let ourselves marinate in the silence. It was in such moments that our lives, memories, and choices were the loudest. But in the end, the seconds marched on with or without you.

And the regret of not taking action would weigh more heavily on me than failure. Because at least in failing, I would know I had tried.

I placed my elbows on my knees. "Let's go through the plan again."

Mama clasped her hands atop the table and nodded to the vrykas. They and the siren joined us, leaving the centaur to debate with another rebel. Pip draped across Thesa's shoulder, the pixie now on her belly, tracing circles on the vryka's leather vest.

We'd spent the last few days scheming, crafting a plan on

how to get into Phobetor's dungeon. A strategy to rescue Gavrel —and Melina. My mouth puckered, irritation boiling at the thought of helping her. But we needed the Elder for Ascension.

Or at least her ember.

The day before, I'd asked my mother how she knew so much about Ascension.

"Morpheus spoke of it often," she'd said. *"Ascension always demands sacrifice. An Elder gives up their gifts, and the Scion offers blood and ember to the Elysium Tree. If the banyan deems the Scion worthy, it accepts the oath and sends them back ... stronger than before."*

I thumbed my rune talisman, and Mama smiled. I mirrored her expression, let it fall, and my fingers drifted to the new amulet resting over my collarbone. Tingles zipped over my skin.

Therrok's rumbling voice broke into my thoughts. "... and we leave tonight. Make it to the shores by midday, when the sky is at its darkest." He lifted his thick jaw toward Galeyn, the siren.

Rolling her eyes, she tilted her head, azure waves and thin braids flowing over her shoulders like a current. "Yes, a few from my khorus will be there." Her words poured out smoothly, lyrically. Just on the edge of intoxicating. If Galeyn freed her voice ember instead of dampening it, I suspected it would be nearly impossible to resist.

The sirens' lore had always enraptured me. Enchanting creatures who could walk on land, their legs morphing into shimmering tails in the sea. Their voices lured unsuspecting prey to their watery graves. Not merely with song, but by unraveling emotions, bending desire into obedience.

I imagined their power was the fountain from which Haadran ember was first drawn, when the Ancients bestowed such gifts upon mortals.

Sirens were neither good nor evil. Some khoruses—clans born of blood or bound by choice—emerged from the Nether

Void, their songs heavy with shadows. Others from Surrelia, brighter but no less perilous.

According to Galeyn, the most powerful among them could breach the barriers between realms, pressing through in the darkest depths of the Insomnis. She'd giggled when she'd told me, and my eyebrows had flown to my hairline.

Breaking my pondering, Breena jabbed her forefinger in the air, mimicking Therrok's tone. "And we'll find an opening in Phobetor's tunnel situation. Like Firefly did with Morpheus' dungeon, what with them being mirrors of one another."

"And I'll distract my uncle," I added. Breena high-fived me and then pumped her fist in the air.

Mama's lips pressed thin, her silence meaningful. She no longer objected to the plan we'd settled on, but her hazel eyes betrayed her. There wasn't much that could distract Phobetor.

Except perhaps the one thing he would never resist—using me to hurt his brother.

I'd make him believe I was his blade.

The question remained: how would he try to wield me?

19

DEMI-DAUGHTER

SERYN

We set off in the dead of night, when the pale cyan sky glowed brightest.

We'd made our way over the Gloaming Weald's plateau, and my calves burned from the steep paths we'd traversed. Mama was in no mood to deal with the forest's umbras or the Mourning Pass.

I agreed. Today would be challenging enough.

Finally, our feet planted on flat banestone, leaving the Weald behind us. I craned my neck, taking in the dark moon and stars, their violet edges flickering in the light cradling them. Outside this realm, the stars winked cheerfully, giddy to be beheld. Here, they were black voids pierced into the aether's fabric, ready to swallow anyone who dared look too long.

I sighed as we skirted the cliffs and plateaus, making our way down, down, down. Fortune smiled upon us; we navigated the craggy, flame-ridden landscape without incident, each lost to their own thoughts. Even Breena was quiet, gnawing the inside of her cheek, caught in whatever reveries had claimed her.

Thesa walked beside my mother, shoulders and wings taut, ready to take flight. Pip napped in a pocket of the vryka's leather vest. Her brother trailed behind Breena and me, his boots thumping rhythmically. Galeyn led, her movements graceful and languid, as if she were already swimming.

After countless footsteps, the blackened sun nudged its way into the sky, slipping dusky apricot light across the horizon, where a sliver of ruddy ocean finally rippled into view.

"Not long now," Galeyn announced, her hair whipping behind her. "The others will find us below."

The banestone shingle crunched under our toes when we reached the base of the final cliff. A narrow strip of beach wound along the massive wall, cloaking the shore in deepening shadows. In the distance, Phobetor's palace lurked, rising high atop the black-fire-opal islet.

Thesa snapped her fingers in front of Breena and my face, garnering our attention. "Watch your step. All manner of creatures lurk under the gravel."

Breena's lip curled as she eyed the pebbles, treading carefully.

We stayed near the water's edge, letting the dim light and Galeyn guide our way.

"How weary you must be, travelers." I spun to the newcomer on our right, hand around my dagger's hilt.

The male siren smiled, water dripping from his indigo hair, running in rivulets down his bare torso as he bobbed close to the shore. His aura swelled with liquid sparkles the same color as his hair. "Come, let us help you."

His throat glowed as he spoke, his energy rippling through the air with each word. They wrapped around me like a gentle caress, and my feet carried me toward him. Toward the two other beautiful females behind him.

Galeyn's arm whipped across my chest, breaking the spell. "Still your tongue, friend."

The male pouted playfully, the halo melting away.

"Maya, you'll go with me. Breena and Seryn with the others." Galeyn waved her hand toward her companion and then narrowed her eyes at him. "Behave, Ronen."

"I don't bite," he crooned at Breena, caressing the top of the water with long, elegant fingers.

He most certainly did.

She smirked. "I do."

He threw his head back, genuine amusement spilling from him. "Then we'll get along just fine, mortal."

Unabashedly, Galeyn stepped out of her breeches and into the water. My mouth parted as her aura shimmered, swirling around her in glittering aqua light. Her legs knit together, scales the same shade as her ember rippling over her skin. She dove beneath the surf just as a magnificent, semi-translucent tail unfurled behind her. She surfaced beside Ronen and the others with a satisfied smile.

It was the same expression I wore in Evergryn. And in the Perilous Bogs now. Both places were home.

Before Breena could go near the waves, a stifled yelp rent the air. My gaze snapped to the sound, and a flurry of movement confused my senses.

In a blur of bluish-gray and blue-veined wings, Thesa darted toward Mama, whose lips pulled back with shock. Pip tumbled from Thesa's vest pocket, wings flailing as the pixie tried to right itself mid-fall. Thesa's glaive arced through the air in my mother's direction, forcing her to stumble back.

Pip landed on the ground with a soft squeak, blinking up at the chaos as if entirely unbothered.

Thinking she was attacking Mama, I lunged, ready to rip the vryka's wings from her back, but Therrok caught me mid-leap by the vest.

"Get off me!" I shouted.

"Hold, little Nightshade." His words were clipped as he swept Breena's legs out from beneath her. Cursing, she hit the pebbles, daggers clattering at her sides.

Thesa sheathed her weapon as swiftly as it had appeared. A wispy trail of Nyxvein slithered back into the gravel between her and my mother.

"What the ever-loving feck was that?" Breena squealed.

I tore free from Therrok's grip and rushed to Mama's side. At her feet lay the severed head of a serpent-like creature. Liquid shadows seeped from between its shiny, black scales. Blood dripped from one of its fangs.

Mama winced as she held her side. "Bane vipers. Its nest was hiding underfoot." She nodded at the female vryka as Breena scrambled to her feet. "Thank you, Thesa."

She rolled her shoulders, a shiver running through her wings. "My pleasure." Her nostrils flared. "Nasty little beasts."

I wrapped my arm around Mama, steadying her. "It bit you."

Thesa scoffed, rolling her eyes. "It barely grazed her. Poison didn't even loose."

My mother pressed against her flank harder with a grimace. "Don't worry, Little Star. Looks worse than it is. The aether won't claim me anytime soon."

I toed the creature's remains with my boot, and it erupted into a billow of dust, sinking into the banestone shore. "Don't you mean the Stygian Murk?"

Mama's eyes didn't meet mine. After several seconds, my shoulders inched up when no one answered my question.

Thesa's wings twitched as she shifted her gaze elsewhere. "Come, Pip," she muttered, holding her pocket open for the pixie. She glanced at Mama. "We'll meet you there and scout for an opening."

Therrok ran his tongue over one fang. "And take out any waiting guards."

Breena crossed her arms, eyes fixed on the retreating wings skimming low over the water. "Still think we should've gone with them. We're like baggage no one wants."

Mama's lips curved faintly. "Better baggage than dead weight. You know carrying us would have weakened them." Her smile lingered, but her gaze was on the dark horizon. "And you'll be grateful for their strong wings soon enough. What waits inside will test every one of us."

Breena's smirk wavered, betraying the rare flicker of nerves she tried to bury under bravado. She muttered, "You really know how to ruin a perfectly good whinge."

Mama's eyes softened, but she let the silence stretch rather than respond. With a grunt, she lowered herself onto a nearby boulder and lifted her tunic.

My stomach dropped. A finger-length cut scored the skin just below her ribcage, the edges angry, though the bleeding had already slowed. I let out a shaky breath.

"Breena, fetch my pack. Needle, thread, and noirshade," Mama instructed, her voice steady.

Breena's amusement returned as she dug in the bag. "Now, Maya—I'll never say no to a nip of wine, but is this really the time?" she joked before handing over the bottle.

Mama chuffed a laugh that turned into a wince as she poured the navy alcohol over the gash. It hissed and fizzed as it disinfected the wound.

I clenched my fists when she sucked in air between her teeth.

Then she took several swallows of noirshade, wiping her mouth with the back of her hand before managing a crooked, pained smirk. "It'll make me forget the pain for a while."

My eyebrows creased as I watched them. Mama still hadn't answered my earlier question.

Breena produced the needle and thread with a flourish and then crouched beside her. "I'll stitch you up quick. Hold still, Mama Nightshade."

My mother brushed her fingers over Breena's shoulder, gentle despite the tremor in her hand. I moved to her other side, steadying her with my palm resting against her back.

Dread stiffened my shoulder blades. In Midst Fall, when someone died, their astral form was pulled to limbo. From there, they went to the dream or nightmare realms after judgment. Or if they'd been soul-wandering, like we did during Dormancy, their astral form went to the Murk, their body remaining in stasis.

But … she wasn't in her own realm, and hadn't been for a long time.

I squeezed my mother's shoulder, my voice more insistent. "Mama, don't you mean you won't be pulled to the *Stygian Murk* any time soon?"

Breena tied off the end of her sutures and brushed her hands on her breeches before rising. "Mighty fine handiwork, if I say so myself." Her tone wobbled at the end as if she were trying to change the subject.

She grabbed the noirshade and took a pull, holding the bottle out to me. "Have a fecking nip, Firefly."

Irritation bubbled. Pushing the bottle away, I ignored her and glared at my mother. "Answer me," I demanded.

Mama offered Breena a grateful look and then tucked a damp curl behind her ear. She pressed her lips together, standing and placing both hands on my cheeks. Her skin was warm and rough from turns of hard survival. "Seryn, I know you understand."

My pulse stuttered. I chose the path of willful denial. "Understand what?"

But I understood. I'd known the whole time, but I'd pushed the truth deep down, defiantly refusing to acknowledge it.

Because after all the many long turns without my mother, I finally had her back. My chin jutted forward, and I bit the side of my cheek, still fighting with myself.

Her physical form had been pulled to her as Kaden's had been in the nightmare prison. It wasn't safe in a pod, tethering her soul. It wasn't there to yank her astral form back, like an elastic band, to limbo if destroyed.

She tilted her head, eyebrows pushing together, and regret lining her mouth. Liquid welled along my lower lashes, and I blinked, unashamed when a tear spilled over and dampened my cheek.

"Mama," I whispered, burying my face in her neck and gently wrapping my arms around her.

My mother wouldn't be coming home to Evergryn. And if she sustained fatal injuries here, the aether would claim her like it had done to Hestia. Because she'd been in a realm not her own for too long. Her corporeal body was stolen turns ago. Her astral form trapped and left to wander the Nether Void all this time.

"You … you died," I breathed. The weight of my words was too much. I would surely sink beneath the banestone at any moment, its darkness trapping me here with her.

My mind spun, desperate for a loophole. "I could visit you during the full moons. Letti, too." My voice trembled. "There must be a way."

Mama's smile was tender, sorrowful. "No, Little Star. Each time mortals cross the veil, it frays. It pulls at the threads that bind your body and soul. Thins the boundaries between life and death, dream and waking. Yet another reason the Dormancy is so malevolent—why the pods must be destroyed once and for all."

My heart dropped into my stomach. I knew she was right. The longer we stayed, the more the Oneiric realms would try to claim us. The more the portals would strain and weaken until nightmares completely bled into the living plane.

Gently, her fingers smoothed my hair before tipping my chin up. "Don't despair. Home is gone to me, yes—but Surrelia,

Morpheus … there may yet be a place I can begin again. And one day, you and Letti will find me there. For what is death but a dream?"

AFTER DEPOSITING me at the base of the islet, Mama and Breena had gone with Galeyn and the other sirens, approaching the palace under the cover of darkness and waves.

My wet clothes chilled my flesh, and I shook out my hands, trying to rid myself of shivers, breath clouding the space before me.

My thighs burned from climbing the crooked stairs that coiled around the islet. Each step pitched outward, a threat of air and nothing below; there was no railing, no handhold but my resolve. I pressed my palm to the fire-opal wall, ignoring the nerves clawing at my belly.

Images skittered through my head like chasm spiders. Gavrel, broken and bruised. Mama, bursting into ashes. Everyone I loved crumpled and bloodied, pulled screaming into the aether.

Stop.

I couldn't lose myself here. Not now.

I drew in three slow breaths, counting each one against my heartbeat. With each measured exhale, the panic leaked away. My world narrowed to the steps beneath my soles and the rhythm of the Shadowvault Amulet and my rune stone thumping against my chest.

Gavrel had to be alive. I would have felt it if he weren't. *Right?* The question echoed through my skull, but the faint hum against my ribs eased the sharpest edges of my concern.

The air thickened the higher I climbed; rank with iron and

smoke, coating my tongue. Shadows leaked along the edges of each stair, creeping closer.

My ember purred against my scar, reminding me who I was. Determined, I set my jaw and pressed on, shoving aside my doubts. Whatever happened today, we would endure.

I would find Gavrel. I would save him. I would end this.

The twisted copper gate loomed ahead at last. Carved bane-stone sentinels flanked it, their rocky faces twisted into screams.

I touched the hilt at my side, comforted that I wasn't walking into this unarmed.

This wasn't a dream. It wasn't sparring or memory. This was the threshold of nightmare itself. And I was done running.

I squared my shoulders. Steadily, my ember vibrated inside me. Whatever waited beyond this gate, it would not break me.

For I was already broken. And I had learned to carve my own path with the beautifully scarred edges of my soul.

I wrapped my palm around a metal bar, letting its chill anchor me.

I grinned at the new image emerging in my mind.

One of Phobetor on his knees, his shadows torn, ground into dust.

20

THIS BLOODY DUNGEON

GAVREL

This bloody dungeon.

It was nearly identical to Morpheus'. Was Phobetor so obsessed with his brother that any originality had escaped him? Or was it simply the nature of the Oneiric realms, the echoing balance between them? Either way, it seemed like a defensive oversight to have them so similar.

I had glimpsed that liquid metal, albeit copper-tinged, pool below before being tossed in my cell. It would likely be the quickest way to portal back to Surrelia.

I'd searched the entire chamber for any vulnerable spot to aid my escape, but I had come up short. I leaned against the wall, clenching my teeth as the ache in my ribs twinged, then winced when my frown tugged at my split lip and battered face.

Phobetor had learned that Seryn was his niece. That she was my khorda. About Maya. About Morpheus being released.

Thanks to Melina.

Venom raged inside me, crawling over my tongue.

I should have killed her the moment we landed in this realm.

Should have put her down turns ago.

I wrenched against my handcuffs.

"Looks like you want to have a chat again," the demon guard said, two curved horns jutting from the top of his head.

By "chat," he meant another thrashing while manacles shackled me to a chair and prevented me from beating him to a pulp.

"I'd enjoy *chatting* without these." I jerked my wrists, the chains clanging against the floor.

He scoffed. "Mortal, it matters not if you are bound. The result would be the same. Besides, you need to be conscious when your fated arrives."

Phobetor knew Seryn would come for me. It was a trap— and the thought of losing her, of her being used or hurt, set fire crawling up my spine.

I lurched forward, restraints biting into my wrists.

The demon chortled. A throaty, grating sound.

I'd rip his fucking horns off if he touched her.

He slapped his knee, a raucous guffaw echoing through the pit as he moved up the corkscrew incline. His laughter broke into a hacking cough, and I smirked.

Good. Let him choke on it.

Wait.

He was choking. I strained against the bars, rattling my chains, until a pair of boots flopped into view and metal jangled.

"Look alive, Commander," Breena whisper-yelled, shoving the guard's key into the lock.

"Seryn?" I demanded, holding up my cuffs as the door rolled open.

"Nice to see you, too," Breena muttered.

I nodded at her and looked at Maya as she slipped into the cell and helped undo my tethers. Her jaw clenched. "She's with Phobetor."

I shoved through the opening, nearly colliding with Therrok and Thesa. "We have to get to her."

"Yes, Commander Obvious." Breena rolled her eyes. "That is, in fact, the next part of the plan."

The horned creature lay on the ground, his eyes bulging, his veined neck raw from strangulation. I removed his baldric and secured it across my chest. I slid the sword from its sheath, the thick, curved blade shining in the dim light while I studied it.

Its guard consisted of two platinum interlocking crescent moons that rested snugly against my fist, the intricately etched banestone hilt gleaming. A small smile tugged at my mouth as I admired the craftsmanship. The demon had likely stolen it from another, so I didn't feel the slightest ounce of guilt commandeering the piece. I was due a new blade.

Therrok wiped the demon's blood from a metal rope wrapped in his fists and then clipped it securely on his belt. "Onward."

"This is a trap. He knew she'd come," I muttered, taking the lead up the spiraling path.

Unlike Morpheus', his brother's dungeon seemed to be at full capacity. Creatures and astrals cried out from their cells, claws and hands snatching at us as we passed.

Maya pushed forward. "I figured as much. Let's make haste."

Flaming orb lanterns bobbed along the walls, shadows lurching across black opal walls, and gleaming patches winked like neon-colored eyes.

From above, heavy footfalls hammered against stone. Metal clanged, and shadows swarmed along the walls, rushing toward us.

"We did not make *enough* haste," Therrok said dryly.

Breena's aura flared, lighting all of us in an eerie red glow.

The top of the pixie's head poked out from Thesa's vest pocket, copper eyes flicking about nervously. "Stay hidden, Pip," the female vryka snapped. The pixie stuck its jade tongue out, then burrowed deeper.

My eyebrows rose. Thesa narrowed her eyes, scanning our path. "In here," she snarled, dodging into a tunnel.

We didn't get far before a horde of demonic guards blocked the passage, teeth gnashing and weapons slicing the air.

Breena hurled a sparking ball of ember toward them as we backtracked, and pained cries chased us.

Phobetor's minions closed in along the ramp—a tide of horns and fangs, deformed faces twisting with malice, their ragged armor clattering like bones in a tomb.

There was nowhere to go but through them.

"Cut down every last demon," I ordered and stepped toward the first line of attackers. The carved ledge was only wide enough for three bodies abreast, and I counted at least a hundred bodies rushing toward us from both ends.

I'd faced worse odds.

My rune tattoo blazed, and I pushed its energy over my new sword, the edge flashing. A slow smile spread over my face, and the closest guard narrowed his eyes, his throat bobbing. I lunged, slashing my blade diagonally. His mouth dropped open, revealing rows of sharp, crooked teeth as the metal cut through his wrist like butter.

Blood sprayed. An opus of battle cries and clashing steel swallowed his howl.

Therrok charged ahead, barreling into our enemies, his war hammer shattering shields and bones. With a feral grin, he sent several guards screaming over the edge and into the pit. His wings twitched, half flaring, but he stayed grounded. He was a wall of brute force.

I spun, slicing into another demon's guts. And another. Another. Until we inched our way up the incline.

Breena darted past, a blur of heat and steel. She carved through throats and bellies. Gracefully, she tossed her daggers into the air, flung her power into an advancing foe, and then caught the hilts. One guard charged at her from the side, but she stabbed one dagger into his neck, caught his wrist, twisted, and then shoved the other blade into his chest before kicking him off her steel and into the well.

Calculated and merciless, Thesa moved like a shadow, polearm sweeping in lethal arcs. She was supernaturally fast, her movements barely registering between each blink. A guard's head toppled, and another fell yowling as her blade severed his leg at the knee. Her wings flexed, angling for balance.

A sparkling, midnight aura burst past my left shoulder as I yanked my weapon from an enemy's flank. Maya's shadowy ribbons caught hold of a guard's gray aura, yanking on her ember as though it were a rope. The demon jerked, but Maya's energy was stronger as it slammed the female into the wall and knocked her out.

We made progress. Even so, they kept coming. Kept swarming. More adversaries spilled onto the ramp from side tunnels above us.

"We're being herded," I growled, parrying a strike and ramming an elbow into a guard's jaw. His teeth cracked under the blow.

Maya whipped toward me. "We have to descend. There are too many coming from above!"

Fucking void.

She was right.

We hacked our way downward, Breena's ember and blades dancing around her, Maya pitting auras against their owners.

Thesa and Therrok took to the air, attacking from above. Demons plunged past, smashing into stone or the molten pool at the bottom of the pit. Steam exploded upward with a hiss, flesh peeling from bone in seconds before the rest disintegrated.

My chest tightened. Void take me—was that what the pit did

when the moon wasn't full? A portal one moment, a cauldron of death the next.

I squared my jaw, driving my blade into another guard.

If Seryn was anywhere near it—

I gritted my teeth, rage coiling within me. I couldn't allow myself to imagine her falling into that.

Exhaustion gnawed at the edges of my muscles, but I refused to slow. I would not falter, not while there was breath in my lungs. A heartbeat in my chest.

Not while my fated was near.

21

A RUNEBOUND BARGAIN

Seryn

"Who goes there?" the imposing troll bellowed, stabbing a spike-riddled club in my direction.

Here goes nothing.

I pushed my shoulders back. "I'm here to see the Ancient of Nightmares."

The other troll dragged his dark, beady eyes over my body. He chortled. "He'll be the last thing you see."

The first beast guffawed and slapped his thigh. "'Tis true! You're as good as burnt niblets!"

My nostrils flared as I fought not to roll my eyes. The trek up the islet's winding staircase had been arduous. My leg muscles burned. Breathing labored. Patience nonexistent.

"Tell Phobetor his niece wants to see him," I snapped.

That quieted them. Both of their ledge-shaped brows lifted so high I thought the dark tufts of hair at their crowns might tumble off their scalps.

"Let her in."

The familiar singsong voice still sent a chill over me. The jagged copper gates creaked open as the trolls did as Melina said. She stood in the open entrance, a feral grin plastered over her face.

She was a damned roach. Hard to kill and cunning enough to survive the most hostile of situations.

"Phobetor will be so pleased to see *family*," she taunted. "Quite the secret you've held onto."

"It wasn't mine to hold until recently," I muttered.

I followed her as she sashayed into the foyer, the fitted, black silk dress hugging her curves.

As suspected, the palace had a similar layout to Morpheus', with a pair of grand fire-opal staircases curving along the rounded banestone walls, a balcony above, copper doors with beautiful swirling designs, and an impressive copper chandelier above, dripping with hundreds of cracked, smoky quartz crystals that both glimmered and consumed the light.

Directly ahead was a Great Hall, but we turned right, Melina pausing at the first door we reached. She rapped on the etched metal, and I held my breath for a few heartbeats.

"Enter!" a commanding voice boomed.

Melina ran her tongue over her bottom lip and swiped her hand through the air, ushering me inside.

The study was dark and lavishly Gothic. Soft, red textures vied for attention with sharp, black stone furnishings.

Elder Harrow pushed against my biceps, forcing me to take a seat in an intricately carved chair opposite the Ancient of Nightmares. I jerked away from her, repulsed by her chilled touch. She sniggered, claiming a seat on a plush sofa in the corner, her usual crimson lipstick the same shade as the velvet.

My star-shaped scar thrummed while Phobetor studied me from under dark lashes. His lean yet muscular figure lounged in an imposing, high-backed chair, his night-colored robes nearly blending into the banestone. He dragged his eyes over me, his scrutiny lingering at the Shadowvault Amulet resting against my collarbone.

"How well you look, *niece*. Imagine my surprise when I learned of our relation. My brother was never one to spread his seed frivolously," he drawled, studying his trimmed fingernails on one hand.

He was baiting me. Prodding to find the cracks. He wouldn't find any. "It's not my concern what Morpheus does."

Phobetor looked at me from the corner of his eye. "Ah, but are there not tender feelings between a father and his sprout?"

"Do you have tender feelings for those you've sired?" I threw back. There were countless tales of Phobetor's exploits. Of how he swiftly executed all of his progenies so they'd never challenge him for his throne.

"Love is a crutch invented by the fragile to distract from the emptiness of their pitiful existence." His mouth pursed, and a slight shrug moved one shoulder. "It's not a pursuit I take part in."

What a dismal reality he lived in.

I imagined Gavrel imprisoned below, filling me with the will to get through this. If love were a crutch, I'd happily lean on it for the rest of my turns.

By now, my mother, Breena, and the Grim Twins may have found a way into the dungeon as planned.

"Well, he's never been a part of my life. Never helped my mother. He can rot for all I care."

Amused air blew from Phobetor's straight, regal nose. "Is that so? Yes, Maya, is it? She is the leader of some useless band of misfits running around my realm. She's only recently become interesting."

I pushed my spine into the back of my chair, keeping my mask of indifference fixed on my face. He paused for a touch too long, his eyes boring into mine, marinating in the uncomfortable silence.

He'd be waiting a long while.

The straight seam between his lips quirked. "I've heard how exceptional your gifts are." His voice was silk-wrapped razors.

Malice and charm seeped into his smile, his high cheekbones lifting over the sharp angles of his features. "Melina tells me your mother was her Scion. Shame Maya couldn't claim her place." Long, elegant fingers stroked his chin.

My fists clenched, nails digging into my palms. The reminder that my mother was an astral—was dead—pinched my heart.

Elders Harrow, Ash, and Craven had imprisoned her. Played Phobetor's games. Led her to her demise.

Melina looked pleased with herself, the corners of her mouth twitching like a cat being scratched behind the ear.

They would pay.

And so would my uncle.

Phobetor leaned forward. "Maya couldn't. But you can."

"My liege—" Melina started, eyebrows furrowing.

"Silence!" Phobetor barked. His dark eyes flashed, aura puffing around him like a poisonous smog, and she cowered. I'd *never* seen her cower. "You remain here only as long as you are useful or entertaining. I fail to see how you are either."

I braced my elbows against the armrests, and my seat creaked under me. Phobetor's attention slid back to me. "Scions have a purpose." He leaned forward. "You have a purpose. It's why I didn't allow the Elders to rid themselves entirely of you or the others."

My eyes narrowed a bit. I peeked at Melina. Her nails dug into the cushion under her.

He smirked. "Scions are, as you know, very gifted. Their energy is a vital source of power in my Epiales Tombs. And to me."

My molars were going to crack. Heat rushed over my cheeks.

He either didn't notice or didn't care. Probably the latter. Likely believed I wasn't a threat.

Not yet, anyway.

He continued, "And then there's the prophecy of the child who'll use their gifts against the Ancients." He waved one hand in the air.

A recollection needled the back of my mind. Phantasos, as the Augur, had once mentioned the story of her brothers' demise.

My shoulders tensed. "And what? You think I'm the one? I think you overestimate my gifts. You cursed the mortal realm—imprisoned countless mortals. To what—avoid defeat? Make Morpheus suffer? To … to bring forth the Dark Reaping? Seems counterintuitive. If mortals perish, you will, too." My words were clipped, dripping with venom.

I took a quick sip of air, knowing I'd gone too far. Let my mask slip.

Bollocks.

His palm cracked against his armrest, making me jump. "You foolish girl. I *am* the darkness, the son of Night and Day. Nightmares linger beyond time. Beyond Kosmos and Khaos. I care not what happens to mere mortals. You are but a bug under my thumb. Even in death, I'd squash you."

I let the moment simmer before responding. When his shoulders relaxed once more, my chin lifted. "What do you want in exchange for the commander?"

"Ah, your khorda. Such predictable, feeble beings your lot are," he lamented, running his teeth over his bottom lip. "I'll release your lover." The Ancient grinned, and Melina's mouth arched downward. "But only if you drain your father of his ember—and his life. Every last drop, until there's nothing left but an empty husk."

My mouth pressed into a hard line. He truly believed I could turn my gift against the Ancients, but a mortal was incapable of doing so.

It defied scripture.

There was design and balance to everything. To ember.

But you're part Ancient.

My heart skipped a beat.

"You think I'm the child Phantasos told me about—the one who can steal an Ancient's power."

He steepled his fingers in front of his mouth, but it didn't hide the way his lips curved over his teeth. "My darling sister was always so fond of riddles. She failed to mention the most important part." His voice lowered, cruel and eager. "The prophecy speaks of a *daughter* born of an Oneiroi. And you, dear niece, are the only female offspring who lives."

I clenched my fists. "Until recently, you didn't even know I existed. There could be others."

"But you are the only one here. With promising abilities"— his hand slashed toward me, shadows coiling in his palm—"and I hold your mirrored soul. Your other half. It's a wager I'll gladly make. Refuse your end of the bargain, or try to harm me, and your lover will suffer in ways you cannot yet begin to imagine."

My nails dug into my palm, surely leaving crescent marks, threatening to break the skin. It didn't matter. I'd say whatever I needed to. To save Gavrel. To make my uncle believe he had won.

"I accept. Morpheus is nothing to me," I lied, the words tasting like ash.

One of his brows arched, and his eyes narrowed. He stood, a cloud of darkness pouring over him. "Deal."

He snapped his fingers, and his ember lashed out.

Agony seared my flesh, claws sinking into my nape, shadows burrowing deep until they hit bone. By the time I released a pained gasp, Phobetor's ember was gone.

"You know, there are so few things that can bind an

Ancient," my uncle purred. "A runebound bargain"—he traced a cold fingertip over the tender skin at my nape—"and Nyxvein. How positively delightful that my brother will have suffered because of both."

Disgust and indignation crept up my back.

The Ancient mistook my silence for intrigue. His smile widened across his teeth as he brushed his thumb over the Shadowvault Amulet before letting it fall. It vibrated softly against my skin. "Haven't seen this in quite a while. Fitting that you should be the one to wear it now."

I held my breath, thinking that he would push the issue, but he didn't. The necklace meant little to him, as most things did, aside from harming Morpheus. I realized the irony; creating the amulet had probably warped his mind even further.

"Your father. Always so pliable. So insufferable in his fond-ness for mortals. That's how I caught him." He tilted his head toward Melina. "I had this one dangle what he most desired— his first *human* wife. The fool believed she still lived after the Nightbloom Sundering. After I executed her."

He closed his eyes as though relishing the memory. Then his eyes snapped open and locked on mine. I sat straighter in my chair, shifting uncomfortably. His words cut into me like shards of ice. "He followed the hope of her straight into his dungeon, and when he reached for her hand at the bottom..." Phobetor bared his teeth. "The Nyxvein claimed him. Coiled tight and solidified into amber. An Ancient reduced to a relic."

He sniffed disdainfully, then turned as if bored. "Bring her to the pit to claim her mortal," he ordered Melina. He paused at the threshold, offering me his profile, a grin splitting it before he sank into the shadows.

Melina unfurled herself and sauntered toward me. I slapped her hand away before she could touch me. She was so close, her rose and bitter almond scent drifted over my face, and I scrunched my nose.

She grinned, sweeping aside her curtain of platinum hair to reveal the gilded brand. "He'll find you now—wherever you hide. It's how he tracked me down." Melina let her strands cascade over her back. "It seems you belong to him just as much as I do, *pet.*"

"We are not the same," I spat. "I didn't curse an entire realm for my own gain."

She tittered, flicking one hand in the air. "Not yet. Do you think you control how this ends? Over the Ancients?" Her sneer deepened. "You're even more foolish than I thought. The Withering was inevitable. Mortals would've damned Midst Fall in due time. The Nyxvein simply hastened the impending rot."

Touching the tender skin next to my scar, I swallowed the acid rushing up my throat. I traced the etched, geometric lines and knew it matched Melina's—molten gold twisted into the shape of a snake coiling around a crescent moon.

Strangling it.

Bloody void.

I had made a deal with a nightmare. And now, the shackles it forged were mine to break … or die trying.

22

LIKE FATHER, LIKE DAUGHTER

GAVREL

As we neared the bottom, a whirring sounded far above. My gaze snapped up. A billow of blackened haze cradled a descending amber glass platform.

Two forms were scuffling atop the conveyor, shadow and prismatic light battling for dominance.

I stilled, the heel of my palm pressing into my scar as the chaos continued around me.

I felt her before I saw her.

Saw her arms windmill, glowing dagger clutched in her hand, and a ribbon of iridescence sucking in Melina's dark halo.

She teetered on the edge, and a burst of shadow slammed into her.

My heart stilled in that moment before gravity claimed her —before she toppled off the thick glass. Everyone and everything else disappeared.

Her scream ripped through the pit, colliding with the bellow that tore from my very core. "Seryn!"

My sword sheathed, I lunged toward the abyss, desperate to break her fall, but before I could leap, Thesa plummeted, her wings tucked tight and her features hardened into single-minded resolve.

The muscle in my chest nearly seized as the vryka snatched the back of Seryn's vest mid-air. Their forms jolted like puppets when Thesa's wings snapped wide to slow their descent. Thesa's grimace deepened with effort. Pip peeked out, latching onto the end of Seryn's plait.

Wearing a look of relief and determination, my fated focused on the guards still scattered around the edges of the pit. Seryn flung her dagger out, and the blade embedded itself with a meaty thud into a demon's chest. She called it back, aimed, and lobbed it into another's eyeball.

Again and again it flew, a deadly blur carving a path of ruin until she was so close I could almost reach her.

Her glacial-blue eyes met mine at last, burning with unguarded joy and fierce relief. I jumped down from the path, landing in a crouch on the wide stone slab at the heart of the churning reservoir.

Thesa released her into my arms. I pulled Seryn against me, her warmth searing into my chest as she shuddered, breathing my name. My pulse lurched back to life at hearing her voice.

Seryn nodded at the vryka, eyes shining.

"Mind your female, Commander," Thesa called out before rocketing once more into the fray. I could've sworn the corners of her lips curved, just slightly.

With one hand, I cupped Seryn's jaw, the other locked around her waist. "Little Star." My words trembled at the edges.

"I found you," she whispered. "And how fucking dare you make me actually go to the Nether Void to do it."

A laugh spilled from me, all the tension I'd shoved deep down bubbling over. She grinned, staring at my dimple before roaming over my face. Tenderly, her fingertips traced my split lip, then brushed over my cheeks.

"You're hurt," she growled.

I pulled her closer. "It's nothing."

Her palms pressed against my chest, heat seeping through the torn fabric. My eyes locked on hers, and for a breath, the battle above—the nightmare we were living—fell away. Time stilled.

My star.

My mouth crashed against hers, pain pinching my lip. I welcomed it. Relished it. The pain meant I was alive. She was alive. In my arms.

Her fingers fisted into my tunic, clutching me as if I might fade like a figment of her imagination. Her lips moved with mine, desperate and claiming.

I squeezed her waist, aching to become whole with her.

Body.

Mind.

Soul.

Breathless, she broke away just enough to run her fingertips over my stubble. "Never sacrifice yourself again."

"You know I can't make that promise." My thumb brushed her cheek. "When it comes to you, I'd gladly tear my heart out." I pressed a kiss to her forehead.

Her eyes narrowed, and she huffed a small, trembling laugh. "Then at least consider every alternative first. I rather like your heart where it is."

She tucked her cheek against my chest, and I savored the feel of her for a moment before the scene around us started reemerging.

Shouting, broken bodies, and flashing ember.

Blood and shadow and gore.

A growing shade seeped over us and the landing across the basin.

I tucked Seryn behind me as the conveyor settled with a whoosh over the magma, creating a bridge between us and the stone ledge.

"What a touching reunion," Melina scorned, smoothing her messy strands. Her whole face curled with disdain as she looked at Seryn.

Breena and Maya rushed down the ramp, stepping over the smashed husks of defeated guards. They positioned themselves behind the Elder, their skin bloodied and soot-covered.

With her smoky energy wavering around her, Melina ran her tongue over one incisor and turned leisurely to the side. "Together again at last. Maya, it's been too long."

Maya snarled at the Elder before her gaze flicked past me.

Dazzling iridescence, so out of place in this dark realm, spilled over my shoulder. Seryn moved forward, her aura swirling furiously.

"It hasn't been long enough." And before her last word, she thrust her palms out, not waiting for the retort that tipped Melina's tongue. Seryn's halo latched onto the Elder's, slurping in the dark fumes.

Melina's eyes widened, and she backed away, her hands pushing against some unseen force. Or perhaps trying to untangle her gift from my khorda's. Melina's body jerked, and she dropped to her knees, joints cracking against the amber glass.

In awe, Seryn's mother stepped closer, but halted when Breena flung her arm across her chest, eyes snapping up.

Then everyone's attention followed, except Seryn's. My fated grinned, consuming Elder Harrow's power.

The demons slipped into the shadows and tunnels like scurrying insects, leaving their broken comrades scattered across the solid surfaces. A swirling black smog plummeted down, its tendrils scratching the opal walls. Raspy, wet clicking echoed through the space as if the cloud was made of frenzied tomb beetles.

I grabbed Seryn's shoulder, and her halo quivered. She looked at me, and I tilted my chin up. Finally, she lifted her gaze, noticing the commotion above. Her mouth parted, and we edged back as far as we could without tipping off the slab.

Seryn's ember pulsed, drawing in a few last smoky wisps of Melina's power like threads being pulled from a tangle. The corners of her mouth curled as energy swirled above her palms for a heartbeat, then instinctively she pressed the fragments against a new amulet at her chest.

My brows scrunched when the suspended black stone morphed into amber as the stolen energy sank into it, then blinked back to ebony, quivering faintly with its new occupant.

Her gift released Melina's, and the female slumped, breathing hard, her complexion sickly pale. The Elder glared at my fated, eyes burning with fury.

She was lucky Seryn hadn't taken the rest of her ember, and her life with it.

For now.

A chill poured over us, and I braced against whatever was approaching.

In an explosion of soot and shadow, Phobetor landed before us, one knee and fist touching the stone. The Ancient of Nightmares slowly looked up, a wicked grin seeping across his wide mouth, his shadows slithering around him like besotted snakes.

I grabbed Seryn's hand. Her breaths were shallow and uneven, each tugging at something deep inside my ribs. But her chin lifted, and her jaw set, refusing to smother her gift. It glimmered around her defiantly.

Ancients, I would never get enough of this woman.

I narrowed my eyes at her uncle.

"What is the mortal saying?" He rose slowly, a nightmare creeping out of the darkness. "Like father, like daughter."

23

INEVITABLE

SERYN

There was nowhere to retreat, and Gavrel's vise-like grip on my hand told me he wouldn't let go. He tried to nudge me behind him, but I planted my heels, refusing to move.

Like I always would.

If he sacrificed himself, so would I.

Tendrils of night crept toward our feet. My heartbeat thundered, nerves and ember vibrating under my skin.

Therrok and Thesa landed beside my mother, fists clenched around bloodied weapons. Melina tilted her head, excitement gleaming in her eyes despite her wilted form.

I braced against my uncle's darkness, but it veered around our boots and poured over the slab's edge.

The black, copper-lined liquid fizzed and splattered as if it wanted to flee Phobetor's ember. Gavrel and I edged back, but the inky veins tore free of the metallic substance and leaped, latching onto the toe of his boot.

He froze, muscles locking as it slithered up his legs.

"I can't move," he growled.

I tugged on his hands.

"Don't bother." Phobetor stalked closer. "The Nyxvein has taken hold. Did you not listen when I told you of Morpheus' entrapment?"

The darkness climbed Gavrel's hips as Phobetor went on, voice almost amused. "Our mother gave Morpheus and me mirrored doorways into other realms. But her essence poisoned them—made them quite useful. That's how I delivered my Dormancy pods to the mortal realm. How I trapped my brother."

At last, Melina rose, her voice trembling with sycophantic devotion. "It was an honor, my liege. My Akridais and I are forever in your serv—"

Phobetor's hand snapped out, and a cloud of shadow slashed over her face. In its wake, black twine sewed Melina's lips shut.

A muffled shriek slipped between her fingers as they clawed at her mouth. Smoky energy burst from her like an extinguished fire, cracking the glass conveyor under her.

Breena hissed, and her aura flickered. Even Mama stepped back, wary of the toxic outburst.

Phobetor sneered, "I tire of you." With a flick of his wrist, Melina collapsed. She writhed against his domination, pewter eyes fixed on me, burning with venom. She smiled, lips tugging at the twine as if she knew her hatred would outlive this battle.

Her tendrils brushed my ankle before my uncle's power jerked her back.

"Contain yourself," he hissed, shadows coiling around like chains. "Your spite fouls even my air."

"If you want something done, best do it yourself." His attention swung to me. "Now, niece. Nyxvein and amber"—he twirled his hand in the air toward Gavrel—"bit more poetic, isn't it? Motivating."

"We had a deal," I spat.

"I said I would release him. I never said *when*."

Rage surged along with my aura, fists trembling with the effort to contain it.

My uncle clucked his tongue. "Careful. You'll only hurt yourself. And everyone else." He gestured toward the others.

Gavrel strained against the darkness climbing his arms. Amber had already encased his lower half. His emerald eyes pleaded with me to run, though we knew there was nowhere beyond Phobetor's reach—not in this realm.

Panic hollowed my chest. I caught Mama's eyes, then Breena's. Both their auras blazed.

Phobetor turned to my mother with an unsettling smile. "At last, we meet. Maya, the vessel for my brother's seed. Clever enough to turn an Ancient's head while imprisoned … You must be his khorda. No mortal could reach him otherwise in such a state." He scoffed, aura darkening. "And yet, it hardly ended well for you."

Mama's voice cut sharply. "Nor for you. What a pitiful existence—jealous of your brother, trapped in a realm of scraps. You cursed Midst Fall, and still he bested you."

His jaw clenched. "Shame his end will come at the hands of his daughter. And he will never reunite with his fated."

The mist climbed Gavrel's neck. "Move!" he bellowed as Phobetor's hands snapped forward.

Breena braced herself, a radiant shield flaring out before them. Mama's ember lashed at Phobetor's, but his shadows tore free and slammed into the red barrier.

My ability thrashed, and my arms flung out, our auras colliding. My fractured rainbows clung to his darkness when it tried to slip away. But then he grinned and tossed aside my energy.

"Seryn!" Mama called, pushing her ember toward me.

I latched onto it. Breena followed, scarlet waves weaving

with Mama's midnight ropes. My iridescence drank them in, hues bleeding into mine, melting together in a rush of color.

The teardrop-shaped amulet throbbed faintly against my collarbone. Melina's stolen ember hummed in time with my own. Its presence was unmistakable, a tether to the Elder that I couldn't wait to be rid of, but at least it was caged. For now.

Heat seared through me, through every joint and sinew. It sizzled along the glowing boughs of my forearms. My head craned back, irises illuminating.

Too much. It would tear me—and this realm—apart.

I am you, and you are me, I screamed in my mind.

We are one, my ember whispered back.

I thrust a hand toward Gavrel. The Nyxvein shrieked, recoiling. The amber splintered, then shattered into golden shards.

He rushed to me, one arm locking around my waist. His tattoo glowed white, and calm washed over me.

He was my anchor in a sea of chaotic, cosmic bedlam.

I squinted at my uncle and cupped my hands around the orb forming between them. Lustrous fragments of light coalesced into something otherworldly—a bottomless, star-flecked void.

This time, I didn't fear it.

And it hungered. Yearned to become one with the celestial force before me.

So, I let it feast.

Phobetor's shadows reared back at my assault, his shocked gaze snapping to mine.

He couldn't free his darkness in time.

Destroy, my ember chanted within me.

"Finish it, Asteria," Gavrel murmured into my hair.

With a cry, I unleashed my power. The orb inverted, and pulsing, star-struck blackness devoured the surrounding nimbus.

Phobetor paled; worry flitted across his sharp features.

I lifted my chin. "Perhaps you were right." I curled my fingers around my dark creation. "Like father, like daughter."

Searing energy zipped up my spine. Phobetor's body arched, shadows peeling from him, sucked into the black hole I'd created.

It grew. Seeped over my arms, staining the branch patterns with star-lined ebony.

I was invincible.

Indestructible.

Inevitable.

Phobetor's mouth gaped on a silent roar. Loathing burned in his eyes as he hurled one last wave of darkness, swiping his thumb over the tourmaline ring on his middle finger.

Gavrel and I staggered under the icy weight, aura fizzling. My knees buckled as my body took the brunt of my spent energy. Gavrel caught me before I crashed into the stone.

My vision blurred, but I forced my eyelids to stay open. Faintly heard Mama and Breena calling my name.

A vortex of haze twirled around the slab, splashing thick, Nyxvein-streaked copper on the edges. My mother's ember lashed toward Phobetor before he vanished into the portal he'd opened, his enraged roar chasing him.

Once released from the Ancient's hold, Melina's metallic eyes met mine, flickering with odium and malice—a promise that she wasn't finished with me.

With a sharp nail, she sliced the twine binding her mouth, a wicked grin twisting her lips before she dragged herself into the whirlpool, letting it swallow her.

No!

They couldn't get away. I wouldn't let them.

"Let's go!" I screamed before the portal could close, brushing over my own celestial key. Hoping the threshold wouldn't tear us apart since there wasn't currently a full moon. Hoping it ripped Melina to shreds.

Heat vibrated against my finger, and I tried to picture Phobetor so we'd be sure to follow him, but consciousness was slipping away from me.

Therrok and Thesa scooped up Breena and Mama, flying over the crumbling conveyor and landing on the floating slab.

I grabbed Breena's wrist, forcing my ember into her. Her eyes widened. "Use it to shield us," I ordered.

She nodded, her aura blazing brighter than ever. A sparking, scarlet shield slammed around us. Gavrel held me close as I crushed my eyes shut, but I felt everyone's touch on my shoulders and arms, surrounding me. My last thought before we toppled into the molten depths was not of my uncle.

But of bright skies and those I loved.

24

WHO IS YOUR DADDY?

GAVREL

We crashed unceremoniously, soft grass breaking our fall. I squinted against the sky, so blue and bright, after being trapped in a world of darkness.

Groaning, I pushed to my feet, every inch of my body a throbbing bruise. My gaze swept the training field, heart clenching, then easing.

No Phobetor. No Melina.

Relief warred with frustration within me.

"I lost them," Seryn murmured at my side.

I pulled her into my arms. "*We* did. But not for long."

She pressed her forehead into my chest, drawing slow, deliberate breaths until the tension fell from her shoulders.

Therrok squinted, eyeing the distant barracks and the electric hues of the Reverie Weald. Thesa walked along the rail-and-post fence by the cliff. Pip darted in circles around the vryka, squeaking gleefully.

Maya sat up, lashes shimmering with unshed tears. Breena offered a hand, helping her to her feet. Seryn wrapped her mother in a hug.

Holding her daughter at arm's length, Maya's thumb and forefinger tugged at Seryn's amulet. With a grin, she let it drop. "You did it, Little Star."

The corners of my lips curled at the nickname. I rubbed the back of Seryn's neck, fingers toying with the chain.

Seryn glanced at me with a soft smile. "It's the Shadowvault Amulet. It traps embers."

Breena snorted. "Modest shite. She fought the Minotaur. Fought a cunty, Nyxvein version of herself in front of Melina's khorda *and* the rest of Nekrionn, *in* an Ancients-damned pit her primeval grandmother smashed into existence. *Then* she gobbled up Melina's aura and locked it in there." Sucking in a breath, Breena jabbed the air with both forefingers. "Oh, and let's not forget she just made Phobetor piss 'imself and drank his aura like a goblet of mead!"

Before Seryn could protest, Breena lunged at her, hugging her tightly.

"Bree!" Seryn laughed, but didn't pull away.

"Take it!" Breena squeezed again before releasing her, cheeks flushed.

Therrok coughed, shuffling over to the fence to join his sister.

I leaned close, my words only for my fated. "You're magnificent." I brushed my thumb over the shell of her ear, and she shivered.

A blaze of light snapped behind us. "Maya," the deep baritone voice rumbled through the air.

Maya's entire frame seemed to melt. Tears rolled freely down her face now as she surged forward. Morpheus met her in a few strides, and they crashed into one another's arms, clinging as though they might split apart again. He looked at Seryn, pride shining in his blue eyes. "You did well, daughter."

Nodding, Seryn watched as Morpheus rested his cheek on the top of Maya's head, closing his eyes.

Seryn's face was a storm of confusion, wonder, and grief. She was processing—her mother found, her true father revealed, her family reshaping before her eyes. I wrapped my arms around her, anchoring her as she gripped my forearms and rested her head against me.

After a moment, her body relaxed, and I kissed her crown. A sharp pang spiked through my chest, and I winced.

She glanced up at me. "You all right, Gav?"

I breathed in, letting the pain dissipate. "More than all right. Just a few scrapes and bruises."

She arched one brow, but didn't argue. Taking her hand, we made our way to Morpheus' palace. Pip darted around the group one last time.

"Thank you for all your help, Pip," Seryn said.

The pixie tugged Seryn's braid with a smirk and then poked Thesa on the nose with a tiny squeak. The vryka's mouth twitched. With a cheeky chirp and a softening of its metallic eyes, Pip zipped off toward the forest, prismatic wings glinting.

Morpheus could barely keep his eyes off Maya. I knew the feeling well. The longing of being separated from your khorda was unbearable at best.

I peeked at Seryn, her eyes bright as she chatted with her parents and the others. This was how she was meant to look.

Sated. Content. *Happy.*

I rubbed my hand over my scar, and it pulsed under my touch.

I would make it my mission to keep her this way—simply to keep her—and I would die to make it so. *At least consider every alternative first. I rather like your heart where it is.* Seryn's words echoed in my mind.

I pulled her closer, tucking her arm in the crook of my elbow.

As did I.

IT WAS SO MUCH EASIER to breathe in Surrelia. Clean, crisp air flowed into my lungs as if it could purify the banestone soot coating them.

Boots pounded down the hall as we entered the foyer, crystalline stars scattering rainbows everywhere from the chandelier above. Thesa's wings flared, and Therrok widened his stance as Kaden burst in, a wide grin plastered on his face. He scooped Seryn in a tight hug before setting her down. I pressed my lips together, tucking away the smile threatening to surface.

Any lingering jealousy faded. Although my brother would always be her best friend, and they had a history, Seryn was mine, and mine alone. Both things were true. As it was meant to be.

His joy was contagious as he embraced me, clapping my back.

"Welcome back, brother. The Nether Void didn't kill you, and smiling won't either," Kaden teased.

I grunted, refusing to indulge him.

When he turned, his mouth fell open. "Maya?"

Seryn's mother smiled, gathering him in her arms. He buried his face in her hair, then lifted her off the ground, swinging them both around. "Maya! Holy shite!"

She laughed, cupping his jaw when he set her down. "As cheeky as ever, Kaden. Meet Therrok and Thesa Flint." The siblings lifted their chins in quiet acknowledgment, eyeing my brother.

He grinned at them, and both of their gazes narrowed.

Kaden rubbed his nape, cheeks puffed. "Marek and Rhaegar returned to Midst Fall. Daddy Dream and the pixies helped them find a portal shortly after you all went on your *adventure*."

"Ancients," Seryn whispered, hand tightening in mine. "I hope they find Yaya."

Kaden nodded, brushing her biceps. "I'm certain they will, Ser."

Elders Marah Strom and Endurst Guust met us in the foyer. In a flurry of lemon-colored robes, Endurst bowed. "Welcome ba-back." He swallowed, pausing for a moment. "We're pleased you've returned. News of Melina?" he asked carefully, as if saying it faster would make her appear.

"She followed Phobetor into a portal, but it didn't seem that they were on the best of terms," I answered.

Marah inhaled for several seconds and then smiled softly, eyes landing on Maya. Color rose in her pale cheeks. "I am so very sorry for our part in your imprisonment."

Maya squeezed her hands. "Think nothing of it. Melina made prisoners of us all."

Marah nodded, her eyes darting between Seryn and me. She opened her mouth but then closed it, trapping her next words. Instead, one hand fluttered to her chest, she closed her eyes, and then turned down the hall.

"Please excuse us. We're still re-recovering." Endurst patted Kaden's shoulder. "With the help of this fine young man."

Kaden wiggled his eyebrows. "You hear that? Fine young man."

Smiling, Endurst dipped his chin and bid us farewell before following the other Elder.

Seryn's stomach rumbled. Kaden smirked, throwing an arm over her shoulders, nudging me aside. "Time to eat. What has Maya been feeding you down there?"

"*Insolent* young man," Maya retorted, swatting his arm.

"Ah, but Seryn eats men for breakfast." He tapped his chin, a smirk tipping the corner of his mouth.

"Kaden," I growled. Seryn rolled her eyes.

He lifted his hands in surrender, chuckling. "I jest. Let's eat, be merry, and figure out how to save the realms."

Maya turned to Seryn, brushing a thumb over her cheek. "We'll find you later. But for now ..." Her eyes flicked to Morpheus. "There are things long overdue."

Seryn nodded before the words fully left her lips. "Go."

Maya smiled and let her hand fall away. She went to Therrok, whispered, and put something in his hand. With a grunt, he tucked away whatever she'd given him in his vest pocket.

Seryn's gaze lingered on her parents for a moment.

As we entered the Great Hall, I studied my brother. His humor. The ever-present grin. He was acting more like himself. But I wasn't sure whether I should be relieved or worried.

I rested my hand on Kaden's shoulder. "Why didn't you portal to Midst Fall with the others?"

He shrugged. "I needed to know you both came back safely. Besides, there were the Elders to heal. Ancients to schmooze." He waved his hand dismissively. "And I promised Marek I'd keep an eye on—"

His eyes shifted behind us, a flash of clover rippling over the irises. I blinked, unsure if I'd imagined it. He continued with less humor, "—her. It was all I could do to keep him from killing the woman. The bastard packs a fucking punch."

He wiggled his jaw as soft footfalls sounded, and Seryn flinched as a figure emerged.

"What's she fecking doing here?" Breena hissed, moving forward. "Ready to stab us all in the back again?"

Kaden stepped into her path, but Breena elbowed him in the side. The exhale whooshed from his nostrils. "Damn it, woman."

Caelora Aundyne raised her pretty, oval face, her back

perfectly straight. "I deserve that. But I assure you, I didn't mean for anyone in Helos to get hurt."

Seryn grabbed the back of Breena's breeches just as she lunged for the other female. Violet burst around Caelora just as Breena's aura ignited.

Breena gritted her teeth. "Let go, Ryn. I need to *accidentally* hurt her."

Seryn yanked on her friend. "Just a moment, Bree. There's a reason she's here, roaming freely."

Thesa and Therrok watched the scene unfold from the corners of their eyes.

"I missed your logic, Ser," Kaden muttered, holding his side and glaring at Breena.

Breena stopped struggling and crossed her arms. Seryn looked at Caelora, eyes narrowing.

Caelora's mouth flattened, and she tucked her dark, golden-blonde waves behind her ears. "Thank y—"

Seryn held up a palm. "I don't need your gratitude. I need you to explain. Your choices led to my grandmother's capture. To Helos burning."

The slightest hint of remorse swept over her features before she tucked away her gift, purple waves vanishing into the air.

"Please, sit." She went to the table filled with various cuts of meat and fresh produce, not waiting to see if we followed.

Kaden waved his arm, inviting us to sit, a new smile plastered on his face. Breena nudged his shoulder as she passed him with a huff, and he shook his head.

Seryn and I sat across from Caelora and Kaden as she folded her hands atop the wood. Everyone took a seat, a heavy silence blanketing the space.

One of Thesa's nostrils lifted as she studied the spread. "I'll find us something to eat," she mumbled, marching from the room.

Therrok shrugged and pushed his bulk onto the bench next

to Kaden, who scrunched his brows and shifted closer to Caelora.

My hand found Seryn's on her lap, and I twined my fingers with hers. "Best if you start at the beginning, Miss Aundyne."

She drew in a breath, eyes drifting over the moon-phase windows.

"Someone once told me," she murmured, "the price of vengeance is mercy. I did what I thought I had to do … and I paid the price." She plucked at her lavender-colored dress. "*Helos* paid the price."

"And when the Akridais and Draumrs spilled through the illusion border you opened?" Seryn pressed. "What could Melina possibly have offered you to betray Yaya and the people who took you in so profoundly?"

"After the Winnowing Trials, Melina took an interest in me —my blended ember. She gifted me my memories and this rune." Her fingertips scrubbed at two interlocking decagons on her left hand. "She tried to recruit me to the Akridais, but I refused. Then she learned of the one thing I've always wanted … something I thought I'd lost forever. She sent a missive by harbinger starling, promising it if I merely dropped the barrier so she could meet with Yaya to discuss an armistice. I—"

Breena snorted, but Seryn lifted a hand, waiting.

Caelora sighed, pressing her palms flat against the table top. "After my mother died, I waited so long. I didn't know what Melina had truly planned, and she promised no harm would come to anyone."

"And you believed her?" Breena scoffed. "Clearly, you've suffered multiple head injuries throughout your turns."

"And if I did that," Caelora continued, unfazed, "she'd grant me a meeting with my father. I didn't think she'd stage a full attack just yet. Our intel suggested the Elders weren't aware of our numbers in Helos. I admit my selfishness—my desire to meet my father after all this time blinded me. I wanted—no, *needed*—him to pay for what he did to my mother."

Seryn's fingers stiffened in my hold.

My forehead creased, and my eyes narrowed. "And *who* is your father?"

She frowned as if the name tasted bitter. "Elder Ryboas Ash."

Breena shot back to her feet. "Bollocks!"

25

CALM YOUR TEETS

SERYN

$\mathcal{M}$outh puckering, I placed one hand on Breena's wrist, ignoring her simmering aura. She was struggling to keep her temper at bay. I understood the anger and disgust, but I also believed Caelora didn't mean to hurt anyone in Helos.

They'd taken her in when she had nowhere else to go. The shame slightly curling her usually straight back was obvious. Maybe just to me. Because I knew what it was to want vengeance. To risk everything to grasp it.

The thought of my grandmother being culled weighed on me, but I had to hope she was alive and put the blame where it was due.

Firmly in Melina Harrow's hands.

I reached for a flaky piece of bread, broke it in half, and offered it to Caelora. Kaden's mouth quirked. Her features twisted in gratitude before she realized I had offered her at least my understanding if not my absolution. She nodded, took the bread from me, and nibbled on the edge.

"And how did you come to be here in Surrelia?" Therrok broke the silence, his question spilling like rocks over the table. After sizing up the group dynamics since we'd arrived, he must have decided the others posed no threat. His leather wings twitched when she didn't answer quickly enough.

Caelora swallowed, and Kaden leaned forward, answering instead, "The pixies found her outside the arch, the portal we come through during the Dormancy."

Her mouth flattened, and Kaden shrugged. "When Melina followed you through the portal at Hallowed End, her two Akridais dragged me with them." Frowning, she dropped the remaining bread on a plate as if it had soured. "And conveniently left me stranded in the Murk after she entered the Epiales Tombs, as she called them."

Breena ran her tongue over one incisor and plopped down onto the bench. "You're sayin' that you survived the Stygian Murk, and made it all the way to the portal … on your own. On those short little legs?"

Caelora's mouth pinched, and she shot Breena a look of mild annoyance. Her mouth parted as if she might reply, but instead she smoothed her hands over her dress and stayed quiet.

Thesa stomped back into the hall, a furry carcass in her hands. She didn't pay us any attention.

Kaden glanced at Caelora, and she dipped her chin, not making eye contact with anyone. Never one to let awkward silences fill a space, he stood and began pouring mead into everyone's goblets. "And now that that's out of the way, how about a drink? Then you can entertain us with stories of the Nether Void."

Raising one dark, thick brow, Therrok jerked his glass away before Kaden could taint it with the honey wine. He passed it to Thesa, who took it and another chalice to the stage along with her kill. I looked away, not wanting to see how she filled the cups.

Kaden shrugged, pouring more mead into his cup, his dimple peeking out.

My mouth tipped up. He seemed to be in better spirits since we had last seen one another. I hoped it wasn't an act; only time would tell. I glanced at Caelora. She hadn't glanced his way once. Was she actively ignoring him? I tilted my head, curiosity kindling in the back of my mind.

"Well, our Firefly here is a top-tier demi-Ancient …" Breena started, pulling my attention back to her. Animatedly, she spun our tale for the others as we filled our bellies and wet our tongues with the sweet golden liquid.

In this moment, it all seemed like a bad memory. Like hope and providence were the only things to look forward to in the next part of our journeys.

Absently, Gavrel rubbed one hand over his chest, his other hand never leaving me. His thumb brushed back and forth over my thigh, and tingles buzzed along my skin. Gratitude flowed over me in waves that kept cresting and breaking. He was here. Safe.

So was my mother. My father. Kaden. Breena. And even the Grim Twins.

I didn't want to think about needing to leave Surrelia. Perhaps I would be all right, being a demi-Ancient. But if the others lingered beyond the next full moon, the aether would come for them.

Kaden leaned back, brows furrowed. "Morpheus gathered loyalists from the realm to guard the palace and grounds." He set his goblet down with a clink. "Elders Ash and Craven likely escaped to Midst Fall. There's been no sign of them here or in the city."

Caelora's nostrils flared delicately. He glanced at her and then clutched his glass once more. "Where do we think

Phobetor and Melina fled to?"

Gavrel cupped his chin and scraped his fingers over his stubble. "Seryn significantly weakened him. You could see it in his eyes; he was stunned by what she did. My coin would be on the Epiales Tombs."

I nodded. "He'd have had access to the energy source at the center of the prison. All those stolen nightmares while he recovered."

Therrok shifted, licking the crimson off his lips. "He'll likely be there for at least a couple of days. The Murk will work against his recovery. And he won't have *this* to help him travel."

His sister peeked at him, sipping from her chalice. The male vryka dug in his leather vest, pulling out a twisted black ring. He held it up, then slipped it on his thick, blue-gray pinky.

I coughed, almost choking on a bit of food. My eyes darted to my tourmaline ring. "How?"

"Calm your teets," Therrok grumbled, rubbing his belly. "Mama Nightshade stole it from the bawbag before 'e scampered away like a void rodent."

A recollection flashed in my mind. My mother's ember lashing out before Phobetor disappeared. I grinned.

With a laugh, Breena raised her cup to the vryka. "Bloody brilliant, Rocky."

His mouth twisted to the side, and Kaden chuckled. Thesa's black gaze snapped to him, and he gulped back his mirth.

My amusement morphed into something else entirely as Gavrel leaned into me, tucking strands behind my ear. "Are you … feeling weary, Asteria?"

I turned to him, cupping my heated cheek. I bit my bottom lip, searching his eyes. His pupils dilated, gaze darkening.

"Not one bit, Commander," I lied.

He frowned, and I ran my thumb over the crease between his eyebrows, and giggled, my voice low so only he could hear me as I continued, "Care to join me in my chambers, regardless?"

His fingers tightened on my thigh, and his dimple flashed. "We bid you all a good evening."

"It's only midday," Breena sing-songed.

I shrugged, waving my hand in the air. "Must be the realm change."

Breena winked and popped a magenta mirberry in her mouth while nudging Thesa with her shoulder. Thesa didn't budge, the tops of her wings twitching.

Kaden offered me a smile, dipping his head. "Have a good night, you two."

Caelora rose and wandered out of the hall without a word, her footfalls steady.

Gavrel and I had almost reached the wide entry when Therrok called out gruffly, "Little Nightshade." I turned, and he stood and lifted his nose. "Well done today. You didn't die."

I pressed my lips together, holding in my amusement.

Gavrel took my hand in his.

The vryka was right.

We hadn't died.

26

MAKE ME FORGET

SERYN

We rushed down the hall toward the illusioned wall. His strides were so long that I could barely keep up, his hand gripping mine, my messy braid whipping behind me.

"Can't wait to show me your chambers, Gav?" I teased. He abruptly stopped, and I nearly crashed into him before he grabbed my waist and shoved me against the moonstone wall.

He winced, and my eyes darted over the lingering bruises and shallow cuts scattering his face. "We should have Kaden take a look—"

"I'll heal on my own. And the only thing I'm concerned about is my inability to keep my hands off you."

"Your room seems a bit far away."

His nostrils flared, and a wicked smile spread over his lips, threatening to reopen the cut in his lip. He rested his forehead against mine, his knee wedging between my thighs. I shuddered at the friction.

"Don't tempt me." His palm pressed beside my temple, the other curling around my nape. "Unless you've forgotten where we are—how everyone will hear you scream my name."

I ran my fingers over his sides, pulling him harder into me. His chest heaved, straining against the leather strap. His jaw clenched, and I cupped it, thumbs brushing the hinge where it ticked. When his eyes searched mine, desire seeped over the jeweled depths.

I ran my teeth over my bottom lip. "Make me forget," I breathed.

A growl rumbled in his chest before he scooped me over his shoulder, disregarding any of his injuries. A squeal fled from me, but he simply clamped his hand over the back of my thigh and strode ahead once more.

There was a dance of light and rippling moonstone, and I wriggled in his hold as the wall sealed behind us and he made his way up the spiral stairwell. "Gavrel, put me down," I demanded, the blood rushing to my head, and absently noticing the new sword he'd confiscated in the Void as the sheathed tip bounced below me.

He paused, lowering me, helping my body slide down his.

Every.

Delicious.

Inch.

Until I stood on the step above him. Sunlight shone through the quartz ceiling high above, the crystal prisms sprinkling rainbows everywhere.

My nape thrummed in time with my racing pulse, and a pleasant dizzy feeling swept over me.

Before I could get my bearings, Gavrel pushed me against the wall again, fingers ripping at the ties of my vest. His mouth crashed into mine, teeth clacking, and tongues clashing.

My lips met his again and again, the subtle taste of iron and salt mingling with the leather and sweat coating our bodies.

I clawed at his tunic, frustrated when it caught his baldric, wanting nothing more than to feel his warm, hard flesh against mine.

How *fucking dare* anyone or anything try to separate us.

I moaned into our kiss, my teeth scraping over his bottom lip. The tip of my vest loosened, and too impatient, he yanked it down, trapping my elbows against my sides.

He grinned before kissing his way along my jaw. His arm locked around my waist, cinching the garment tighter around me. "Don't move," he ordered.

Immediately, I struggled against my bindings, and he tore my tunic open to my navel, the crisp air sneaking under the loose material, pebbling my nipples.

"So defiant," he murmured, nipping at the peak through the rough linen.

I cursed at the pain, and then moaned when he pushed aside the fabric and laved the bud, sucking it into his wet mouth.

His free hand roamed over my stomach, spread my leg to the side, propping it on the step above. He drew tortuously slow circles along my inner thigh with his thumb. When I quivered, his hold tightened around my waist.

Another garbled sound spilled from me as he sucked on my other nipple, untied my breeches, and slipped his touch beneath my underwear.

He groaned against my breast, dipping two fingers into my already drenched center. Sliding them back out, the sound of my lust echoed through the stairwell.

"Do you hear how fucking wet you are, Asteria?" His erection pushed into my hip, and I trembled. He pumped his fingers inside me, and then slid from me, my core clenching at the emptiness.

"Gavrel," I whimpered.

He caught my lips once more with his and glided the tips of his fingers up my exposed stomach and chest, circling my nipple. Evidence of my desire trailed in their wake, goosebumps following. "Do you feel how soaked you are?"

"Yes." I was ready to combust. He flicked the tip of my breast. "Fucking yes," I cried.

"Good. I never want you to *forget* what I do to you." He pinched my nipple and shoved his hand back into my pants. "But you *will* scream my name."

Three fingers slammed into me, and my neck arched. His thumb pressed and rubbed and circled the throbbing at my apex.

He buried his face in my neck, finally untangling his hold, the vest going slack. I tugged my arms free, desperate to feel his skin as his fingers moved in and over my most sensitive parts.

I clung to him, nails digging into his back under his tunic. Pressure built at the base of my spine. Unbearable heat raced down my flesh, my breasts, my stomach. My channel clenched around his fingers, and he pumped faster, sucking and licking my nipples. My neck. Whispering my name. His hot breath against my damp skin.

My whole body trembled, and his palm slapped against me, my achy clit pulsing.

"Come for me," he whispered raggedly in my ear.

And I did. The wave finally burst, crashing violently, shaking me to my very soul to the sound of his name ripping from my throat.

Gently, he slipped his hand from me, scooping my limp, sated body into his arms before my legs gave out.

I was too depleted to object, so I rested my head against him and let myself be carried to his room. Exhaustion washed over me—born of what he'd just given, everything we'd endured these last days, and the ember I'd spent.

Sometimes it took a lot of energy to hold your head high.

But I didn't want to waste a moment with him. "I'm not

tired," I uttered, eyelids fluttering as we entered his old room, and he set me on the bed.

He helped me undress and carried me to the waiting bathtub. I let the steamy water sink into my sore muscles, lulled by the popping, lavender-scented bubbles.

My eyes closed despite my best efforts. The water splashed over the sides as Gavrel slid into the water behind me. His length pressed into my backside, and I squirmed, eyes fluttering open a crack. Already wanting him again.

"Later, my star. For now, rest." He positioned himself so that he was holding me in his arms, safe and cherished. His nimble fingers massaged and stroked my muscles until there was nothing left to do but surrender.

His touch glided in geometric patterns over my nape. And I ignored the thought of the golden lines he was tracing.

Because for the first time in a long while, I wanted to forget.

What came next.

What we needed to do.

What I'd promised.

But never him.

27

NOTHING GOOD

GAVREL

A tendril trickled over her forehead like a gentle, twirling stream in the dim morning light. I smoothed it behind her ear, my thumb lingering as it brushed the dip beneath her cheekbone.

Seryn nestled against my bare chest, palm resting upon my scar. Beneath her touch, my heart thumped languidly as my gaze roamed over her sleeping form.

For everyone, dreams had returned; it was true. But I still couldn't fathom how my khorda was here in my arms. How she was mine. This was something I never dared to hope for. Never believed would come to pass.

And she was so at peace. I feared that if she awoke, she might never breathe this easily again. Because what was to come surely would steal more of these moments from us. And from those whom the nightmares would reap.

She stirred, limbs going taut as she inhaled and shifted her warm body against mine.

A smile curved my mouth.

Yesterday, she'd fallen into a deep slumber in the tub as I'd explored the new rune on her neck. A tangle of golden lines, the image of a snake strangling a crescent moon.

I was certain that the tattoo meant nothing good. But Seryn needed to rest, especially after all the power she'd expended. While last night was not the time for more questions—and admittedly, we were *preoccupied*—I knew the sunrise would bring answers.

So, I'd let sleep take us for a bit before we'd bathed, enjoying one another in the soapy water.

Ancients, I loved her hair. Enjoyed unbraiding it and the feel of its wildfire between my fingers. And then that led to me needing every inch of her beneath my touch. Over. Under. Any way I could have her.

And last night, once we made it to the silken sheets, she'd called my name like a prayer into the moonlit darkness as I sank myself into her again and again.

With a satisfied inhale, I cupped her rounded cheek and pulled her supple curves more snugly against my side.

My cock stirred, ready to take her once more. Bloody void. I would never get enough of my khorda.

My dimple indented at the thought.

Seryn's eyelids fluttered, and she rubbed her hand over my chest and then my stomach. My length twitched under the sheets, eager for her attention.

A lazy smile spilled over her beautiful face, messy curls creating a soft, cinder-hued halo around her visage as pink and peach sunbeams painted the contours of her bare hip and thigh.

I dragged my gaze over her, hands itching to follow. Instead, my thumb grazed her jaw. "You're a painting come to life," I murmured.

She giggled, propping herself up on her elbow and skimming her fingers over my stubble. "Good morning." She pressed a kiss to my lips, and the contact swept to my tailbone.

Turning toward her, I hooked my ankle over hers and wrapped my arm around her waist. "Did you sleep well?"

She nodded, looking up at me through thick lashes. "And you?"

"Better than I have in a long time. Although I'm surprised you got any rest considering you *weren't* tired."

She swatted my chest and then sat up abruptly. Her fingertips prodded the skin above my heart. "What the void is this?"

My eyebrows rose, the haze of contentment flitting away. I glanced down, and instantly, my jaw clenched.

Black, fragmented lines splintered out from my scar, ink creeping along my arteries across my left pectoral.

Well, damn.

If I hadn't been so exhausted and stupidly drunk on having her beside me, perhaps I might have worried sooner. Yesterday, the aching twinges had been easy to ignore; pain was old company for me.

I pushed upright, muscles bunching. "Nothing good, I suppose."

Seryn frowned, sitting up. "Damn it, Gav. When did this start?"

"Since we left the Void, it's been more bothersome." I glanced out one of the circular windows along the wall, watching the sun push into the sky.

Trembling, her hand left the mark. Her fingertips met her lips. "Why didn't you say something? We should've—We need to fix this."

I caught her hand in mine and brought it to my mouth, brushing a kiss across her knuckles. "To be fair, the streaks are new as of this morning."

Her chin dipped. "Gav, I think … I think this is my fault."

I shook my head. "It's likely a side effect of the nightmare realm. The banestone, the Nyxvein—take your pick."

"No." Her voice cracked, sharp and high-pitched. "I know you saw my rune mark." Turning, she swept her hair aside. Dread prickled over my flesh as I studied the tattoo more closely.

I gathered her strands and leaned in to place a kiss in the curve of her neck. She smelled of lavender-tinged honey. I began braiding her hair. "Tell me."

With a few deep breaths, her shoulders sagged. "We needed Phobetor to believe I hated Morpheus—that I'd do *anything* to get you back." Her knees folded into her chest, and she wrapped her arms around her legs. "But the price was you. I didn't have enough time to think it through. I'm supposed to steal my father's ember—"

"He thinks you're who the Fates foretold," I interrupted quietly, tying off the end of the plait. "The one Phantasos told us of."

Seryn's eyes met mine, wide and troubled. She nodded.

"I don't think Phobetor's wrong, Little Star. Not after what you did to him."

She glowered. "He said it was a *daughter* born of an Oneiroi. And if I tried to harm him—or didn't drain Morpheus—you'd suffer." Her words stuck in the back of her throat, tears coating her eyes. "And I think … you already are."

I swiped my thumbs under her lash line, cupped her jaw, and kissed her softly. Relished the feel of her lips on mine and her flesh under my fingers. "We've suffered enough. If this curse is runebound, we'll break it. Together."

She drooped, cheek pressed to my chest. My heart pinched, and I held back a grimace.

"I can't lose you again, Gavrel," she whispered. "Not when we've only just begun. I won't have it."

I kissed her temple before I shook with silent laughter at her pervasive stubbornness.

"This isn't funny."

"I know." I rested my chin on the top of her head. "All I want is a day without any threats to our lives."

After a moment, she tilted her face toward mine, worry knitting her brow. I smoothed the wrinkle, the way she often did for me. My fingers rested below her chin.

"How is it," I started softly, "that I want to shake you for always putting yourself in harm's way—and worship you for being brave enough to do it?"

She gave me a watery smile. "It's a talent. And how dare you," she teased, nipping my thumb. A solemn expression overtook her playfulness. "To the Nether Void ..."

"And beyond," I finished. My chest tightened, love and pain tangling in the same breath.

Fucking void.

The world was crumbling, trying to tear us apart. Elders were missing, and Phobetor was now on the loose. We stood with one foot in a long-brewing rebellion, born of corrupt leadership and unspeakable injustices. Once news that the Elders were divided and missing spread, their flock would be in upheaval. People would scramble for power and control to fill the space the oligarchy had left behind.

Whatever poison the Ancient of Nightmare had woven into that bargain was slithering through my veins, bit by bit, unmaking me. Trying to rip my heart apart at the seams, thread by thread. And I couldn't allow it to spill into our bond.

But, for now, I still had *this*.

Her.

"Seryn." My voice was rough, splintered with everything I couldn't say. She propped herself up on one elbow, her braid spilling over her shoulder and draping across her breasts.

Ancients, she was beautiful. Like light itself, even when I was already fading into shadow.

"I need you to know." My words caught in my throat. "I want nothing more than to bind myself to you for the rest of our lives, but I—"

She silenced me with her fingers against my mouth, then lowered her lips to the marred flesh above my heart. "I know," she breathed. "But we don't need a ceremony to prove it. The Fates can carve their runes wherever they want ... Our souls were stitched together long before they noticed."

The corners of my mouth lifted. "Just to be clear: you are my everything. No curse, no runebound bargain can touch that. You're mine, and I'm yours. Across every thread of time, every realm."

Light flashed across her icy blue gaze. "Even if the stars burn out?"

"Especially then. You're the only star I'll ever need, Asteria."

Her laugh was quiet, broken. "Don't make promises Kosmos can hear."

"Too late," I muttered.

My lips found hers, and I sank into her warmth. The kiss wasn't about hunger; it was a vow woven from defiance and devotion.

Somewhere, I swore the air shifted, as though unseen hands tugged invisible spider silk around us. The amulet she wore warmed between us, but I ignored it. I disregarded the ache under my rune stone.

Because, in this moment, it didn't matter that the world was unraveling.

We were the thread holding one another together.

Her chest flushed, lips curving. "Gavrel Larkin," she whispered, sliding her hand beneath the sheets. My breath caught, and then her touch drew a groan from me. "Let me show you"—

her murmur brushed against my lips—"how completely you belong to me."

28

AWAY, AWAY, AWAY

SERYN

Finally, I left the warmth of our bed after a morning of bittersweet pleasure. The darkness staining Gavrel's skin was my doing. How cruelly fitting that the deal I'd made to save him was now trying to destroy him. Exactly as my uncle intended.

I padded across the room and took one of Gavrel's white tunics from the armoire. Feeling his eyes on me, I glanced at him. "Enjoying the view?"

"Immensely," he rasped.

With a smile, I slipped the garment over my head and scooped my belt off the ground.

Gavrel's arms wrapped around me, his mouth meeting my neck.

A firm knock sounded, and he reluctantly released me. Frowning, he opened the door to a flurry of movement.

Derya Atwater pushed into the room. "Miss! Oh, by the Ancients, you gave me such a scare, you did."

"Derya!" I cried, running into the older female's arms. "What are you doing here? I thought you were only at the palace during the Dormancies."

"Times are changing, my dear. Morpheus has returned, and what with Melina gone and the other two rotters fleeing. It's a relief to say that for other ears to hear." She flapped one hand and shifted a bundle of clothes under her arm. "And when Mr. Burlam sent word that you'd gone to retrieve the Commander from the Nether *and* that you'd brought your mother back. I came as soon as I heard, I did."

My smile grew. "I knew Mr. Burlam cared."

"But don't be pointing it out to him," she scolded.

And I suppressed the urge to giggle.

Her eyes softened as she studied me and Gavrel, her hand covering her heart. "It pleases me, it does, to see you finding one another at last. It's a waste of time to be so stubborn." She clucked her tongue.

I pulled her into another hug before my smile faltered as an idea crossed my mind. Derya was a skilled alchemist. Perhaps she knew something of curses. She often was a deep chasm of hidden information. "Derya, you wouldn't happen to have any experience with runebound bargains?"

The chambermaid's nose scrunched. "Not in the slightest."

Damn me to the Murk.

Consolingly, she patted my shoulder, one worried eyebrow rising. "But there might be someone who has. Everything tip-top?"

"Here in Surrelia?" Gavrel asked, sidestepping her question.

Derya set the clothes on the edge of the bed, giving him a sidelong glance. "Of course, dears." She cupped my cheek before flitting toward the door, her navy skirt flaring behind her. "The runemaster is here for tonight's ceremony."

"What ceremony?" I called after her.

"Oh my, yes. Yes, that's why I came up. I've brought you clothes for your parents' Kollao ceremony, of course."

"What?!" I squealed, surprise squeezing my windpipe.

"Your father said they've waited long enough to join souls." Derya shrugged. And with that, she flew out the door like a flighty bird. One that had dropped an egg on your head.

"A KOLLAO CEREMONY, HUH?" I asked, but not really wondering. If Gavrel and I could, we'd undergo the ritual ourselves. I couldn't imagine how my mother and father had suffered all these turns. Only seeing one another in a dream every so often.

"Is that even a question?" Mama smiled knowingly.

I chuckled. "No. I'm grateful you're both free and finally together. You deserve all the happiness, Mama." An image of my sister as a child dancing with my mother and me flickered in my mind. My shoulders slumped. "I miss Letti. It feels like turns since I left her. She'll be so heartbroken she missed this."

Mama's head dipped. "Give her my love and tell her I can't wait to see you both again someday." She put her arm around my waist. "I'll be waiting for you, my beautiful girls. Always."

I slid my hand to the back of her shoulder and squeezed gently. This life could be so very cruel. I blinked away the dampness trying to slip from my eyes. But my mother was safe, and she would be with her fated for the rest of eternity. I hoped it would comfort my sister knowing Mama was finally at peace.

What is death but a dream? The words echoed in my memory as we wandered the halls after lunch. Gavrel had gone to find Kaden.

We paused, examining a painting of the Moon Ancient, Selene. The female draped over the inside curve of a crescent moon, nearly falling off the tip, reaching for her lover's outstretched hand far below. My heart pounded against my ribs.

"I'm surprised you and Gavrel aren't binding."

"We don't need the ceremony to love one another. But regardless, there … there are complications," I said, glancing at her profile.

She kept studying the painting. "Never knew you to curl up in a ball of defeat, sweetheart."

I smiled. "Well, first we need to figure out how to break Phobetor's runebound bargain." I showed her my tattoo, and her eyes widened. "Because it's poisoning Gavrel. And then we need to remove the rune stone over his heart … that Morpheus showed Hestia in a dream." Mama's mouth dropped open. "It prevents him from talking about our bond. Although it likely protected him from Melina's emb—"

"That … that bloody wanker!"

I clapped my hand over my lips to stifle the burst of laughter. She so rarely cursed. That didn't bode well for Morpheus. My mother grabbed my hand and rushed through the halls and up the stairwell until we reached a massive study on the upper floor. It reminded me of Phobetor's, but in shades of silver and opalescence.

The Ancient of Dreams sat at an intricately carved desk, concentrating on various papers and books. His golden hair shone in the fractured sunlight dripping through the crystal ceiling.

He looked up, eyes practically glowing when they landed on my mother.

"My dream, what ails you?"

Mama stomped toward him, and he smiled. She poked a finger into the wall of his chest. "What have you done? You're the reason Gavrel has a rune in his chest. The reason *our* daughter can't bond with him. How could you?"

He held his hands up in surrender. I hadn't really thought to be upset with him, especially with everything else that had happened in recent days. And seeing him, an Ancient, being reprimanded by my very mortal mother was causing a twinge of sympathy to course through me.

"Maya, let me explain." Pausing, he looked at me, genuine regret framing his gaze. "My sincere apologies, daughter."

When he called me that now, it didn't feel odd. It felt … *right.* I realized I'd been thinking of him as my father more and more.

He continued, "We are all at the whims of the Fates, as you know full well. They offered me a way to protect you, and I'm not ashamed that I took it."

I tilted my head, eyes narrowing. Mama wore much the same expression.

"Fates help me," Morpheus muttered, eyes darting between us.

"They won't be able to get here quickly enough to help you," Mama threatened between her teeth.

He swallowed. Coming out from behind his desk, he waved to the cushioned seating area in front of a hearth on the other side of the room. He snapped his fingers, and a crackling fire ignited while we sat.

Mama crossed her arms. My father went on, "They said you would one day be in grave danger because of your gifts. That if your khorda and you bonded too soon, the prophecy and path laid out would collapse. That those who wished you harm would find you too soon … and all the realms would fall into Khaos."

My fingers dug into my thighs, breathing shallow. "So, it is true."

"What is, Little Star?" Mama's soft voice comforted me.

"That I can consume an Ancient's power." After what had happened in the Nether Void, that kernel of truth had tunneled under my skull, but hearing the Ancient of Dreams say it now. It was too much. It was *real*.

Mama glared at Morpheus. "*This* is why? Why I had to run from the Bogs? Implant her rune? I knew she'd be more, but I thought it was because she was half Druik, half demi-Ancient. I didn't know *she* was the prophecy." She ran her hands through her curls, causing them to fluff in a halo around her cheeks. "I'm so sorry, sweetheart."

I stood, toying with my talisman, pushing my shoulders back. "How do we remove Gavrel's rune?"

Morpheus closed his eyes for a moment, shame digging into the line of his lips. His gaze flicked to my blade—once his— before locking onto mine. "You must pierce his heart with *that* dagger."

"But he'll die. Why not just remove the stone?" The words were brittle on my tongue.

Morpheus dipped his head. "The symbol's ember would have bound itself to his heart. You can't remove it simply by cutting it from him."

"Then what's the use if it kills him?"

He steepled his fingers. "It isn't for us to bend the will of the Fates."

I scoffed. "Damn the Fates."

My father frowned. He'd ignored the three sisters and paid dearly for it.

Pursing my mouth, I inhaled deeply. "And how do I break my runebound bargain with your brother? It's already poisoning Gavrel," I bit out.

"You can't," he responded gently. "Unless you fulfill the terms."

"What was the deal?" Mama asked.

Staying silent, I crushed one fist closed and gripped my dagger, the metal hilt cold against my skin. I couldn't form the words yet. Couldn't tell them what Phobetor made me promise.

It was either Gavrel or my father. I drifted out of the study, thumb rubbing absently over the pommel.

Away from my parents and their troubled expressions.

Away from the nauseating truth.

Away from any sense of hope I clung to.

29

SCATTERED TOMES

Seryn

"I'm not sure there's another way, Ryn-Ryn," Breena groaned, another book slamming against the table.

We'd spent hours scouring the library for ways to break my oath and to rid Gavrel of his cursed rune stone. I hadn't brought myself to tell Gavrel what I'd learned. I sighed, flipping through the pages before me.

Kaden pulled the new book toward himself. "She's right. As much as it pains me to admit it."

Breena smiled smugly, eyeing him with interest. "If it came to it, your gift might be strong enough to heal your brother, eh?"

Kaden shrugged. "It's not a risk I want to take. If he could die simply from removing the talisman, the rune itself might be entirely too powerful. There's no telling if I'd be able to heal him quickly enough."

"You're not wrong, Lark," the deep, smooth voice said from behind us. Breena's eyebrows lifted as we turned in the male's direction. There was only one person who called Kaden that.

Kaden immediately scowled, and I jumped to my feet, throwing my arms around the male. "Magister Barden!"

He smiled, giving me a tight hug before holding me at arm's length.

"*That's* your ol' teacher?" Her eyes dragged over him, his well-fitting breeches, plain tunic, and chocolate-colored overcoat. She winked at him. "Well, hello, Magister."

With a polite smile, he inclined his head. "Jace, please."

Kaden stood, offering him a stiff handshake. "What brings you to the dream realm, Magister? You finally choke on your lessons?"

Jace's mouth flattened, shoulders pushing back. "I see your temperament reigns true, Lark." He glanced at me, eyes direct but the corners softening a little. "Morpheus summoned me to officiate the binding. Congratulations on learning your true heritage, Seryn. Fascinating, isn't it?"

Kaden sidled next to me. "She's not something to dissect and study."

I bumped my shoulder into his, unsure why he was being so combative, and he shrugged. I shook my head. Although now that I thought of it, Kaden had often provoked Magister Barden during our lessons when we were young.

A yellow glow—only my gift allowed me to see—flickered around Jace, like the morning sun when it spilled into a room. Kaden was getting under his skin, his tightly wound emotions loosing his aura.

He pushed one hand through his thick, blond waves, which were neatly trimmed and swept back to his ears.

He always looked suspiciously young for his assumed age— possibly mid-thirties. But now that I knew he was a Druik, it made sense.

"We're all meant to be studied. It's how one learns to deal with others. How we avoid making the same mistakes," Jace responded coolly. "How to conduct yourself."

Kaden's tongue pushed against the inside of his cheek, trapping any retort he might've had.

One corner of my lips quirked. "Quite the secret keeper, Magister. Not only are you a Druik, but you're a runemaster as well. I'm impressed."

"Says the demi-Ancient Scion." Breena chuckled.

I rolled my eyes, unease fluttering in my belly.

"Secrets are needed when they are the only thing standing in the way of survival," he said while gesturing to my nape. "May I? Maya mentioned you made a runebound bargain."

I gathered my hair and showed him the mark. His warm touch traced the lines.

"This type of oath, especially with an Ancient, is notoriously malignant until it's fulfilled." He squeezed my shoulder with a frown. "Let me think on it. If I can find a way to unravel it, I'll let you know."

My shoulders drooped. "Thank you, Magister Barden."

His attention flicked above. "It's Jace," he murmured.

I followed his line of sight and noticed Caelora wandering the second-floor balcony, her dark blonde waves spilling down her back as she searched the shelves.

Jace's aura glowed again before vanishing. "Pleasure seeing you all. If you would excuse me." He nodded and then stalked toward the curling stairs in the back of the library.

Kaden glared at him as he left.

"Don't fancy the Magister, do ya, Larkin?" Breena ruffled his hair, and his scowl deepened. "Really gets your panties in a twist, eh?"

"He's always been so damned pompous." He crossed his arms. "Hey, I'm sure you miss Marek, yeah?"

Breena's lips pinched as she blinked slowly at Kaden. He smirked in response.

I tipped my head to my friends. "All right. Why don't you two go spar outside? See you at the ceremony."

"Yes, Ma'am," Breena teased. "Come on, Larkin. I've been meaning to stab you in your bits."

With a huff, Kaden followed her.

A wry laugh shook my body as I refocused on the books strewn across the table. Disappointment festered as I turned each page without an answer.

Soft footfalls sounded behind me. "Like an astra poppy to the sunlight." Gavrel kissed the top of my head. "I knew I'd find you here. We need to get ready for the Kollao."

He bent, gathering the scattered books, running his thumb over the worn titles. "*Blood and Bonds. Runes for the Ages.*" A faint smile ghosted his mouth. "Just some light reading?"

I snatched up the last books, turning to the stacks. "I thought I might find something to help us ... but there's bloody nothing."

I shoved a book into its spot a little too aggressively. "After everything we've been through,"—another book slammed into place—"and now I have to fucking *kill* you to get your rune out, or kill my father, or let the curse finish what it started. Ancients damn it!"

He shelved his last tome and then closed the distance between us, his fingers finding mine, rough and steady. "Breathe," he murmured. "I'm not dying today. And neither is your father."

My forehead met his chest, the rhythm of his pulse anchored me even as it made me ache.

"But what was that about *you* killing me?" he asked softly.

I shuddered, my words spilling down his tunic. "Morpheus ... he said my dagger could remove your stone. But I'd have to pierce your heart. And it might—" My throat closed. "It might kill you."

"That's not ideal," he said, rubbing my back.

I looked up, his face composed. He was always so damned unruffled. "How can you be so Ancients-damned calm, Gav? We have to figure this out before it's too late."

"I'm calm because I'm here with you," he replied simply. "And that's what matters. Let's celebrate your parents, and then we'll face whatever comes next."

My back hit the shelf, the cool wood pressing into my borrowed tunic. I relished the scrape of it against my skin. I dragged my teeth over my bottom lip, fighting the flood of conflicting emotions. My fear. Irritation. Gratitude. Love. The hunger that always simmered beneath my flesh when he was near.

His eyes darkened, flicking to my mouth. He leaned in, bracing both hands on either side of my head. His breath was cool against my damp lips. "Or perhaps," he murmured, voice rough and low around the edges, "we can reverse that. *Come first. Celebrate after.*"

"How do you do that?" I breathed, chest rising against his.

He arched one brow, stepping closer until the space between us was barely existent.

"How do you calm me one moment and set me on fire the next?" I whispered.

A hint of a smile tugged at his mouth—just enough to reveal his fleeting dimple. He swept my curls aside, lips grazing the shell of my ear. "Because you are mine just as much as I am yours. Two halves of a whole that can't stop calling to the other."

He traced the line of my jaw, pausing over my pulse. His other hand gripped the shelf so tightly the wood creaked. "Can you feel what you do to me, Asteria? How my heart races. How it demands that you answer it?"

My hands fisted his tunic, breath catching. His heartbeat thudded beneath my knuckles. "Yes."

His touch slid down my neck, long fingers encircling me, thumbs pressing into the hollow above my collarbone. "Then listen to it. Every time it beats, it's calling for you."

I swallowed hard, the ache in my chest pounding throughout my body. In my core. "You make it sound so easy."

He swept a hand over my shoulder, fabric slipping down my biceps. "It's never been easy, but it's always been *right*."

Heat washed over me, my collarbone and face warming. For a breath, I forgot the curse, the coming ceremony, the world beyond us. There was only him and me. This beautiful, infuriating man who never stopped choosing me, even when it broke him.

When I didn't move, he did. His forehead pressed against mine, our breaths mingling in the infinitesimal space between. "If this is all we have," he whispered, "then let it be enough."

Something inside me snapped. I closed the distance by yanking on his tunic, and his mouth slammed into mine. He was my salvation and devastation all at once. I needed him more than air. More than my pulse.

The air shimmered around us, my aura fracturing and his rune tattoo casting a glow that spilled down the leather-bound treasures as he pressed his hands into my lower back. The shelves bit into my shoulder blades and backside.

The bite of pain seeped into me, but I didn't care. Forgot to care if anyone caught us in the stacks.

My focus narrowed in on the feel of his body against mine. Of the taste of him. I groaned, and the sound vibrated between our tongues and mouths as we collided and fed on one another.

"You look good in my clothes." His hand glided down my hip, fingers warm against my bare thigh. "But you look even better out of them." His hand whipped up, tugging the tunic down my chest. My breast fell heavy into his palm, his touch rough and possessive.

"The feel of you. Your taste. I can't get enough," he rasped against my neck, nipping and licking me.

I was burning up, my wet core already clenching at the

emptiness. Needing him to fill me. If he didn't claim what was his, I would ignite and burn all my beloved books to the stone.

Fucking void.

He kissed a path across my collarbone, up my chin, and then claimed my mouth again. He consumed me, kissed me so hard and deep, as if he feared I'd slip away.

Seeking friction, his length pushed into my belly, and my hips answered in kind.

His left bicep flexed against my temple, wood groaning under his grip before he slid it down my side, squeezing my waist. I whimpered when his right hand kneaded my breast. He smiled against my lips and then pinched my achy nipple.

My mouth wrenched away from his, and I sucked in a breath before nipping his bottom lip. Something between a moan and a growl rumbled in his chest, and his fingers slipped under the tunic at my thighs, between my legs. They burrowed under my underwear and then sank into my heat.

He grinned, thrusting his fingers inside me twice before swirling my wet desire over my pulsing clit. "I want your fucking books to see you come all over me."

My cheeks flamed at his wicked words, and my knees trembled.

He flicked the tender bundle at my apex as his eyes dragged over my puckered nipples. I groaned his name, and before my legs gave out, he gripped my thighs and hoisted me up, slamming my back against the stacks. Books trembled, shifting precariously toward the edge.

He reached between us, freeing his erection while my boots dug into the firm muscles of his backside.

When his lips claimed mine once more, and his hand returned to squeeze my thigh, my eyes fluttered closed, core quivering in anticipation.

He stilled, and my eyes snapped open. In my next breath, he slammed his cock into me, and I clenched around him.

Sweat beaded on his temple as he thrust, every inch of him dragging over every sensitive nerve within me. He pushed in, whispering sinful, sweet nothings in my ear, and then pulled out.

Again and again.

"Harder," I whimpered, not giving a damn when several books started toppling around us and pounding against the floor in time with his thrusts. In time with my cries and back slapping against the shelves.

"Asteria, drench me."

I cried out, and he kissed me, swallowing my plea. Desire scorched my spine, my pulse throbbing in my head. In my convulsing cunt.

He buried his face in the curve of my neck, fingers digging into my flesh. Bruising me. I bit my bottom lip, my aura trembling around me and behind my eyelids.

With a final groan, he rammed into me, and my body shook around him as an explosive wave of need burst between us.

He shuddered, his sweat dripping onto my damp chest and slipping between my breasts.

"Gavrel," I uttered. "Holy void."

His shoulders shook with quiet amusement as he slipped out of me, our desire coating his manhood. Gently, he lowered me until my boots hit the floor. He brushed back wayward strands and cupped my jaw before placing a kiss on my forehead.

I traced the inky lines peeking over the V of his dark tunic, then gripped the fabric over his scar. "Just one day will never be enough."

He wrapped his arms around me and rested his chin on the crown of my head. I listened to his heart steady itself, felt the rise and fall of his thick pectoral muscles.

"I know." His answer dropped among the scattered books at our feet.

30

THREADS BOUND ETERNAL

SERYN

wilight cloaked the Elysium Tree in shades of violet and coral. Fireflies danced among us as we waited for the ritual to begin. Embered orb lanterns bobbed on invisible tethers among the weeping branches and round, semitranslucent leaves the color of sweet apricot marmalade.

It was a smallish gathering for an Ancient's Kollao ceremony. But it's what my parents wanted. They'd both waited long enough and didn't want to make the journey to Aion for a more formal ceremony. Morpheus mentioned they could organize a larger celebration in the coming months.

One I wouldn't be able to attend.

I sighed wistfully, grateful to be a part of this, regardless.

Earlier, I had helped my mother get ready. She had laughed and twirled in her room. I'd never seen her so carefree and joyful. The memory stirred in my mind, bringing a smile to my face.

"Hold still," I'd murmured, tucking the last blue flower into her curls.

She didn't hold still. Instead, she turned toward me, eyes shining. "You don't need to fuss over me."

With a smile, I smoothed a braid into place on the top of her head and pinned it. "Someone has to."

She caught my hands before I could pull away, and for a moment, neither of us moved. She studied my face as though memorizing it, like I'd spent my whole life trying to remember hers.

"You've grown so much. I've missed so much," she murmured.

Words escaped me, so I only squeezed her fingers.

She continued, her voice hitching, "We won't get many more moments like this before you leave. Moments where I remember who I was, and who I always wanted to be as a mother when you were little."

"Now is all that matters, Mama. And it's enough." I leaned my forehead against hers, and she breathed the moment in.

"My little star," she whispered. "I'm so proud of the woman you've become."

"I've learned from the best, Mama."

We shared a long embrace before she sighed and kissed my cheek. "Let's get me to the ceremony, shall we?" She spun in place, her dress glittering in the sunlight.

"Yes, let's. It's about time."

We laughed, walking elbow in elbow as we left her room.

I blinked, coming back to the present. I'd cherish the moments I'd had with my mother in recent days. Hold them tight in my heart so I could take them out like paintings to study and feel the love and warmth I'd known in them.

Mama practically glowed in a flowing dress the color of midnight. Delicate sparkles shimmered over the material when she shifted, sheer sleeves fluttering in the breeze to her wrists. The deep V down the front exposed most of her sternum. Dainty blue flowers weaved throughout her curls, and thin piles of braids wound atop her head in a crown.

Uneasily, Therrok and Thesa shifted, wings twitching, while they lingered at my mother's back like foreboding shadows. The rest of us, including Elders Guust and Strom, gathered in a semicircle around them. Derya dabbed a handkerchief under her lashes, and Mr. Burlam patted her shoulder with the least severe frown I'd ever seen him wear.

I swore Breena's eyes were shining more than usual. She gave me a watery smile when she noticed me looking and then shrugged, making the bright red, strapless dress she wore shift against her thighs. The light caught on the three pink, raised scars on each of her shoulders, a permanent reminder of the dream reaper's attack in the Epiales Tombs when we'd saved Kaden.

My father stood before my mother in golden robes, his chest exposed and white breeches slung low on his hips. A gold diadem, with stars and leaf patterns, circled his crown atop thick, wavy flaxen hair that reached his chin. He looked at her in awe, hands embracing hers. He kissed her knuckles, and she smiled, cheeks flushing.

My heart fluttered at the pure devotion written across their features.

Before I'd gone to her chambers, I'd checked on Morpheus. My lips curved at the encounter only hours earlier.

I'd found him in his study, the air warm from the flickering hearth. He sat hunched in his chair, elbows on his knees, hands buried in his pale hair. The firelight caught on the dreamlike haze drifting about the room, as though his aura was weaving a spell around him. Or perhaps he was trying to soothe himself.

"Everything all right?" I asked gently.

He didn't lift his head at first. "You'd think," he murmured, voice catching like fingers running the wrong way over velvet, "that after existing for an eternity, I'd have learned to trust the path laid before me."

I stepped closer. "Are you worried about the ceremony? About binding with Mama?"

A small laugh broke from him. "Ah, you see through me too easily. I've never feared the bond with Maya, but, yes—the ceremony. I've disregarded the three sisters before and paid dearly for it. Perhaps that was always their intent. I would never have found Maya without my imprisonment. And you wouldn't have been born from a dream." His cheeks puffed out with an exhale. "The Fates do so love the symmetry of it all—taking two halves and pretending they invented wholeness."

I hesitated. "You don't sound sure."

His gaze found mine, eyes crinkling at the corners. "I've never loved someone as I do your mother. Every promise is a double-edged sword meant to protect, yet ready to slice your soul to ribbons. Still, I would choose her every time. Suffer any destiny if it meant she remained my other half. Because she's worth it. In this, as you said, damn the Fates."

Something inside me squeezed. "I understand the feeling." I sank into the chair opposite him, the flames crackling at my side. "Though the Sisters weave every web—and choice may very well be part of their illusion—I like to think I can take my dagger to their strings whenever I please."

A smile ghosted over Morpheus' face. "You have her defiance. But you carry something else, too. Something I can't quite name yet."

"Panic and a chronic inability to breathe?"

Chuckling, he shook his head. "No. Fire." He looked at the hearth, its flames dancing over the ice of his irises. "That's why Kosmos marked you, daughter. You're both starlight and shadow, and neither has ever bowed."

I hesitated, unsure of what to say.

"So," he went on, "for all our sakes, I'll follow your lead and believe in choice ... believe that it's real."

"I hope so," I whispered.

"Keep that hope close." He looked up, and for a heartbeat, the Ancient of Dreams vanished, and just a father remained, staring at a *future he couldn't stop. "When the time comes, and the Fates demand a choice, don't do it for duty. Don't do it for your mother or me. Choose because your heart refuses not to."*

I blinked, caught off guard. "You ... you sound like you know more than you're saying."

He sighed. "Perhaps. It's the curse of walking through others' dreams." He reached out, thumb brushing my jaw. "Don't be afraid of what's inside you, Seryn. Even stars need the dark to burn."

A floral breeze tossed a curl over my nose, and I brushed it away, along with the memory.

Gavrel's fingers tightened around mine, and his lips pressed against my temple for a moment. I leaned into him, closing my eyes and relishing the warmth of his minty breath as it glided over my cheek.

"You are beautiful," he whispered in my ear.

"Thank you." I opened my eyes, following the path of my thumb as it traced the lines on his palm. I refused to look at his arms, at the inky darkness that had crept over the length of his left limb.

We had found nothing in the library to offer a resolution. And although Gavrel had allowed his brother a shot at healing the infection, his aura had practically recoiled from the streaks, and I swore they had stretched further along my fated's flesh before Kaden wrenched his ember back, cursing.

Magister Barden—*Jace*, I reminded myself—had yet to find a counter rune or a way to rid me of the mark. The Druik in question approached the couple, his posture perfectly aligned.

He wore a simple, but neatly tailored brown overcoat over a crisp, pale tunic and breeches. His smattering of rune tattoos peeked over the edges of his tunic, glowing in soft, buttery yellow hues against his tanned skin.

I was still a bit stunned that he was a prominent runemaster. A highly skilled Druik who'd been hiding all these turns in Evergryn.

On my left, Kaden leaned into me, glaring at our former educator. "Barden is hiding more than we know, I'm sure of it," he whispered, loud enough that one of Jace's eyebrows lifted, his fingers tightening on the golden bowl he held in one hand.

"You're a thorn in everyone's backside," Caelora hissed from behind us. I flinched, surprised at her outburst. She had said little since we'd arrived. Actually, she'd made herself scarce; she seemed skilled at making herself fade into the background.

But who would miss the opportunity to see a Kollao ceremony when they were so rare nowadays? Giggling, I shrugged. "She isn't wrong, Kade. You think everyone is hiding something."

His face crumpled. "Because it's true," he huffed, crossing his arms and giving me and Gavrel an accusatory look.

Rolling my eyes, I tipped my chin toward Jace. "I'm sure there was a good reason for him to hide his skills and identity. He's lucky the Elders didn't keep him locked up in the dungeon. Who knows what's become of their runemaster."

He narrowed his eyes at the male, lips pressed in a thin line.

I glanced at Gavrel, and he smiled, although it wobbled at the corners as if he was holding back a wince. I brushed my fingers along his jawline. "You're in pain."

His gaze dragged down my dress. The silk shifted between silver and gray where the light hit, like moonlight over water. Three glittering, slender straps draped from each shoulder and crisscrossed over my collarbone, holding the fitted bodice that curved along the top of my breasts. Tiny, silver-threaded flowers and vines clustered along the hem, the blooms scattering as they climbed toward my waist.

"And you are stunning," he responded, cupping my chin and bringing my mouth to his.

"Thank you, but flattery won't distract me. As soon as this is done, we're doing more research."

He bent down, whispering into my ear, palm warming my thigh. "I have plenty to *research*."

Heat crept up my breasts and neck. I squeezed his hand, biting my lower lip.

"We'll begin." Jace's voice rang out, deep and resonant as it echoed through the trees. Everyone breathed in at once; even the fireflies and swaying vines seemed to still.

He lifted a slender gilded dagger. Light from the hovering orbs rippled over its surface, spilling molten gold across his hands.

"Since the birth of the stars," he intoned, "until the end of all turns."

My mother raised her palm in offering.

"With the blood of your fated," Jace recited, and the blade sliced into her skin. She flinched, but her hand didn't waver as her blood welled and then spilled into the waiting bowl when she squeezed her fist. My father followed, his hand steady as Jace opened his flesh, and his blood mingled with my mother's.

"May Kosmos bless this union," Jace called out, lifting the bowl between them. "For we are all but halves adrift in the aether, seeking the pieces that make us whole."

Morpheus laced his fingers with Mama's. Red dripped over their joined hands and onto the roots of the Elysium Tree. A low thrum pulsed beneath the moss.

"As crimson begets gold," Jace declared, "threads are bound eternal. Mind, body, soul, and ember—one flame. So speaks Kosmos."

"So speaks Kosmos," my parents echoed.

Their auras shimmered around them, my mother's halo of sparkling night brushing against my father's gilded starlight. Jace's own soft yellow radiance pulsed over him. Every inch of him now ablaze with intricate, geometric markings as if his flesh kept a record of each rune he learned.

Gavrel's hand slipped around my waist, grounding me.

Everyone had gone utterly still—even Kaden's usual smirk had vanished.

The runemaster moved one hand, fingers sketching lines of glowing gold in the air, suspended above the bowl. Threads bent and twined, forming a sigil: twin crescents that interlocked as they faced opposite directions, an infinity loop tying them together. At the point where their curves crossed at the top, a flame perched.

He exhaled, and the symbol sank into the mingled blood. The liquid bubbled before swirling into molten gold.

"Although we are born with part of their soul, we have Eros, the Ancient of Love, to praise for the Kollao ceremony. He believed that khordas have a connection so rare that they deserved the chance to reunite the thread that binds them."

His gaze swept over us. "This binding is sacred; not even the Fates can deny it. Two souls will fuse—their lifeblood, ember, and soul entwined. The mark shall be carved where breath and pulse and life meet. Do you accept this joining?"

"So be it," my parents replied together.

Jace dipped the blade into the golden ichor, and his dagger gleamed. My mother tightened her grip on Morpheus' hand.

The runemaster worked swiftly, slicing through skin, muscle, then bone. Morpheus' breath caught, his body straining as Jace carved the mirrored crescents and flame into his rib, light poured from the wound, gold replacing blood. The glow pulsed once, sank deep, and then sealed itself beneath healed muscle and skin. My father slumped forward and then arched in a silent scream. When he straightened, the faint sigil shimmered over his chest.

Jace turned to my mother. She pushed her shoulders back and crushed her eyes closed. When the blade met her sternum, he repeated the ritual. After he finished, tears spilled over her cheeks. Morpheus caught her when her knees faltered. The luminosity between them merged along with their auras. They were two halves of a cosmic star collapsing into one brilliant whole.

As we cheered, waves of light pulsated from the sacred banyan's roots and over its bark. I thought it was part of the ceremony until my father tensed, and my mother's narrowed gaze snapped behind him.

My breath caught as a violent vortex burst into existence, and a dream reaper flew out of the portal. It screeched, its gauzy veil flying up and exposing its gruesome skull and fire-filled hollows beneath.

Damn me to the Murk.

The ritual must have torn a rift between realms, and Phobetor had scraped together enough nightmare ember to rip it open.

31

PAPA

SERYN

Jace spun, flinging out his hand. Ember and runes flared along his arm like molten script; the light slashed across the nearest reaper's throat, lopping its head off. Its skull cracked to the ground as more creatures poured from the portal, skeletal forms spilling through the veil.

"Huh. So that's how you kill 'em," Breena chuffed.

Gavrel brandished his sword, but then doubled over in the next moment—the ebony curse creeping over his other arm.

"Get back, Gav," I cried. "It's getting worse!"

He shook his head, tried to stand his ground, then staggered backward.

Weapons and auras flared, bursts of multicolored energy tearing through the air as skulls slammed onto the earth. A few demon warriors slipped through the threshold, their black, beady eyes squinting in the neon bright of the Reverie Weald.

I threw my dagger dead center into a charging, horned beast. It collapsed at Mr. Burlam's boots, and he harrumphed.

"Get Derya and Iben inside! Defend the palace! Gather more forces!" I shouted toward Marah and Endurst, who snapped into action, rushing toward the palace.

A disembodied voice cut through the mist, cold and amused. "How vulgar not to invite me to your Kollao, brother."

My breath hitched.

Phobetor.

Horror flickered over everyone's faces, even the Grim Twins. If the Ancient of Nightmares crossed into Surrelia, the treaty would be broken. And the Fates would likely summon the Primevals.

"Phobi has finally lost his last fecking thread of sanity," Breena snarled, raising an embered shield against an oncoming reaper.

Morpheus shoved my mother behind him as Jace decapitated two more reapers, who fell in front of them.

"Stop him!" I yelled, sprinting toward the portal. Gavrel's shout followed me, and everything in me wanted to heed his voice.

But I couldn't allow Phobetor to enter this realm.

My iridescence burned around me, and I dodged another monster.

My parents leaped over piles of bones and bloody remains. Caelora's lavender fire clung to the demon at my side. Its screech tore through my ears.

Shadows whirled in the center of the portal. The firefly-like orbs were being swallowed into the darkness. My uncle's silhouette sharpened.

Everything sped up: My name shouted in a chorus of voices. Phobetor's chiseled angles came into focus. Gavrel stumbled toward me, sword arm slackening.

I flung my hands out, branch-like patterns blazing up my arms, and plunged into the maelstrom. Gavrel collided with me, solid and warm, before the mist took us both.

"Not without me," he grunted, locking his hold around my waist as we plummeted, weightless, spinning through a dizzying tunnel of light and shadow.

Before I could catch my breath, our knees cracked against the stone. Forms crashed around us; everyone had followed.

Bloody fucking void!

I jolted to my feet. When my sight adjusted, I recognized the molten metal sloshing beside us, veins of light pulling into the pool from thousands of amber globes.

The Epiales Tombs.

Therrok grumbled as his wings snapped out, and he hauled Thesa and Mama up. Weapons and ember flew as reapers and demons closed in.

Morpheus charged at his brother. Phobetor grinned. With a snap of his fingers, the nightmare prisons burst to life—thousands of captives writhing inside amber glass spheres and mist, their screams silent.

Morpheus hurled a stream of twinkling gold. Phobetor dodged and threw shadows back.

On the far side of the embered basin, Melina was imprisoned, terror twisting her features. Hordes of reapers indulged themselves, fed on the fear radiating from her cell and all the others.

"Morpheus!" Mama called out, bending a demon's aura against it like a weapon. "Free them!"

Morpheus' gilded stars struck Phobetor, stunning him for a heartbeat. I lunged forward, my gift latching onto him. My father stepped closer to the enchanted pool, hands directing its energy, blending it with his. Dreams and starlight melded with the stolen nightmares, the veins of light quivering with his ministrations.

Phobetor's enraged bellow bounced off the banestone, more furious at his brother than with me. He pulled, clawing at my ember's hold, veins standing proud along his neck.

Morpheus arched, light exploding from the pool. From him. Surging through the room in a roaring wave. It knocked everyone off their feet as the light blinked out from all the globes.

My back slammed into the stone, knocking the air from my lungs. Within my next breath, the sound of splintering glass shrieked through the place, the orbs glowing white as cracks spider-webbed over their surfaces.

Gavrel threw himself over me just as they shattered and shards showered us. Bodies hit stone all around, and I winced. When I peeked from beneath my khorda's arm, Jace, Mama, the Flints, and Morpheus were doing everything they could to catch or slow the falling captives.

Breena, Caelora, and Kaden fought off those demons and reapers bold enough to attack once more.

Gavrel clutched his chest with a groan, face pinching. I screamed his name as he pitched forward. I caught his head before it cracked against the ground. My parents ran to us, hearing my cry.

Phobetor swept his hands outward and shadows surged, sealing me, Gavrel, and my parents inside a dome of churning black.

Reapers scratched at the surface. Thesa slammed it with her polearm, but it bounced off uselessly. Caelora's liquid fire coated three demons, igniting their pallid bones in violet hues before they crumbled into nothing.

Therrok swooped over the dome, the obsidian ring on his finger glinting as he summoned another inter-realm passage from the pool.

Kaden and Breena threw themselves at the barrier, fists and weapons hammering. Jace called the others, hoisting an unconscious Melina over his shoulder.

With a final flick of Phobetor's wrists, shadows thickened around the dome, swallowing the last glimpse of my friends.

"Interesting how my poison spreads faster the closer I am, isn't it?" Phobetor crooned, eyeing Gavrel as he lay in my arms. He had my mother pinned, shadows binding her arms and muffling her voice. The sight of his boot digging into her side had me grinding my teeth. "Looks like your time is up, niece. Who will you choose? Your mortal, or your father?"

"Seryn," Morpheus barked. I looked at him, agony pouring from my eyes. Morpheus' golden aura swelled, and he thrust out his hand. "Take it."

"I can't. We've only just found one another," I sobbed.

My heart slammed into my throat. Shame and regret rushed through my senses. Everything I'd lost, every mistake I'd made, had led me here. Could I destroy him to save the man I loved?

"You can, and you will." My father ... my fucking *father's* voice was unyielding.

"Papa," I whimpered. His eyes softened. Mama choked back a sob.

I cradled Gavrel's head and recalled Morpheus' words.

Choose because your heart refuses not to.

Tears slipped free as I let my iridescence rise. Let it thread itself through my fingers and latch onto him.

The rune burned against my neck, my ember pulsating through me as I drank my father's power in. He paled, and his eyes rolled back into his head.

Pure glee flashed over Phobetor's features, his lips wet from his tongue, fists clutching greedily at the lapels of his robes.

The dark universe formed within my orb, its utter blackness sprinkled with starlight. Raw, vibrant energy vibrated through my every sinew, eyes, and limbs, glowing with celestial light.

More, my gift demanded. *More!*

I kept taking what my father offered. Long after he crumpled in a heap. Well after Mama's cries faded from my attention.

My body levitated with the force of my newfound power.

Prickling, like that of a hundred needles, stung along my

nape. Like threads ripping from my flesh. *The runebound bargain,* I thought with both relief and despair. It was satisfied. Because I'd drained my father—until he was an empty husk, as my uncle had put it.

With a strangled whimper, I forced my ember to unlatch from Morpheus as the small universe gyrated in my palms.

"Release her," I ordered, voice low and not entirely my own. My rune burned before the glowing image of a snake coiled around a crescent moon slid off my skin and hovered above me. Geometric lines shifting, the snake slithered away from the moon before dissolving into shadow.

Phobetor's darkness peeled away from Mama, and she crawled over to my father, cupping his face.

Power surged through me, raw and dizzying.

Gavrel coughed, the ebony in his veins receding.

I raised the orb, ready to destroy the Ancient of Nightmares, but froze as the banestone pendant seared my sternum. With a sharp gasp, I clutched it. The amulet's black hue bled into amber. Instantly, the pressure crushing my skull eased as my father's stolen ember surged into the stone and purged Melina's, its smoke spilling at my feet.

Unbidden tears blurred my vision. My power could enhance another's ember, but it couldn't restore what was lost.

The amulet could.

Strong arms wrapped around my middle. "Breathe, Asteria," Gavrel ordered, his voice rough and grounding.

Confusion raced over Phobetor's face, then realization. His aura burst outward, shadows whipping around him as his arms flung wide.

Gavrel's tattoo ignited, rune flaring in perfect harmony with my power. His energy bled into me, steady and fierce, as I thrust ember at my uncle. The blast slammed into his chest and knocked him into his own collapsing dome.

The last of Morpheus' ember sealed within the amulet as the

veil fizzled out. A sea of broken glass and scattered bodies was all that remained.

Phobetor stirred. Our eyes met, ice colliding with a black void. I curled my fingers around the amulet, feeling the pulse inside. My ember—I ... We—reached for the coiling energy within the banestone teardrop. Connected. *Communed.* Drew it out.

A sweet pressure released within my chest, and I *knew*. Felt it in my very marrow that I controlled the stolen power.

I turned the flow toward my father.

But Phobetor roared, his shadows slashing through the link. The surge scorched through my veins, blistering my palms. I faltered, Morpheus' dream ember seeping wild and molten between my fingers.

I stopped trying to catch it. There wasn't time.

"Sweet dreams, uncle," I taunted, tearing the chain from my neck and slamming the amulet to the ground. It cracked beneath my heel, and light erupted.

Morpheus' power spewed from the banestone and crashed into my father's chest. His back arched, gasp scraping through the air. Ire-coated fear flashed over my uncle's features, and he scrambled away on all fours.

Mama cried out.

Phobetor lobbed a shadowy dart toward me. My knees buckled, vision blurring.

Gavrel swung us around, and the shadow sliced into him. He'd taken the strike meant for me. I think I called his name— just his name—because it was the only thing I wanted on my lips before death took me.

The thread binding our ribs stretched painfully thin. So taut, I wasn't sure if it had snapped. We tumbled together, limbs tangled, breath shallow.

Another molten whirlwind.

Boots thundered.

Flame-like shadows collided with nightmarish billows.

Shouting. Cursing.

Bodies slamming.

Mama's hands brushed my cheek.

"Find me … in dreams." Her voice sounded far away, every other word slipping into the unknown.

Tears fell onto my skin.

Then.

Darkness.

32

WAKE UP

S ERYN

My legs were trapped. I kicked my feet, panic flitting through my limbs. The rustle of layered fabric calmed me when I realized I was still wearing the dress from my parents' Kollao ceremony.

My tongue was sandpaper, throat so dry it was about to split. I sat up, pain slicing across my brow. The rickety bed creaked under my weight as I shook my head and rubbed my eyes, which apparently were also made of sand. I slumped onto the bed, crushing my eyelids closed to shut out the light.

"Ser, take it slow," a soft voice said.

I must have smashed my brain in because I swore I heard my sister.

"When has she ever taken anything slow?" another voice retorted.

All right. I was hallucinating Yaya now.

Just open your fucking eyes, I snapped within myself. A chorus

215

of gilly toads and crickets undulated on a damp breeze that caressed my exposed skin.

Images flit through my mind, dread sinking into my stomach.

My parents.

Phobetor.

The Epiales Tombs.

Gavrel.

"Gavrel!" I bolted up, ignoring my aches.

"Whoa—steady," Letti scolded, pressing a cup of water into my hands.

Tears blurred my vision. My grandmother stood behind my sister, hands propped on her hips. Her intricate braids and silver curls spilled over her shoulders as she smiled.

"Letti? Yaya?" I stumbled over my words. "How?"

Letti ran her hand over my forearm. "Hush now. You're safe." She pushed the cup closer, and I took it with shaky hands. "Drink," she urged.

The foot of the bed dipped under Yaya's weight. "We're in Helos," she explained briskly. "Marek and Rhaegar rallied what ravens they could, took the Draumr's stationed here, and freed us. Much of the Order defected when word spread of the Elders being dismantled. Melina thought so little of Helos that she left no Akridais to defend what they'd taken."

Blinking rapidly, I still struggled to believe they were both here with me.

Letti nodded, smoothing a hand over my hair. "Once Melina went missing, Lucan fled to Evergryn. Declared martial law. Luckily, Xeni got Rhaegar's harbinger starling in time, and she, Father, and I escaped to Helos before the borders closed."

Her mention of Gideon made something twist in my stomach. I ignored it. Being near my sister only sharpened the truth: he'd never been a father to me. Stubbornly, he'd kept his distance from me for so long that he'd made sure he never resembled one.

And thinking about that made the loss of Morpheus hit harder—made me relive the moment I'd drained him.

I pushed the memory away as Yaya rested a hand on Letti's shoulder. "And now I have both my granddaughters with me."

My sister grinned, tapping the bottom of my cup.

I should have asked about their reunion. How Letti had felt meeting our grandmother for the first time. Told them about Mama.

Instead, I took another sip, my voice steadier. "And where do they think Ryboas fled?"

Yaya smirked. "Ah, there she is." She patted my ankle. "Ravens spotted Ash heading toward the mountains." She scoffed. "We're letting him think he's safe for now. Let him skulk about in the wilds a bit. Unlike Lucan, he's not a problem until he gathers more followers."

The Elders were an issue for another day. "Where's Gavrel?" I asked again, handing my cup to my sister. She helped me stand as my knees wobbled.

"He's in your old cabin." Her lips pressed into a thin line. "He hasn't woken yet."

My feet moved before my brain could stop them. I wrestled with my dress, yanked it over my head, and let it fall where it landed.

The damp, charcoal-tinged air clung to my skin, stifling against my thin, satin shift. I stumbled across the short bridge, the wood groaning under my bare soles. All around me, the city lay in ruin, and I swallowed the furious pain clogging the back of my throat.

The attack had left its mark, not only on the people but on the city itself. Broken, scorched bones of homes gouged the gray air petulantly. Causeways shivered, their edges cloaked in char and ash.

I burst into the hut, and Kaden looked up, eyes tired. "I've tried everything," he said without preamble. "I've healed the worst of his injuries, but my ember can't break through whatever nightmare holds him."

"He took the blow," I murmured, sinking onto the edge of Gavrel's bed. He was so damned pale. Like a shell that had been stitched together. Bandages crisscrossed his chest. Purple darkened his beautiful face as if it were a bruised fruit.

I looked at my best friend, tears welling in my eyes. "Phobetor's attack. It was meant for me. I—"

"Stop." Kaden shot me a look that held no patience and shoved one hand through his messy waves. "This isn't your fault, Ser." He paused, brushing his hand over my shoulder. "At least we have Phobetor and Melina contained." With a heavy sigh, he shrugged and headed toward the door. "I'll give you a moment with him."

When the door clicked, tears flowed over my cheeks as if a dam had burst. I curled into the crook of Gavrel's arm and laid my hand over his bare, bandaged chest. He was cold. So cold.

Fuck!

Once again, he'd sacrificed himself for me. And my choices had put him in the position. I'd asked him to consider the alternatives before doing such a thing, but I now knew that wasn't fair.

There hadn't been time to think, and without a thought, I would have done the same for him. It was who we were, and how we showed our love.

But damn him for doing so.

And damn me for constantly hurting those I loved.

Bloody void, take me. I was spiraling, my lungs grasping for air.

I inhaled and exhaled, paced my breaths with his. There was a steady thump—a faint, stubborn heartbeat beneath my palm.

My muscles relaxed.

He was alive, but his mind was trapped somewhere I couldn't reach.

For hours, I stared at the wall, refusing to leave his side. As if my touch was single-handedly keeping his heart pumping.

The daylight crept like a living thing, slinking over the wall planks. The afternoon morphed into the twilight, its dusky hues lurking in the grains of wood.

With the subtle rise and fall of my cheek against Gavrel's chest, I let the swamp's melodious hum wash over me.

Let sleep claim me.

Let it guide me to him.

HE STOOD in the center of Aion's citadel, in the capital's heart. It was almost like the night we'd celebrated the Moon Ancient, rain pouring down outside, visible between the open-air columns. The temple's turret was open, its golden edges peeled back in a starburst to reveal a waxing moon with a crimson ring hugging its edges. The soft thud of flowers hitting the floor echoed around us, but this time, unseen hands dropped them from above. This time, the petals curled in on themselves in sickly, black contortions, wilted and rotting.

I ran my fingers down the burnished copper of my silk sheath dress from that night as I went to him. Not a muscle moved under his silver overcoat, but still his form glided away from me with each step.

"Gavrel," I whimpered, hand stretching toward him. But as I reached the center, the space twisted, time elongated, and he arched away, his body lifting into the air.

As my feet met his shadow, I leaped into the air to grab hold of him, but he was just out of reach, his body limp.

"Selene!" I cried out, beseeching the moon. Begging her to

forgive me for whatever transgression I'd committed. Was she punishing me like she and her lover had once been punished … forever kept apart and only able to see one another from afar?

All at once, the moon blinked out, and Gavrel plummeted, but before he crushed me, he vanished in a billow of sparkling motes. Blinded, I waved my hands through the cloud. Before my vision cleared, I fell to my knees, clawing at the opal. Terrified that the taut thread pulling at my ribs would snap, that I would lose Gavrel if it did.

I crushed my eyes closed, concentrating on the golden string, and imagined clutching it so hard that it would pull me straight through the piles of dead flowers and stone. Our bond jerked in my grip, and I held tight until the temple trembled.

The ground crumbled beneath me, and weightlessness took me as I fell through time and earth and ember. Within my next breath, I landed on my bottom, my teeth clacking against one another from the jarring impact.

Nothing but darkness enveloped me. "Gavrel!" I called out, feeling the buzz along our bond.

Through the all-consuming blackness, a familiar hand reached down to help me stand, and I choked back a sob.

"No need to fret, Little Star," Gavrel said, his dimple peeking out. He wore Marek's overcoat, the fabric too snug on his biceps. The glint of black iridescent thread glinted along my body. I was wearing the gorgeous dress Breena had gifted me for the Moonbud Revelry.

Slowly, I rose, and Helos' square, just like it had looked during the celebration, materialized, as if we were in the center of a painting being created stroke by stroke.

Bobbing embered orbs flickered above us, and *Fated*—our song now—drifted on a gentle breeze.

He wrapped his arm around my waist, taking my hand in his. "It's been too long since we danced. You were meant to dance among the stars." The corners of his eyes softened as his hands brushed over my face.

My fingers toyed with the hair on his nape. "I don't want to dance among the stars unless you're with me."

"Always."

I closed my eyes, trying to recall why I'd been so scared a moment ago.

There'd been something.

Something I had to do.

We swayed to the haunting melody, each note hanging on the strings that played them. Our matched pulses keeping time.

The wooden boards creaked under our feet.

There was something I needed to do, but it was just out of reach.

He spun me out slowly and then pulled me back into his embrace, kissing my forehead. "Where are you now?"

"What?" I blinked, and his image flickered, his touch fading. Fear ripped through me once more, awareness clicking into place.

My nails dug into his shoulders. "No! Stay with me, my love."

Confusion rippled across the chiseled angles of his face; his body solidified. "I'm here. The Fates themselves couldn't keep me from you." He cupped my cheeks and brushed his thumbs against the apples. "My love?"

My heart thumped unevenly against my ribs, a shaky smile tugging at my lips.

Light flickered over his emerald eyes as he kissed me. Just the softest brush of his lips against mine. The cord connecting us hummed when he drew back.

"You need …" I paused, sliding my thumb over his mouth. "You need to wake up—we need to—before it's too late."

His gaze lifted. "I'm not sure I can."

I traced my fingers along his jaw until he met my eyes again.

"Gavrel, you can. Wake up. Come back to me." My exhale shuddered out of me. "I need you."

He pressed his palm over my heart. "Say it again."

I curled my fingers over his. "I need you."

There went his dimple again. "No, the other thing."

My grip tightened, and the beat beneath my sternum hammered against both our hands.

He searched my eyes, waiting for me to say the words he needed. The words we'd danced around all these turns.

All this time, he lay himself bare. Made it clear he'd rip his own heart out to ensure my happiness, even if it meant sacrificing himself: mind, body, and soul.

But I was terrified. If I said the words out loud and he couldn't return …

It.

Would.

Destroy.

Me.

I'd bury myself in our dreams and never wake up. Would spend the rest of my days chasing him through the twists and turns of our minds and memories.

He faded again, evaporating like mist into the Bogs. "Don't go," I breathed. "Please wake up."

He bent, his form nearly translucent now, his mouth was a whisper against mine. A promise.

My eyelids fluttered closed, and a tear glided over my cheek. "*My love,*" I murmured into the dark.

But he was gone.

TO THE NETHER VOID AND BEYOND

Gavrel

A gasp pulled her out of our shared dream. Her arm clung to me, dampness coating my chest where she nuzzled.

"Little Star." My ragged words bordered on a pained groan.

She jerked upright, and I winced at the ache in my ribs. I didn't think they were broken, likely just bruised. And my damned lip had split again, but I didn't care as long as she was near.

"Thank the Ancients," she cried out, flinging her body over my torso and peppering kisses along my jaw.

I grunted at the impact, and Seryn leaned back. "Sorry, I'm just so happy you came back to me."

"The Fates couldn't stop me," I murmured, burying my fingers in her hair. "Bring those lips back here."

She frowned and gently slid her hand over the bandage across my chest. "But I'll hurt you."

"You would deny a man his last dying wish?" I raised one eyebrow.

Seryn swallowed a giggle. "That *would* be very uncouth." She tapped a pointer finger against her cheek. "Hmm."

I narrowed my eyes and then tugged her curls. Amusement curved into a smile before her lips met mine. She pulled away and kissed my nose, then my brow. She trailed her fingertips over my biceps. "The poison left you."

"It did."

"We're back in Helos."

I smiled, glancing around the cabin. "I figured as much."

"Marek and Rhaegar saved Yaya; they took back the city. Although when news spread that the Elders were missing, many of the Draumrs defected. Xeni, Letti, and my fath—Gideon—are here. I don't know what happened to Mama. Bloody void, I—"

"I'm happy to hear about Neoma and the rest," I interrupted gently, rubbing her forearm. "But for now, breathe. Tell me."

For a few moments, I wasn't sure she would speak any more. Her brows scrunched, and then her shoulders fell. "I don't know what I would have done if I'd lost you," she said at last, words catching in her throat.

My eyes dragged over her face. "You would live, *my love*."

Heat bloomed from her chest to her cheeks. "So, you remember that."

It wasn't a question.

"I remember everything when it comes to you." And I'd be damned if I let her take back what she'd said. I tucked my khorda's hair behind her ear and cupped her nape.

Claimed her.

"There's no point pretending any longer. These past months have made it painfully clear that our time together is short. You know I'm yours." The straight line of my lips softened into a smile. "I think you've always known—how deeply I've loved you, even from afar. Only you, Asteria. Until the aether claims me, and even then, I'll find a way to keep loving you."

"Ancients damn it, Gav."

I chuckled, my hold tightening.

She rested her palm over my scar. "I'm yours as much as you are mine. I love you so much it hurts. And it scares me what I'd do for you. For *us*."

My scar thrummed, sending a shiver over my flesh. "Then we'll suffer together." I lifted her hand and placed a kiss on the palm before setting it on my chest again. "And if you want to be someone's nightmare, I'll gladly be your right hand."

She snorted, resting her forehead on my shoulder. "Just another day for us then."

I grinned and tipped up her chin. "To me, every day with you is a dream."

She searched my eyes, tucking her lips between her teeth. If she were looking for the lie, she wouldn't find it.

Whether she was a dream or a nightmare, I loved her.

Would take her anyway I could.

Would help her burn the world down until we were the only ones left. And if it was wrong … well, it wasn't. Because she was everything right.

Slowly, she leaned down, lips meeting mine. She was so soft, but so fucking strong.

I lifted into her body, ignoring the spasm in my ribs. My mouth pressed into hers to deepen the kiss, and my tongue prodded the seam until she opened for me.

Carefully, she straddled me, burying her hands in my hair. Her chest rose and fell fitfully as she pulled away, thumbs brushing my temples. Her eyes asked a silent question.

"I promise you can't hurt me, but I might perish if you stop." I wrapped my hands around her hips, pulling her center against my erection. This woman needed only to breathe in my direction, and my cock stood at attention.

Fucking void.

She bit her bottom lip, and a delicate line creased her brow. "Gavrel…"

My hands skimmed up her sides, pushing the fabric of her shift over her head.

She sighed as I splayed my fingers over her ribs, beneath her heavy breasts. Her nipples puckered as I beheld her.

"I won't ever get my fill of you," I said, brushing the tips of her breasts with my thumbs.

Her head tilted, curls spilling over her shoulders, tickling my hands. My touch slid down her belly, memorizing every soft curve.

I leaned forward and winced as my ribs protested the movement. Gently, she pushed me back onto the pillows and slowly untied my breeches, her gaze never wavering from mine as she released my cock, palmed it. My hips followed her grip as she moved it over the tip. "Don't move, my love. Let me take care of you," she whispered.

My tongue wet my bottom lip as I watched her like the dream she was. All starlight and fire as her hot, wet center sank down my length.

She moved over me, her cunt clenching and pumping. Her body lifted, then down, circled, and gripped. I dug my fingers into her thighs, holding onto her as if fearful she'd slip away. As if I were still dreaming.

She squeezed her breasts, chest and neck flushing as she moved.

If I had died and our astral forms had been taken to Surrelia, I never wished to return.

Her chest heaved, curls bouncing around.

With each slick slide of her core over me, my balls tightened, muscles tensing as thick, molten desire rushed to my tailbone.

I ignored the nips of pain spiking through my body, my

focus wholly on the vision before me, the warmth surrounding my cock.

Her hand drifted down her belly. The other clamped around the top of my straining thigh, fingers digging in hard enough to bruise. A guttural sound tore from my throat when she arched into her own touch, rubbing her clit in messy, desperate circles.

I called her name among garbled promises and cursing as our eyes met, her hips pistoning faster.

Bloody Ancients.

The sight of my cock slick with her desire, sliding in and out of her tight cunt, mesmerized me. She bit her bottom lip, her body jerking chaotically.

My nails dug into her hips, staccato groans catching in my chest.

Her heat squeezed, convulsed. Breathy moans spilled from her.

Her whole body trembled, and she cried out my name over and over.

As she tipped over the edge, I fell with her.

My cock thickened as my desire spilled into her. Fingers flexing, every muscle in my body taut as she took everything I had to give.

My soul. Desire. *Everything.*

Exposed and raw. Her eyes darted over mine, shiny and sated as she leaned forward and kissed me gently.

"I love you, Little Star," I breathed, wrapping her in my arms and stroking her hair when she rested her cheek upon my chest.

"I know, my love." She brushed her fingers over my bandaged chest. "And I you. To the Nether Void and beyond."

34

LOOK THE BASTARD IN THE EYES

SERYN

*L*ater in the day, Kaden came to check on his brother. I gave them time alone, despite my reluctance to leave Gavrel. Kaden shooed me out the door, teasing that I needed a bath anyway. I stuck out my tongue, but my chest was tight as I made my way to my sister's lodging. Even the sunlight couldn't chase away the lingering shadows beneath my skin.

Letti had left a note on the table, telling me she'd gone to Yaya's home. I smiled at her foresight, at how she knew I'd come back. I prepared my bath, sinking into the tepid water with a sigh.

After cleaning up, I went to my grandmother's cabin; each step up the coiling staircase had my breath hitching. I needed to tell her and my sister. All of it. About the Nether Void. Mama.

When I reached the floor hatch, I peeked inside and smiled when I saw Yaya and Letti, admiring her privacy screen painted with a wooded scene from Evergryn. The delicate brushstrokes caught the afternoon light, making the trees appear to be sway-ing, ravens soaring over them.

My pulse skipped a beat when I noticed Gideon drumming his fingers on Yaya's kitchen table. Pushing my shoulders back, I entered. My ember tapped under my star-shaped scar. I breathed in, the air thick with the scent of vegetable stew and smoke.

I held my breath as every eye in the room turned to me. I shook out my hands and exhaled.

"I need to tell you all something. About what happened in the Nether Void," I began, straightening my spine. "Will you sit with me?"

"Er, it's never great when she asks you to sit down," Letti joked, sliding into a seat at Yaya's table next to her father. Her attempt at levity gave me the courage to go on.

Gideon sniffed, eyes flicking toward me, like a hawk assessing its prey. His fingers twitched slightly on the table's edge.

Yaya went to the kitchenette and grabbed a bottle of mire-berry wine and four cups. She poured a splash into each, plunked them down in front of us, and settled into a rickety chair across from us. She took a long sip, filled her cup with the lavender liquid again, and then clasped her hands atop the table.

"All right, start from the beginning." Her gaze was steady and patient. It was the same unwavering look she always wore—that of a rebel leader. That of someone who refused to break, even with so much loss carved into her turns.

Gideon pushed his cup away, and Letti pulled it toward her before drinking from her first chalice.

I drew in a steadying breath. There was no use taking the long way around.

"Well, to start, Morpheus is my father." I paused, letting the words hang in the air. I couldn't help glancing at Gideon. His mouth tightened, nearly disappearing behind the pale line left behind. "He's the one we freed from the amber in the dungeon."

"Get on with it, girl," he snapped, voice brittle. "This is old news."

"Hold your tongue, Gideon," Yaya barked. "I asked her to start at the beginning. She might have details Rhaegar hadn't known."

Letti nudged my knee with hers under the table, offering me comfort as she so often did when Gideon had treated me unkindly.

I continued, "Mama and Morpheus are khorda. He asked me to find her in the nightmare realm." Just thinking of that dismal place made my stomach churn.

Letti covered her mouth, fingers fluttering over it. Yaya leaned forward, eyes wide.

I rubbed my hands over my thighs. "And I did. She had been trapped there all this time. Melina found out that Mama was her Scion. She imprisoned her in the Epiales Tombs. Phantasos helped her escape, but the portal led to the Void." I took a drink, trying to swallow the lump in my throat.

"Some Ancient Morpheus is. Couldn't even save his fated," Gideon sneered.

"Bloody void, man. Do you not know your history? Not only was he trapped for nigh a century, but the Nightbloom Sundering treaty prevented him from entering his brother's realm." Yaya shook her head. "Unless you want the Aetherbind to unravel and have the Primevals destroy us all."

Her measured words rumbled over the table, and I shivered at the reminder that our lives were merely threads in a tapestry far larger and more ominous than any of us could fully grasp.

Crossing his arms, he huffed, glaring out the window.

Already, I was tired of him. And somehow, knowing that he wasn't my father was freeing. Like the chains I hadn't realized I'd carried my whole life had fallen away. I wasn't the unlovable one. He was the one who refused to open his heart to me.

I pushed my shoulders back, a weight drifting from them.

I went on, "They had their Kollao ceremony. It was beautiful. Well, until Phobetor showed up."

"I'm so sad I missed that, but you have no idea how happy I am." Letti brushed the liquid sheen under her lash line. *It's such a relief to finally know what happened to her.* Her fingers trembled as they fell to her lap.

"That's my girl. Always was a fighter." My grandmother lifted her cup in a salute before drinking. "Surviving in the Nether all this time. Extraordinary."

I smiled. "And she formed a band of rebels that loathe Phobetor and the Elders. Sound familiar?" I teased.

She smirked, tapping her forefinger hard on the table. "Well, we might need all the help we can get if this war spreads across realms. And I don't doubt that it will." Her hazel eyes brightened as she met mine.

The weight of her words, of my legacy, pressed down on me. No matter how often we pushed against the Fates, it still seemed that destiny would catch us in the end.

Letti glanced at her father, then back at me, eyebrows furrowing. "Why did Mama leave the Bogs in the first place? She would've been around my age, I think."

Yaya nodded, closing her eyes momentarily.

"Morpheus came to her in a dream. Said that she and her future children would be in danger if she didn't flee and hide her identity." I toyed with my cup. "She was the Scion, but—but she died in the nightmare realm after being stuck there so long." I could almost imagine Mama, standing in the endless darkness all those turns ago, as her physical body was taken from her.

Letti's bottom lip wobbled, but she bit down on it, holding back the tears still lining her eyelashes.

I looked between her and Yaya. "Mama says she loves you

both and is saving a spot for us in Surrelia." The corners of Yaya and Letti's eyes softened.

I glanced at Gideon. "She sends you the deepest gratitude for everything you did for her … for *us*. And that you'll always have a place in her heart."

His jaw was so rigid I thought it might crack. Grief etched itself into every line on his face. A twinge of sympathy struck me. He really loved my mother. I couldn't imagine what it cost him to lose her, even knowing she was never his to keep.

Every day must have been a fresh heartbreak. And I had been the reminder.

Yaya slapped his shoulder. "You did well. It takes a real man to love someone unconditionally and care for a child not his own. I'm in debt to you, Gideon." She leaned forward, voice low. "But if you *ever* betray my granddaughters or me again, I will cut off your balls. Your spying days are over."

He gulped. "I would never put *my* daughter in harm's way." His eyes softened as he looked at Letti.

My sister reached across the table and squeezed his hand. "Father." She waited until his gaze met hers. "When you hurt my sister, you hurt me."

He frowned, but dipped his chin and then patted her hand.

After a moment, he sniffed. "Perhaps I've not been the father you deserved. When your mother disappeared, I did what I had to do to keep you safe. To make sure we had food and the roof over our heads. Spying for the Elders kept their eyes off us." He stood, his chair scraping over the planks. "And I won't apologize for that. Especially since the Somneia is far behind me."

The tip of my tongue pressed against one incisor. It was the closest to an apology he'd ever offer.

"That's to be seen," Yaya muttered, her words a quiet warning. The past was never fully behind us; it lingered like smoke after a bonfire, clinging to our backs.

Gideon's face pinched, nostrils flaring before he marched down the stairs.

Letti rubbed my forearm. "He'll come around."

I shrugged. For the first time, I didn't carry the burden of what the man did or didn't do. Gideon was not my father, and he'd held himself so far out of my reach that he never was one to me anyway. My gaze lingered on the window, the gray coating the sky outside. The air was thick with possibilities and dangers yet to come.

Somewhere beyond the walls, the faintest whisper of the Void stirred. The Ancient of Nightmares waited, no doubt plotting his escape. His revenge.

But I wouldn't let him.

My ember purred against my nape, and I finished the rest of my wine. "Tell me how we captured Phobetor."

Standing, Yaya grabbed the bottle. "Better yet, granddaughters." She tilted her head toward the hatch. "Let's look the bastard in the eye while I do."

35

FATES' PUPPETS

SERYN

On the way to Hallowed End, I told my sister and Yaya about the runebound bargain and about our journey through the Void. And then even my grandmother's eyes held a wistful sheen when I relived the Kollao ceremony.

"Did the words 'Magister Barden is a Druik runemaster' just come out of your mouth?" Letti squealed.

I laughed. "Yes! He was incredible, with all these glowing tattoos—it's like he can manipulate the air, draw runes with it."

Yaya smiled, marching ahead. "Jace has been with the Korax longer than you realize."

My mouth fell open.

"No one really knows the full extent of his gift; he keeps that to himself." She shrugged. "But he's guided countless Druiks to strongholds throughout Midst Fall." He even helped Caelora get here when she was younger."

We reached the long bridge that led to our sacred destination. I squinted through the haze. "Ah, so that's why he seemed so curious about her in Surrelia."

Letti nudged my shoulder. "I would think that kind of journey bonds people," she offered.

My mouth pinched in thought. "You've forgiven her, then?" I asked my grandmother.

"In times like these, you learn to forgive when you can." Her fists tightened at her side. "But I won't forget."

After a few moments of silence, I tucked my hair behind my ears. "I … I wanted to apologize for how I acted when I first woke up here. I am so happy to see you both, and you deserve better."

Yaya flapped her hand in the air. "Nonsense, girl. You barely escaped Phobetor and the Void. Your fated was injured. Ancients, what matters is that we are all here, ready to take on the next day."

I touched her arm, dipping my chin. Letti gave me a side hug. "Yes, what Yaya said." She giggled, and the sound washed over me. "I'm proud of you, sis. You've become someone the Ancients need to fear."

I scoffed. "I think you might have suffered a head injury." Her quiet shrug answered me, her compliment left to simmer. I continued, "And I'm grateful for Xeni. Are you two happy?"

Her smile lit up her eyes. "We are. She's everything I didn't realize I needed in a partner. And you should see how unbothered she is around Fath—my father," she corrected herself.

"You deserve every happiness," I said.

"You both do. We *all* do," Yaya murmured.

Heavy footsteps echoed behind us. I spun, hand on my dagger.

I was a bit jumpy these days.

"Easy, cousin." Marek held his quarterstaff diagonally before him.

My shoulders relaxed, and I wrapped my arms around him

before thinking better of it. He stiffened, then patted my back awkwardly.

Rhaegar grinned behind him. I leaped into his arms; he squeezed me tight. "Safe and sound, I see," he said affectionately.

"Same to you. Well done on taking back Helos. What, no Bree? Hiding from her?" I peeked behind his broad frame.

Marek scowled.

"No one hides from that woman," Rhaegar guffawed. "She's like a bloodhound. No, she's likely stalking some poor fellow, or stabbing someone."

Marek's frown ground deeper into his face.

A soft rustle brought my attention to Xeni, waiting patiently. "A pleasure to see you again, Seryn," she said as Letti linked arms with her.

My sister studied Marek with a stern eye. He was her cousin, too, but she clearly hadn't spent enough time with him to get under his skin yet. The corners of my lips quirked. Letti would have him wrapped around her little finger in due time.

"You as well." I touched Xeni's forearm. "Thank you for watching over my sister."

"Think nothing of it," she replied, brushing her fingers over Letti's. "I would have done it even if you hadn't asked."

Letti kissed her cheek, and I glanced at my cousin as he leaned closer to Yaya.

"Did I hear you speak of the traitor?" Marek bit the last word out.

"How long were you back there stalking us?" Letti teased.

He glowered, mumbling, "I should've ended her in Surrelia. The pretty boy better be keeping his word."

Yaya swatted his chest and led us onto the swaying bridge. "Kaden's been her shadow, much to her dismay. Caelora's always kept to herself. If she'd told us who her father was sooner, she might've avoided a good deal of trouble. The ravens would've backed her. But what's done is done. She'll be the first to volunteer to hunt him down, I'm sure."

"And you trust her after what she did?" Marek accused.

Our grandmother narrowed her eyes. "I trust she wants revenge on Elder Ash, and that we're aligned in taking down the rest. For now, that's enough."

A throbbing hum sliced through the damp haze ahead. Light bled away from the center of the platform, rippling along a glowing semicircle curving around the back edges.

My gaze dragged over the three massive conservatories, half-submerged in mucky water. Their glass domes peeled back to expose the pulsating radiance from within. Swirling liquid-like blackness leaked from the activated amber vessels.

Ice skittered up my back. "Dormancy pods?" I croaked.

Yaya circled the perimeter and pointed up. "Look him in the eye."

My attention snapped upward. Nyxvein slithered from each pod and condensed into a furious eddy high above the platform. It hissed and popped. And in the center of the roiling tangle was the Ancient of Nightmares, his body writhing and contorting. His eyes, blacker than night, pinned me where I stood, hatred boiling in them. His aura leaked from his misty bindings, only to be swallowed by them. Even trapped, he oozed menace.

Marek came to my side. "You weakened him enough to make him malleable. We dragged him here while he was unconscious. Jace made quick work of locking him up."

Etched symbols glowed atop the planks under the Ancient's shadow, golden motes floating from the rune before vanishing into the mist.

"Give yourself credit where credit is due, boy," Yaya called.

Ignoring our grandmother, my cousin's sapphire eyes bored into Phobetor as he cracked his neck from side to side, hand gripping his staff. His muscles bunched under his bare, scarred torso, and a flicker of his black flames shivered over his body.

Rhaegar scrubbed a large hand over his chin. "Your cousin opened the pods. Quite impressive. Never seen anyone but the Elders or Akridais do that."

My mouth pulled to the side. The image of the Akridais who'd opened Hestia's pod during her culling flashed behind my eyes. I pushed it away; the memory of dark ember clashing in Phobetor's nightmare prison replaced them. "You were in the tombs, cousin?"

Marek nodded. "The vryka used Phobetor's ring to open the portal for the others. Pretty boy found me."

I waited for him to continue, but he clamped his mouth shut, gaze flicking toward the shadows where the Nyxvein writhed.

Xeni's eyes never left the Ancient, her hand locked around Letti's. "Marek insisted on going back through. Said he'd be damned if he let his cousin rot in limbo," she added matter-of-factly.

My sister grinned, and I bit down on my bottom lip.

With a glower, Marek walked away, inspecting the conservatories and poking them with his quarterstaff.

"So, Thesa and Therrok didn't come through?" I asked.

"The vrykas? No," Rhaegar answered. "They stayed with your parents."

I exhaled, feeling the loss of my new friends, but grateful that they'd be there to protect Mama.

Xeni's delicate eyebrows furrowed as Yaya joined us again. "If I'm understanding correctly, the portal shouldn't have opened yet. Not without an Ancient, or a full moon."

I shrugged. "The Murk messes with everything. Or maybe when Morpheus destroyed the Epiales Tombs, ember flooded the prison. Hard to say."

Yaya scratched her chin. "The rift is widening; the Aetherbind is too strained. With Nether beasts slipping through, and both Morpheus and Phobetor weakened while in limbo, there's no telling the impact. If we don't find the rest of the Scions and complete Ascension soon … the Hollowed Stars prophecy won't wait. We'll have far bigger problems than a single portal."

Above, Phobetor's shadows pulsed like a creeping omen.

I gritted my teeth, meeting his glare whenever it found mine as he revolved. "Where's Melina?" I asked.

Rhaegar tilted his head toward the far end. I wandered across and peered into the open conservatory beyond the towering doombarks that anchored the platform. Embered manacles cuffed her wrists and ankles as she sat cross-legged among the ten Dormancy pods. A yellow, swaying film enclosed her in a dome, runes floating along its invisible surface. She was trapped inside a giant ebony flower. Beautiful, but deadly.

"Jace's handiwork." Yaya stood next to me, eyeing the Elder. "He said it'll hold, especially when surrounded by the pods' ember."

"Nyxvein," I explained, giving her a brief rundown of the energy running through the banestone.

"Ah, so your other grandmother is *also* difficult," Yaya quipped.

I chuckled, my smile widening when Melina glared at me from the confines of her prison.

Rhaegar leaned against a nearby tree. "Jace's runecraft is quite impressive."

I nodded, ignoring the anxious feeling creeping along my nape. There had to be a limit to what the sigils could do. Only so much time to drag the inevitable along—or worse, before Melina and Phobetor somehow slipped their binds.

Resentment and dread coiled through me like sticky threads, tightening with each breath. Every turn, every decision—had any of my choices ever been mine? Or were we all just dancing to the Fates' rhythm, our limbs tangled in the strings they wove eons ago?

I drew in a steady breath, rolling my shoulders back and

straightening my spine. Even if we were the Fates' puppets, we still had teeth. We could cut the tapestry, tear free, if only between one heartbeat and the next.

Though freedom came with new tethers. Duty. Promise. Love. The bindings we chose ourselves.

My chest expanded, lungs burning. Was I ready?

Maybe not.

No one ever truly was.

But I could face it one breath at a time, as I always had. I exhaled, nostrils flaring.

I had my kin. My friends. Gavrel.

I would accept whatever destiny waited for me—no matter whose hands wove the pattern.

Because there were still realms to heal.

People to save.

Monsters to slay.

I met everyone's gaze before turning toward Melina. "There's no use waiting any longer. It's time."

"For?" Letti asked at my side.

Melina's face twisted into something cruel, her mask of beauty painted in odium.

We both knew what came next.

"My Ascension."

36

WE'RE ONE, YOU AND I

G AVREL

C andlelight flickered across the walls of my cabin. The low flames guttered in a damp draft sneaking through the cracks, shadows swaying like restless phantoms. A soft breeze rocked the nearest bridges outside, and they creaked among a chorus of crickets and gilly toads. The swamp never really slept; it simply changed its tune as the day turned into night.

I leaned back in my chair, mouth pinching as pain lanced through my ribs with every slight movement. It wasn't just the bruises. Something deeper ached, a lingering throb where my rune was buried. Absently, I rubbed the spot, feeling the faint pulse of heat beneath my skin before shaking it off.

It was exhaustion, it had to be. The runebound bargain had been fulfilled. Seryn had brought me back from the nightmare that clung to me once we'd escaped the Murk.

"How are you holding up?" Kaden asked, handing me a cup

of water. We'd gone over what happened in the Void and what still needed to be done, but even after hours, we'd barely scratched the surface.

He slumped into the chair across from me, eyes ringed with fatigue. He'd stayed with me when we first returned, healed me. My brother was so much *more* than he gave himself credit for, and I hoped he'd believe it sooner than later.

"I've had worse," I muttered, though my words had a rougher edge than I intended.

He chuckled. "You always say that. Even if your arm was hanging half off." He clapped a hand on my shoulder. I grimaced, and his grin widened. "You'll live another day, brother."

"Indeed," I replied dryly. My brother had offered to do another round of healing, but I'd declined the offer. Like he said, I'd live.

Kaden palmed the back of his neck and sighed. "I'm glad you made it back. Sweet Surrelia, I was ready to burn the palace down waiting for you and Ser to return."

I dipped my chin. "Glad to be here, but the path ahead is long."

He waved a dismissive hand. "Let me have one moment without doom lurking over us, Gav. There are no wyverns to slay right now."

For a few minutes, we listened in companionable silence. The hum of dusk taking over the day, the gentle splash of water lapping against sodden wood. The world was peaceful, deceptively so. I traced the grain of the table with my thumb, grounding myself in the mundane rhythm of the movement.

"You ever think about what comes after all this?" Kaden murmured.

"What do you mean?"

"When the war is won. The realms healed, or all of them defeated. What then?"

I exhaled slowly. "We rebuild. Then we rest. Or try to."

He barked a laugh. "You, rest? I'll believe that when I see it."

"Then you'll never see it."

His shoulders shook, but there was something tired in his eyes. The kind of weariness that no amount of laughter could wash away.

Studying him, I echoed his earlier question, "How are you holding up?"

"Oh, you know—defying death, mingling with Ancients, and minding traitors." He scratched his stomach and then brushed a hand over his chest. "Just a typical day."

"Caelora doesn't seem to be causing trouble." Footfalls echoed over nearby bridges, and I tilted my ear toward the creaking.

Kaden's smile returned. "Seryn will be back soon." He rubbed his lips together. "And no. Caelora isn't a problem. At least not to the Korax. I think she made a terrible mistake chasing Ash, and it backfired spectacularly."

One of my eyebrows lifted. "So you trust her?"

He smirked. "Not one bit. But it hasn't been a hardship to watch her." He ran a hand through his shaggy hair. "She mostly ignores me."

"I'm sure that's a first."

He dragged his tongue over his top teeth. "Anyway, I'd like to keep my chompers where they are, so I'll do as promised until instructed otherwise. Fucking Marek," he grumbled.

"I'm sure a team will be sent to the mountains soon to hunt for Ryboas. She'll want to go."

"Then I'll go. I need something to do besides chasing a short, headstrong female around." He wiggled his eyebrows. "With the roundest, most delicious ass I've ever seen."

I rolled my eyes.

The door groaned, and Seryn returned. A faint smile softened her face as she took us in. "Who has the most delicious backside?"

Kaden's hand went to his chest in mock offense. "How dare you? A gentleman never tells."

She snorted and shoved his shoulder, nearly tipping him off the chair. "Gentleman, my ass."

"You also have a fine ass, Ser. Don't get your panties in a twist about it," he teased.

My jaw tightened at the reminder that they'd been intimate.

"Relax, brother," Kaden chided. "You don't want to pop a vein."

"Leave," I said flatly.

Kaden snickered, but stood, stretching like a cat.

"Wait," Seryn put a hand on his wrist. "Before you go—there's something I need to tell you both." She exhaled, the weight of her next words hanging between us. "I've decided to ascend."

Kaden's mouth dropped open. "Well, bloody fucking fuck, Ser. Should I bow down and kiss your Elder toes?"

Her lips curved, though she shifted uneasily before sitting on my knee, and my arm immediately wrapped around her waist. We moved without thought, needing to be near one another, two stars in a perfectly synchronized orbit.

Kaden brushed a wayward curl behind her ear. "I'm here for you. Just say when."

She squeezed his hand. "Thank you."

When the door clicked behind him, the sounds of the swamp mingled with our silence.

"Are you sure, Little Star?" I asked, cupping her chin.

She nodded, eyes searching mine. "Yes, but are you all right with it?"

Ancients, she was incredible. She'd always been resilient, but I'd watched her become the fiercest woman I'd ever known. She'd never cease to amaze me.

"Whatever you decide, whoever you become, I'll be by your side."

The rune above my heart stung, sharp enough to steal a breath. I ignored it, pressing my thumb along her jaw instead.

With a sigh, she leaned into my touch, her soft breath brushing against my flesh. "We're one, you and I. Every choice affects the other. And if we ever get that talisman out of you, our bond will be even stronger."

I swept my thumb over her cheek and kissed her forehead. "You were born to lead, Seryn. You'll be a damn worthy Elder. Just say the word, and I'll be the most devoted consort the realms have ever seen."

Contentedly, she curled into my embrace and toyed with her rune stone necklace. The candlelight danced over her curls, melding with the fiery twists. I sank my fingers into the soft strands.

She dropped her talisman, her expression determined.

I knew that look. She'd worn it so many times, perfected it by the time she was old enough to walk. That was so long ago now—back when our biggest worry was finding the next meal. Void, even a couple of months ago, felt like turns. And never once did I imagine she'd end up here, in my arms.

I loved this woman more than anything this realm—or any other—could offer. For so long, I pushed that love down, buried it so deep I nearly drowned in it. Until it clawed its way back up and became the air I breathed. I would tear my own fucking heart out if it meant keeping hers beating. If it meant keeping her afloat.

She nestled against me, warm and content. I rested my chin atop her curls and inhaled her sweet scent. Relished the feel of her, the gentle rise and fall of her breath. Through my tunic and bandages, her fingers traced over the thick starburst of scar tissue above my rune stone. I stilled, willing away the unsettling prickle that stalked her touch beneath my skin.

Two days' time was the next full moon. In two days, every-thing shifted once more.

Some things changed the moment you named them, willed them into existence. Others, the moment you pretended they wouldn't.

37

SOUL-WANDERING

SERYN

Our names echoed through the moonstone halls like a chant lost in time and space. The rumble of Gavrel's voice sounded ahead of me, then behind, and then everywhere all at once. He was close; our bond vibrated against my ribs as if he'd plucked the golden string.

The air shimmered, and I blinked, trying to focus. Fuzzy, multicolored hues lingered in my periphery, and no matter where I looked, they remained. I reached out, grasping at glowing motes that moved like stars underwater. My body swayed, and my mind felt … stretched, coated in swirling light and shadow.

I murmured his name, though I wasn't sure if I'd spoken aloud.

Moonbeams speared through the vaulted quartz ceiling, fracturing into ribbons of blurred rainbows that stuck to everything—the rippling pewter doors lining the long hall, the curving stairwell hugging the foyer, and the glittering star-shaped crystals hanging from the chandelier above.

"Seryn?" My mother's voice whispered to my left. I turned; no one was there.

"You're here." The echo swept from my right. I spun again. Nothing.

"Mama?" I cried.

"Seryn?" This time it was Gavrel's voice, and he caught me around the waist as I stumbled in surprise. "Where are we?" he asked, words warm on my cheek.

"I think …" I hesitated, fingers gripping his hand. "We're dreaming again. Back in Surrelia."

Mama's whisper ricocheted around me, "You're close."

"Mama!" I called again.

The prismatic light quivered, and before us, my mother stepped out of it. My chest ached at the sight of her.

She pulled me into a hug, her embrace solid but not, as if she were made of chalk that would break into dust if I squeezed too hard. She cupped my cheek and then smiled, leading us into the Great Hall.

Then a deeper voice rumbled from ahead. "Daughter."

Papa.

The Ancient of Dreams sat tall on the obsidian throne atop the dais. His gilded eyes sparkled as they landed first on me, and then, his fated.

Morpheus rose, descending the stairs with impossible grace. "You've come farther than I expected."

"We didn't portal," I murmured, words laced with confusion. "We just … were here. Are you in our dreams?"

He grinned. "On the contrary … You're in ours."

Mama went to his side. "Little Star, you *wandered.*"

The word hit me straight in my stomach. "Soul-wandering," I breathed, recalling the term Melina had used when describing what happened to our astral bodies during the Dormancy.

Gavrel's grip tightened, and I glimpsed awe and something like dread in his eyes.

My father's smile widened impossibly, pride and amusement threaded through it. "You've touched the Aetherbind that connects our realms. Not with your body or ember, but with your will."

"I didn't mean to—"

"Intent is irrelevant. My blood runs through your veins," he interrupted gently, his golden robes sparkling in the moonlight spraying through the lunar-phase windows behind him. "You're dream-born, daughter. Descendant of Night and Day, of the Oneiroi."

He gestured toward the exit, and we followed. Luminescence undulated as we meandered down the hall, doors opening as we passed them.

Through each one, glimpses of other dreams flashed. A city of floating lanterns. An ocean so still I thought it was made of glass until sirens and all manner of aquatic creatures suddenly danced in the depths. A sleeping child clutching a whittled wooden toy in the shape of a wyvern.

Gavrel turned, wonder and unease chasing each other across his features. "These are … other people's dreams?"

Morpheus nodded. "The collective unconsciousness of the mortal realm. Every soul that slumbers sends a ripple here. But you, Seryn—you can ride those waves."

I swallowed hard. "As you do."

He chuckled, warm and deep. "No. My influence is akin to how the moon and sun command the ocean's tides. You're more of a swimmer."

"As long as I'm not drowning," I muttered.

A new, melodic voice resonated across the hall. "It's possible. You must beware the undertow of the Somnis, Belladonna."

The light shifted, and gilded sparkles poured from one of the pewter doorways.

"Phantasos," I murmured as she stepped out, pale hair and dress flowing about her. She wore the face of the young seer from Ceto, skin smooth and dewy. Her strands twisted into intricate braids with gilded beads sprinkled throughout.

"You always had a flair for making an entrance," Mama muttered, though fondness softened her words.

"You look well, Maya. I am pleased you are here." The Ancient of Illusions smiled, then leaned toward Morpheus, the delicate slashes of her eyebrows lifting. "Brother."

"Sister," he responded, inclining his head. "It's been too long."

"It has." She touched his shoulder lightly. "Welcome home."

"A bit late, yes?" The corner of his lips curled.

"I go where the wilds call me." She waved one hand and twirled toward Gavrel and me. "The Somnis hummed with your arrival, child."

Morpheus sighed. "Don't start."

I held in a nervous giggle. It was fascinating to see the two Ancient siblings interacting, affection and a hint of irritation blending.

"Start?" she echoed, the outline of her body flickering. "I only listen to the Fates' whispers, the dreamers, to the wilds. They all must wake, and so shall she. The Elysium Tree will make certain of it."

A chill slipped over my spine. "You know about the Ascension?"

Her form wavered, but her luminous gaze didn't as it fell on me. She brushed her fingers along my jaw. "I know the cost of becoming. Every seed must break before it blooms."

Her enigmas had never been threatening, but there was something more ominous lurking beneath them this time. I stiffened, and Gavrel stepped forward. "That's enough."

My aunt tilted her head as though listening to something distant. "The Fates weave threads, whether or not you approve."

She looked at me again. "When the tide comes, look not to the stars, but to what hides beyond them."

I rolled my eyes. "Bloody Vo—"

"Child," she interrupted, and then her eyes darted up as if she were listening to something. She leaned toward me, eyes narrowing. "To cage one nightmare is to unleash another."

Before I could respond, her form unraveled and fluttered away in a cloud of glittering dust.

Morpheus exhaled through his nose, tension etched into his face. "She delights in being nonsensical."

My tongue pressed against the back of my teeth. I didn't entirely agree. Her words held a warning of consequences to come. Frustrating as she was, Phantasos had helped us more than once, and her riddles tended to make sense only when they counted most. Still, now wasn't the time or place to argue with my father.

And what was the use in allowing my mind to spiral from her words? Of course, there would be consequences to whatever path we chose.

Mama's hand brushed mine, and I felt the faintest pulse of her midnight ember. "Back to the matter at hand—my daughter, the soul-wanderer." She smiled. "What was your original plan for the ceremony?"

"Well, I thought I could just portal when it was time for the Ascension," I admitted and then wiggled my fingers. "And what the void is the 'Insomnis'? Like the sea?"

Mama's eyes softened. "*Somnis*, sweetheart."

Morpheus inclined his head. "You've touched Surrelia and the Nether Void's surfaces, yes. The dreamlands that shelter astrals during death or Dormancy, and the nightmarescapes that punish." He circled his hand in the air, and threads of golden light spiraled outward like ripples across still water. "But hidden between the seams flows the *Somnis*, where memories and souls become one. It is the tide of dreaming itself. It is there that the Oneiroi guide dreams and navigate the currents of the psyche."

His expression darkened slightly, expression reverent and somber. "It is not unlike the Insomnis Sea. Both are boundless and connect distant shores, their depths holding many wonders and terrors alike. And both can drag you into their darkness if you stray too far from the light."

My hand fluttered to my neck, and I gulped, trying to ignore the flicker of old memories. The rush of cold water pulling me down, filling my lungs.

Gavrel weaved his fingers through mine. "The Elysium Tree—"

Morpheus continued, "Its roots burrow deep into that space and act as a conduit. With the sea, the body needs breath and soul to survive. But with the Somnis, you must let your spirit splinter from flesh, offer your breath and blood to the banyan so it may anchor you in the tide."

"So my body—"

"Must stay in Midst Fall," Mama finished. "But your astral body can travel. It won't be easy, but that's what the ritual demands."

Gavrel frowned. "Why?"

The Ancient's golden gaze swept over us. "You think Ascension is a simple ceremony. A task you finish."

I sighed. "Isn't it?"

A bittersweet smile curled Mama's lips. "No. I know better now. It's not just an offering. It's *surrender*." She placed her palm over my heart for a moment. "You give everything you are, so something greater may decide if you're worthy to keep it."

I lifted my gaze to the prisms above, ignoring the prickles needling my spine. "Mama … I thought you once told me that every time a mortal crossed, it frayed the Aetherbind."

"Reckless crossings do," she responded softly. "Slipping into dreams outside of your khorda's tears at the veil. But a ritual crossing is different. The Elysium Tree holds the boundary steady, so it isn't harmed."

Morpheus stepped closer, each of his words careful. Deliberate. "Because Ascension is a convergence. The full moon cracks open the Oneiric gate between the Somnis and the realms, and the banyan links them. When flesh and spirit divide, the sacred tree weighs a Scion's worth and forges the bond that ties them to Kosmos itself."

"And if the tree finds me wanting?"

"Then it won't bind you," he replied simply. "Your ember and physical form will wither, and your soul will drown in the aether."

"Bloody fucking Void," Gavrel hissed, his jaw tensing.

Silence swelled through the hall. The splintered moonlight danced across everyone's faces.

"But you won't fail," Mama stated firmly. "The Elysium Tree has known you since before your first breath—since the moment you were conceived in the Somnis."

I looked away, my throat choking on a response.

"You're telling us that the bloody tree found *Melina* worthy? Lucan and Ryboas?" Gavrel growled, disbelief roughening his tone.

Morpheus' nostrils flared, but his voice remained even. "It weighs a Scion's worth at that moment in time, their potential to ascend. What happens beyond that is between the Elder and the Fates."

Gavrel's stance widened, hand flexing at his side. "What happens if Seryn can't come back?"

My mother's expression softened. "Your bond will anchor her. It's how you keep finding one another."

Gavrel and I exchanged a glance, and my eyes drifted to his tunic, where his scar lay hidden.

Morpheus waved his fingers between Gavrel and me. "That thread was forged the moment your souls were torn apart.

Though his talisman dulls it, no rune can fully sever a khorda bond."

I rubbed my thumb over the etched pendant at my throat, and Mama's eyes followed the motion. "And Melina?" I asked, trying to keep the tremor from my voice.

"She needs to be near you in Midst Fall." Mama tucked my wayward curls behind my ear. "Her gift will respond to the ritual—it'll *know* you. She'll resist, but she won't be able to hide from your ember, Little Star. Though the ceremony typically needs full cooperation—"

"I can drain her without it." My tone came out harsher than I meant, the words tasting bitter on my tongue.

"You could, but the Elysium Tree weighs the spirit as well. Taking her energy by force could leave a lasting stain," Mama said softly.

My brow furrowed. "I'm not planning to hurt her. But if she attacks first—"

"She will," Gavrel said grimly.

"Then it isn't a choice," I murmured.

"It always is." Mama took my hand in hers and squeezed. "You'll know the difference between mercy and vengeance when the moment comes. Trust that you'll choose right."

I wanted to believe her. And despite my aversion to the Fates, I wanted to think I could still do this the way they intended. Through offering, not theft.

But deep down, I knew Melina would never kneel, would never yield her power willingly.

Not to me.

Not to *anyone*.

I clutched my rune stone. "If the Elysium Tree demands her ember, I'll make sure it gets it. One way or another."

38

SCARRED BUT UNBROKEN

GAVREL

The next morning, she gasped awake, body swaying and breaths hitching as if her world tilted violently. As if surfacing from deep water.

I caught her before she tipped forward, my hand bracing her shoulder. "Easy, my love," I murmured, though my heart slammed repeatedly into my ribs.

She could soul-wander. It was how we'd met so often in my dreams. My scar stung as if a handful of barbs stabbed under the thickened flesh.

"Gav …" she whispered. "Was it real?"

I met her gaze, unable to speak past the weight of what we'd learned, and simply nodded.

She ran her hands over her stomach and arms, grounding herself, ensuring she was still whole. Then her expression hardened with sudden resolve. "Then it's settled."

Before I could stop her, she swung her legs off the bed and slipped into her breeches, then yanked on one of my tunics without bothering to lace it. The fabric hung loose at her collar-bones, and determination burned bright in her eyes. "We need to tell the others."

"Now?" I asked, arching a brow.

"Before anything else can go wrong," she said, already heading for the door.

We found the others gathered at *The Boggy Grog* for breakfast. The air was thick with the aroma of roasted root vegetables, but their conversation stilled when Seryn approached.

She explained everything—about soul-wandering, the Elysium Tree, the Somnis, and the ritual that would decide her worth. By the time she finished, a shroud of silence hung over the table.

Marek leaned back in his chair, eyes narrowed in thought. Neoma's fingers tapped against her bowl like the ticking of a clock. Breena's mouth puckered, while Rhaegar and Xeni only nodded grimly, jaws tight. Kaden crossed his arms, and Letti quietly held her sister's hand.

Neoma broke the silence. "I knew you were special, girl, just didn't know the extent."

Seryn's cheeks blanched before a rush of flame coated the pale skin.

"We'll all be there with you," Letti assured, squeezing her fingers. Seryn gave her a grateful look.

Kaden scooped some sort of vegetable porridge into his mouth and smiled around the bite, nodding enthusiastically.

"Wouldn't miss it for the world. And if any of ya were thinking you wouldn't be there ..." Breena slid her thumb over the edge of one dagger.

Marek's nose scrunched, and he sniffed.

Rhaegar chuckled, raising a goblet. "To the soul-wandering raven, may her wings carry us through the Somnis."

I lifted my cup with the others, and a few other patrons in

the pub as well. I sipped the sweet juice, letting it soothe the trepidation skulking within me.

Neoma stood, punctuating the end of our conversation with a hearty slap on the table. "All hands to the square. There's a lot of work to do before tonight's feast."

Kaden snorted. "How many celebrations do the Korax have?" He touched his chest, his hand forming a tent over it. "Don't get me wrong. I'm all for as much wine as I can get. And dancing with lovely maidens."

Seryn tucked her bottom lip behind her top teeth, stifling her amusement.

"Some levity would do this city good after everything we've been through, yes?" Neoma replied, narrowing her eyes at my brother.

He held up his hands in surrender.

Breena nudged him in the side with her elbow. "Gotta love a city that celebrates often. Isn't it the Mireberry Moon?"

"Yes," Marek mumbled.

Kaden smirked. "Sounds like my kind of moon."

When we left the tavern, the weight of the risks and what was coming pressed down on the group, crushing our usual banter. Breena and Rhaegar stayed behind, chatting with some visiting ravens.

Rhaegar's friends, Korax recruiters from the Pneumali region, had arrived early this morning with a slew of new ravens to help rebuild. Seryn hugged Keethan and Eliz Wynt, her smile wide when they'd entered on our way out.

I shook their hands, Eliz cupping our grip with both hands. "So good to see you both again. I hear congratulations are in order, Seryn."

Her eyebrows rose. "Er, in what regard?"

Keethan chuckled, "So modest. You'll do well as the new Bogs Elder, my dear."

Her chin lifted. "News travels fast."

Eliz smiled. "As swiftly as the raven flies."

With pride shining over her features, Neoma's hand rubbed Seryn's biceps. "You'll need to get used to the attention, granddaughter. You'll be doing great things for our realm. I've no doubt."

Seryn's back straightened even more, and she rubbed her lips together. I wove my fingers with hers, and she held on tightly.

"Any news from the north or east?" Neoma asked Keethan.

"Lucan's rule is burrowing deep in Evergryn. A few Korax are still stationed there, but we can't be sure they'll make it tonight," he reported.

Eliz leaned in. "Ryboas is still fumbling around the mountains, last we heard. In better news, Neris, Zeph, and Drakon should arrive shortly."

I glanced at the Korax leader, and she stretched her neck to the side, answering before I could even ask. "Korax commanders from Haadra, Pneumali, and Pyria Island. It's time we gathered to discuss what the cause must do next. When they arrive, find me in the war cabin."

The line of Neoma's lips stiffened. "I'll see you all tonight." She squeezed Seryn's shoulder before she went off in the other direction. Seryn watched her go.

Outside, Helos was alive with motion and the tireless work of repair. The city still stood, scarred but unbroken, and its people refused to let ruin have the last word.

In the main square, we joined them and spent the rest of the day helping to rebuild.

My ribs were stiff and sore, but it was a small price to pay to see Helos still standing. There was work to be done. There always was.

While we were lost to the Void, the city's people had fought to reclaim what was theirs after the Draumrs and Akridais had scurried away.

New timber bridged the gaps where fire had eaten through the walkways. Smoke-stained walls were scrubbed. Some homes had been restored completely; others were singed but holding strong.

I lifted another plank into place while Kaden hammered a nail into the side of the shop we were working on. The main square was bustling with the rhythmic clang of tools, the rasp of saws biting into doombarks, and the grunts and shouts of people working together.

Sweat beaded at my temple, stinging as it slipped over the healing cut on my cheek. The scent of smoke still lingered in the air, faint but stubborn, a reminder of how close the city had come to destruction. But also of how it survived. Just like the Korax.

Kaden wiped the back of his hand over his brow, glancing at me. "You look like you're enjoying this."

"Beats being forced to stay in bed while you mother me," I quipped, fitting a board into position.

He chuckled and drove another nail home. Around us, children carried scraps of wood, women patched roofs, and two old men argued over where to hang new lanterns. Helos was slowly putting itself back together, piece by piece.

Kaden's attention drifted across the square to where Caelora handed Jace a tool. The male's well-honed muscles flexed beneath his ivory tunic as he worked.

I brushed my left thumb over the spot where my hidden tattoo lay. Like me, his skin was unmarked in the mortal realm, but the Oneiric realms, or when he was actively using ember, revealed the intricate runes scrawled across his flesh. I was curious what other abilities his gift afforded him.

A sharp thwack broke my focus. Kaden hissed through his teeth, shaking his hand as a string of spectacular curses followed.

Caelora's head snapped in his direction, her mouth pinching

tight before she dropped a pile of wood at Jace's feet. The Magister's brow lifted, his gaze flicking between her and my brother with a mix of annoyance and intrigue.

I bent, retrieved the hammer, and held it out. "You okay?"

"I'm fine," he snapped.

"They seem to have reconnected." I nodded toward Caelora and Jace. "I hear he brought her here after her mother died."

Kaden only shrugged and went back to hammering, jaw tight.

Seryn wandered over, offering us water. "How's your thumb, Kade?" she asked, rubbing his shoulder.

He grumbled, thrust the injured thumb out, and let a shimmer of clover energy ripple over it. After gulping down the water, he handed the cup back with a curt, "Fine."

Seryn smirked at me over the rim of her drink. I shook my head and pulled her into my arms. She laughed, squeezing my waist as her gaze swept over the piazza. "It's remarkable how far the people of Helos have come."

I kissed her forehead. "It is."

Voices rose from around the square, breaking the quiet. Kaden charged toward the commotion, hammer clenched in his palm. Seryn and I followed.

"Why is she loose?" one man barked, his pudgy finger jabbing at Caelora. "She's the reason our city's in shambles!"

Murmurs rippled through the growing crowd. Some shifted uneasily; others clenched their fists.

Jace stepped close to Caelora. "Just a minute, that's not the whole story. Let's all keep our heads."

Caelora lowered her gaze for a moment, then touched his forearm. "I'm deeply sorry for the harm I caused. I only hope to rebuild our home—and earn back your trust."

"This ain't your home no more, girl," the man spat. He turned to the crowd. "She should be tied up with the Elder bitch!"

More people nodded, several shouts of agreement peppering the air. Two more men flanked him, sneers twisting their features.

Kaden's jaw ticked, his biceps bunching as he gripped his tool. I laid a hand on his arm. "Kaden ..."

He shrugged me off, pushing through the crowd until he planted himself in front of Caelora. "Best you move along." His words were low and dangerous.

The man snorted, glancing at his companions. "You wanna join her, boy?"

Kaden growled, mallet inching higher as he advanced.

Before violence could erupt, Caelora reached for my brother's hand, fingers curling over the handle. He froze, and Jace stayed close, eyes sharp, observing their every movement. She tilted her head, amethyst eyes meeting Kaden's. His shoulders sank.

Seryn drew in a quick breath. "Her aura ..." she whispered.

I squinted, but saw no trace of ember as I scanned Caelora.

The female crushed her eyes closed, then opened them before addressing the crowd with calm authority. "Everything will be fine. Return to your work. Let's rebuild together in peace." Her words rolled over the mob, melodic and compelling. The tension in the square exhaled, the crowd releasing a collective, soothing breath.

I blinked, and Seryn grabbed my hand. "She ... she did something with her gift."

My eyebrows lifted. "I didn't see her aura, though."

She shrugged. "I did. Her emotions were heightened. Her throat glowed as she talked, and energy poured out of her. It was almost like ..." Her words drifted off.

"Like what?"

"Like the sirens I met."

I brushed a hand over my jaw. "Anything's possible. Could others see their song?"

Seryn nodded. "When it wasn't directed at them, yes." She watched the others dissipate and resume their work as if the whole situation had never happened.

Kaden shook his head, gave Caelora and Jace one last scowl, and then stomped off in the other direction. Caelora pushed her shoulders back and left the square. Jace hesitated but followed her.

"Let's find Yaya," Seryn said, pulling me after her.

39

THE BLOOMLESS

GAVREL

"Caelora's hiding more than she lets on," Seryn announced, arms crossed as she stood beside Neoma's desk. During Helos' reconstruction, the citizens had built a hut near the leader's for larger rebellion meetings—a war shanty nestled between bridges, blending in among the surrounding homes.

"Obviously," Marek muttered from his corner.

Inside was simple: a desk, a table, and scattered parchments. Neoma insisted most Korax plans stayed in people's heads, exchanged as coded messages much like the Bogs' history, only rarely written. Parchment—easily destroyed by shifting landscapes or attacks—was used sparingly. The rebels would burn the cabin with everything inside before letting it fall into enemy hands.

The older woman tapped the pile of weathered maps, lips pursed.

"If I may," Jace began, stepping into the dim light of the

cabin. "It isn't my place to speak for her, but whatever secrets Miss Aundyne keeps, she must have her reasons."

Marek scoffed. "Yes, well, last time she *had her reasons*, half the city burned."

Jace's jaw flexed, but his tone remained calm; patient in that dangerously composed way he so often used on disobedient students before he flayed them with his words. "Forgiveness isn't blindness, Marek. It's strategy."

Marek's nostrils flared, but he didn't rise to the bait.

"I'll keep an eye on her," the Magister continued, turning to Neoma.

Seryn arched an eyebrow. "Ah, so now she needs two men shadowing her every move?"

"I assure you," Jace replied smoothly, "It's for her own safety. She means to leave for the Ourea Peaks—to find Ryboas. Ascension is the priority, after all, and that can't happen without all the Elders."

"But she's not going there to reason with him," I asserted. "She's going to kill him."

A murmur spread across the room.

Jace held up one hand. "Which is precisely why it isn't unreasonable for Lark and me to accompany her. A few ravens as well. The more caution, the better."

The nickname caught my ear, and I shifted my scrutiny to the Magister.

Kaden wasn't even here to bristle over it, yet Jace said it too naturally for a man who spent half his time pretending my brother didn't get under his skin.

I didn't know what to make of that—or of him.

For turns, I'd suspected he was Druik, but I also had been relieved he'd worn his lies like armor. It had spared me from hunting him down at Melina's behest.

I glanced at Neoma. "I agree. Did your last scouting party ever report back? The one that followed your man Oren's group?" Not long ago, Marek mentioned winged creatures had attacked them in the mountains.

The Korax leader exhaled, rubbing her temples. "No. No missives since." She looked at Jace. "Fine. Take what you need and in a few days' time, leave at dawn. Find Ash and the others if you can. If not—find answers."

Jace bowed his head. "Yes, ma'am."

Marek's scowl deepened, though I couldn't tell if he directed it at Jace, his grandmother, or no one in particular.

Just then, Breena burst through the door, a pint in hand. "What's this? A party and no one thought to invite me?"

"Precisely," Marek mumbled. He gave her drink a pointed look. "Starting early? It's only half past noon."

Breena's eyes sparkled. "And you're drinking what? A tall glass of misery? How shocking." She glanced at Neoma, adding, "You must be so proud he can tell the time."

The older woman's lips twitched, but she dipped her head before a smirk could fully form.

Rhaegar strolled in with a bright smile and clapped a hand on my shoulder. "I see we've already lost control of this meeting." Then, he lowered his voice. "Yaya, some chaps at *The Boggy Grog* were asking for you. Quite insistent they were. Didn't look like locals."

Breena cocked her head. "Definitely not from the Bogs, that's for damn certain." She lifted her pint, using it to gesture —not so subtly—toward Marek. "Maybe someone should fix the illusion barrier so every stray knobshite can't just wander in."

Marek glared at her. "What's the point? You're already here."

Breena's grin cut deeper. "You bloody bas—"

"For the love of Ancients, *enough!*" Neoma snapped, slamming her palm on her desk. The room stilled. "We'll meet them at the pub. If they're trouble, I'd rather have witnesses—and half the Korax at my back."

THEY WERE TROUBLE.

The pub quieted when we entered, the smell of charred peat and ale hanging heavy in the air.

In the far corner, a group of men and women in pure white robes sat in unnatural stillness, their eyes following us. As they rose in unison, their uniforms rustled like baleful whispers.

A tall, pale man with colorless hair stepped forward. "Through Dormancy, we blossom," he intoned, bowing his head and touching his chin, then his heart.

Neoma raised an unimpressed eyebrow. "No, we bloody well don't. Who are you, and what do you want?"

I bit back a smile. The Korax leader had clearly lost all patience for ceremony.

The man stiffened, affronted. "I'm Ahlux. Speaker for the Bloomless. We were sent to petition for Elder Harrow's release."

Marek moved closer, planting his staff beside his boots. "Who is *we*, and who sent you?"

Seryn squinted, releasing her gift and studying the zealots. "They're all human. No Druiks among them."

Ahlux lifted his chin, nose scrunching. "*We* are the faithful. The Elders are the chosen of the three sisters. To chain them, to exile them from Surrelia, is blasphemy. Elder Lucan Craven has given us sanctuary in Evergryn—and the authority to retrieve Elder Harrow and locate Elder Ash."

"How do you know all this—*remember* all this?" I asked, tone clipped.

As one, the Bloomless raised their unmarked palms.

Seryn's eyebrows lifted, seeing what no one else could. "They have memory runes. Silver decagons with an eye at the center."

Breena tilted her head. "They just handin' those out like sweeties now, eh?"

"We, the devoted, are blessed by the Elders indeed," remarked a short, dark-haired woman at Ahlux's right. Her words were almost dreamy, reverent in a way that sent a chill crawling up my back.

"You, the *devoted*," Neoma retorted, "will need to move along. Petition denied."

"This is most unacceptable," Ahlux bit out, his composure cracking.

Breena snorted. "Life's unfair, which you'd know if you didn't have your heads up the Elders' arses."

Marek stepped forward, dark flames licking at his bare torso. "Melina Harrow will face her judgment here—and here she'll stay until her sentence is fulfilled."

Seryn cupped her chin, eyes imploring. "If you truly worship the Elders, tell me, doesn't it strike you as odd that there hasn't been an Ascension in nearly a century? Doesn't that defy your sacred doctrine?"

A few of the Bloomless wavered, uncertainty flickering across their countenances. But most stood unshaken, with petulant glares and rigid spines.

"Don't speak of what you cannot comprehend, heathen," one hissed.

My jaw ticked, but Seryn grabbed my wrist before I could do something I wouldn't regret.

Ahlux's voice rose over the wave of mutters. "The Elders are law. They will lead us through what is coming, along a righteous path. You'll see." His mouth puckered. "I am disappointed in this encounter."

Something between a growl and a grunt vibrated in Marek's chest, but Ahlux held up his palms.

Word had not spread beyond the Korax about Seryn's

Ascension. Admiration filled me at how organized and enigmatic the rebels were.

The cult turned in eerie unison, exiting the pub like a fog retreating.

Silence lingered in their wake. Even the barkeep stopped pouring drinks.

Neoma propped her hands on her hips. "We'll need more ravens guarding Melina. They'll be back sooner than we hope."

My heels dug into the floor. "Then we make sure they don't get what they came for."

She looked at Seryn. "Your Ascension. It happens tomorrow, as soon as the Mireberry Moon calls to you."

My fated nodded. "My parents will meet me at the Elysium Tree. I'll need Melina close. But I can't have her distracting me."

"I can help with that," Jace offered.

"As will I," I added.

Breena slung her arm over Seryn's shoulders. "We'll all be there, Firefly. Wouldn't miss watching you go full demi-Ancient on the bastards."

Seryn chuckled, but it didn't reach her eyes.

Neoma's gaze lingered on the door, where the white-robed cult had vanished. "The devoted don't wander without a shepherd," she murmured. "If they've come this far, someone's pulling the strings. Someone other than the Elders."

The Korax leader looked at Seryn, pride and warning mingling in her hazel eyes. "So be ready, granddaughter. Tomorrow won't just be your Ascension. It'll be a reckoning."

40

COMMANDERS AND MIREBERRIES

S ERYN

"I love this dress on you," Breena said, plucking teasingly at the fabric along my shoulder. "Looks like someone fixed these. I wonder what could have happened to them in the first place?"

I giggled as she winked. Letti had mended the dress Breena had gifted me for the Moonbud Revelry. Wistfully, my fingers glided over the delicate, sheer strip of chiffon that followed the plunging neckline.

My thighs pressed together at the memory of Gavrel snapping the thin, braided straps as easily as if they were blades of grass, and then taking me against a doombark that night. With a smile, I smoothed my hands over the dress's black, kaleidoscopic threads. The necklace Gavrel had made for me dangled against my chest, the rune stone warm against my skin.

Gavrel pushed my loose curls over one shoulder as he met us, placing a gentle kiss in the curve of my neck. "It's none of your concern, Cadell."

She snorted, patting him on the cheek and rushing off to get another goblet. Her olive skin glowed, cheeks flushed from the drinks she'd imbibed throughout the afternoon.

Her deep red dress danced around her thighs as she sidled next to Kaden and Caelora at a table, Letti and Xeni across from them.

Breena waved animatedly with whatever story she was telling, a chunk of cheese clutched in her fingers. Even Xeni and Caelora's mouths quirked as she went on.

The main square's construction was nearly finished. A tepid breeze carrying notes of freshly cut doombarks, damp mud, and brine pushed away the lingering scent of smoke.

A mystical magenta light cast upon the night, and a rosy blush shaded the moon, its form lingering closer to the horizon even at its full height. Tomorrow, the full Mireberry Moon would be a sight to behold.

But only the Ancients knew what tomorrow held for me, or if I'd even get the chance to appreciate it.

Firelight flickered within little glass balls that dangled from interwoven strings in the trees. The crowd wasn't as big as at the Moonbud Revelry, but new and familiar faces gathered. Laughter and lively chatter bopped among the long tables circling the square, each spread littered with goblets of mireberry wine, ale, and an assortment of meats, vegetables, and fruits. A small ensemble of fiddlers played at one end, their lively tunes bouncing off the trees.

A smile curved my lips. Helos would always rise from the mire. No matter what skirmish or disaster befell them, or tried to steal what was theirs. Like their battle plans, history, and scriptures, the community's bond burned in their minds and hearts, and no one could take that from them.

From across the platform, Yaya beckoned us over, and we joined her, sitting on a bench across from her and three others. Marek, Rhaegar, Keethan, and Eliz sat on either side of us.

She gestured toward Gavrel and me. "This is Commander Gavrel Larkin and my granddaughter, our future Elder, Seryn Nightshade." A note of pride lifted her voice at the end.

I dipped my chin in greeting, and Gavrel shook each of their hands, his polite nod carrying the weight of respect between leaders.

Yaya introduced the two seated to her right. "Commanders Neris Kymara of Haadra, and Zeph Stratos of Pneumali."

Neris was stunning. Her skin was a deep umber, and her hair woven into dozens of neat braids threaded with silver wire that caught the firelight. Her eyes, sharp and assessing, softened when they landed on me. She wore a royal-blue jacket fastened with silver clasps, its sleeves rolled to the elbow to reveal forearms dusted with faint burns, which I took as proof of someone who'd survived. An opalescent raven feather trailed from the side of her right wrist all the way to her elbow. "An honor, Elder Nightshade," she said, her tone smooth and measured. "Your reputation precedes you. Let's hope your head's as clear as your courage."

I smiled faintly. "Depends on the day."

Her laugh was genuine, and I decided I liked her immediately.

Beside her, Zeph was the opposite in temperament, his sharp features carved into a stern expression. A scar traced a line from his right jaw to his temple, marring his pale skin and vanishing into the graying blond sweep of his cropped hair. Just under the right side of his jawline, in black ink, the head of a screeching raven peeked out from his collar. His pristine uniform was grayish yellow with white piping, like the sun trying to break through dark clouds after a storm. His lean form sat tall in his seat, eyes shrewdly studying everyone around us. He inclined his head in greeting. "Your efforts in the coming days will inspire many to our cause. That is no small feat."

His voice was level but not cold.

I tilted my head. "Yours as well. Thank you."

"And this," Yaya continued, turning toward the broad-shouldered man to her left, "is Commander Drakon Valyn from Pyria Island."

The man rose, sunlight catching the amber in his eyes. A strip of red cloth tied his dark hair back. His sleeveless burgundy tunic exposed biceps, which were honed and covered in various tattoos of creatures dancing among liquid fire. There were so many, I couldn't find where his Korax tattoo was yet. A pendant of lava rock rested against his light brown chest. "It's an honor to meet you both," he said, voice smooth as tide-worn stone. "The tales of your adventures have reached even our shores."

Gavrel's lips flattened. "Don't believe everything you hear." His gaze softened as he glanced at me. "Unless it's about her brilliance. That is accurate."

Drakon laughed, and it was a deep, rolling sound that carried across the platform. "Brilliant, yes. And I'd wager there was much left out. We do like our legends to be a little mysterious, their stories blazing through the ears of all who revere them."

A flicker of discomfort made me shift in my seat, and Gavrel traced a slow pattern along my lower back. I eased into his touch.

"Blazing, is it? Fitting," Neris murmured, sipping her drink. "You command the Fire Island, after all."

He winked. "And you command my respect, strategist."

Zeph's sigh was barely audible, but his lips twitched. "Ancients save us from Pyrians and their charm."

The table chuckled, and for a fleeting moment, the weight of war lifted.

Yaya leaned forward, eyes gleaming. "We'll talk strategy after the feast," she said, her voice low but sure. "The rebellion's threads are tightening, and soon we'll have to pull."

Neris nodded. "We're ready. The sea routes are secure, and our spies within Evergryn report Lucan's Draumr movements have lulled."

"He's becoming too complacent," Zeph added. "Could be an opening—or a trap."

Drakon crossed his arms. "Either way, we strike before they do."

Yaya looked between them, then at me. "And that is where your part begins."

Their attention shifted my way. Three commanders, each shaped by a unique elemental bloodline but united under one cause. The subtle glow of their auras revealed their rising emotions, each color matching their attire.

Neris' gaze was calm and calculating, Drakon's unwavering and strong, Zeph's sharp and focused.

Their faith weighed on me, heavier than any crown.

I was no longer an anonymous Druik. Now, I was a crucial link that joined them, the prophecy, our cause, and our realm's salvation together.

"We will rise." Yaya's voice cut through the jubilant music bouncing around us. "But you, granddaughter, have given us hope—the proof that the prophecies are true and that all we've worked for was not in vain. You are the spark that ignites our fight, reminding the Korax of their true purpose."

A chill ran down my spine, half awe, half dread. Gavrel's arm, tight around my waist, anchored me as I thought of my responsibilities and the war to come.

I straightened, swallowing the lump that rose in my throat. "Then I'll do my part."

Drakon's lips curved. "That's the spirit."

Neris inclined her head in quiet approval. Zeph simply leaned back, satisfied with my response, and bit into a piece of meat.

Gavrel stood, offering me his hand. "It was a pleasure meeting you all, but if you'll excuse us."

I bowed my head to each of them and went with my fated. The hum of laughter and music faded into something softer as he led me toward the center of the platform. The stringed globes flickered above, and pinkish hues spilled over his dark tunic and breeches, catching on my dress's iridescent threads.

I was untethered, adrift in a dark ocean. Perhaps in the deepest zeniths of the Insomnis Sea, the space where its boundary separated the Oneiric realms.

Gavrel turned to me, cupping my jaw with a calloused hand. "Little Star," he murmured, voice low enough that only I could hear. "You won't carry this alone. And not all at once."

My chest ached. "It feels like I already am."

His thumb brushed my cheek. "Then let me carry some. We share the weight. Always."

Before I could answer, he tugged me closer, one arm circling my waist as the music swelled. He moved with effortless grace that made my pulse stumble. The song was a haunting, lilting tune, a melody written for the stars.

"You've already done the impossible," he whispered against my hair. "You've fought against nightmares, defied the Ancients, and you're still standing. Whatever comes next—you'll rise to meet it."

I pressed my cheek to his chest, letting his words flow through me. Letting his love course through my veins.

I can do this.

My ember thrummed against my nape, and I looked up, eyes grazing over his striking face. "You have a lot of faith in me."

His dimple flickered before he spun me out and back again. "Faith? No. I *see* you, Seryn Nightshade. You don't need faith when you already know the truth."

Around us, the celebration was in full motion. Caelora shook her head as Jace offered his hand, only for Kaden to stride in and claim it instead. She frowned but let him pull her onto the dance floor. Jace's jaw worked as he watched them, something burning beneath his mask of poise.

At the far end, Breena danced beside Rhaegar, her drink sloshing dangerously close to his boots. He threw his hands up, and then his chest shook with laughter. A few paces away, Marek stood, arms crossed, trying and failing to look unaffected as her wide hips swayed under her red dress. Something tugged at the corners of his lips before he turned away, knuckles whitening at his sides.

Gavrel's hand slid to my hip, pulling me back to him. "You know what this dress does to me."

I smiled, hands trailing over the hard planes of his chest. "I do. And I wouldn't mind a repeat."

His hands ran up my spine, and I shivered. "Oh, there will be. Several, once the night quiets. But for now …" His lips brushed the shell of my ear. "We dance."

The world blurred around us, light and sound and color dissolving until there was only him and me, and the steady rhythm of our steps. The fiddled chords bounced around us and the others on the dance floor.

For the first time in ages, I felt *alive*.

The music soared, and he lifted my hand, twirling me once more. The world spun out of focus, except for him. Only him, as he drew me close into his warmth.

When the final note vanished into the night sky, I rested my forehead against his as he leaned in. My pulse was steady, thumping in time with his.

Was I still terrified? Absolutely.

Did I know what the void I was doing? Definitely not.

Would I fight for Midst Fall and do whatever was needed to save it? Would I love this man with everything I had until my final breath?

"Always," I whispered against his lips.

41

UNWORTHY

SERYN

By the time the next day's dusk fell, the songs and laughter of the feast had faded into memory. The whole day had been subdued as if holding its breath, and when the sun dipped, mist spilled over the bog like it finally exhaled over cold glass.

Each step toward Hallowed End drove another lance into my belly.

The air was damp and smelled faintly of smoke, tinged with decay, but also with the richness of wet soil, algae, and fresh doombarks. With the promise of new life and new beginnings.

Sunset bled across the horizon, smearing crimson over the swamp like spilled blood—mine, maybe, or the realm's. It was too easy to imagine it seeping from my heart and into the murky water.

Unworthy.

The thought scraped against my skull, and I ground my teeth together, crushing my insecurities between the enamel.

Not here. Not now.

Gavrel's hand brushed against my lower back as if sensing the storm inside me. His touch was a gentle reminder that he was there. But I knew. His presence never left me, even when we were apart.

My palms glided down the length of my white dress. I hadn't worn white since the Dormancy; wearing it now felt like reclamation. The soft fabric flowed over me like moonlight, the slender straps resting on my shoulders. Along the hem, clusters of gilded stars shimmered where Letti had stitched them. She'd gifted me the dress before we left, insisting that an Elder needed proper ceremonial attire.

Rhythmically, I pulled in a lungful of air, held it for longer than usual, and exhaled as if my breath could slow the seconds slipping through my fingers.

The bridge swayed beneath us, the creaking of shifting wood, leather, and sheathed weapons serenading our trek. One boot in front of the other. The faint outline of Selene's full moon pierced the darkening sky, bathing the wooden decagon in silver. I whispered an entreaty to her—and to my father—that my Ascension would go smoothly.

It had to. I wouldn't accept failure. Of course, I didn't want the aether to claim me, but it was more than that. I didn't want to let down those I loved. Didn't want to doom them and all the citizens of Midst Fall. If ascending meant being one step closer to healing the mortal realm, then my sacrifice would be worth it.

I had a legacy to uphold. A prophecy to slide another piece into.

And I would make it so.

Ahead, the shadowed mass of my uncle writhed, a living darkness suspended above the center of the platform. I refused to meet his ebony gaze. Refused to give him any satisfaction.

But his anger was palpable, a curling menace that jerked against his restraints.

Jace and Kaden moved toward the conservatory, where Melina was held. The Magister's aura spilled like melted butter over the floating symbols that tethered her. With a flick of his wrists, the ignited runes coalesced into a glittering net. Melina shrieked as it tightened, hauling her up by the manacles and pulling her to the edge of the platform.

Her disheveled platinum strands fell across the smudged darkness under her lash line. I moved closer, head tilting. Yes, faint lines were wrinkling her usually smooth face. Time was clawing back the turns she'd stolen.

She sneered, pewter irises flashing as they bore into mine. "You won't succeed! The aether will tear you to pieces, you pathet—"

Jace slammed the flickering veil over her once more, and her tirade cut off mid-word, swallowed by the barrier.

He nodded once and stepped to the side. "The runes should hold, but I'll keep watch."

"We'll all be here, Ser," Kaden added with a smirk. "You've got this. Nothing to it."

"Letti …" I began, glancing at my sister, who stood beside Xeni at the other end.

Kaden hugged me and then kissed my forehead. "Will be here when you return."

I brushed my fingers over Kaden's cheek before turning away. Around me, the others waited in silence, the air thick with apprehension and hope. Words of affection, veiled good-byes—I'd said them already. No need to delay the inevitable any longer.

Gavrel waited for me in the center, his figure tall, solid. The Nyxvein writhed above us, its slithering darkness licking at our moonlit skin. He stepped forward as I approached, hands sliding into my curls, smoothing them back with deliberate care. Like he was memorizing how they felt.

"My star," he murmured, his voice steady despite the tension vibrating through him. "You're extraordinary. You always were."

The lump in my throat was almost too big to swallow.

His thumb traced along my jaw. "I told you I'd believe it enough for the both of us until you came around. Looks like you finally have." His dimple peeked out, tenderness brightening his emerald pools. "You stand before Ancients and beasts—and still, you outshine them. Midst Fall will be fortunate to have you as its Elder."

He kissed me. It was a promise sealed in moonlight and shadow. "Now go," he whispered. "Be brilliant, Asteria. I'll see you soon."

"To the *aether* and beyond?" My smirk wobbled.

"Always, my love."

This time, his lips met mine with fierce urgency. He pulled away, jaw tight, and without another word went to stand beside his brother.

I sat cross-legged, my dagger resting in my right palm, my tourmaline ring warm against my forefinger. Phobetor's shadow cloaked me. I gritted my teeth and ignored his hovering presence.

Focus.

Crushing my eyes closed, I willed the lids to relax and muscles to slacken. Neck. Shoulders. Jaw. Back. Every joint. Every thread.

Breathe In.

Breathe Out.

My aura flowed outward, iridescent against the creeping darkness.

I am you, and you are me.

In.

Out.

Crickets hummed, the soft drone a fragile melody that anchored me to Hallowed End even as the city faded from my awareness. Little by little, the platform, the edges, and the others receded.

Only the Elysium Tree remained in my mind, shimmering with celestial power. I drew it closer, embracing the warmth prickling through my limbs. My ember thrummed gently against my star-shaped scar, sending pulses down my spine, along every nerve.

The Dormancy pods lurked in the corners of my mind. Ghosts of violence and subjugation. I shivered.

Stop.

Images of the glossy vessels collapsed inward, folding like smoke and vanishing. Instead, the banyan's outline flickered, elusive.

My brow furrowed. A cool breeze brushed against my cheek, and the bright, crisp scent and the sound of swishing vines filled my senses.

The Reverie Weald.

I opened my eyes. The sacred tree materialized before me.

I'd done it. A grin tugged at my lips.

I'd bloody well soul-wandered into Surrelia *on purpose*, without a portal.

It was odd to be in both places at once. One foot in a dream, the other in the waking. I sensed my body in the mortal realm. And I felt an echo of it here in my astral form, the glowing strings of my soul tethering one to the other.

I looked at my hands, bottom lip dropping at the sight of my semitransparent, glittering form. It was like my very essence was made of stardust. Was I finally seeing my astral body in its true form now that I was actively soul-wandering?

The ground trembled, and my arms shot out to the side for balance. The tree's roots illuminated, reacting to my presence.

Above, the air warped and twisted with the distant hum of divine energy. A distorted window into Midst Fall.

I knew Phobetor was watching, waiting—his fury coiled like a serpent ready to strike.

Around my physical form, the atmosphere seemed to throb, a heartbeat resonating through the edges of the decagon where my allies stood. Where my khorda waited. I could almost feel their breathing syncing with mine. Every whispered prayer and every lingering gaze anchored me to the mortal realm.

But this moment—this leap across the threshold—belonged to me alone.

I inhaled deeply and exhaled, letting the banyan's energy slide over me.

"Little Star." Mama appeared at my side. She stood with my father, pride etched on their countenances, and the breeze rustling their golden robes.

"Well done, daughter," Morpheus praised.

Mama squeezed my hand, and I felt the warmth of her skin both here and in the mortal realm. "Are you ready?"

I lifted my chin. "As I'll ever be."

The Ancient of Dreams looked at the Elysium Tree, and a glow shivered over its gnarled bark. "It's time."

42

WEAVE ME THROUGH YOUR ROOTS

SERYN

I gripped the astral version of my dagger, its cool platinum hilt heavy in my palm. The wavy edges of its chiseled obsidian blade glinted, and the faceted diamond at its pommel filled with swirling iridescence.

This blade was part of me. It had chosen me. And it was the only thing that could remove Gavrel's rune. But what did that matter if it would kill him? I was damned tired of the games the Fates played.

My gaze followed the dips and curves of the radiant tree before me, and I bowed my head. At least there were things far greater than the whims of celestial beings, and this tree that stood unyielding, rooted in the very essence of life and ember, was proof of that.

With a long inhale, I lifted the blade.

Here goes nothing.

The slick bite of its edge slid across my flesh, and I hissed, crimson pooling in the hollow of my hand. I exhaled, looking at my father.

He brushed his thumb over my cheek. "Repeat after me, daughter."

His words fell over me like hot, gilded wax. Ethereal and sealing my fate.

"I come with my heart and breath and ember," Morpheus intoned.

I echoed him, forcing myself to respire so my spirit wouldn't recoil into the comfort of Midst Fall. So my body wouldn't betray me.

The roots of the banyan trembled, sending a tremor up my spine.

"Body bound and spirit free.
Weave me through your roots."

I mirrored Morpheus' cadence, letting the syllables hum in my chest. Blood dripped from my cut, seeping into the moss.

"Let my will be tested.
Let my essence prove true.
I surrender so the Somnis may guide me,
and bind me with Kosmos anew."

With a final shudder, the tree's radiance pulsed three times before blinking out. The floral-scented breeze stilled, my curls settling around my cheeks.

A deep line of confusion etched between my brows, and I glanced at my parents. But before I could speak, the banyan exploded in light.

The world warped, reality folding inward like a sheet drawn into the roots by its center. My stomach flipped, and I clamped my eyes shut against the nausea clawing up my throat.

Then—impact.

I slammed into roiling liquid. Tendrils of ice and flame licked over my skin in the same moment. I spun, tumbling through rivers of stars and prismatic hues, my very being a streak of consciousness cast between the currents.

Disoriented, I flung out my limbs, trying to stabilize. My vision swam as the flux snatched me, carried me away on a coiling channel.

Faces and scenes zoomed past me.

Children laughing.

Kaden and Gavrel sparring.

My mother's eyes in the firelight.

Sirens singing death-songs across glassy oceans.

A wyvern hatching from its metallic egg.

Lives I'd touched. Lives I hadn't yet.

Another wave slammed into me. Air fled my lungs. I plummeted straight into a sea of stars and sank as the tide wrapped around me. My scream smashed against my closed lips so the luminous substance wouldn't fill my throat. Panic flared within me. I thrashed about, fingernails clawing at the shifting shimmers above, but the Somnis dragged me deeper. The midnight unknown caressed my body. Picking me apart.

I was both here and elsewhere.

Time fractured.

Slowed down.

Sped up.

Condensed.

Folded.

Reversed.

I was everything.

I was nothing.

Breathe. Gavrel's voice bounced through my skull.

I couldn't fucking breathe! I was drowning. My body stilled. I let the Somnis claim me.

Be brilliant, Asteria.

I wasn't brilliant. I was broken.

Unworthy.

My throat closed, despair pressing on my chest.

Enough.

My fist clenched around my dagger. Its diamond pommel glinted, my ember alive within it.

I was *enough.*

I was *more.*

And I was *needed.*

My gaze lifted. A speck of light gleamed above, impossibly distant. My aura shimmered around me, calling to the motes of starlight at the edges of my vision. Heat cocooned me. Electricity vibrated from my crown to my toes.

When the tide comes, look not to the stars, but to what hides beyond them. Phantasos' words flickered through me. *Beyond.*

I thought of Gavrel. Of Mama. Letti. My friends. They were *my* beyond—the reason I'd fight through whatever void waited.

What was beyond the stars?

Death? The unknown? Destiny?

All those things. But it was not for me or anyone else to comprehend.

Sometimes you had to surrender to the chasm to become who you were always meant to be.

I leaned back, letting the current cradle me. The fizzing stars condensed, sinking into the glowing branch patterns on my arms. My gift thrummed; a chorus of water, laughter, and endless silence filled my ears.

Then my lips parted, and I let the molten beyond pour into me. It filled my lungs and stole my breath. Shadows and stars streaked across my vision, but I didn't flinch. I let it consume me, embrace me.

It was terrifying and exquisite. The tide pulled me in all directions, a thousand dreamers' thoughts brushing against my skin.

And then, with my next fluttering heartbeat, my body heaved upward, breaking the surface. A sputtering gasp tore from me, melted starlight spilling from my lips.

The sea descended, and I floated weightlessly, my dress soaked with the dreams of others. Wind whirled around me, drying me in a rush of warmth.

All around, ribbons of imagination wove through the molten firmament, brushing my astral form. Echoes of lives I'd never known whispered my name.

"Breathe," I told myself, my voice reverberating across the expanse. "Breathe and *stay*."

Below me, my physical body glowed hazily in Midst Fall as I sat cross-legged in a trance.

Above, Surrelia and the Elysium Tree hovered, almost calling to mind the floating islets in the Stygian Murk. The banyan's long roots dangled from the bottom of the earth, stretching and weaving through the currents.

"They're coming," the familiar voice rasped. "They want Elder Harrow—mean to free her!"

Time quivered, and the sensation of dropping plopped heavy in my belly.

"Father?" My sister's voice echoed around me.

"It's too late," Gideon spat. "Letti, get behind me."

Thundering footsteps.

Shouts.

"Hold your ground!" Yaya yelled.

Then a scream sliced through the Somnis.

Melina.

The platform of Hallowed End flickered into being beneath my astral feet—half real, half dream. Smoke curled, thick and choking. I sliced through it with my blade, my power lashing out.

And there, one golden string burned brighter than the rest.

Brighter than the dreams and stars and the unknown. My khorda bond.

I seized it, wrapping the cord around my left wrist, feeling it pull at my ribs. A tether between soul and body.

The battle surrounded me in blurred flashes. Like splashes of splattered watercolors.

Gavrel, Kaden, Breena, Jace, and the others—all fighting across overlapping planes. The Bloomless had returned. They'd freed Melina and brought loyalist Draumrs and Akridais with them.

Locust tattoos glowed like infected wounds over the enforcers' throats as they whipped their oily energy at the Korax.

Breena's scarlet shield flared in front of her, Gideon, and Letti, who dropped to her knees and stabbed their attacker in the ankle. Gideon slashed a knife toward a cultist reaching for my sister.

Trees bent to Kaden's ember, thrashing their foes into the swamp water, the muckweeds holding them under. Jace's runes traced in the air, and Caelora's lavender-tinged power spilled over screaming bodies. Marek's illusioned flames clung inside the skulls of his victims.

Gavrel lunged, his ten-point star igniting, the blaze illuminating his blade as it met Melina's smoke. She shrieked again, pewter eyes gleaming, and slammed her power into him. He flew backward, crashing through warriors who'd been attacking Xeni, Rhaegar, and Yaya.

Gavrel lay, unmoving, in front of my prone form, his chest rising and falling fitfully.

A feral grin split Melina's mouth, and her features twisted into something grotesque. Slowly, she inched toward me, savoring the hunt. "Do you feel it, pet?" she crooned. "How close you are to death? I'll take you piece by piece until there's nothing left to save."

43

WORTHY

Seryn

I widened my stance on the trembling dream platform. Energy surged over my skin, through the threads that bound me across planes and time.

The roots of the banyan.

My khorda bond.

My ember.

My very fucking will to survive.

I braided them into a resolve.

She would not take me.

My power buzzed in my ears; it surged through me, searing and euphoric as it drank in the dream prisms and stars.

My spine arched. Then I lurched forward, curls flicking around me like flames.

A piece of my soul snapped into my body.

My eyes opened in Midst Fall, breath ragged, hands splayed on the wood.

Both versions of me—astral and corporeal—rose in perfect synchrony.

"Sorry to disappoint you, but you can't have me, *pet*." My words echoed in both worlds.

Melina faltered. For the first time, fear cracked plainly through her perfect composure.

Everyone paused for a split second, gasps and awe saturating the air before the clang of weapons and whirring of ember resounded once more.

Around us, the fight continued, Phobetor still suspended above. But they all fell away. It was just Gavrel, me, and the Elder who had terrorized us all these turns. Who'd brutalized so many others for nigh a century.

I lifted my right hand. My weapon shimmered. And when I flung it, both my astral and physical forms moved as one. The blade sliced through dream and reality, twin streaks of black stone and rainbow-hued tails.

Melina dove aside, snarling. My ability called to my weapon, and it raced into my hand in each plane like twin comets returning home.

My limbs moved as if pulled by a single cord; astral and corporeal matched step for step. I was both puppet and master. Every breath I took in the Somnis flowed through my lungs in Midst Fall.

The Elder huffed, black smoke coiling around her. She charged, throwing everything she had at me. Darkness, teeth, the raw cruelty she'd hoarded for so long.

She wanted me to suffer. Wanted Gavrel. She wanted to tear out the thing that bound us.

I didn't hesitate, my blade singing through the air once more. It cleaved through the starlit aether of the Somnis, cut through Melina's haze, and buried itself in her flank.

Her eyes went wide, not from surprise, but with pure, animalistic panic. She tugged my dagger from her, letting its blood-coated blade clunk against the planks. Her arms flung out as she stumbled. Her ember slammed into me, cinching around Gavrel and me in a choking, prickly embrace.

The burn of it lanced through my mind, and Gavrel groaned, pushing up shakily on his elbows. I freed my power in both worlds, its force crashing into hers, slurping it in. It tasted of smoke and iron and every cruelty she'd ever committed.

My eyes illuminated, cutting through her darkness and that of the Somnis.

And I *took*.

Let her power absorb into me. Urged my ember to take all it wanted.

Mine! it purred.

"Little Star—" Gavrel's voice cracked somewhere between, raw with warning. Not through fear of hurting Melina, but of losing myself.

But I was more myself than I'd ever been.

Worthy.

Inevitable.

Melina's talons dug into my shoulder, her mask of rage appearing in front of me out of our clashing ember. I welcomed the pain as it surged over my physical and astral bodies.

I tugged harder, her dark aura diminishing, her stolen ink-dark energy sifting through the boughs along my forearms. She released me, fingers tearing at the air, trying to claw her gift back, to keep the thing that had kept her beautiful and terrible.

"You can't have it! You can't have *him*," she spat, deep wrinkles etching into her face, hair turning brittle. "Not yours. *Not yours!*"

Something like desperation and wrath flickered over her aging visage, ugly and human, before she shrieked. Even this close to death, she still obsessed over Gavrel.

But she couldn't have him.

He had always been *mine*.

My physical body pulsed, our ember and something other-worldly vibrating under my flesh and through my bones.

I was going to split at the seams.

It is time. Morpheus' voice broke through. Like all the other times, he'd found a way to guide me.

My muscles tensed, and I channeled my and Melina's joined ember, offering them to the Somnis. To the Elysium Tree.

Both versions of Elder Harrow dropped to their knees, blood and pieces of crumbling flesh falling to the wooden planks. Coating my boots in the Somnis. For she was also both here and there. I'd dragged her astral form to the sparkling unknown with me.

She sneered, blackened blood spilling over her bottom lip.

I kept taking. Not because I wasn't in control of my gift, for we were one and the same. No, I kept taking because sometimes violence was necessary.

And this was the only way she'd kneel.

The only way to stop her.

Ascension insisted on the offering, and even though she was unwilling, something in me knew the tree would accept it all the same. Because there was no other path, and …

It was time.

My arms flung upward, and I funneled what remained of her ember into the tree's roots, somewhere far above. The Somnis hummed with approval; the liquid stars blazing bright and currents stilling for but a moment.

So it is done, a voice echoed, but I wasn't sure from where or who it came this time.

A searing heat sliced down the base of my skull, burned over my flesh in waves, like thousands of tiny paper cuts. I gasped as my ember sank into my stinging flesh.

Melina's body unstitched itself as she fell forward in slow motion. First the edges, then her hair, then her torso and limbs. Noxious smoke, laced with the scent of bitter almond and roses, curled and then shimmered as sparkling motes consumed her.

She did not die with a gasp or a whimper. That wouldn't have been fitting. Her wrinkled face cracked like a sculpture, bit by bit, grain by grain. As she evaporated into ash, disbelief lined her expression. Hatred. Fear, maybe.

"Pet," she croaked, and then nothing. The rest of her imploded, bursting into the aether as if she'd never existed at all.

I closed my fingers around the hilt of my dagger in a prayer, willing my soul to return home. My physical body lurched in Midst Fall; my knees cracking against the planks hard, and I bit down on a sharp intake of air.

Around me, our allies staggered, wounds and breath ragged.

"Hold—" Jace shouted as new runes floated around Melina's ashes. He flicked his wrists, and they vanished, her remains drifting away on a damp breeze.

With a stifled cry, I fell onto my hands, and Gavrel crawled to me, pulling me into his lap. Slowly, golden patterns seeped over my hands and wrists along the usually hidden bough patterns.

"By the ravens, it worked," Yaya murmured.

Gavrel kissed my temple, smoothing my damp curls from my cheeks. "You did it, my love. It is done."

There were no signs of the Bloomless. The fighting had ceased, the cowards fleeing when I pulled Melina's soul to the Somnis. Perhaps they weren't so faithful after all.

The few Akridais and Draumrs who remained took a knee, bowing their heads toward me in respect.

Gideon lifted his nose, observing them and the aftermath with shrewd eyes. He put his arm around Letti, and she hugged him before rushing into Xeni's arms.

Kaden stared numbly at the spot Melina had last been, shoulders slumping and hands running through his hair. Jace peeked at him from the corner of his eyes, lips pressing into a firm line before he went to Caelora.

I brushed my fingers over Gavrel's cheeks; his beautiful, bruised face bathed in moonbeams. A residual tingle tickled my flesh, as if the Somnis was still fluttering along the edges of my reality, beckoning me back.

My heart stuttered, unease tapping against my nape.

I stilled.

Something in the air had shifted. I felt the tremor along my marrow, my soul, and gifts now connected to Kosmos.

As the new Elder of the Perilous Bogs.

Wait.

Why was the moon shining fully on us?

My gaze whipped up, Gavrel and I staggering to our feet. Everyone's attention followed.

"Where is Phobetor?" I whispered.

44

SISTER

SERYN

A raven flew across the star-speckled sky, glossy wings slicing through the haze above the muddy water. Its shadow glided over the platform, between the Nyxvein tendrils slinking back into the conservatories.

It banked sharply, letting out a caw that made every hair on my arms stand. When it landed, it burst into a billow of stars, and the Ancient of Illusions emerged. She stood at the edge, her eyes shining as if cut from glass.

"Phantasos—" I breathed, relief and question twining through my voice.

She inclined her head; her smile pressed between the thin seam of her lips. "Balance."

The word dropped at my boots, where Jace's runes were nothing but charred etchings, the wood splintered through the symbol.

Marek stomped forward, his quarterstaff gripped tight in his hand. "What have you done?"

Yaya's palm whipped out before him, firm and commanding. "Mind yourself."

But the Ancient's gaze had already slid toward him—brief, assessing—something uncanny flickering in her expression. "So much of him in you," she murmured, more to herself than anyone else.

I glanced at my cousin, and he squinted, a vein pulsing in his temple as if his mind was racing, chewing on her meaning. As far as I knew, his childhood was a blur to him. He didn't even remember how he'd gotten scarred.

I moved between them, anger thrumming against my jaw. "What balance requires freeing a monster?" I demanded. "You saw what he did. To the realms, to the people in Midst Fall—"

"The Fates know what must be done," she cut in smoothly. "Death unbalances what they have decreed. He is the darkness that gives your light meaning."

Breena scoffed. "Bloody *living* gives life meaning."

"The Fates weigh more than mortal hearts," Phantasos replied.

Gavrel's hand found my lower back. "Ancients and mortals alike will perish if Phobetor has his way."

The platform quaked beneath us. The gilly toads fell silent in the distance.

"You—" I started, but the words caught in the back of my throat as a deep, resonant groan rose from beneath the decagon.

With a thunderous boom, the wood split at her feet, and a swarm of shadows exploded in a vortex of shrieking wind and black mist. The impact threw several of us backward.

Phantasos hovered above, unmoving, ribbons of light spiraling lazily around her.

Then the shadows condensed. They pulled inward, writhing like a storm forced into a human shape. But this Ancient was anything but human. The darkness melted away, and Phobetor stepped forward, a satisfied grin hanging off his incisors.

"Sister," he drawled.

Phantasos' form flickered, her face shifting into a blur of many, like reflections in rippling water. "Brother." The word was hollow.

His smile twitched, gaze flicking to me. "Ah, niece. The little dirtling who thought she could cage an Ancient."

I raised my dagger, though my hand shook. "I did more than just think."

He licked his bottom lip. "You have your father's arrogance."

Marek moved to my other side. "And our family's stubbornness," he barked.

Phobetor's head tilted, something unreadable passing over his expression as he studied Marek. A faint line carved between his brows. "Curious."

The ground convulsed again, my uncle's shadows arching like stretching cats beneath the planks.

Phantasos turned to face me; her metallic eyes, the only stable feature on her countenance, flashed. "Belladonna, heed my words. What follows was always meant."

"No," I spat the word. "Damn you to the Murk. Both of you."

Her lips quirked, and she sighed. "Perhaps."

And then she spread her arms wide and vanished, dissolving into a flurry of glittering dust.

The silence that followed was unbearable.

Then Phobetor snickered. A low, grating sound that made the doombarks quiver. "Now," he purred, "let's see what the Fates have chosen for you, Elder."

45

A DARK SUPERNOVA

S ERYN

P hobetor whipped his arms out, and the world split apart. Shadows peeled off him in thick ribbons, ripping through the air and knocking us all back. My teeth cracked together as I braced myself, my halo igniting.

A second dark wave undulated, skittering like a mass of spiders over the planks. It slid between them and cascaded off the edges.

The muck gurgled, groans breaking free with each burst bubble. Swollen shapes twisted beneath the surface.

"What the void is that?" a young Draumr cried out. I glanced at the small group of them and Akridais, who lingered near the bridge. Likely deciding whether they could safely make it across if they chose to flee.

Breena's shield flared just in time to repel the first wave of darkness before it slammed into us. "He's raising the fecking bog bodies!"

And she was right. All around us, the water broke open, clammy hands clawing up from the depths. The dead. Old and new. The ones Melina's recent attack had sacrificed to fuel her madness.

"Back!" I shouted, but it was too late.

The first corpse lurched over the ledge, cracking joints, limbs reaching, bloated skin slick and pallid, eyes glassy, filled with celestial darkness.

Letti screamed as it reached for her and grabbed the hem of her dress, dragging her toward the edge.

"Letti!" Her name tore from me as I lunged, but a clammy hand snagged my ankle, yanking me back.

"Get away from her!" Gideon's shout tore through the chaos. He barreled past Xeni as her sword flashed, slicing clean through another monster's neck.

He slashed downward with the borrowed sword, severing the corpse's arm, then shoved my sister behind him.

"Stay close!" Yaya barked. Her arrow flew, piercing through a bulging eyeball. The creature tipped back with a moan.

Rhaegar planted himself at her flank, his battle-axe whirling in wide, brutal arcs. "Try to touch her, I bleeding dare you," he grunted and cleaved the next monster that lunged in half. "Two for one. Anyone keeping count?"

"Three, you cur!" Breena bragged, her focus unbroken as she poured scarlet heat from her palms in wavering sheets while yanking her dagger out of a monster.

Caelora rolled her eyes, pushing her liquid fire over two more decaying bodies. When lavender coated the reanimated, they froze mid-step, their grotesque movements hesitating before they burst into flames.

Phobetor squinted toward the Akridais. "Ah, how fortunate. Melina did something right. Nyxvein in the ink."

He crooked his pointer finger, and their neon-yellow tattoos flared, black seeping over their eyes. They turned as one, hurling oiled power at me.

"Move!" Gavrel's arm shot around my waist, yanking me aside as boards cracked beneath us.

The attack flew toward my sister, and she screamed. Before I could think, my thumb brushed over my tourmaline ring. In a crack of bright light, I condensed and reappeared next to Letti just as Gideon pushed her away, taking the full brunt of the Akridai's attack.

I grabbed her before she could fall.

His gasp took my breath away. Blood poured from his mouth. And he looked at me, eyes wide with disbelief and a strange, fragile relief. "Take care of her, Elder," he rasped.

Letti sobbed as he staggered into the dark water.

My heart solidified into stone, and I spun toward the Ancient of Nightmares, fingers curling into claws.

Phobetor's smile split wider. "You think your embers and blades will save you, little dreamers?" His eyes filled with ebony. "We gave you these gifts. Gave you life. And we can unmake you just the same." His shadows pulsed, and we all stumbled, auras jerking around us.

The air thinned like the membrane between the Somnis and Midst Fall had been torn. I sensed it deep in my marrow. Phobetor's nightmares bled into the waking.

A scorching pain ripped through my mind, vision going dark. Reality splintered into dozens of twisted versions of itself. Each horror-fueled nightmare slammed into the other, filling my awareness until I crashed to my knees, fingernails digging into my scalp.

I was helpless against each wave of images; wanted to curl in a ball and fade into the muck. Rhaegar and Breena were buried under an endless tide of corpses. Gavrel lay with his eyes vacant. Mama and Letti skinned alive. Black char poured from

Marek and Yaya's mouths. On and on, I tumbled through each vision, tasting iron on my tongue. Drowning.

"Cousin, fight! They aren't real!" Marek's demand broke through.

I blinked, half in and half out of reality. The world was a smear of this realm and the Void. He'd torn a rift, and the nightmarescape was trickling in. He was turning our realm inside out, making it in his image.

Phobetor raised his hands, and the sky itself warped, his form fracturing into overlapping shadows. "You call yourself an Elder, niece?" His voice was discordant. "Let me show you the truth of power."

Before I could answer, the platform completely cracked in half.

In a blur, Marek was already moving.

He landed in a crouch, pitch-black flames blazing around him. His tattoo gleamed with dark iridescence, making it look like the branded raven flew over his shoulder blades.

Marek's ember thrashed against Phobetor's. His sapphire eyes burned with fury. "All you wield are lies," he growled. His voice wasn't fully his—it was deeper, older, laced with something primal. "And they won't save you."

The inferno around my cousin condensed, then erupted outward. It struck the Ancient's shifting outline in its center, sending my uncle staggering backward with a bellow. His body solidified once more, shadows fluttering like misty gnats around him. A ring of whitish gray showed around Phobetor's dark irises, and his lips pulled over his teeth in a snarl.

I jerked, released from the trance he'd had me and the others in.

"Now!" Jace shouted from across the chaos, slashing runes through the air. Symbols flared around the perimeter of the broken decagon. He slammed his palm against the planks, and they knitted together. Light climbed up the Ancient's legs.

Phobetor's snarl rattled the trees. "You dare to bind me with my own sigils, boy?"

"Poetic, isn't it?" the Magister shot back, blood slicking his temple. "You always said imitation was the sincerest form of flattery."

The air vibrated with so much energy that Hallowed End whirred.

Kaden raised his hands; a wave of his verdant healing ember cascaded outward, sweeping through our ranks, sealing shallow wounds and keeping us upright. The doombarks leaned in, branches spreading wide, like fingers ready to catch something.

"Ser, your move!" he hollered.

I shook my head, gathering my senses. My fingers weaved, gathering my ember between them. The orb quivered between my palms, straining for release. "Let's see how the Fates like *this*," I whispered and hurled it.

The comet struck the Ancient in the chest. He reeled, form flickering and blackness spraying from the wound. But instead of dissipating, his shadows coiled tighter around him, plugging the injury.

He grinned, liquid night dripping over his teeth. "Ah, niece … you underestimate me."

I planted my heels, stiffening my spine. The platform trembled. But not with Phobetor's energy.

Mine.

My ember was more powerful now. I was connected to Somnis. To Kosmos itself. I was the prism, splintering color and light, drawing it to me.

From the wild kaleidoscope twisting around me, glittering gold emerged, dancing within.

The Akridais and bog bodies slumped, released from the Ancient's hold.

On a roar, my power blasted forward. It coiled around him, lifting him off his feet.

With deliberate steps, I shifted toward the platform's center, bypassing the fissures and hopping over the crack that ran through it.

The Ancient of Nightmares would not win this battle.

Or ever again.

Balance be damned.

For I was of the stars and the Night. Of hope and the light of Day. Nyxvein ran through me as well as resplendent, celestial ember.

Nightshade and Dream.

A dark supernova who refused ...

That's it.

I simply refused.

Phobetor would not take what wasn't his. He wouldn't continue to reap sorrow, rot, and terror upon this realm or any other.

Fates be damned.

My uncle's grin drooped, worry lining his brow.

The air crackled like splintered glass under strain. Marek and I stood shoulder-to-shoulder, his dark flames lashing at the air on my right. "Finish him. Now."

Gavrel stood close, his right arm wrapped around me, holding me steady.

"Together," he murmured in my ear, voice low but steady. "You and me." His rune blazed, shining white against my stomach. So pure against my soiled dress. My aura caressed it lovingly.

My ember clung to Phobetor's, drinking it in and seeping into the wound I'd inflicted on him.

Another sparkling orb gyrated between my palms, my new gilded star-like ember folding into the center. The boughs along my arms were now filled with liquid gold.

"Marek, the pods," I gritted out.

Phobetor's form convulsed, his shadows shredding as I

consumed his power. He struggled against his rune bindings, the light fraying in sections.

"Now," I ordered, balancing my creation in one palm, the other resting on Marek's shoulder. I pushed the filtered energy into my cousin, and an obsidian blaze whipped around him, the air shrieking.

His muscles tensed, his tattoo gleaming and black seeping over the many scars that riddled his torso. The veins in his neck bulged, his teeth grinding as a roar reverberated from him.

His arms and quarterstaff thrust out, flaming umbras exploding outward.

Every single conservatory lining the city blazed open with amber light, the Nyxvein roots pouring from the pods. Coming straight for Marek and me.

My orb twisted in on itself, the starry black hole taking shape. Marek slumped at my side, falling to his knees, his breath heaving in ragged huffs.

There were so many Nyxvein tentacles coming from the circumference of the city that their liquid inkiness blotted the moonlight out, creating a writhing, ebony dome. They fused into one twisting spiral.

Before it could smash into us, I thrust my mini universe into it. It reared back, the mist shaking, stunned. Phobetor roared again, and the Nyxvein twirled, focusing on the Ancient.

With a final twisted sneer, Phobetor's fingers lashed out, and a barb of shadow shot toward us.

I pushed away from Marek, knocking him to the side as Gavrel and I tumbled in the other direction.

The Nyxvein hissed and then attacked the Ancient, sinking into his flesh and nose, eyes, ears, and mouth. Anywhere it could find. His garbled screams spilled as it ripped his body apart, stole bits of his unraveling essence, and dragged them back to their respective pods like pieces of treasure.

The aether didn't even have the chance to claim his soul for itself.

One by one, the pods sealed. Sickly shades of burnished crimson, like dried blood, bloomed beneath the amber glass before it turned obsidian once more.

Jace's embered runes evaporated.

I sagged forward, Gavrel's arm slipping from me. The scent of scorched flesh and smoke hung thick in the air.

"He's gone," Marek rasped, gripping his weapon.

I wanted to believe him. Believe what my eyes had seen. Phobetor was dead, no doubt. And I hoped that whatever the pods stole from him stayed buried.

My ember sank into my flesh, but the gold branch tattoos didn't vanish; in fact, they swept over my biceps, connecting over my shoulder blades and clavicle.

I lifted my chin, acknowledging the Elysium Tree's gift as its song hummed through me. As Somnis fully accepted me, and Kosmos bonded with me.

My Ascension was complete.

It should have ended there.

All at once, the moonlight shifted. A pulse of something *wrong* flitted through Hallowed End.

I flinched as gasps rent the air. I braced for an attack that never came.

A dull thud sounded behind me.

"Gavrel?" I cried.

He was propped on one knee, eyes wide and unseeing. Shadow coiled from the rune over his heart, his tunic torn open, showcasing his flesh. The star-shaped scar at its center corroded with spreading darkness.

Phobetor's final attack hadn't missed its mark after all.

"No—" My voice tore free as I lunged toward him. Kaden caught his brother before his head hit the planks.

Every color drained from the world until all that remained was darkness.

The others shouted, distant, warped by the roar in my ears.

"Stay with me," I pleaded, cupping his face between my hands. "Gavrel, look at me!"

His lips moved—my name, I think—but no sound reached me.

My ember zoomed over my flesh, answering the scream I didn't have enough breath for.

46

THROUGH THE DARK

GAVREL

Her fingers trembled as they traced the blackened rune over my heart. The mark pulsed, slow and sick, each throb echoing like poison through my veins. Her eyes were glassy with starlight and terror. I'd never seen her so afraid.

"It's spreading. His talisman was already vulnerable to Phobetor's ember. Or perhaps a piece of the curse never left him," Jace murmured from somewhere behind us. "If it reaches his heart, he'll—"

"I know!" she cried, her voice sharp enough to split the air.

My vision was fading; all I needed to see was Seryn. She was the only thing that mattered to me before I slipped into the aether.

Her aura flickered as she looked back at me, searching my face as if she could anchor herself there. "There's only one way to get it out," she whispered, her trembling hand going to her dagger.

My hand found hers, weak but sure. "Do it."

She shook her head, tears cutting tracks through the grime and blood coating her cheeks. "There has to be—"

"Do it, Little Star." I coughed, blood dribbling from the corners of my lips.

She pressed her forehead to mine, her words shuddering on an exhale. "You bloody stubborn—"

"I love you, too."

Slowly, she straddled my waist, her weapon in her grip, the moon glinting off the black stone. The pommel danced with radiance. She raised it, her entire body shaking.

I swore the faint outline of the Elysium Tree fluttered behind her, but I blinked, and it was gone.

"I'm sorry," she whimpered, and drove the blade into me.

Searing pain like fire-coated lightning exploded through my chest. My body bowed, a raw cry tearing from my throat and Seryn's.

Then … nothing.

The world blinked out.

Weightless. Soundless.

Only her voice broke through the emptiness, calling my name as if she could chase me through the darkness.

47

TWO HOLLOWED STARS

SERYN

Trembling, I clenched the bloodied dagger so hard, the swirling carvings in the hilt bit into my palm. Gavrel's body stilled, the light fading from his eyes—and from the rune tattoo on his hand.

My heart lurched, the thread around my ribs limp and lifeless.

No! I screamed in my mind, chest heaving.

Dark ichor pooled, thick as grymseed oil. Blood and curse fused together.

And within that mutilated hollow, the talisman glinted. Cracks riddled its surface. My blade had cleaved it straight through the center of what might once have been a lightning bolt etched down the middle of a decagon.

My breath hitched as the fractured pieces rose, tugged from his flesh by something unseen.

No.

By me.

The rune's power called to my ember, which now thrashed around me. My gift seized, instinctive and desperate, clinging to the energy bleeding out of him, coiling around the shards and pulling them free.

My hand shook as the rune stone remnants hovered between us. Our bond twitched, and it felt like hundreds of glass slivers needling into my own heart.

The talisman's essence and the curse tangled together in a shimmering web that held to his lesion. The sticky, glittering strands fought to snap toward him like spider legs writhing, ready to scurry back into the darkness.

"No," I hissed, summoning my ember from its deepest core; the place now bound to Kosmos, to my demi-Ancient lineage. It boiled through me, eager to oblige.

I let it feast.

The rune shuddered as I drained its power. Light burst from within it, imploding first, then exploded into dust.

For a heartbeat, I thought I'd won.

Then the poisoned strands reared back and burrowed into his chest.

I screamed, the sound raw and jagged, shattering against the trees.

"No. No, no, no—"

I dragged him against me, my hands shaking so violently they could barely hold his weight. His skin was already cooling. The wound over his heart had gone dull. It was empty. Hollow. Stained with Phobetor's lingering poison.

Suddenly, Kaden was beside me, nudging me aside. "Let me try."

He pushed his clover-colored ember into the injury, sweat dripping down his face.

And nothing.

Kaden cursed, slamming his fists against Gavrel's chest. "Come on, you fucking wanker!"

I shoved him away, draping my body over my love, his blood and darkness coating my already stained dress.

"He's gone," Caelora whispered, her voice a fragile thread somewhere at my side.

I reached within, heard the dim hum of my bond, felt it sting as I plucked it. Fading fast, barely there among the aether.

"He's *not*," I snarled, my power surging. "He's not gone!"

"Stay calm," Caelora murmured, a lavender glow drifting toward me.

My halo flared, eyes bursting in icy illumination. "Don't you dare fucking touch us!" Caelora's gift reared back, and she dipped her chin.

Breena rubbed my back, and I flinched. "Ryn—" she started softly.

"I'm not leaving him!" I screamed, and she straightened, eyes soft and fists clenched.

In an instant, Jace was beside me, his tattoos blazing across every inch of exposed skin. "The Kollao Ceremony. It might—"

Kaden grabbed his shoulder, nodding once. "Do it."

They knelt on either side of us, Jace etching circles and sigils in the air.

"May Kosmos bless this union," he began, grabbing Kaden's hands and forming a makeshift bowl above Gavrel's pectorals.

Jace's blade sliced into my palm. I didn't feel the pain, my mind turning inward as I stared blankly at Gavrel's lifeless eyes.

He made an incision on Gavrel's palm; the blood there was untainted. I took my fated's icy hand, letting the sticky, wet warmth coat my skin. Kaden held his cupped hands beneath, crimson filling them.

Jace's words scattered through the air, words of devotion and bonds and Ancients.

"Seryn," Yaya's shout broke through the fog, but only for a moment.

What was the point? I needed to follow Gavrel into the

aether before our cord unraveled completely. I bent forward, our blood staining the golden tattoos lining my arms and collarbone.

"Calm her," Jace bit out at Caelora. I'd never heard the Magister use that tone before.

This time, before I could stop her, her spoken energy flowed over me like a cool breeze. And then, peace. Serenity and hope fluttered in the back of my mind.

Color crept into the world once more. My vision cleared.

I sat up, sucking in the smoky air. Let it fill my lungs.

Hastily, Jace continued, dipping his blade into the now-golden liquid in Kaden's palms, "This binding is sacred, and not even the Fates can deny it. Two souls will fuse—their lifeblood, ember, and soul entwined. The mark shall be carved where breath and pulse and life meet. Do you accept this joining?"

"Yes!" I cried out, realizing what was happening. "Kosmos, help us."

Energy zipped over my back, and my gilded tattoos warmed, chasing away the chill. My fingers tingled with renewed feeling, sticky with mine and Gavrel's blood and poison.

I tore the rest of Gavrel's tunic down the center, fully exposing his torso. I ripped my dress just enough to expose the space above my heart.

"Do it!" I demanded, teeth gritting.

Jace worked swiftly, carving through my skin and muscle, etching the mirrored crescents and flame into my rib. My molars clenched so tight I thought they would crack as a sharp, searing heat separated my tissues. The high-pitched scratching against my bone zinged through my back teeth.

But I didn't cry out, I held the scream in my soul, even when it bent my spine backward. And yet the pain didn't matter. The agony of losing Gavrel was far worse than the blade slicing through my body.

It didn't fucking matter.

Because this had to work.

Had to bring him back to me.

That was all that mattered.

He was all that mattered.

Radiance erupted from the incision, gold replacing the scarlet. The symbol sank deep into my bone, and then my muscles and flesh knit themselves whole. The sigil shimmered over my heart as I watched Jace repeat the act with Gavrel.

When he finished, the ritual's power sealed his flesh, and Gavrel's golden mark lifted over the star-shaped scar. But the inky stains remained, his veins branching outward in a dark starburst around our Kollao emblem.

Yaya gasped, her words flitting over us, but I barely heard them. "Lest rise Dark Reaping from the scars. Make haste with hollowing of the stars."

The others drew in a collective breath.

"Come back to me," I whispered, pressing my palms against his healed mark, ringed with poison. "Please."

A tingle thrummed under the scar on my nape. Incessant, and I closed my eyes, listening. A universe of fractured rainbows and swimming stars and hope and pain filled my mind.

Somnis called to me. I beseeched it, my fated khorda's name a repeated echo through my mind.

Helos fell away.

Hallowed End. Gone.

The others. Gone.

It was just Gavrel and me. Us.

Then Kosmos answered.

A blinding light shot through me, snaking over my entire body. My bough markings ignited—the gold lingering along my collarbone, shoulders, and biceps, while splintered prisms rippled down my forearms and hands.

My aura burned bright. It sought the poisoned curse still lingering within him, coiling around us like a vine.

It burned—Ancients, it *burned*—draining through me, sucking the poison out of him and into my own veins.

For three long breaths, I felt his death inside me.

The sickly chill.

The emptiness.

The collapse of everything I loved.

I slumped, my ember finally having had enough. Too expended.

And then the rune tattoo on his hand flared along with his new khorda mark.

A pulse, and then two beats beneath my palm.

I gasped and pushed harder, letting my aura pour into him. All of it, until I thought I would come apart.

Without a barrier, our golden thread, thick and gleaming, shone between us.

His chest heaved—and he *breathed*.

A sob tore from my chest, and my opalescent halo collapsed around us. Helos and the others reappeared as if a veil had been lifted.

Gavrel coughed, air and starlight spilling from his lips as his eyes flew open.

His hand shot up, catching mine, gripping it like a lifeline. "Asteria—" His voice broke. "You called me back."

I collapsed against him, laughter and sobs tangling in my throat. "To the fucking beyond, Gav. Don't you ever make me do that again," I whispered raggedly.

His dimple peeked out as he brushed a tear from my cheek.

His hand tattoo still glowed. Its energy and our bond sank into me. My joints. My heart. Like a wellspring replenishing and strengthening me.

Around us, the others exhaled in disbelief, exhaustion, and celebration. The air was thick with the echo of what we'd done —what we'd *survived*.

And above, the moon had traveled closer to the horizon, but

its beams still slanted over the splintered, sacred place, pure and rose-tinged silver.

It seemed like Selene was blessing us, the new demi-Ancient Elder and the man who died for her ...

Who returned from the beyond *for her*.

48

AS ONE

SERYN

*H*allowed End was quiet now, the echoes of battle still thrumming in my bones.

Marek leaned against a doombark, hands clenched around his quarterstaff as if it were the only thing keeping him upright. His sapphire gaze was glued to the brightened horizon.

My sister sobbed quietly, legs dangling off the edge where her father had fallen, Xeni's hand brushing over her back and golden hair.

Gideon.

My chest tightened at the memory of his final cry; the way he'd thrown himself in front of Letti to shield her. I wasn't sure I could fully grieve him, but his absence was a dull ache. My sister's grief was pressing into me, making me want to swallow her pain.

I went to her, kissing the top of her head. Her eyes shone as she looked at me, sorrow lining her features.

"I'm here, sis. Whenever you're ready."

She nodded and folded into Xeni's embrace.

I touched the warrior's shoulder and then shared quiet looks with all who remained.

Now wasn't the time for words. The shock of everything needed to settle over each of us in our own time and way.

Gavrel stirred beside me, fingers brushing my wrist in quiet solidarity. His eyes met mine, and I felt the weight of all we had carried.

The blood.

The ruin.

The pieces of ourselves we'd left behind in the process of saving the realms.

"Now, we rest." Yaya's soft order broke through the silence, through the stun.

As we crossed the swaying bridge, Yaya, Rhaegar, and Breena uttered words of rebellion yet to come. The next steps we had to take. Of prophecy. I listened with half an ear, too drained to care.

My grandmother's touch brushed over my curls, so like her own, before Gavrel and I parted from the rest.

"You did well, granddaughter." She traced a gilded bough. "This isn't the mark of the Ascension," she added as an afterthought.

"What?" I murmured.

"Our scriptures speak of gold markings like these—those of a demi-Ancient. I think that's what this is. Your heritage revealing itself at last."

I tilted my head, words escaping me.

"I love you, Yaya."

She smiled, her thumb gliding over my cheek. "And I you. Now, go. Rest."

We made our way to our cabin. As we stepped inside, I pushed away the memory of the battles.

My eyes dragged over Gavrel's bloodied chest, and I waved my hand toward the bath. "Get in."

He didn't argue. Undressed, he sank into the cooled water. I joined him, scrubbing away the grime, blood, and remnants of war. My hands glided over his skin, over the new bond marks that vibrated beneath my fingertips.

He leaned back, letting me take care of him, which was proof of how spent he truly was. He'd died, after all.

When we were done, we curled against one another in bed, legs twining, and let much-needed rest claim us.

MY LASHES FLUTTERED OPEN, blue skylight spilling through. A spotted moth wobbled above us.

I had brought us here.

Not in body, but in soul. To the place that had always called to me—the seam between waking and dreaming.

The Somnis had answered my call without hesitation, unfolding my meadow on a sigh, just as it was before the Withering sank its teeth in.

We weren't in Evergryn, not truly. But I'd brought a piece to us—shaped this dream from memory and longing. A place of stillness, somewhere that wasn't ravaged by war or nightmares.

A sanctuary between the realms.

The Somnis pulsed softly behind the meadow's edges, motes of my ember drifting lazily through the air like fireflies.

My eyes darted to the edge of the fantasy, half expecting Melina or my uncle to materialize. To take what was mine again.

They are gone. Breathe, Little Star.

I balked at the voice in my head.

Are you in my fucking head?

Gavrel chuckled, rubbing his hand over my bare stomach.

"It's the bond, remember? We'll have to get used to it."

Don't bounce around in here all the time, I countered in our heads, not truly upset. The thought of sharing my mind—my fears, my shadows—was unnerving.

He shifted onto his side, and I rolled toward him. "You think I care what darkness is inside you? My love, I've seen you at your fiercest and your weakest. Nothing in you could ever turn me away."

His words curled around something raw inside me.

"Gavrel," I breathed, threading my fingers with his. "I love you. And I … I can't lose you again."

He pressed his forehead against mine. "You won't. Even in death, even if the realms fall apart—we'll find one another. That's what this bond means. Across dreams, across aether, across all that was and will be."

A breath shuddered through me. "Then we'll never be lost again."

Never, Asteria.

His promise reverberated within me as he unraveled our fingers, bringing both of his hands to my jaw.

His touch was warm and tender, but with an undercurrent prickling under it. All the desperation and rage and terror we'd experienced in these last few months had finally crashed around us.

In those moments, when I believed I'd finally lost him, all I wanted was to join him in the darkness. Nothing else mattered.

That kind of love—that kind of reckless abandon—should have terrified me. But it didn't. It only made me more feral.

Because we shared something impenetrable. A devotion that would not yield. That would defy Khaos itself.

Tears lined my lower lash line, muscles softening even as my heart slammed against our bond. His fingers rested in the space just below my jawline, claiming me. His emerald eyes searched mine, as if he'd dive into their icy depths to save me from drowning once more.

His right hand drifted down and traced the gold outline along my clavicle. A tingle unfurled low in my belly, spreading outward. It felt like he was touching me everywhere. I rubbed my thighs together, savoring the soft heat beginning to pulse in my core.

His hand went lower, grazing the side of my breast, following the curve of my waist. Warm white light spilled over me as his rune tattoo kindled.

His gaze met mine once more, nostrils flaring.

"Gavrel," I whispered a second before his lips crashed into mine.

His tongue pushed inside, and I met it stroke for stroke. This kiss was more, deeper than it had ever been, our bond ravenous for us to fully connect for the first time.

Our mouths danced and pressed and sucked, and I swore my body felt what his felt. That our lips and tongues—skin and hearts—were one and the same.

His groan spilled into my mouth, and he wrenched me closer, his stiff length pushing against my thigh.

I caught his plump lower lip, sucking on it hard and scraping my nails down his back.

"Fucking vo—" he moaned, and I swallowed the rest of the word, meeting his lips again. Demanding more as I dug my fingers into his muscled backside.

His hand slipped over my bottom and squeezed, kneading the round cheeks before running down my thigh and dragging it over his.

The warm air brushed against my wet sex, making me shiver and moan his name, and rock against him, desperate for purchase. My desire coated his lower abdomen.

His hand slid along my thigh, the tips of his fingers featherlight, teasing the sensitive, swollen flesh around my channel.

My neck craned back, and my palms brushed over his spine, feeling a tingle go up mine. I buried my fingers in his hair, and I tugged, thrusting my hips in impatient circles.

A smirk tipped his mouth before he bent forward, feasting on my neck, teeth nipping, his tongue leaving a soft, wet trail along my skin.

A low rumble sounded in my throat.

His smile widened, eyes dazed with lust as he finally dipped two fingers into my wet heat.

It wasn't enough. My core clenched at him, seeking more.

He pulled his fingers out and rolled me onto my back, his weight pinning me down. The soft grass tickled my skin, and the reeds and flowers around us swayed.

I gasped as his hand slipped between us, his thumb finding the sensitive bundle at my apex. He circled it, pressing and sliding against it. Heat buzzed over my spine, and I whimpered, gripping his bulging biceps as he braced himself above me on one forearm.

"You are so perfect, Asteria. Every. Single. Inch." His thumb punctuated his words, flicking my clit. He leaned down and sucked one nipple into his mouth, and I groaned, cradling his head in my left hand and biting my lower lip.

An invisible line of energy ignited, tethering my pleasure points. From my nipple, taut and sensitive, to my swollen clit, heat zinged, hips thrusting against him wildly.

My aura purred under my skin, illuminating the golden boughs, making them dance along my skin.

"I need you. All of you," I whimpered, head lolling to the side.

He released my nipple with a damp pop and met my heavy-lidded gaze.

"And you'll have me."

He positioned his hips, right hand shifting to my waist. And with a fierce thrust, he filled me to the hilt.

My eyes rolled back, a gasp clogging my windpipe.

"So beautiful, my love. So fucking wet." Gavrel growled, sliding out and squeezing his thick cock back in.

Light shifted over our khorda runes, warmth shimmering through our connection.

His eyes snapped to mine, full of shock and lust.

I felt … everything.

We were feeling *everything.*

The slide and pulsing of his cock inside me. My wet heat trembling and gripping him. It was as if our minds and bodies were one, slipping into the other and experiencing the pure, unadulterated desire coursing through us, within us.

"Fucking void, Gavrel. It's too much. I … I …"

He shoved into me again, sweat beading on his skin, dripping on my breasts. "Look at me. I want to see your eyes when you scream my name."

I groaned, and he moved faster. The sound of slapping skin rent the air. He pounded me into the grass, muscles corded and straining, refusing to slow.

Liquid heat poured down to the base of my spine. I called his name over and over like a prayer, or a plea. I wasn't sure.

Come for me, my love. Drench me.

The demand barged into my mind, and my sex convulsed, squeezing him. His pupils dilated, jaw clenched as he moved.

In. Out.

In.

Out.

The pace raged in time with our shared heartbeats.

His cock lengthened, balls tightening.

Gavrel! I screamed in our heads and out loud, echoing

through the meadow. And my body exploded into pure iridescence, stars and golden threads wrapping around us as we reached our release together. Wrung every last ounce of our souls and pleasure from us.

As one.

49

THE CONSTELLATIONS OF DREAMERS

Seryn

My flesh and bones still buzzed from the ritual and the victories that followed. Our triumphs and grief and hope. Our lovemaking. Every nerve quivered, echoing with memories of power and blood and infinite love.

I inhaled, letting it all wash over me, relishing the sweet and comforting scent of the meadow and astra poppies.

Evergryn seemed so far away. And it was, but it would always be my beginning. My roots.

But I'd finally bloomed, found myself along the winding, jagged journey we'd traversed.

I exhaled, emptying myself of the tension.

Blessedly hollow.

I kissed Gavrel's forehead, savoring the earthy scent of him like leather and smoke and something wilder.

We were *the* two hollowed stars.

The next part of the prophecy had been satisfied.

Another testament of the Fates getting their fucking way.

The reeds whispered in the breeze, their soft rustling carrying through the dream meadow. The flowers shivered, their cerise petals glowing faintly, pulsing with the light of the Somnis.

Gavrel lay against me, his head resting on my breast, his chest pressing against my side with every breath. My fingers slipped through his dark hair, my golden tattoos casting a metallic sheen against his glossy strands.

He was alive.

He was *here*.

And that was enough.

For now.

The nightmares were silenced, and I was grateful for the fragile reprieve Midst Fall was granted.

But I could still feel the ripple of what we'd done humming throughout the realms. The balance had been tipped, and it would need to be restored—that much was true.

The Fates always came to collect what they were owed.

I thought of Phantasos. Her betrayal was a delicate piece of glass that had shattered around us in those last moments. Bitterness rolled over my tongue.

She wasn't evil. Merely devoted. To symmetry, to the Fates' eternal designs. Devout. Dangerous.

And I understood her now in a way I hadn't before. The Ancients were no better, no different from the mortals they'd created. They, too, were driven by longing, jealousy, and hope. Capable of tenderness and ruin.

She would do whatever it took to maintain balance. To ensure the Aetherbind didn't fray.

And that, in its own right, was admirable.

But if she—or anyone, Ancient or mortal—tried to take what was mine again, it would be the last thing they ever did.

My aunt's words echoed in my memory: *The dawn does not fear the night. Protect the balance. Persevere.*

And I would.

Between light and dark. Dream and waking. Life and death.

I—the woman who was once afraid of all these things—had become the bridge between them.

My gaze drifted upward, scanning the shimmering stars above us. They were clearer here, in our dreams, than in any realm of the living. The constellations looked almost alive, each line of light bending, whispering the language of the Ancients.

"Asteria," Gavrel mumbled against my skin, as if he'd heard my thoughts. His breath slowed again, lulled by sleep.

The Somnis stirred within me … the demi-Ancient part of me. The Elysium Tree had accepted me as an Elder, though the ritual was incomplete until all five regions were represented. Yaya had made sure to remind me of that.

My golden tattoos gleamed under the starlight; the marks of my true lineage.

It was strange to think of where I had begun. Of how I once trembled at my own ember.

I was never meant to cage it, nor was it meant to consume me.

It showed me I could contain both light and shadow. Love and fury. Mortality and Eternity.

And I was still *me*.

The girl who used to sneak out to the meadow and listen to the frogs sing with her best friend.

The one who laughed when Kaden and Gavrel fell into Oleander Cove, the grym needles poking my bare soles.

Who dove headlong into the Nether Void for the ones she loved.

And the woman who had faced an Ancient—and refused to yield.

All of her lived here.

In this dream.

Across the realms.

Within me.

Gavrel stirred, the softest sound escaping him. He tilted his head to look at me, lashes heavy, emerald eyes glassy with sleep and starlight.

"Where'd you go, my love?" I whispered, brushing my thumb over his cheekbone.

His mouth quirked, dimple peeking through the stubble along his jaw. "Nowhere. Everywhere. To the beyond. Does it matter, as long as you were with me?"

"It matters to me."

He smiled as I traced the golden mark over his ribs—the Kollao sigil that mirrored mine. It twinkled faintly under my touch, our bond pulsing between us like a gilded vein.

"The beyond suits you," I murmured.

He laughed softly, a rare and wondrous sound. "Then it's settled. We'll stay there."

I arched a brow. "Is that so?"

He propped himself up on one elbow. His gaze roved over me, memorizing every inch in quiet reverence.

Always. And only for you, he answered in my mind.

He kissed me then, slowly and deeply.

Our bond vibrant, humming in the space between thought and breath.

When we parted, the meadow faded into the twilight, the poppies bending.

My eyelashes fluttered. For a heartbeat—or perhaps an eternity—there was only our breathing and the rustling of grass.

I thought of Marek, standing on the edge of a battlefield in the Void, his flames blending into the nightmarescapes.

Of Yaya's laughter echoing over maps and bottles of mireberry wine.

Of Kaden and Jace arguing about runes in the mountains.

Caelora's haunting songs.

Breena's sharp tongue and sharper blades.

Rhaegar's exasperated sighs.

Xeni's quiet, steady loyalty.

Letti's wisdom and bravery.

And Gideon's final shout—the man who'd never called me daughter, yet gave his life to save his own.

They were pieces of me, too.

Every one of them.

The stars that made up my constellation.

The path ahead was uncertain, the balance fragile, and Kosmos restless. But I was no longer afraid.

The Fates might have woven the threads of destiny, but I would choose where mine led.

Gavrel stood, offering me his hand. His fingers intertwined with mine, grounding me as always.

"I used to say, 'only the Fates know,'" I murmured.

"And now?"

"Now," I smiled toward the horizon, "only we do. The people. The dreamers."

His thumb brushed the pulse at my wrist.

I leaned into him, resting my temple against his shoulder. "We'll make something new. Something beautiful out of all the hollow places."

He kissed the top of my head. "You already have, Little Star."

My chest flushed, and I closed my eyes. "Then let's rest. Just for a while."

The poppies and reeds and all living things sighed around us. At the edges, the Somnis' prismatic lining shimmered. The stars shifted above, forming new patterns I didn't yet know but somehow recognized, like a promise waiting in the dark.

I am not afraid, my ember and I whispered in the quiet of my mind.

Let it come, Gavrel responded within me.

My lips curved.

I'd finally taken my broken pieces and made something wholly exquisite—mine.

No, *ours.*

And it was indeed sharp enough to carve through the nightmares.

A month had passed since the destruction of Elder Harrow and Phobetor. Since Seryn Nightshade's Ascension. The atmosphere in Helos carried a tentative peace, but the city's scars lingered in the charred wood and the splintered but repaired Hallowed End.

A multitude of hours had been spent debriefing, planning, and rebuilding.

Each of the Korax members, for they were all officially ravens now, had a part to play. A journey to embark on in the turns ahead. Scouts were sent to gather more rebels, to organize across Midst Fall. There wasn't time to waste, with the last pieces of the prophecy on the horizon.

The Perilous Bogs breathed again, albeit bated.

Seryn stood at the edge of the bog field to the west, the hem of her dark dress brushing dew-laden moss, her dagger glinting from her belt. Her golden tattoos caught the dawn.

Mist rolled low over the murky water, curling around doombarks and spongy hummocks, carrying the scent of new life and something older still—an ancient ember that had slept beneath the surface for eons.

The Somnis hummed quietly in her soul, as it always did in these early hours, when the moon's memory lingered. The bond was faint but persistent. It was a tether to the dreaming world, an invitation. It pulsed in her sinew, steadying her, whispering that her purpose had not yet ended with Phobetor's fall.

Behind her, Gavrel moved with careful grace, his steps soundless, the hummock bobbing gently under their feet. Every now and then, his eyes found hers as though to reassure himself she was still here, still real.

Seryn had tried to visit the Augur's cabin in the bogs a couple of weeks past, but the Ancient of Illusions had moved on; the embered archway had vanished.

It was doubtful the night of the Hallowed End battle would be the last anyone saw of Phantasos. For mortal dreams would never be rid of illusions.

Sometimes, when the veil between realms thinned, Seryn still felt the pull—the whisper of the Somnis inviting her into its tides. Soul-wandering wasn't the same as portaling between realms, but it carried its own peril. When she let her spirit drift, the Aetherbind quivered, the thread between soul and flesh stretching thinner.

She had learned that Kosmos always asked for something in return.

With Gavrel, it was different. Their soul was a single flame split in two, the divine tether between them holding firm. When she found him in dreams, their joined light moved as one, neither straining nor fraying the veil.

But with others … the cost was heavier.

She had done it once for Letti and Yaya—only once—to draw her sister and grandmother into the Somnis so they could see Mama again.

Letti's dream had burned bright, darting through the dreamscape like a star refusing to be caught.

Yaya's was equally stubborn. It had taken all of Seryn's

strength, will, and the lingering grace of the Somnis to reach them. And when she finally did, something in herself stretched thin, fragile as spun glass.

Yet, it'd been worth it. Beneath the Elysium Tree, she'd been granted time with her mother, grandmother, and sister. They'd spoken of home, of Midst Fall, and of what still needed mending.

When Seryn returned, the Somnis trembled inside her for days; her essence shaken and her aura buzzing angrily under her flesh.

After that, she made herself a promise. She wouldn't seek out other people's dreams again. Not unless the need outweighed the cost.

For a long moment, she and Gavrel simply stood there, letting the morning stretch around them. Gavrel's thumb brushed over her knuckles. The fog curled, and somewhere in the distance, something vigilant watched and waited. She did not need to name it.

Thoughts of what must come next replaced her memories of what once was. Helos would recover, but the realm was still dying. Elder Lucan Craven reigned in Evergryn, poisoning her home with his greed and toxicity.

And Elder Ash still had to be found. She hoped Kaden, Caelora, and Jace found him before trouble found them. They'd left weeks ago, amid a flurry of bickering. She sent a prayer to Tyche that she would pave their journey in luck.

Seryn tightened her grip on her khorda's hand and stepped forward to the edge of the knoll. The sun fully broke over the horizon, painting the mist in rose gold and peach. She couldn't help but feel the shift settling deep within her.

The Perilous Bogs seemed to shiver. The future stretched wide and uncertain before them. Elder Nightshade inhaled the scent of moss and brine, and in that breath, she knew hope. She would be ready.

They would all be ready.

In that moment, the Perilous Bogs fell silent again when the sun's base clung to the skyline—but it was not the silence of endings.

It was the silence of a beginning.

NOT YET THE END ...

<u>WANT MORE?</u>

BOOK 4: Don't miss the start of a new romance in the Fate of the Embered series—where vengeance, healing, and the fragile line between control and surrender collide.

Between Lark and Lore is available on Amazon at:
https://books2read.com/betweenlarkandlore

EXCLUSIVE CONTENT: Be the first to learn about Rowyn Adelaide's new releases and receive exclusive content!

Join Rowyn's author newsletter:
WWW.AUTHORROWYNADELAIDE.COM

RA

GLOSSARY/PRONUNCIATION GUIDE

CHARACTERS/CREATURES

- **Akridai (Ack-reh-die)** – very powerful, elite Druik enforcers who wield their power at the discretion of the Elders and the Elder Laws.
- **Alette Vawn (A-let Vawn)** – a.k.a. Letti. Younger sister of Seryn Vawn. From Evergryn.
- **Alweo (Al-weh-oh)** – Seryn's chestnut stallion.
- **Ancients** – powerful gods who created the mortal realm and gifted magic to certain mortal bloodlines.
- **Argedes (Ar-guh-deez)** – a member of the Hespira rebel crew. A centaur who hails from Surrelia.
- **Asteria (A-stare-ee-ah)** – The Ancient of Stars.
- **Augur (Awe-grr)** – a revered female of the Perilous Bogs who offers prophetic counsel to those who seek it.
- **Breena Cadell (Bree-nah Kah-dell)** – friend of Seryn Vawn. Lives in Pneumali City, but originally from Pyria Island. Possesses red, fire-related magic.

- **Caelora Aundyne (Kay-lor-a Awn-deen)** – a half-borne Druik that was in the final Winnowing trial with Seryn and Kaden. Her combined lineage hails from both Haadra and Pyria Island. She has a violet-colored aura, which manifests as lavender water that turns into flames on contact.
- **Chasm spider** – giant, cave-dwelling spider beasts with camouflage abilities.
- **Derya Atwater (Dair-yah At-water)** – friend of Seryn Vawn and her chambermaid. Lives in Surrelia, but originally from Haadra. Possesses blue, water-related magic.
- **Drakon Valyn (Dray-con Vay-lin)** – a Korax Commander who hails from Pyria Island.
- **Draumr (Draw-mer)** – warriors in the Elders' warrior legion, the Order of Draumr. Uphold laws and order within realms.
- **Dream Reapers** – skeletal, cloaked Void creatures that feed on people's fear and nightmares.
- **Druik (Drew-ick)** – one who wields magic. Lives longer than non-magic mortals/humans.
- **Elders** – extremely powerful, chosen/ascended Druiks granted extra celestial powers through the Ancients' Ascension ceremony and rule the mortal realm as an Oligarchy. They hail from divine lineage from one of the **five founding bloodlines**:
    - **Aerides (Air-id-eez)** of Pneumali
    - **Celosia (Suh-low-sha)** of Pyria
    - **Lotus** of Haadra
    - **Nightshade** of Perilous Bogs
    - **Oleander (Oh-lee-an-dur)** of Evergryn

Current Elders:

- o **Endurst Guust (En-derst Goo-st)** of Pneumali – possesses yellow, air-like magic.
- o **Lucan Craven (Loo-can Cray-ven)** of Evergryn – possesses green, earth-like magic.
- o **Marah Strom (Mar-ah Strawm)** of Haadra – possesses blue, water-like magic.
- o **Melina Harrow (Meh-leena Hair-oh)** of the Perilous Bogs – possesses smoky, memory-erasing magic.
- o **Ryboas Ash (Rye-bow-es Ash)** of Pyria Island – possesses red, fire-like magic.
- **Eliz Wynt (Ee-lie-z Win-t)** – friend of Rhaegar and fated khorda of Keethan Wynt. Keethan and Eliz are recruitment scouts for the Korax and recruited Rhaegar for the rebel cause.
- **Elysium (Eh-lis-ee-um) Tree** – the oldest and most sacred, banyan-like tree in all of existence. A source of life-giving ember. A place to pray or offer oaths to the Ancients.
- **Emmet Larkin** – Gavrel and Kaden Larkin's father. Husband of Hestia Larkin. Died shortly after his wife was culled.
- **Fates** – three powerful sister entities who write, alter, and determine the destiny of mortals, realms, creatures, and Ancients alike.
- **Gavrel (Gav (like have)-rel (like fell)) Larkin** – Seryn Vawn's neighbor and friend. Brother of Kaden Larkin. Elite Commander in the Order of Draumr. Has a rune tattoo on his right hand that grants him some ember and enhanced strength/stamina.
- **Gideon Vawn (Gid-ee-on Vawn)** – Seryn and Alette Vawn's father. Husband of Maya Vawn.

- **Gryvak Leystaes (G-rye-vack Lay-stay-s)** – the leader of the Nether Void gang called the Scourge. Elder Melina Harrow's khorda, whom she murdered.
- **Half-borne** – Druiks born of two lineages and display mixed ember abilities.
- **Harbinger starling** – starling-like birds that deliver missives across the realm.
- **Hemeros (H-eh-mer-ohs)** – the father of the Oneiroi. Primeval of day and light.
- **Hespira (Hess-pee-rah)** – the rebel group fighting against Phobetor and surviving in the Nether Void. The leader is Maya Nightshade from the Perilous Bogs.
- **Hestia Larkin (Hess-tee-ah Larkin)** – Gavrel and Kaden Larkin's mother. Wife of Emmet Larkin. Was culled when Gavrel was eighteen turns old and Kaden was thirteen turns old. Possessed green, earth-like and healing magic.
- **Horai (Ho-rye)** – the Ancients of Hours. Twelve Ancients who once guarded Aion, the Surrelian capital.
- **Iben Burlam (Eye-ben Burr-lamb)** – librarian and begrudging friend of Seryn Vawn. Lives in Surrelia, but originally from Evergryn. Possesses brownish, earth-related magic.
- **Jace Barden (Jay-s Bar-den)** – otherwise known as Magister Barden. He arrived in Evergryn several decades ago. He teaches the students of the region. Runemaster. Possesses yellow, air-related magic.
- **Kaden Larkin (Kay-den Larkin)** – Seryn Vawn's best friend. Brother to Gavrel Larkin. Possesses green, earth-related and healing magic.

- **Keethan Wynt (Keith-an Win-t)** – friend of Rhaegar and fated khorda of Eliz Wynt. Keethan and Eliz are recruitment scouts for the Korax and recruited Rhaegar for the rebel cause.
- **Korax (Core-ax)** – the rebel group fighting against the Elders and their Laws. The leader is Neoma Skiya (i.e. Nightshade) from the Perilous Bogs.
- **Mare wyrm (Worm)** – Nether Void, leech-like creature that tricks you into thinking it is your loved one. Once they have you in their slimy hold, they suck the life and magic out of you.
- **Marek (Mare-ick) Nightshade (formerly Skiya (Skee-yah)** – member of the rebel group called the Korax. His hidden lineage hails from the Nightshade bloodline of the Perilous Bogs. Grandson of Neoma Nightshade.
- **Maya Nightshade (formerly Vawn)** – Seryn and Alette Vawn's mother. Morpheus' fated khorda. Has some sort of magic related to the Perilous Bogs, where she was originally from.
- **Mormo (More-mow)** – a demon-like nightmare creature that hails from the Nether Void. A bogey that is said to feast on children and marrow.
- **Morpheus (More-fee-us)** – the supreme Ancient of Dreams. Presides over Surrelia. Maya Nightshade's fated khorda.
- **Neoma (Nay-oh-ma) Nightshade (formerly Skiya (Skee-yah))** – the leader of the rebel group called the Korax. Her hidden lineage hails from the Nightshade bloodline of the Perilous Bogs. Grandmother to Marek Skiya.
- **Neris Kymara (Nair-iss K-eye-mar-ah)** – a Korax Commander who hails from Haadra.

- **Nyx (Nicks)** – the Primeval of Night. Mother of the Oneiroi and paternal grandmother to Seryn.
- **Oneiroi (Oh-knee-roy)** – the dream Ancients. Siblings. (Also see Morpheus, Phantasos, and Phobetor).
- **Order of Draumr (Draw-mer)** – the Elders' warrior legion.
- **Pegasus (Peg-ah-sus)** – Surrelian winged, horse creature. Mortal-bred horses that were gifted wings by the Ancients once they reached Surrelia. Very rare.
- **Phantasos (Fan-taz-ohs)** – Ancient of Illusions (and surreal dreams). Wanders across the realms and likes wild landscapes.
- **Phobetor (Foe-beh-tore)** – Ancient of Nightmares. Presides over the Nether Void.
- **Pixie** – mischievous, winged creatures that are as big as a mortal hand. Reside in Surrelia in the Reverie Weald. Skilled at finding portals in Reverie Weald.
- **Primevals (Prime-evils)** – the first beings that ever were and always have been. The very personifications of creation itself. If released, would cause the Dark Reaping.
- **Rhaegar Hale (Rag-ar Hail)** – friend of Seryn Vawn. Gavrel Larkin's second-in-command in the Order of Draumr.
- **Scion (Sigh-on)** – descendants of one of the five founding bloodlines. The only type of Druik that can undergo the Ascension to become an Elder. Only one exists at a time.
- **Selene (Suh-leh-nee)** – The Moon Ancient. Her true love was a mortal named Endymion. He was put to sleep eternally so she could visit him every night for eternity.

- **Seryn (Sair-in or like the name Erin) Nightshade (formerly Vawn)** – our main female leading character. Alette is her younger sister. Morpheus and Maya are her parents. Is a demi-Ancient with magic that hails from the Perilous Bogs and celestial power. Has lived in Evergryn her whole life.
- **Somneia (Som-nee-ah)** – the Elders' covert network of spies.
- **Therrok Flint (Thair-awk)** – a member of the Hespira rebel crew. Brother to Thesa Flint. A reformed vryka who hails from the Nether Void.
- **Thesa Flint (Thess-ah)** – a member of the Hespira rebel crew. Sister to Therrok Flint. A reformed vryka who hails from the Nether Void.
- **Tyche (Tie-kee)** – the Ancient of Luck.
- **Vryka (Vree-kah)** – a Nether Void being that has blueish-gray skin, black leathery wings, and fangs. They are known to dwell in the dark and are said to feast on the blood and flesh of mortals.
- **Wyvern (Why-vern)** – Surrelian creature that lives along the cliffs in the Reverie Weald. Massive, reptilian-like creature with wings, feathers, scales, and two forelegs. It can spray poisonous spit. Protects the Mirage Orchid.
- **Xeni Reed (Zen-ee Reed)** – friend of Seryn Vawn. Girlfriend of Alette Vawn. Warrior in Gavrel's elite Draumr unit.
- **Zeph Stratos (Zeff St-rat-ohs)** – a Korax Commander who hails from Pneumali.

PLACES

- **Aion (Ah-ee-own)** – capital city of Surrelia.

- **Cradle of Nyx (Nicks)** – a banestone pit that was created after the primeval Nyx fell through the aether. Nekrionn and the rest of the Nether Void was created from this impact.
- **Ceto (See-toe)** – capital city of the region of Haadra.
- **Epiales Tombs (Eh-pee-ah-less Tombs)** – Phobetor's nightmare prison hidden in the Stygian Murk where prisoners are trapped in glass orbs reliving their nightmares. Dream reapers guard the tombs.
- **Evergryn (Ever-grin)** – Northern, wooded region of the mortal realm. Magic that hails from here is earth-related and often shades of green and brown.
- **Gloaming Weald (Glow-ming Wheeled)** – a terrifying forest with pale trees and banestone gravel that runs along the northeastern region of the Nether Void. There is a massive plateau that splits it in two, and it is home to several Void creatures as well as the Hespira's den hideout.
- **Haadra (High-druh)** – Eastern, water-ridden region of the mortal realm. Magic that hails from here is water-related and often shades of blue and aqua.
- **Hallowed End** – A sacred place at the edge of Helos where Seryn opens a portal that leads into the Stygian Murk.
- **Helos (He-low-s)** – capital city of the Perilous Bogs region.
- **Insomnis Sea (In-sawm-niss Sea)** – fabled dream realm sea that surrounds Surrelia. It is also in the Nether Void, but its colors are inverted in shades of orangish-red and black.
- **Lochs of Haadra (Locks of High-druh)** – a series of three large, brackish lochs that border the Haadran border. The northernmost loch between Haadra and

the Ourea Peaks is Lotus Loch. Below that, Inksalt Loch borders Haadra, the Ourea Peaks, and the Perilous Bogs. Aerides Loch, the southernmost loch that borders Haadra and Pneumali.

- **Midst Fall** – the mortal realm
- **Mourning Pass** – an area in the northern part of the Nether Void where living skulls and bones spread across the landscape. Most were victims of the Gloaming Weald.
- **Nekrionn (Neck-ree-on)** – capital city of the Nether Void.
- **Nether Void** – ancient nightmare realm. Phobetor presides over this realm. It is a terrifying, dark realm where those who pass on may live out their eternity in eternal suffering.
- **Ourea (Oo-reh-ah) Peaks** – mountain range that borders the easternmost edge of Evergryn and westernmost edge of Haadra.
- **Perilous Bogs** – Western and center, swamp/bog region of the mortal realm. People avoid this area and not much is known. Magic that hails from this area is mysterious and can manifest in many different ways and is often shades of black or iridescent.
- **Pneumali (New-mall-ee)** – Southern, desert region of the mortal realm. Magic that hails from here is air-related and often shades of yellow and orange.
- **Pyria (Pie-ree-ah) Island** – Southernmost, volcanic island of the mortal realm. Magic that hails from here is fire-related and often shades of red.
- **Reverie Weald (Rev-er-ee Wheeled)** – a beautiful and neon-colored forest that separates Morpheus' land and palace from the rest of Surrelia.

- **Somnis (Sawm-niss)** – a place hidden between the seams of reality where memories and souls become one. It's the tide of dreaming itself, and it is there that the Oneiroi guide dreams and navigate the currents of the psyche.
- **Stygian (Sti-jee-uhn) Murk** – a colorless portal realm or limbo between realms where time slows and travelers easily get lost while their will to survive and exist is drained.
- **Surrelia (Sir-el-ee-ah)** – Ancient dream realm. Morpheus presides over this realm. It is a beautiful, vibrant realm where those who pass on live out eternity.

TERMS

- **Aether (Eth-er)** – the pure, invisible essence that permeates space and time throughout all the realms. The fabric of the universe.
- **Aetherbind (Eth-er-bye-nd)** – the seam that holds the aether and everything within it together. The very thing that keeps Kosmos in check.
- **Ascension** - the ritual in which the Scion metamorphoses into the new Elder.
- **Banestone (Bane-stone)** – the black stone that originates in the Nether Void. It is what the Dormancy pods are made from. Nyxvein runs through it. When dormant, it looks like obsidian. When active, it looks like amber glass.
- **Dark Reaping** – in the event that the Primevals are unleashed, they would destroy every living being in Midst Fall. Without worshippers, the Ancients demise would soon follow.

- **Dormancy** – the process the mortal realm is mandated to undergo from every Autumn Equinox to Spring Equinox in order to preserve resources.
- **Ember** – magic that was gifted by the Ancients to Druiks and is inherited through bloodlines.
- **Fated khorda (Core-duh)**– a Druik's mirrored or twin soul. The three sister Fates helped the Ancients weaken Druiks so that mortal ember would not become overwhelmingly powerful. It was believed that Druiks were born with half their soul, the other half cleaved from them and gifted to another—Druik or human.
- **Hollowed Stars Prophecy** – The prophecy warning of the end of Midst Fall once various omens come about, and potentially how to prevent this. The Korax believe it is the path to saving Midst Fall.

Prophecy/Song:

Behold the call of the end,

When lo, the Aetherbind's seams do bend.

As withered roots the earth doth take,

The battle 'gainst the curse shall break.

Dark beasts through veils shall creep,

And dreams shall rot in mortal sleep.

Unless the stone of light shall fall,

Within obsidian, night devours all.

Lest rise Dark Reaping from the scars,

Make haste with hollowing of the stars.

Earth harvests breath and misted pyre,

And flame be quenched by blackened fire.

One shall be two, and two turn three,

To break the curse o'er land and sea.
When the final threads are fully weaved,
Only then shall Khaos be cleaved.

So speaks Kosmos.

- **Khaos (Kay-ah-s)** – unstable, chaotic nothingness. The opposite of Kosmos, which is balance and order.
  - **Proverb:** "What binds, protects. What breaks, devours."
- **Kollao (Kah-lay-oh) Ceremony** – the ritual through which a Druik is bound to their fated khorda and becomes whole in soul and magic. Their life is also bound together.
- **Kosmos (Caws-mows)** – Fates' most precious gift to all living things. It is balance and order. Life and death. Ancients and mortals. Dreams and waking. If it isn't maintained, then everything spirals into Khaos—unbalanced, chaotic nothingness.
  - **Proverb:** "What binds, protects. What breaks, devours."
- **Nightbloom Sundering** – A monumental war that spanned nearly a century and crossed multiple realms. The conflict erupted when humans were first gifted ember, leading to chaos throughout Midst Fall. The empire collapsed, and the Druiks, left unchecked, unleashed destruction upon the realm. Seizing this opportunity, Phobetor killed Morpheus' wife. In response, Morpheus infused dreams into the slumbering, banishing his brother's nightmares. This rivalry ignited a war across both the dream and nightmare realms among the Ancients. After nearly a century of turmoil, the Fates finally intervened, as the Aetherbind had become vulnerable. They threatened

the release of the Primevals, which would trigger the Dark Reaping.

- **Nyxvein (Nicks-vain)** – the inky mist that runs through banestone, which originates from the Nether Void. It feeds off your essence, fears, and is what essentially created all life in the Nether Void.
- **Shadowvault Amulet** – amulet that Phobetor created out of banestone for Morpheus first wife. It can hold another's ember within.
- **Turn** – one year
- **Winnowing Trials** – a Surrelian festivity at the end of the Dormancy where Druiks and Draumrs can compete to win a grand prize.
  - **Weeding** – first trial of the Winnowing Trials
  - **Wilting** – second trial of the Winnowing Trials
  - **Winnowing** – grande finale trial of the Winnowing Trials
- **Withering** – the progressive decay of the land in Midst Fall.

ACKNOWLEDGMENTS

I'm so grateful that you, reader, are sharing this wickedly dreamy ride with me. I'm filled with so many emotions after finishing this trilogy. I seriously can't believe Seryn and Gavrel's love story is finished. Well, never truly finished. You'll see them again in the future. *Wink wink.* Thinking back on the last couple years, it feels like an actual dream. I wouldn't have been able to do any of this wild author stuff without the support and encouragement from my husband, friends, family, and readers like you! I'd like to give a ridiculously huge thank you to my husband for his endless patience and cheerleading. To the Nether Void and beyond, my love.

Thank you to Bethany, Courtney, Chey, Christine, Sami, Kaileigh, Jessie, and Maeghan. Their constant encouragement, guidance, and support as my beta readers was indispensable. I wouldn't have been able to push through this third book without them. You all are the real MVPs. Now, I'm going to go cry in a corner thinking about how grateful I am for each of you.

Katie (Spice Me Up Editing), my wonderful editor, thank you so very much for your expertise, your humor, and patience through this whole process. You are an amazing editor and all-around human!

Thank you to all of my readers, my Wicked Dreamers Street Team, ARC readers, and reviewers who took a chance on an indie romance author with a dream and a magical, steamy story to tell. I appreciate each and every one of you for reading, reviewing, sharing, making reels/posts, and generally just being amazing.

I can't even with my character art. Check out my socials for all the amazing artists I've worked with and brought my characters to life!

ABOUT THE AUTHOR

Rowyn Adelaide is an insatiable romance reader, advanced practice MSW social worker, and the author of the *Fate of the Embered* series. Her debut novel, *Of Withering Dreams*, launched the dark fantasy romance series with a haunting blend of passion and peril. Her work fuses atmospheric world-building with emotionally driven romance, often exploring themes of transformation, angst, and resilience. When she's not writing or devouring stacks of romance novels, she's usually globe-trotting, rocking out at concerts, counting down to spooky season, or singing karaoke (very poorly). She lives in the Midwest with her favorite creatures: her husband, their dog Audrey Shepburn (aka the goodest girl that ever lived), and their chaotic cat Stormy, who is equal parts villain and sidekick. For more information, visit www.AuthorRowynAdelaide.com.

Get your books, follow Rowyn, get updates, & join her newsletter!